Joshua Chamberlain and the Civil War

At Every Hazard

Where they stood, the ground was brown as if grass knew better than to grow here, a few scrubby bushes protruding from the boulder-strewn ground. On the very top of the hill grew a scattering of trees, all bare of leaves, their branches wavering eerily in the light breeze of the day. It was an ugly little hill; an appropriate spot for killing, and the men of the 20th Maine marked it in respectful silence.

Linda,

Enjoy my history of Joshua,

Matthew Langdon Cost

A novel detailing the life of Joshua Lawrence Chamberlain during the Civil War

Cover Art by Debbie Harper Cost

Table of Contents

The Early Life of Joshua Chamberlain

* *Born September 28, 1828 in Brewer, Maine*

* *Entered Major Whiting's Military and Classical School in 1842*

* *Began teaching in North Milford at a boarding school to pay for his education in 1846*

* *Entered Bowdoin College in 1848*

* *Met Harriet Beecher Stowe in 1851 as she was working on novel "Uncle Tom's Cabin"*

* *Met and began 'wooing' Fanny Adams in 1851*

* *Graduated Bowdoin College in 1852 and began studies at Bangor Theological Seminary*

* *Graduated from Bangor Theological Seminary in 1853*

* *Became instructor of Theology at Bowdoin College in September 1855*

* *Married Fanny Adams on December 7, 1855*

* *Daughter Grace "Daisy" Dupee born in 1856*

* *Son Harold Wyllys born in 1858*

* *Became Professor of Modern Languages at Bowdoin College in 1861*

* *Surrender of Fort Sumter to the South on April 14, 1861, sparking the Civil War*

* *Appointed Lieutenant Colonel of the 20th Maine on August 8, 1862*

Prologue

July 1, 1862

The Great War, begun with such fanfare at Fort Sumter in April of 1861, had not taken just a few short months as many had predicted but was now well into its second year. The Union's Army of the Potomac had been reorganizing and preparing for a new offensive since the disaster at Bull Run in the summer of 1861 during which it had been completely overrun. Most of the major battles were taking place in the Western Theater states of Kentucky and Tennessee leading up to the ferociously bloody battle of Shiloh on April 6-7 of 1862. This was but a day after General McClellan, Commander in Chief of all Union operations, had unveiled a new strategy, beginning a massive troop movement to Fort Monroe on a southeastern peninsula just sixty miles from Richmond. This deployment of 120,000 soldiers was only possible because, despite reverses on land, the Union was more successful in naval battles, never more obvious than the terrific clash between the Monitor and CSS Virginia.

The CSS Virginia was a brand new invention, a steam-powered ship that, much like a knight from the medieval era, had been cloaked in 800 tons of iron. This hulking colossus of a Confederate warship came steaming into Hampton Roads, the channel connecting Virginia's James River with the Chesapeake Bay, determined to smash the blockade that the Union Army had set in place. The Union Navy sent its own ironclad, the Monitor, to combat this threat. This first sea battle between iron-plated ships ended with no clear victor, though the CSS Virginia eventually retreated, allowing the blockade to continue and giving the Union Army access to the James River.

General McClellan took advantage of this naval superiority and immediately laid siege to the town of Yorktown. The ensuing month-long delay during which the Union prepared to shell the city into submission with a formidable array of artillery, gave the Confederates time to reinforce their defense of Richmond, their capital city, just up the river. Before the attack on Yorktown actually began, the vulnerable Confederates under General Johnston had begun to retreat, fighting a delaying battle as they moved back to join Richmond's defense. By the time the Union reached the outskirts of Richmond, the Confederates were deeply dug in and heavily fortified. Even with his superior numbers, General McClellan was afraid to attack, deceived by faulty intelligence into believing he was outnumbered. On June 26th, 1862 the Confederates surprised the Union by attacking at Beaver Dam Creek and then following up with lightning strikes at Gaines's Mill, Savage Station, and the Turkey Station. Still convinced that he was outnumbered, General McClellan, hoping to reach Harrison Landing and naval support, continued to fall back down the Virginia Peninsula in the face of the attacks, even though the Union forces more than held their own in these battles. McClellan was facing another newly appointed Commander, General Robert E. Lee, leading the Army of Northern Virginia.

*****

Unaware of the machinations of either Commander but cursing them both, the Union soldier lay with his arms protecting his head as the artillery shelling continued without pause, the only positive aspect being that they had been ordered to lie down and take cover. It was impossible to tell which side was winning this exchange from his vantage point and thus he made no effort. He was sure that his time would come, as he and the 2nd Maine Regiment from Bangor had been placed dead smack in the middle of the defense atop Malvern Hill. That morning, before the artillery barrage had begun, he had appreciated the beauty of the spot with the James River furling around the hill from the rear and then to his left, steep cliffs looking down upon the river below. It was the perfect spot to defend with the river on the left and the vertiginous hills and cliffs to the right and rear preventing any flanking movements by the Confederates. The Union Army was perched on a hill that stretched into a field more than a half-mile wide in front of them, the far side being marked by some tree cover in which lurked Lee's Confederate Army of Northern Virginia.

That morning about ten batteries had been positioned, most on the west and in the middle of the defensive positions on the top of Malvern Hill, between the infantry and the massing Confederate army of 90,000 men. Each battery consisted of six artillery pieces, the twelve-pound, five-and-a-half foot long bronze Napoleons and the smaller ten-pound Parrots. Each unit was pulled into position by six horses working together, with three drivers riding those on the left side of the team, ready to pull the gun back should it be in danger of being overrun. Nine men worked each gun, first with an intricate dance of load, then tamp, then sponge down, and finally, aim, ignite, and fire. There were more artillery units held in reserve, the thin crest of the hill called Malvern having no room for them. The rebels had begun the exchange of fire around ten this morning, and now several hours later there had been no let-up.

The soldier, John Collins, picked up his head, looking down the line to make sure that his two boys were fine, having been separated from them by about forty feet. He saw them, William and Daniel, sitting up and conversing in apparent good humor. As he watched, Daniel, at eighteen the younger by two years, broke into a laugh that shook his whole body. At that age, they're too dumb "to know better," he thought shaking his head. He started to yell to them to lie down and take cover, but there was no chance of being heard above the pounding roar of the huge guns firing their twelve-pound shells. Cursing, he wriggled forward on his elbows and knees, keeping his head low.

A hand grabbed his leg and a whiskered face with breath raw enough to make him wince, even in this god-forsaken place, confronted him. "Collins! Where in bloody hell are ya goin?" It was the company sergeant, a decent enough man who lived just about two miles from him back in Brewer. A man with a wife and two children of his own, all of whom were back safely in Maine. The soldier jerked his thumb down the line and mumbled something about boys that knew not better. The sergeant looked and saw two boys who might have been out picnicking with a pretty girl, so carefree and gay they were as a war raged around them. With a curse, the sergeant let go of his leg, "Just keep your head down," he said. "I don't want to be the one to have to bring the news to your widow." The soldier continued crawling on, not bothering to tell the sergeant that his wife had died several months earlier, or so the letter in his pocket claimed.

There was a whistling that Collins knew meant impending doom and then an enormous explosion raised the ground underneath him, levitating him into the air for a moment and then hurtling him back to the earth. He lay there for a moment in confusion before he realized that a mortar shell had landed just yards away. He immediately ran his hands over his face and body, making sure that there were no missing parts. Through the ringing in his ears, he heard a soldier crawl past him, yelling that lightning never struck twice in the same spot and crawling into the crater left behind. Collins felt a trickle of blood from his nose, but other than that everything seemed fine. The wind had changed direction, blowing the smoke from the Union artillery back towards their infantry line and creating a smokescreen so that the soldier couldn't see his sons not twenty feet away. He rose to his hands and knees and scuttled down to where the boys had been. He found them looking worried for a change, as if they were concerned that he had not survived the blast. "What in tarnation are you two doin?"

William looked surprised. "Waitin for our turn to kill some Rebs," he said. "That is, if Colonel Hunt don't kill them all first." Colonel Henry Hunt was in charge of the artillery raining destruction down upon the Confederates. "Do you see what he's doin, Pa? Every time them Rebs set up a battery, he concentrates the fire of four or five of our batteries, twenty-five to thirty pieces in all, on that spot until he knocks it out of commission. The man's a genius."

"No, I haven't been watchin cause Captain Sargent said we was to keep our heads down!"

Daniel chuckled at that. "I don't rightly see how keepin our heads down is gonna help at all," he said. "This is just the fireworks portion of the show, and there ain't nobody shootin at us. One of those Napoleon shells hits us, it ain't gonna matter if our head is down or up."

"Is it true that Little Mac ain't even here on the hill but back on that gunboat, the Galena, down on the river?" William piped up, referring to the rumor that General McClellan wasn't feeling up to being present and had left command of the army to his Brigadier Generals. In reality, thus far anyway, it was a colonel, Henry Hunt, who was running the battle.

"That's what I heard." John Collins replied, not weighing in on the merits of the commanding officer allowing his subordinates to direct the battle. At that moment, a ten-pound Parrot cannon, about fifty feet in front of them took a direct hit, causing the shell in the barrel to explode as well. John Collins watched in horror as the explosion ripped the arms off the loader. He saw a piece of the wheel splinter off and imbed itself in the neck of the man holding the lanyard as he fell to the ground, his legs turned into bloody stumps by the first shell. For a brief moment, he saw the man tamping the round standing upright even though his head was completely and cleanly severed from his shoulders. Almost immediately he heard a second explosion as the extra rounds stored in the limber and caisson, about ten feet behind the Parrot, ignited, incinerating the face of a man leaning to reach for another shell, instantly burning the skin from his skull as the gunpowder flashed, the man stumbling back and screaming from a hole in front of his head that could no longer be called a mouth. The three men from Brewer stared in shock at the carnage in front of them but were interrupted as an officer began screaming for them to make way. Dumbly, they turned to see General Fitz John Porter approaching astride a horse, parting the infantry to make way for Colonel Hunt and the team bringing up another Parrot to replace the destroyed gun. Alongside of them ran the ambulance crew searching vainly for survivors.

At that moment the gray and butternut colors of the Confederate infantry broke from the tree line some 800 yards distant and began to march steadily across the open field, approaching on the Union left. Almost immediately, another line of Confederate troops broke from the woods directly across from where the 2nd Maine lay in support behind the 22nd Massachusetts. "That looks like General Harvey Hill's men," William muttered.

"That's Colonel Gordon's brigade there on the left," Daniel replied. "I'd know it anywhere. Look at how he rides a horse."

The father and sons from Brewer watched as the Confederates crossed the field, all the while being decimated by the artillery fire that Colonel Hunt rained down upon them. They had changed the cannon fire from the solid shot to shrapnel, more effective against infantry at this distance, each shell spraying its seventy-eight musket balls in a deadly arc into the advancing Confederates. Sporadically, groups of men in butternut uniforms suddenly sank to their knees, fell backward, or merely stumbled and continued on as the musket balls ripped through them. Still, they pressed forward, having moved to a light jog, their rebel screams piercing the din of battle, a wailing, eerie sound that sunk into the bones of the Union soldiers who waited their turn for confrontation. At 350 yards, the artillery switched to canister shot, a combination of anything and everything—pieces of metal, nails, rocks—all of which ripped through the advancing troops like a hot knife through butter. Still, the men from the South continued forward, what was left of them, after more than half lay on the field, the dying and the dead, as well as those who had fallen in pretense, no longer able to face the carnage that rained down upon them. The remaining Confederates were close enough to fire a volley in the chaos, patchy though it may have been, and several of the Union artillerymen stumbled and fell. Brigadier General Charles Griffin rode his horse in front of the 2nd Maine and ordered General Martindale of the 22nd Massachusetts to move forward to defend the artillery batteries from the approaching infantry. Lieutenant Colonel Roberts of Maine stood and ordered his regiment to their feet, the men from Maine moving forward to the spot vacated by Massachusetts before once more hunkering down. The artillery fire had done most of the work, and the few Confederates who reached the battery fell from the fire of the infantry or quickly surrendered. A few men managed to flee back into the Southern lines and escape injury.

"We almost had our chance to get us some Rebs." Daniel remarked sadly, as they watched the charge falter and disintegrate.

"Break ranks to let a new battery through." Lieutenant Colonel Roberts ordered, for a reserve battery of six guns was being brought forward to relieve the one in front.

"Pa, ya can pick your head up now, they's done retreated." William said, shaking his father's shoulder. The soldier's head flopped loosely to the side, exposing a gaping hole where his left eye had been.

William and Daniel buried their father later that night, just before General McClellan ordered a retreat, even though the Union had won the day. In their father's coat pocket they found a letter that he hadn't yet gotten a chance to mail; it was addressed to their younger brother still home in Brewer, Maine. Before moving out, Daniel jotted a quick note to go with the letter, telling the boy, Emmett, that their pa was dead, killed by a minié ball at the Battle of Malvern Hill. He also urged his younger brother to follow the advice given in the letter and promised that he would see him soon.

*****

Emmett Collins touched the unopened letter in his pocket as he trudged down the road from the post office on his way home. It was the first piece of mail that he'd ever received in his fourteen years of life, with his name right there on top of the address in Brewer, Maine, in what he thought was his Dad's handwriting. He walked the three miles to his house, refusing the urge to hurry as he savored the crackle of the thin, stiff, paper envelope. His father had gone off to fight the Confederacy, not that Emmett really understood who the Confederacy even was, other than they were made up of states from down south, had slaves to do their work for them, and had decided they didn't want to be part of the United States of America anymore. He passed the Brewer Steam Brick Company, where he occasionally worked, collecting scrap wood from the local sawmills to fire the kiln that hardened the clay dug from the banks of the Penobscot River. Emmett was proud to know that bricks from his company were used all over the world to build houses, bridges, and tall buildings. He'd been told that, between the lumber from across the river in Bangor and the bricks in the twenty brickyards in Brewer, these two towns had built most of the city of Boston. That was something to think on and Emmett hoped that one day he'd get a chance to see that great city. The air was stifling hot and Emmett was glad that he had the day off from the brickyard even though he needed the money.

He reached home, a square, two-story brick house with granite lintels over the windows, Emmett's dad having built it seven years ago after their last home had burned to the ground. His boast was that this house would stand long after he was gone, even long after his own children had passed, and therefore it was well worth the cost and the labor necessary to raise it up. Emmett entered the house and was again struck by the quiet that he would never get used to. It seemed like only yesterday that they'd celebrated his birthday and Ma had made a special chocolate cake and they'd finished the whole thing that very night. Afterwards they'd gone into the parlor and played backgammon, pitting Emmett and his Pa against the elder brothers, Daniel and William, while Ma had played the violin. Daniel had made them all laugh at the jokes he told, and even William had smiled and chuckled.

Then everything changed, a few months later, his father and both older brothers volunteering to go off to fight in the Great War to preserve the Union as part of the 2nd Maine, otherwise known as the 'Bangor Regiment'. Exactly one year after that his mother had died of an infection to her lungs that the doctor called consumption. Emmett could picture his Ma with her coal black hair and green eyes with a smile always in her eyes, playing the violin, walking around the house, and driving the cold and the shadows away. People said that Daniel took after her with his wit and humor, while William took after Pa, and Emmett was a combination of all of them mixed in together.

He had been alone ever since her death and was not sure what to do. Some neighbors had helped out, especially Mrs. Johnson right down the street, who would make him a meal or insist that he come over to eat with her family. But these were tough times, and people had their own problems. Emmett knew that it was time that he became an adult, but he just wasn't quite sure how to get started. Hopefully, the letter in his pocket held the answer, and his father would tell him what he should do. Emmett closed the door carefully and sat down in the chair just inside the room. This chair was not the most comfortable in the house but had the best sun at this time of day, and Emmett took advantage of the light as he studied the envelope closely before taking out his pocketknife to carefully slit its top, careful not to damage the contents. The letter had been written on white paper torn from a field notebook, the page small, folded once neatly, with a few smudges.

June 25
Dear Emmett,
I got your letter about your ma dyin and was deeply upset by that. She was a gud woman and mother to you. I wanted to come home but couldn't git leave as General McClellan called everybody to duty as he tried to sneak us up on the Rebels by boat. I herd thare was one-hundred and twenty thousand of us, all moved by boat to Fort Monroe about sixty miles Southeast of Richmond. We was afraid to attak at first thinkin they had more men but soon enuf we

drove them up the peninsla but finally bogged down outside of Richmond where they is pretty heavily fortified. That is whare I'm at now, staring across to whare I can just about see Richmond but thare is a whole bunch of Confederates between us and that city. I know things must be tuff for you and so this is what I want you to do. I hoped to be home by now and with your ma dyin I sure would like to be there, but I'm stuck here in Virginia fighting the Rebs. Your Ma and I used to keep some money by for hard times such as these. There should be some silver dollars in a purse in her hatbox on top of the wardrobe. Take that money, close up the house tight and go down to Brunswick. An old friend, Lawrence Chamberlain lives on Potter Street right in town thare and will help you out if you tell him of the sichuation. I must go now but will write agin when I can find time.
Your Father,
John Collins, Company G, 2nd Maine

Emmett was a slow reader, having stopped his schooling at eleven, though his mother had continued to work with him on it until her death. It was only after reading the letter a third time, as he went to put it back, that he realized there was another page in the envelope. He pulled out the small scrap of paper, crumpled and dirty, and smoothed it out.

Emmet—I hate to tell ya, but pa was kilt today at a place called Malvern Hill in Virginia. He got shot in the eye and passed without feelin any pain. Don't have time to write more now but you best do what pa told ya and go on down to Brunswick. I will write ya when I get a chance but ya need to write me and tell me where to send it. —Daniel

Emmett did not cry then, but merely stared at the paper, wishing he had not found it, that he'd never seen it, that it would just go away. After a bit, he stood up and went to get the haversack out of his room. In his parent's room he found the hatbox in the top of the wardrobe, and carefully took out his mother's Sunday topper, the one she wore to church and for special occasions. It was not the plain Jane bonnet that she wore in the winter for warmth nor the straw one she wore to protect herself from the sun in the summer.

This was her pride and joy, one that she'd ordered all the way from France, with a red velvet bow and yellow ribbons twisted this way and that and ruffled paper flowers. And, there was a flat purse heavy with coins, twenty in all. He picked up the book he'd been reading with his mother before she died and placed the letter from his father in its pages. Back in the parlor he stared around, his eyes finally coming to rest on a few tintypes on a shelf at the back of the room. He wandered over, remembering when they'd had these made at Mr. Pinkham's Emporium just a few months before his father and brothers had gone off to war. Daniel, as usual, had been making everybody laugh, even Pa had been caught smirking, but the oldest brother William had finally become annoyed and hit him in the back of the head. There had almost been a fight between the boys until Ma had screamed at them to settle down and not ruin her picture. He took just one of the photographs, the one of the five of them together, his father in the rear middle flanked on either side by older sons Daniel and William, while Emmett as the youngest stood with his mother in front. In the tintype Daniel now looked angry and William was smiling, quite the opposite of normal. He slipped this into a separate page of the book and put the book in the haversack with the few pieces of clothing he owned. And that was all there was to take. As an afterthought, he went to his mother's jewelry box, thinking that he might take a necklace to remember her by, but then he saw a small, ornate, hinged case and he carefully picked it up. With cautious fingers he pried open the case, and saw that it was a daguerreotype with two photographs. The one on the left side was him and his brothers from at least ten years earlier, and the photograph on the right was of Mother and Father—much younger—both smiling happily. He tucked this carefully into the sack and then made a sandwich with the last piece of ham and bread from the neighbors and sat down at the table to eat it. He took his time, chewing every bite carefully and washing it down with water. When he was done, he rose to his feet, gathering up the haversack as he stood, hesitating. But there was nothing else to do, nobody to say goodbye to. He paused at the open door, overcome by a strange feeling that he would never be back, and then firmly pulled it shut and began to walk to the train station.

Chapter One

But, I fear, this war, so costly of blood and treasure, will not cease until the men of the North are willing to leave good positions, and sacrifice the dearest personal interests, to rescue our Country from desolation, and defend the National existence against treachery at home and jealousy abroad. This war must be ended, with a swift and strong hand; and every man ought to come forward and ask to be placed at his proper post. –Joshua Lawrence Chamberlain[1]

August 17th, 1862

"Colonel Chamberlain, sah?" The boy stood with a hat twisted in his hands, his clothes rough from travel and neglect, his frame thin from hunger, his eyes marked by exhaustion. The house had been easy to find, just like the stationmaster had said; it was just a short walk up the hill to the church by the college and then take a right. A long, gleaming, white fence marked the house in the late afternoon sun. The largest house on the street, it would have been difficult to miss due to its very size. As he turned off the main road and walked down Potter Street, the house went on and on, almost as if there were four houses, each built behind the other.

"Lieutenant Colonel," the man at the door corrected him softly. He stood with a calm ease, but with piercing steel blue eyes. His hair was dirty blonde and, although brushed carefully, had a ruffled look that made it seem as if he'd just woken from a nap. A bushy mustache drooped to either side of his angular face, hanging down and almost covering a small goatee. He was tall but slight in appearance, with pale skin and a thinness that belonged in the classroom and not on the battlefield.

"Lieutenant Colonel," stammered the boy. "It's me, Emmett Collins, son of John Collins."

Chamberlain stepped from the doorway into the warmth of the early evening August sun. Just a few short weeks ago Joshua Lawrence Chamberlain had been a Professor of Rhetoric at Bowdoin College. Then this war between the northern and southern states had erupted, throwing many lives into chaos. While he was not, by nature, a warrior, his sense of duty had beckoned. But then, if he were truly honest with himself, he'd admit to liking the sense of adventure war brought, too.

"Emmett Collins? Well, of course you are, son. I can see your mother in those green eyes of yours." As Chamberlain spoke, he inspected the lad from head to foot. He was much in need of a haircut as reddish blonde hair streamed out from underneath his cap in every possible direction almost covering, but not quite, large ears that jutted from either side of his head. The face was simple but kind with precocious eyes full of adult emotion and yet frosted with freckles that made him look like the child that he still was. His chin was sharp with a small dimple in the center, hinting at a handsomeness to come when he had filled out a bit. His clothes had seen better days, his trousers patched more than once, a wool overcoat far too warm for the August day and on which Chamberlain fancied he could see the red dust from the brickyards of Brewer, boots worn enough that water would drain out through the holes when it rained. His eyes returned to the boy's face and he asked, "How is your father?"

"Dead, sah," said the boy flatly, looking away. "The Rebs kilt him in Virginia at the battle of Malvern Hill." Emmett's mouth was a thin line and his eyes narrowed suggesting that he had not had much to smile about for some time.

"I am sorry to hear that." Chamberlain replied. "He was with the 2nd Maine, wasn't he?" The 2nd Maine had been the first regiment to march out of the state back in May of 1861, a volunteer regiment from Bangor and Brewer, a little more than a hundred miles north of Brunswick. The Chamberlain family had called Brewer home, and Joshua had spent his first sixteen years there before moving to Brunswick, first to attend college at Bowdoin and then later to take his position as a Professor there. Thus, he knew many of the regiment's men, most by first name.

The boy raised his eyes with a flash of pride and defiance. "He was with the 2nd, that he sure was, sah."

"I read in the Brunswick Telegraph that the boys gave the Confederates a proper beating at Malvern Hill." Chamberlain remarked, thinking back to the article. The journalist had also reported on the Union victories at Gaines Mill and several other battles, but concluded by pointing out that all the while General McClellan had been retreating down the Virginia Peninsula, driven back by the South's new commander, Robert E. Lee.

Emmett did not reply at first, not understanding that a response was expected. When the silence followed, he finally blurted out, "I read about it myself on the train ride here, sah. It was in the Bangor paper that somebody left on the cars, but I don't think I really understand why we was retreating if we was winning?"

"I don't think even Abraham Lincoln understands that question." Chamberlain spoke gently. "But it is enough to be said that your father died in a noble cause."

"When Pa went away, he told me he was sad to go, but he had no choice but to serve." Emmett whispered, not having any idea then or now what his father had been talking about. "I just know that I miss him. And Ma."

Chamberlain looked up, his eyebrows raised in surprise. "What of your mother?"

"She died as well, sah. Last spring." The boy looked at the floor, worrying the material of the cap so intently Chamberlain was amazed it didn't shred. "She came down with a cough that just kept getting worse. I did all I could for her but it got into her lungs." Emmett's voice trembled. It had not been an easy time. "She died back in April on my birthday."

"And your brothers?" Joshua Chamberlain winced as he asked, afraid of the reply. These were difficult times for men, women, and children.

"They're off to the war as well, sah. Both William and Daniel joined up with Pa and went off with the 2nd Maine."

"How old are you Emmett?"

"I'm fourteen, sah, this past April." He was seeing his mother's bedside, holding her hand fiercely. Her eyes had been hard with the pain of each cough, but somehow, after the fit had passed, she would find a rare smile for the boy at her side. Right at the end, her face had softened into peacefulness and then she was gone.

"What have you been doing since your mother died?"

"I've been trying to keep the house together, sah. I've been getting some work in the brickyard, specially with all the men gone off to war, but there ain't much to do right now."

Emmett waited patiently as Joshua Chamberlain became

lost in his thoughts, the memories of when he'd been no older than this boy, taking his first job down at the brickyard. Days of brutally hard labor, early mornings and stifling heat, until finally he had found a mentor in this boy's father, who had helped him along his way. And now here was John Collins' son, a boy in need of a place. Suddenly, Joshua Chamberlain snapped back to the present, realizing that interrogating his young visitor in the dooryard was not the politest of welcomes. "When did you last eat?"

"I had some ham and bread last night before I went over to the train station. Turns out I had to wait until today for there to be a train coming to Brunswick so I just slept there, but I didn't get no food, so I reckon I'm sure hungry enough now."

"You are just in time for dinner. Come in, and let's get you something to eat." Chamberlain stood back and gestured the boy to enter. They stepped through a massive wooden paneled door, an arched window over the top for light, and into the house where an attractive woman waited, drawn by their conversation. "Fanny, we have a guest. This is Emmett Collins. It was his father, John, who helped me out back when I was a boy and needed a job." Fanny knew the painful story well when young Joshua had been forced to seek work at the brickyard as well as take over the farm chores to help save their home after his father had lost the family fortune. The Chamberlains had weathered this difficult period and even bounced back from, their fortunes restored through sheer effort. "Emmett will be staying to dine with us, Fanny. Please set him a plate." The man and boy walked into the house, neither yet aware that these were the first steps down a long, long road they would tread together.

"Dinner will be ready in fifteen minutes." Fanny stood in the entranceway to the dining room, her face red from cooking, her voice suggesting a hint of irritation at her husband's peremptory command. She was not a woman who liked to be ordered around. As a matter of fact, she did not much like the whole idea of cooking, either, and looked forward to the day when a servant might do that for them. "I am pleased to meet you, Emmett." She added warmly, her manners overriding any momentary miff.

Emmett was told to leave his haversack in the children's room, just inside the front door. A cause of annoyance to Fanny was that the house had no proper entrance hall, leaving no place for jackets, boots, and parasols. In the room, he saw a hobbyhorse, a box of wooden toys, and a tin train, all a bit fancier than what he remembered in Brewer. Across the way was a parlor dominated by a large fireplace with a black mantle in striking contrast to the wallpaper, which was bright daisies and greenery on a gray field. Dark, heavy wooden furniture, impressive armchairs, and delicate side-tables holding tintypes crowded the room. Emmett didn't have time to see more as he was led through into the dining room where a gleaming maple table sat beneath a small but intricate wrought iron chandelier. Fanny had retreated to the kitchen, which lay back through the dining room after asking Wyllys to show Emmett to the washroom so that he might clean his hands and face after his long journey.

"How old are you?" Emmett asked when he emerged a few minutes later smelling of soap to find the young boy standing and staring up at him. Wyllys remained mute, merely staring at him with large, serious eyes.

"He's three years old." Daisy Chamberlain said with the authority that only a big sister could convey. "And I'm five. I was sent to make sure that he brought you to the right place as he's not old enough yet to know better." The little girl walked over and took her brother's hand. "My name is Daisy, and this is Wyllys. Mother said that dinner is ready." And with that pronouncement, she walked through to the dining room.

It had been some time since Emmett had sat down and eaten a real, home-cooked meal, and he was barely able to wait through the brief prayer before plunging in. It was pan-fried cod, light and flaky, battered then cooked in lard with potatoes and green beans that Daisy told him came from their own garden. Ever since his Ma had died, Emmett had been scrabbling to get by, eating whatever he could, meaning that cooked food rarely figured in his diet. He was halfway through the meal before taking a breath and looking up from his plate. The Chamberlain family had hardly touched their food but was staring, mouths agape. Even the children were speechless, no less entertained than if they were watching fireworks on the fourth of July.

Fanny Chamberlain cleared her throat with a small polite cough. "Lawrence tells me that you have two brothers who are in the war?" Her face colored slightly, suggesting an awkwardness of manner. She had no concept of what to say to a fourteen-year-old boy but felt she must make an effort. When Emmett merely nodded, Fanny brushed a wisp of hair aside impatiently. "Tell me about them," she said.

"Ma'am? What do you mean?" Emmett carefully took another bite of food, suddenly tongue tied even as his stomach called for more of the sweet tasting fish.

Fanny, barely able to understand even the wants and needs of her own small children, sighed in exasperation. In five days she would be thirty-seven years old, and she was not quite sure that she had made the correct choice in marrying. It was not that she didn't love her husband, for she did, immensely. But she had never been sure that she wanted to marry anybody. She'd become involved in the artistic scene in Portland thirteen years earlier, before meeting Joshua Chamberlain, or Lawrence, as she knew him. It had been hard to leave the intellectual spirit of Portland behind to become a housewife and mother.

When she thought back to her previous life, sometimes she missed it deeply indeed, especially her friends. Friends like Susanna Paine who did portraits. Frustrated with how hard it was for a woman to succeed in the art world, she had written a book with Fanny's help called "Roses and Thorns". Through her, Fanny had met John Tilton and his haunting landscapes in oil. But it was Paul Akers, the sculptor, who had intrigued her most deeply. The two had become close, both once attending a reading by Henry Wadsworth Longfellow from his epic poem Evangeline. After, they spoke with him and his wife, Frances Appleton. There was music, poetry, literature, paintings, sculpture, and fascinating people—all of which she had given up to marry. For, after being wooed by this persistent Bowdoin College student for three years, she had succumbed to his ardent courtship and agreed to the union.

The engagement had been equally long, three years spent mostly apart while Joshua obtained his masters degree from the Bangor Theological Seminary. She had trained musically in New York City and then taught voice and private piano lessons at a girls' school in Georgia. It was New York City that she missed the most, for the arts scene that she was exposed to there made Portland look like the provincial city that it was. It was with trepidation that she continued her engagement, always wondering if there weren't more to life than being a housewife and mother in Brunswick, Maine.

"Ma'am? I'm sorry but what do you want to know about my brothers?"

Fanny came out of her reverie back to the present. "Well, let's see. Perhaps you could start with their names and ages," she said patiently to the boy.

William was the older brother at twenty-one years of age, Emmett explained, and, as most much older siblings, was almost a second father to Emmett. William was stern and driven to succeed, perhaps because as the oldest male, he was expected to inherit and carry on the family name. Daniel, two years younger, acted as the family diplomat and jokester, striving to keep everybody happy. Emmett felt closest to him, an intimacy that bordered on hero-worship. He worked his way through the rest of the meal talking about his brothers between bites. Just when Emmett felt he was about to burst, Fanny disappeared into the kitchen only to emerge with a blueberry pie that made his mouth water.

"Now," said Fanny. "Was that so bad? You're going to have to learn how to talk to women some day, Emmett." The boy ducked his head, his face suddenly crimson.

Chamberlain had been mostly silent, letting Fanny carry the conversation and allowing the boy to eat. Once the pie was done, however, it was time to broach the more serious matter. "Emmett, what is it that you want me to do for you?" He asked, pushing away his empty plate.

"I don't know, sah. After my Ma died, I sent my Pa a letter telling him the news. I just heard back a couple of weeks ago telling me that I should come to see you as the army wasn't letting him come home on account of General McClellan needing every available man to fight, but there was another note in there as well, from Daniel, telling me that Pa was kilt and I should do what he told me. So, here I am." Emmett's words trailed off and suddenly he was no longer a young man but a small, frightened boy, his saucer-like eyes dimming and his tongue thick in his mouth. After a pause that stretched painfully on, he raised his eyes. "On the train down here I saw in that newspaper that you had been put in charge of the 20th Maine." It had been only a few hours earlier but seemed much longer, and he paused to get his thoughts straight. "I thought, sah, that maybe I could come with you."

"This isn't a trip to town, Emmett," Chamberlain commented wryly. "It's a war we're going off to."

"I don't got nowhere else to go," Emmett replied awkwardly, rising to help Fanny clear the table, bringing the dishes into the kitchen off the dining room. It was an odd space with a set of stairs in the middle that led up to a second floor, but one that provided plenty of room for preparing meals. A large Franklin stove, still hot from the cooking, dominated the room next to a second fireplace. Shelves filled with cups, bowls, and plates lined one wall and above the shelves hung various pots and pans of tin and copper. Opposite, a long counter ran underneath the two windows, while a small table stood in the middle of the room for less formal meals. Emmett insisted that he knew how to wash dishes, anxious to show that he could carry his own weight and be useful. Fanny relented to his request, following her husband up the stairs to the bedrooms. As Emmett washed the dishes he could hear snippets of the conversation drifting down the stairs.

"He could stay here and help out around the house while I'm gone."

"...wouldn't be proper to have a boy that age here, Lawrence. What would people think?"

And then more loudly and with a hint of frustration, "What would you have me do? Tell him I'm sorry his parents are dead and then show him the door?"

"I'm not comfortable...Can't he go with you?"

"War is no place for a fourteen-year-old boy. I'm not going to repay his father the debt I owe him by getting his boy killed."

Emmett had finished the dishes and was standing in the middle of the kitchen, the meal sitting suddenly very heavily in his stomach when Daisy surprised him, saying that Wyllys was being a bother. Embarrassed at having been caught eavesdropping, Emmett quickly followed her to the front of the house to see what he could do to entertain the youngest Chamberlain. He had no sooner gotten there than there was a knock at the door. The three of them peered out the window to the left of the front door; three round faces of various heights pressed to the glass, the glare from the descending sun bright as they shaded their eyes to see a man, slightly obscured by the trellis that surrounded the door, standing patiently. His hair was carefully combed to one side, and a beard ran just down his jawline from his ear to the corner of the chin where it swooped up into a mustache and back down around to the far side. He was several inches taller than Emmett but didn't appear to weigh much more, even though he must have been about twenty years of age.

"Uncle Tom!" Daisy shrieked in recognition causing Wyllys to whoop and holler as well. The two children ran to the door throwing it open with excitement.

'Uncle Tom' dropped his bag and swept a child up underneath each arm, swinging them around in circles until he himself stumbled with dizziness, then setting them back to earth where they both promptly twirled and fell, laughing hysterically. "I brought a piece of candy for both of you from my store, and a present as well." He fished into his pocket and gave them each a hard candy. "Who might you be?" He directed the last statement to Emmett who stood awkwardly in the doorway. Then he realized that he'd met this man several years earlier at F.M. Sabines General Store in Bangor.

"Emmett Collins. I met you a few years ago at the store you worked at, my pa was John Collins, he died at Malvern Hill fighting with the 2nd Maine." This last he said rather proudly, daring Tom to somehow doubt the words.

Tom, suddenly the awkward one, nodded, "Sorry to hear that," he replied softly. "Your father was a good man. He was always friendly to me."

Emmett was saved a response as Joshua and Fanny Chamberlain came to the door to greet Tom. They had been expecting him, as he, too, had signed up with the 20th Maine, finally having persuaded their father to let him go to the war as long as he went under the watchful eye of his older brother. For the next hour the brothers caught up with the details of their lives, as they hadn't seen each other for some time. Emmett sat with them in the parlor, perched carefully on a chair that appeared too delicate to sit on, just the three of them as Fanny was putting the children to bed. After a bit, Joshua Chamberlain turned his attention back to Emmett who was suddenly so tired he could hardly keep his eyes open. "I have thought about your situation, Emmett." He said. "I think that the best thing would be to find you a room in town and a job. I have a few ideas and I'll speak to some friends in the morning. As for now, you will of course spend the night here."

Emmett shared a bedroom upstairs with Tom that night, a real bed with a straw mattress. After such a long day, it should have delivered him straight into the arms of sleep, but first he found himself relating his story to Tom. Before very long, a gentle snore told him that the youngest Chamberlain brother was sleeping. For Emmett, the sleep that had threatened retreated even farther, the fateful events of the previous days washing over him like a wave. Tears welled up in his eyes, and he cried silently, thinking of his parents. Finally he drifted off and slept like a rock until just before dawn, awakening with the realization that he had made a decision. He wasn't sure why, but he had a need to go see this Great War that had stolen his father and borrowed his brothers. If Joshua Chamberlain wouldn't bring him to the Great War, he would have to go on his own. He'd heard there was another regiment being organized out of Augusta, the 16th Maine; he would go and join them as a drummer boy. Resolute, and with first light licking at the window, Emmett rolled from bed, pulling his clothes and shoes on, gathering his haversack in the dark and slipping quietly down the stairs. He knew that his resolve would be weak in the light of day, and he didn't want to give in. He would leave now. Potter Street was silent, but there was a stir of activity from town and it was here that Emmett headed, hoping somebody would be able to tell him where the 16th Maine was being mustered into service. He paused at the corner of Potter and Main Street, taking in the wonder of the First Parish Church as broad streaks of sunlight now shot up behind its spire. Out of the blue, Tom Chamberlain appeared at his side, plucking at his coat and then demanding to know what he was doing.

"I'm going looking for the 16th Maine."

"What for?" Tom asked. The creaking of the stairs had woken him to find Emmett's bed empty. His carefully combed hair from the previous day was in disarray, his eyes still puffy from sleep.

26

"Because I'm going to this war and your brother won't let me go with him," he replied vehemently. Emmett felt that he couldn't soften his stance in the slightest or his resolve would fade. He would not spend the war in Brunswick, Maine, and maybe, if his brothers came back, one day in Brewer? No.

Tom considered repeating all the arguments his own parents, especially his father, had thrown at him for the past year. He was only now allowed to join up because his big brother was an officer and could keep an eye on him, and he well understood that the boy didn't want to be told that he was too young and that war was no place for a boy. So he kept his mouth shut. He felt a sudden allegiance stirring within him for this relative stranger, likely from his own frustrations at being held back. "What makes you think that you can still join the 16th? What if they don't need any more boys to play the drum or the fife? Do you even know how to play a fife?"

"Anyone can bang a drum." Emmett retorted. He started walking again, Main Street opening up down the hill from where he was, the train station down on the left and the downtown just beyond. "I guess I'll find out. But I'm not staying here."

"I have an idea," Tom suggested to his retreating back. "You get on the train this morning early, before anybody else is boarding, and I'll take care of Lawrence." Tom assured the boy. "He can be a stubborn cuss once he gets his heels set in, but I can convince him to let you come along once we are all on our way. It'll be that much harder for him to say no. Now let me get back to the house before they realize we're both gone."

When Emmett didn't appear at breakfast, Tom professed ignorance to his whereabouts, claiming he had woken up only to find the boy gone, haversack and all. There wasn't anything to be done and with so much to do before they boarded the ten a.m. train to Portland, they spoke no further about it. Joshua Chamberlain had come downstairs in the full uniform of a Lieutenant Colonel in the Union Army. He wore a frock coat of dark blue cloth, double breasted with two rows of shining gold buttons placed in groups of three. His pants were of the same dark blue hue, with a thin sky blue strip down the side, pressed and without wrinkles, tucked into knee-high leather riding boots. His blue shoulder straps were outlined in gold embroidery with a silver leaf at each end. He wore no sash and had not yet buckled on his saber, but had carried it downstairs and set it carefully in the corner, warning both children to not touch it. Tom Chamberlain, a simple soldier, looked much plainer with sky blue pants over which he wore a single-breasted jacket with gold buttons down the center. His feet were shod in the official 'Jefferson' boot of black leather, ankle length and laced up the front. In his hand he held his kepi, a thin brimmed hat with a flat top. Joshua pointed out that the government was responsible for outfitting regular soldiers, to which Tom replied that their mother had brought these basic pieces as a gift and he knew better than to refuse them. Last minute preparations consumed them until they were boarding the train, Chamberlain standing in the door as the train pulled out, waving to his wife and children, their faces pale and thin on this sunny morning as they bid husband and father farewell.

"They will be fine without you," Tom said gently. "I know that Sae plans on coming down to help out soon." Sae was their beloved sister, always ready to help, especially with the children.

"How does one ever know what is the right thing to do?" Joshua Chamberlain asked, still staring back at the disappearing train station.

"There is nobody I know who better chooses the right thing to do than you." Tom said, putting his hand on his brother's arm.

Joshua turned away from the door, capturing Tom with his intense gaze. "Mother tells me that she is afraid you have been making some bad decisions lately." It was more of a question than said in disapproval. He studied his brother's face, searching the blue eyes that all the Chamberlains had. The eyes were just about the only similarity, Tom being black-haired and almost swarthy to his brother's blond hair and pale skin. Tom was almost as tall as his brother at 5'9", but weighed a paltry 120 pounds, making him appear all angles—elbows, knees, and Adams' apple.

"I believe that the adventures of war will be good for me," Tom replied simply.

"You can't run away from who you are." Joshua said. "Going off to war won't change that."

"Easy for you to say," Tom retorted hotly. "You the golden child who can do no wrong. The firstborn given everything that you asked for and then some. Want to go to Bowdoin

College? Go ahead. Study up more and become a theologian? Go ahead. Marry the woman of your dreams? Sure. It's not so easy for us mere mortals to figure things out always."

"You know that I've worked hard for everything I have." Joshua replied, failing to keep the anger from his voice.

"Not everyone knows what they want." Tom said, following his brother into the rail car. "Sometimes we have to stumble along until we fall into it. Let's just say I'm fairly sure my fate lies elsewhere than in a general store in Bangor."

Chamberlain had stopped still, staring at the figure of Emmett Collins sitting carefully in a seat that faced away from the loading area of the train station. "What are you doing here?" He demanded, in a voice more harsh than intended. Emmett squirmed uncomfortably in his seat, looking to Tom for help. Chamberlain caught the look and swung around. "Are you part of this?"

"His father's last wish was for him to come to you," Tom replied plainly.

"I can assure you that his father's last wish was not for me to lead him to his death in war." Chamberlain's normally calm composure showed the first signs of cracking.

"You can't control everything and everybody around you, Lawrence. He's just going to go off and join the 16th Maine if you don't bring him along. And then who's going to look out for him?"

"Don't call me Lawrence!" Chamberlain snapped. "I told you if you were to join my regiment you were to call me Lieutenant Colonel, or in private, Joshua, but I am no longer Lawrence." His blue eyes blazed in fury at this disruption to his plans on his first day of duties as an officer in the United States Army. "As for Emmett, you may have a point. The choice is a poor one, but a choice to be made all the same. We shall see."

"As I have called you Lawrence for the first twenty-one years of my life, it might take more than a few weeks to change that," Tom responded derisively.

Born Lawrence Joshua Chamberlain and Lawrence to one and all, the older brother had just recently in life begun introducing himself and signing documents as Joshua Lawrence Chamberlain, taking his father's name. "How about I change my name to Davee Thomas Chamberlain, and we'll see how you do?" Tom was thirteen years younger than his brother, and therefore Joshua Chamberlain had been more of mentor and father figure until now, but with Tom's maturity a new competitiveness had sprung up between them.

"Don't act like a child, or I shall send you packing back to Mother and Father," Joshua Chamberlain said hotly.

Tom glared back at him for a long moment and then took a deep breath, his face relaxing into a reckless grin. "You don't have that power, Lieutenant Colonel," he said. "You may discipline me. Court martial me. Even have me executed. But you can't send me home."

Joshua Chamberlain muttered an epithet in exasperation at the frustration only a teasing brother could provoke. He realized that the car was mostly filled with passengers, several of whom he recognized, none of who had said a word during his exchange with Tom. "So," he asked Emmett, "you want to go see the war? I will take you as my personal aide, but make sure you understand firmly that I can send you home at any point. You will stay to the rear out of harms way at all times and you will never, and I repeat, never, listen to the inane ideas that come out of my brother's mouth."

Emmett kept the smile from his face and nodded his head. "Yes, sah, Lieutenant Colonel, sah."

Chapter Two

I feel that we are fighting for our country—for our flag—not as so many stars & stripes, but as the emblem of a great & powerful nation—fighting to settle the question whether we are a nation, or only a basket of chips. Whether we shall leave to our children the country we have inherited—or leave them without a country— without a name—without a citizenship among the great powers of the earth—Joshua Chamberlain[2]

August 18th, 1862

It was only Emmett's second experience on a train, and when it jerked into motion he grabbed for the armrests and held on for dear life. They were almost to Portland before he ventured a glance out the window, and the flashing countryside forced him to hurriedly look down at his lap and hold on tighter. Luckily, it was no time at all before they arrived, a journey so swift that he could barely believe it as they chugged into the Preble Street Station on the northern side of Portland. A line of hacks waited to taxi travelers to wherever they wanted to go, and Chamberlain quickly secured one for the three of them. Knowing that Tom had never before visited Portland and certain that Emmett had not either, he instructed the driver to take them down Commercial Street on the way. Portland was a thriving sea port as ships came into the same harbor with molasses and sugar to be refined and turned into rum, others carrying cotton for the textile mills, as well as multitudes of fishing vessels. Along the wharves was found every other merchant activity, from chandlery to rope and furniture making. They went by a massive church on Congress Avenue, St. Luke's Episcopal, its stone and glass facade soaring so that Emmett could only stare in awe. While the six-and eight-story brick buildings of Congress Avenue loomed over the boy from Brewer, it was only when they turned onto Commercial Street that he was truly struck dumb with wonder. Never had he seen so many people and wagons in one place.

The street was, if possible, even more crowded than Congress, as busy as a beehive, with people rushing in every direction, each on some urgent, unknown mission. The streets had been watered to keep down the dust, but by this time of the day, brown clouds enveloped the pedestrians and obstructed the view, only adding to the confusion. There were sailors in port from the ships, already drunk and walking arm in arm singing sea chanteys, while around them were businessmen in dark suits and derbies hurrying to the office or talking animatedly with one another as they walked along. Meanwhile, workers at the sugar refinery were changing shift, one wave leaving as another swept in, many of them women filling in for the men gone to war. On the harbor side hordes of longshoremen were unloading ships, some bolting in and out of the many taverns and saloons lining the street for a drink between jobs.

Emmett had never seen so many Irish in all of his life and felt strangely unconnected to these burly, red-haired men who spoke in an accent so thick he couldn't even understand it. Black men and women were walking the streets the same as everybody else, with a purpose all their own. There were street musicians on the corners playing fiddles, banjos, and harmonicas, hoping for a penny or a two-penny piece to buy a tin cup of the cheapest rum in one of the drinking establishments. Soldiers on leave or just arriving were everywhere, some in uniform, some with just a cap or jacket. Factories like the J.B. Sugar Refinery and the Portland Star Match Company occupied whole blocks along the waterfront while smaller businesses filled in between. They passed the Grand Trunk Great Eastern Railroad Depot that connected Portland to Montreal, bringing grain from Canada to be shipped to the rest of the world. This booming trade had created a need for the new-fangled steamships that dotted the harbor, bobbing between the square-rigged schooners, sailing sloops, and four-masted barques that had until then carried goods of the world across oceans and up and down the Atlantic Coast. A regular exchange between Portland and Liverpool brought Canadian grain to England and returned with Irish immigrants ready to work as longshoremen or in the factories and mills. As Emmett watched, the steamship Daniel Webster plowed through the harbor, leaving a wake that rocked the surrounding vessels. Thick, oily, black smoke rose from its twin smoke stacks and a horn wailed eerily across the water.

"I wonder if those soldiers are from the 20th Maine?" Tom

said, pointing to a group of men, some of whom wore the fatigue cap of the Union Army, but who were otherwise dressed as civilians. They were obviously drunk, shouting catcalls and stumbling all over the street as they followed a woman who appeared to have just ended her shift at the match factory.

"I certainly hope not," Joshua Chamberlain murmured. "Too much free time certainly brings out the worst in men, and many of our volunteers have been waiting too long to be mustered into service. I don't think there is any sort of system in place to occupy the soldiers who have already arrived." When the call for 300,000 more volunteers had come from Abraham Lincoln after the failure of the Peninsula Campaign, and then the disastrous defeat at the Second Battle of Bull Run, the men of Maine had signed up in droves, overfilling the quota expected of the state and causing this new regiment, the 20th, to be created. It was a regiment that knew no single home but was comprised of the overflow from the 16th from Augusta, the 17th from Cape Elizabeth, the 18th from Bangor, and the 19th from Bath.

"And Colonel Ames won't be getting here for another week?" Tom raised his eyebrows, "Which means that you're in command?"

"Until the men are mustered into service, I don't know if I have any authority whatsoever over them. But yes, I am the ranking officer." Their hack had reached the destination, bringing them as far as the Fore River that split the bustling city of Portland from Cape Elizabeth, where Camp Mason had been established. There was a ferry, supposedly devoted to bringing soldiers back and forth to camp. In reality a lucrative trade had sprung up transporting people for a smaller fee than the toll imposed on the bridge.

After they had clambered aboard, Tom asked, "How many men are we talking about?"

"When everybody has reported for duty, there should be almost 1,000 men in the 20th Maine." Joshua Chamberlain replied, and then added under his breath, "and God only knows what I will do with them." One thousand men under his command, he thought, surveying the sample before him. Men from all over the state, educated men and men who couldn't read or write, family men and boys who were leaving home for the first time, men who were rough and hardworking as well as men escaping something, and then men in it for the meager money offered—and each and every one of them under his command. Unsure of his authority, unsure of the first thing to do with such a large group of men supposedly preparing for war but not yet in possession of their weapons, uniforms, or even canteens, he must somehow bring these men together and train them to be soldiers.

"Ah, only a thousand men with free time on their hands?" Tom broke into his brother's thoughts, smiling broadly. "That should pose no problem for a professor used to having twenty unruly students to deal with."

"Maybe if I made an example of a soldier right at the beginning like I do in the classroom," Chamberlain said, a wry grin seeping forth despite efforts to control it. "I could in effect, kill two birds with one stone."

"Or poke a stick into a hornet's nest, brother." Tom finished drily.

The owner of the barge was a shifty man of middle age missing his left arm from the elbow down, a wound he claimed to have received in the war. About twenty people could fit comfortably into the vessel and there were already twice that, mostly men who also carried bags and who talked with a false bravado, arriving from all over Maine to report to Camp Mason. Most of them were discreetly eyeballing Joshua Chamberlain in his immaculately pressed officer's uniform.

Camp Mason lay just across the Fore River from Portland in the Ligonia section of Cape Elizabeth, which was mostly a mix of Irish and Welsh, the small village having developed into a bustling supplier of many goods to the soldiers who came through. The camp was not much more than an open field with a few wooden structures built to house the post office, and its official Sutler of the camp, who sold the new recruits all manners of goods. On offer were pencils, stationary, combs, brushes, revolvers, knives, bulletproof steel vest protectors, fruits and vegetables and other food, tobacco products like pipes, cigars, chew, snuff, and even alcoholic refreshments. A large tent housed the field hospital, less necessary in this training camp, but still of prime importance. The offices and living quarters of the regimental officers occupied the remaining large canvas structures, while spread out around them in what appeared to be no particular order were 500 or so two-man 'dog' tents. It was important to get along with your tent-mate, for these were barely big enough to squeeze one man into, using his haversack as a pillow and a rubber blanket underneath to protect from the wet ground. The rain of the last few days had created puddles and muddy, ankle-deep ruts down the rows between the tents. Smoke drifted lazily up into the sky as some of the men were cooking, mostly stew with some salt meat and vegetables bought from the Sutler, these being luxury items, though they didn't know it then. The flag of the United States of America flew from a pole in the center by the post office, and in other parts of the encampment flew the various flags of companies of men from all over the state.

Emmett followed a pace behind the two brothers as they walked into the camp a stone's throw from the Fore River. They had just reached the first tent when the stench hit them, the reek of human excrement mixed with body odor, vomit, and rotting food. The latrines were shallow trenches dug into the ground, to be covered back over when full, and these shallow ditches, past and present, were extremely malodorous. Everywhere Emmett looked, men were clustered, talking, playing cards, throwing dice, telling jokes, drinking, and arguing loudly. It reminded him of times when there had been no work in the brickyard up home for long stretches. Emmett was glad to be walking behind the man in charge and not facing this surly group alone, as not a one stood to attention, saluted, or paid any more than the barest attention to their commanding officer as he walked through the camp. These were volunteers to the army, men who had signed up ostensibly to keep their country united, or maybe to fight for their rights, even occasionally to abolish slavery, but likely more often for the $13 a month salary.

"Lieutenant Colonel Chamberlain, sah, there's soldiers here no older than me." Emmett whispered.

"And plenty old enough to be your grandfather." Thomas retorted, wondering if Emmett's grandfather were still alive.

Joshua Chamberlain took a moment before replying. "I'd be careful what I said to any man here. They may be a mix of old and young, rough around the edges and lacking any sort of discipline—but one thing is for certain, they sure are a mean looking lot."

And indeed, they were all correct. There were boys certainly with no more need to shave than Emmett, arms thin and chests not yet filled out into manhood, eyes round with the innocence of youth. Soldiers were supposed to be no younger than eighteen and forty-five at the oldest. The reality was that it was easy to lie about your age, and there many who were too young, too old, and too everything in between. As Emmett looked more closely, he saw one fellow with an eye patch, another with a crutch, and a third whose blank eyes suggested he had no more wits than a laying hen. More than a year into the war, this call for volunteers was scraping the barrel to the very bottom, as many of the most eligible candidates had already joined and been sent to the battlefront.

The doubt filled Emmett's eyes as his gaze swept the rag-tag group of men loitering in the camp. "And to think you're in charge of the whole passel of them," he whispered in awe, not seeing the fleeting panic that briefly passed over Chamberlain's face.

In complete contrast to the groups of disheveled men, an officer in perfect dress uniform emerged from the post office and walked briskly over to them, stopping and snapping a salute. "Major Gilmore, sir." Charles Gilmore was a man to whom order and discipline were important, as any sort of disruption to regulation seemed to upset the very balance of his being. That balance appeared to be careening towards collapse at the moment, if the tightness of his face was any indication. He had originally been mustered into service in 1861 with the 7th Maine, and had seen limited action that had included a slight wound. Somehow, he'd managed to pull some strings to get transferred to the 20th Maine, get a leave of absence, and then be promoted from Captain to Major all in one fell swoop. As his fellow officers would soon learn, he was adept at the politics of war.

Chamberlain returned the salute with less precision but no less gravity. "Lieutenant Colonel Chamberlain." Not even Fanny knew that he had been practicing that salute over and over again in the privacy of their home, working to perfect that simple gesture.

It was a small thing, but it was often the smallest of details that counted.

"Should I call the men up for your inspection, sir?"

Joshua Chamberlain contemplated the mass of men jumbled in disarray about the camp. He nodded. It would not be so much different than taking attendance at Bowdoin upon the commencement of classes each year.

An hour later the men had been split into ten groups, not in rows, not in order, not standing to attention or anything resembling it, but at least in distinct groups. There were no uniforms. No weapons. No haversacks. No canteens. Indeed, not a single item of their kit had been issued as of yet. Each company was about ninety men, but also as yet, no orders had come through from the governor's office in Augusta officially naming any of the Company officers. Unofficially, it was assumed that the men who had recruited their companies would most likely be made their captains. For now, these leaders held the loose responsibility of that potential future duty.

The last company to be assembled was perhaps the worst of the lot. It would seem that one of them had won money at cards the night before, buying several jugs of rum first thing this morning and sharing it with his comrades from just after breakfast until they passed out one by one. The man given the responsibility of gathering them, Chamberlain happened to know, was a lawyer from Rockland, respected in his practice and deferred to in the courtroom, but at a loss of how to deal with drunken men in the afternoon. Even sober, they would have been a surly group, few of them having shaved in weeks, the scruff on their faces holding bits of food and dead bugs that infested the camp, drawn by the open latrines and the warm bodies. One man had dried blood under his nose and down his chin, his vacant gaze seeming to indicate that he was not even aware that he'd been in a fight, much less capable of remembering exactly what had happened. Two men slouched without shirts, their shoulders and backs red from the summer sun while one man appeared without any pants, totally naked from the waist down.

Emmett watched with concern as Major Gilmore grew increasingly red in the face—spit flying from his lips as he yelled orders in vain, his voice growing hoarse. Joshua Chamberlain, in complete contrast, stood unmoving, with no emotion whatsoever crossing his face, watching as a cat watches a bird, biding an opportunity but not wasting energy until certain of success.

"The 20th Maine for your inspection, sir." Major Gilmore stood with ramrod posture, teeth grinding in consternation. "It is the best I can do, sir."

Chamberlain nodded. "Thank you Major." He walked down the ragged line of men as if taking a stroll on a Sunday afternoon. He was as casual as if he were by himself without a care in the world. The air hummed, a low rumble of voices and shifting of feet. Chamberlain paused in front of a man who was sitting on the ground. Silence fell, not in deference to the man or the rank, but from an interest in the possible exchange. "Is that your idea of standing at attention?" Chamberlain's voice was so quiet that even those close by craned to hear his words.

"Why should I be standin at attention?" The husky man boomed back in a deep voice.

Major Gilmore started forward his face flushed, but was only too happy when Chamberlain waved him back. "Your commanding officer is inspecting the men." He said.

The man got to his feet slowly, the muscles cording in his arms as he pushed himself to his feet. "Inspectin them for what?"

Chamberlain ignored the question, partly because he didn't really know the answer, masking his inadequacy with another question. "Do you have no respect for your superiors?"

"Ya might be my commandin officah, but that don't make ya my superior," the man retorted.

Chamberlain again nodded. "What is it that you did for a living before becoming a soldier?"

"I'm a lumberjack." The man proudly replied. Many of the other soldiers hooted in support, obviously of the same profession. Felling trees was brutally hard and dangerous work that forced you to be up before dawn, often trampling through the snow and ice into the wilderness. Once there, you battled trees with an axe and saw, careful to not slip and cut yourself because you were far from help. Even worse were those who worked the log rafts as they floated downstream to the mills. There, a simple slip and a dunk in the water meant instant death crushed between the enormous trunks, perhaps preferable to the slow death the brutally cold water would cause. It was not an occupation for the weak of will or body, much as that of being a soldier was not for the faint of heart.

"Well, perhaps we'll give you a chance to fell a few rebels." Chamberlain smiled dryly.

"I'll do what I havta."

"I'm glad you stepped forward to defend the honor of your country, sir." Chamberlain said easily. In giving the lumberjack his respect, Chamberlain hoped to get some, however gruffly expressed, in return.

"I'm only here 'cause the pay is better than jackin—and shootin down traitors has to be easier than loggin." His whole company jeered and laughed behind him, many of them obviously lumberjacks and proud of it.

"Is that true?" Chamberlain asked, his voice both loud and steely.

"Is what true, sah?"

"Does this country of ours mean no more to you than some greenbacks?"

The lumberjack shifted his feet, fumbling for his reply. "I shore wouldn't want no King or Queen like they got in Britain or that Emperor Nah-poh-lee-yun like in France tellin me stuff like who God is or that somebody else is betta than me because he was born that way, if that's what you mean."

Joshua Chamberlain nodded as if the man had just confirmed his own thoughts. "What is your name, soldier?"

"Paul Gridley, sah."

"God be with you, Paul."

"I left Him watchin over my family," the man shot back. "In all my born days He's pretty much left me to figure things out for myself. I imagine He didn't want to be goin off to war any more than anybody else."

Chamberlain pondered this, his sense of religion offended. But what right did he have to project his views on another? "Well, we're happy to have you, and may God keep your family safe." He said finally, moving on.

The next company seemed slightly better kept and orderly, and the acting officer in front of the men stood at attention, snapping a salute. "Captain Spear, Company G, sir."

"Hello, Ellis," Chamberlain said, happy to see a familiar face. One of Professor Chamberlain's finest students, Ellis had graduated from Bowdoin College in 1858. He was from the town of Warren, just about forty miles northeast of Brunswick. "How are your law studies coming?"

"Sir, they were coming along fine, until the Southern States interrupted them with their rebellion." The men chuckled at the observation, obviously comfortable with their leader. The man was of medium height and of solid build, but his face was so narrow that the goatee that adorned it almost looked fake, a bush of facial hair perched delicately on the thin strip of chin as if stuck there with glue.

"Fine group of men you have." Ellis Spear's soldiers were standing at attention, their bearing slightly more military than the rest of the regiment.

Spear looked around proudly. "I recruited most of these men myself, sir, from Warren and Wiscasset."

"Soon enough we'll get our chance to test how good they are."

"I am sure they will do their duty, sir."

Chamberlain remembered the kind of student Spear had been, one who saw no gray, only black and white, only right and wrong. He did his own work and took responsibility for what he'd done. It was on time and with every detail polished to perfection. If he suspected another student of misconduct or worse, cheating, he would not have hesitated to share his suspicions. "Keep up the good work." Chamberlain finished.

"I will, sir."

Emmett followed Chamberlain and Major Gilmore on down the line, self-conscious to be out in front of the men but unwilling to stay behind, waiting. Tom had joined his company, looking particularly uncomfortable as he tried to show military respect to his brother, the commanding officer, without being totally ridiculed by the other members of the company who slouched indifferently as the Lieutenant Colonel passed by.

"I have my work cut out for me with this bunch." Chamberlain confided to Emmett once they were safely inside the spacious officer's tent. The older man paused, considering anew the boy before him. "Enough of that," he said finally. "I need to know what you are capable of as an aide. Can you read and write?"

"Yes, sah. I went to school until two years ago and my Ma worked with me after that on reading and writing, not so much on numbers, until she died." Emmett replied proudly. He'd done well in school compared to many of the other boys, until his father had determined it was time for him to help out more at home and that was the end of school for him.

Chamberlain nodded gravely, pushing a book across the small table and turning it around at the same time. The tent was more than ten feet on a side, with room for a small table and chairs, both to eat and to plan. "Sit down. Tell me what the title of this book is."

Emmett slid into the chair opposite and pulled the book closer, "Casey's Infantry Tactics, sah."

Chamberlain nodded, noting there had been just a slight hesitation before the word 'tactics' but that the boy had read it correctly. "Skip past the preface and read me the first four steps under Formation of Infantry In Order of Battle, if you would."

Emmett carefully opened the manual, which would eventually be issued to every Union officer as a basic manual to give these volunteers, who often had no military experience at all, a rudimentary idea of how things worked in the army. He began to read.

1. In the formations of Infantry, a Brigade of the Line will constitute the unit, and in every line of battle composed of more than one of these brigades, they will be, posted from right to left, in the order of their numbers.

2. A similar disposition will be made of the regiments in a brigade.

3. In all exercises, manœuvres and evolutions, every regiment of ten companies will take the denomination of battalion, and all the battalions in the same brigade, will be designated, from right to left, first battalion, second battalion, &c., &c. By these designations they will be known in the evolutions.

4. The interval between every two contiguous battalions in the same brigade will be twenty-two paces, and the interval between every two contiguous brigades will habitually be one hundred and fifty paces.

Chamberlain noted that Emmett struggled with many of the words but had done fairly well with this difficult passage, though he was doubly sure that Emmett did not know what much of it meant. "Very good. Your next step," he said, pushing paper, quill, and ink over to him. "Read all eighteen articles of that section and write down the words that you don't know so that we can discuss them later. You can work here if you like."

This had taken Emmett over an hour to do, reading as carefully as he could and then laboriously writing out his letters with the quill. He'd sat for five minutes pretending to read more but actually hesitant to interrupt Chamberlain, intent on his own reading across the table. Shadows had begun to creep into the tent and an oil lantern flickered between them, its light dancing against the canvas. Finally, Emmett summoned the courage and announced that he was done. Chamberlain motioned him away, telling him to leave his list of words and the book where they were as it was time for sleep.

Walking through the camp as dusk fell over the scattered groups of men was scary for the boy, and he hurried along, hoping that Tom was back in the dog-tent assigned to the two of them. Knots of men gathered around crackling fires, gambling and drinking, telling coarse jokes and laughing loudly. A man stumbled out from behind a tent in front of Emmett, buttoning his fly after pissing, and the boy jumped. Some tents had candles flickering in them showing the silhouette of a man reading or writing a letter, but most recruits were out and about, escaping the heat and waiting for the approaching coolness of the night that came with a fresh breeze off the Atlantic Ocean. Emmett soon realized that he was lost and that all of the tents looked exactly alike and he had no idea where his was. He was wishing that he'd paid more attention when it was still light out when loud cursing erupted from the tent opposite where he stood.

"All I'm asking is for a piece," whined a voice from the tent.

"And I'm tellin ya to get lost before I get bell-fired up and knock the devil out of ya."

___

42

"Every night you bring some strumpet back here to screw and you never share with me," complained the first voice. "And I want some if you're all done."

There was an oath that Emmett was unable to understand and then a small thin man came tumbling out of the tent. A burly man with only trousers on and thick curly black hair matting his chest followed him. The thin man had just gotten to his knees when the other kicked him a glancing blow in the stomach. "I told ya to leave her 'lone," he yelled, "and now I'm gonna break your scraggly arse." But the thin man leapt to his feet before another blow fell. A group of men had gathered by now, materializing seemingly out of nowhere, on their faces the feral look of dogs waiting for a fight, illuminated slightly by the moon that now filled the sky. Emmett wanted to break away, to run, but his legs wouldn't work.

The thin man pulled a blade from his pocket, a mean-looking bowie knife. "Don't make me stick you, Frank. All I want is some time with your whore." A woman emerged from the tent, her locks askew, buttoning the top of her blouse with one hand and carrying her shoes in the other. Her eyes flashed angrily at the thin man, and she stopped as if to speak. But then, thinking better of making any comment, she quickly walked away into the darkness.

"I'm gonna take that knife away from ya and break ya like a twig." The burly man gasped, breathing heavily from the exertion. "You go, Frank!" Someone called from the crowd. Thinking that he had the smaller man cornered with his back to a tent, he lunged forward but tripped over a stake in the ground. As he stumbled, the thin man stepped in with the blade and plunged it into his opponent's side, the steel making a wet sound as it split the skin and sank into the man's flesh up to the hilt. "Ya stabbed me," Frank said incredulously, his hand grasping his side as he slumped to his knees.

"Somebody go get the doc," a young voice called.

"Go get him yourself," another yelled back.

Emmett was still rooted to the spot, reeling inwardly from the sudden violence he'd just witnessed, when a firm hand on his arm brought him back to reality. "Let's go back to the tent now." Tom Chamberlain said in a steady voice, guiding the boy away and down several more rows to their tent.

"But I don't understand." Emmett said an hour later, returning to the conversation he'd started once the shock had worn off. They'd retired and blown out the candle in the tent, but the boy was far from sleep. "You say they were fighting over being with a woman." He had only the faintest notion of what 'being with a woman' meant, but had heard some of the men talking in the brickyard and understood that it was something that men wanted. "But wasn't she that big man's wife?"

"She was a prostitute." Tom replied for the third time in the last hour, "A woman who is paid to be with a man for sex." He was not yet ready to explain to Emmett what sex was, never having played the role of older brother before, but he realized that that time was rapidly approaching. "Let's just say there are many women around camp who would be willing to lay with a man for money, and many men with money willing to pay them to do so." Plenty of the new recruits had brought money with them to buy knives, revolvers, food, and items of comfort to prepare for the war—but instead had lost it to gambling, whiskey, and whores.

Emmett had an idea what sex was and had even heard about prostitutes back in Brewer, but why did this make a man stab another? He understood that when a bull and cow mated, that the bull would mount the cow to implant his seed and this would produce a calf eventually, but the complications of lust and love were beyond him. Finally, the exhaustion he had fought for the last few hours won out, and he drifted off into a deep sleep.

The next day was busy as Tom attempted to help put Company I into some semblance of order while Emmett ran errands for the Lieutenant Colonel. That evening, the two sat down to eat supper with Chamberlain and Major Gilmore during which the Major regaled them with previous battles he'd been in and heroically recounting how he'd been injured attempting to turn the tides of battle in favor of the North. After Major Gilmore had retired to his tent for the evening, Tom broached the incident of the night before with his brother. "It was not an isolated event," he remarked. "I would guess that there were more than twenty girls in camp last night, from what I've been hearing around, and that was the one that led to violence."

"Do you know who the two men were?" Chamberlain

asked. When both Tom and Emmett replied to the negative, he asked them to find out by querying around.

"Is that all?" Tom stared at his older brother.

"What more is there?"

"You have to do something about the prostitutes in camp. Heck, you need to do something about the moneylenders and peddlers and the gamblers in camp, too. They're all bad for morale, and you know it."

"It is not my job to judge the morality of the men, but rather to lead them into war," Chamberlain replied stiffly. "God knows that I would like to preach to these men, but I am not here as a man of God, but rather as a man of war."

Tom shook his head, frustrated. "Don't be such a pompous ass. Do you allow bad behavior in your classroom because you are teaching foreign language and not morality?"

"I don't tolerate the fractious or the crude or boisterous if that's what you mean." Joshua Chamberlain snapped at his younger brother. "But learning French and learning how to kill are two different things and you would do well to understand that, little brother."

"Don't give me that rhetorical hogwash!" Tom exploded hotly. "You're just afraid to stand up to them because you don't know what you'll do if they don't listen to you."

The silence that followed was not the companionable quietness of friends. Rather, a suffocating awkwardness enveloped these brothers who had only the day before been a professor and a grocery clerk, but who were now soldiers preparing for war. Emmett began to understand that the world of adults was a lot more complicated that he had thought.

"Perhaps you're right." Chamberlain said in a hushed tone after several minutes had passed. "I have material to read if you two will excuse me. Emmett, perhaps we can find time in the morning to review your reading of last night."

The next morning Major Gilmore assembled the men and informed them that no longer would non-military personnel be allowed at Camp Mason absent the written consent of the Colonel or the Lieutenant Colonel. The Sutler alone could continue his business, but all of the men were aware that prostitutes, gamblers, and peddlers were no longer welcome.

Only an hour later came the first challenge to this new rule. Emmett was going over the words from Casey's Infantry Tactics with Chamberlain when the unofficial captain of Company B burst into the tent. "Lieutenant Colonel, sir, I am having some trouble with one of my men."

"What seems to be the problem?" Chamberlain was not happy at the man's abrupt intrusion.

"Its about the new order of this morning, sir. I just passed one of my men, Walter Billings from Dover, heading to his tent with some harlot."

"And did you remind him that such women were no longer allowed in camp?"

"I did, sir."

"And what was his reply?"

"He told me to," here the man paused, thinking better of repeating word for word what had been said. "He cursed at me, sir, and told me to go practice giving orders somewhere else."

Chamberlain sighed and stood up. "Emmett, you stay here and continue your work. Captain," he gave the man the title he did not yet possess. "Please bring me to Mr. Billings." As soon as they were out through the tent flaps, Emmett closed the book and carefully followed them.

"Walter Billings, come out here right now," the Captain demanded from outside the man's tent. There was a muffled curse from within, then light whispers and a scuffling sound. The Captain pulled back the flap and entered the tent and dragged out a half-naked woman. "You are no longer allowed in Camp Mason," he said, giving her a shove. She stumbled, dropping the blouse she had been clutching to her chest. Chamberlain turned away in embarrassment as the woman scrambled to pull the garment on, just as Billings emerged from the tent and kicked the Captain in the back of his knee, causing him to crumple to the ground.

"Billings!" Chamberlain's voice was like a bayonet, slicing the air open and stopping the man from loosing another kick at the Captain's head.

"This no-good Nancy-boy done interfered with me for the last time and I aim to see him broken on the ground, and there ain't a thing you can do to stop me."

Chamberlain stepped forward and stooped to help the

Captain to his feet, the hair on the back of his neck bristling in anticipation of a blow. As he stood and steadied the Captain on his feet, a gun cocked behind him. "You don't move an inch." Ellis Spear commanded. "Or you will be paying a visit to the surgeon about a hole in your chest." Walter Billings stood frozen with his arm drawn back, having been about to assault his commanding officer.

Chamberlain brushed the dirt off of the Captain's uniform, then directed him to escort the woman from the camp, but to treat her with respect, all the while making it clear that she was not welcome back. Only then, did he look at Ellis Spear, who stood with a pistol aimed at Walter Billings, its hammer ready to fall with the slightest bit of pressure. "Thank you, Captain Spear. Would you help Mr. Billings to find a tree from which he can cut a six-foot length of wood? It should also be of a good width, thick as a hitching post. And then have this strapped to his shoulders for he shall spend the day marching around the perimeter of the camp. If he does a decent job of that, one day will be enough, but make sure that he is on latrine duty for the rest of the week. Thank you." Chamberlain walked away, trembling inside but showing no emotion on his face. It had been a close call and lucky that Ellis Spear had appeared.

There were several more trials of the new camp rule— swiftly followed by onerous punishments. Soon the men got the point that it was easier to take leave and go into Portland if they wanted whores.

Things changed even more drastically later that afternoon when Major Gilmore came to announce that their commander, Colonel Ames, had arrived. Chamberlain and Emmett followed the Major to the parade ground where a thin blade of a man stood, a scowl on his face, hunching forward slightly as if his back pained him. His skin was pure milk white, making his eyes appear to burn from sunken caverns in his oval face. Even though he was only twenty-six, his hair was receding, but still parted carefully to the side. A bushy mustache reached just past the edges of his lips, while a straggle of beard much like the tail of a cat hung down from the center of his mouth. This was Colonel Adelbert Ames.

"Colonel Ames, sir, welcome to Camp Mason." Chamberlain snapped a salute to greet the Colonel.

Emmett fancied he could see relief washing over his mentor's face. Although it was nice to be in charge, it was better to have the commanding officer of the regiment finally arrive. Colonel Ames was a native of Rockland who had already served admirably at Bull Run where he'd been wounded in the thigh. There were rumors that he'd been recommended for the Congressional Medal of Honor for his valor in the face of the enemy. Just as impressive, Ames was 'regular army', having graduated near the top of his class at West Point in 1861, right about the time the war had begun with the attack on Fort Sumter. Now, at twenty-six, he was assuming command of his first regiment.

"Lieutenant Colonel Chamberlain, please draw up the men for inspection."

Emmett saw Chamberlain wince slightly as he passed this order on to Major Gilmore, who went about assembling the men into formation. Emmett stood quietly in the background as Colonel Ames grilled the Lieutenant Colonel about the readiness of the men.

"Discipline and order, Lieutenant Colonel, discipline and order are the only way to run an army." Colonel Ames was pacing back and forth, ignoring the men forming in ranks in front of him as he spoke.

"Yes, sir." Chamberlain mumbled.

"How many hours a day have you been drilling the men?" Ames asked.

Chamberlain was saved a reply that he knew would be inadequate as Ames took his first glance at the regiment.

"Good God," Colonel Ames gasped involuntarily. "What is that?"

"That, sir, is the 20th Maine."

"That is a hell of a regiment," muttered Colonel Ames. Standing in disarray were groups of men, slouched, shifting their feet, in various degrees of attention and attire. "More like degenerates looking for some kind of free meal," he spit out.

"We've been working on their formation, sir." Joshua Chamberlain interjected carefully, "That is as far as we've gotten."

"Why is nobody in uniform?"

"The uniforms have not come in yet."

Colonel Ames turned as if Joshua Chamberlain had perhaps made this up, but shook his head and promised that by tomorrow the men would be in uniform. "Tomorrow the 20th Maine will be mustered into the army of the United States of America, and it would be a sin to Moses to allow that to happen with them looking like this. It would appear that their rifles have not yet arrived either." Colonel Ames spoke slowly in an obvious attempt to control his dismay. "Soon after the men have mustered into service, we will ship out. These men are going off to war, and they do not have the slightest idea of what to expect or how to handle themselves. We have our work cut out for us. Do I make myself clear?"

"Yes, sir."

Colonel Ames strode forward and demanded, "What Company is that?"

"That is G Company, sir."

Colonel Ames approached the uniformed captain of the company, whose ranks were orderly, the men more rather than less at attention. The orders for officers had finally come in from Governor Washburn and, as assumed, the men who had done most of the recruiting had been made captains on the assumption that they must be leaders. "What is your name, Captain?"

"Captain Ellis Spear, sir." Ellis looked very neat and soldierly in his new uniform. The army did not furnish officers with uniforms but rather expected them to take care of this themselves. Spear had been the first to find a tailor and get his trousers, shirt, and jacket made to fit—and fit they did.

"Keep up the good work, Captain." Colonel Ames nodded and continued walking. "That man shows promise, Lieutenant Colonel," he said, as if in rebuke.

The rest of the day was spent in reviewing the men, threatening the men, cursing the men, drilling the men, and then drilling the men some more. Emmett grew hungry at suppertime, but they did not stop then or until well after dark, for that matter. No bother, he thought to himself, it was not the first time he'd been hungry. Before his father had gone off to war, Emmett hadn't ever been hungry, but since, a regular meal had been the exception rather than the rule. Finally, long after dark, Colonel Ames dismissed them, and the men stumbled off to experience their first taste of hardtack. Ames wanted to prepare them for battle rations and a time when hot meals would be few and far between. Hardtack was a biscuit as big as your palm, made of flour, water, and sometimes salt. When in camp, salt pork was often provided, as well dried peas and beans, and of course, coffee, but tonight Colonel Ames was sending a message.

As Ames had promised, the uniforms and equipment, minus the rifles, arrived in the morning. That afternoon Emmett officially entered the United States Army, joining the fight to halt Southern secession. Nine-hundred-and-sixty-one men were mustered into service for the Federal Government. After the men had been formed into ten companies of just under a hundred men each, the drilling resumed. From first light until long after dark, Colonel Ames drove the men relentlessly. They marched endlessly, this way and that way, wheeling about and then about again. After awhile, Emmett's head spun and he grew numb, following orders without thought or question.

"Why do we need to drill so much? Certainly all this marching back and forth is not going to help these boys fight any better." Chamberlain spoke carefully to his superior officer, not wanting to offend.

Adelbert Ames looked quizzically at this soft-spoken professor in front of him. The man truly appeared to want to understand, to make himself a better soldier, to become a leader— but he had not the first inkling of what made a soldier. Although Ames was only a young man himself, nearly ten years younger than Chamberlain, in fact, Colonel Ames had a keen insight into the workings of the war machine.

"I grew up working on a clipper ship out of Rockland." Ames explained, trying to order his thoughts for the other man. "And working on a sailing ship and being in the army are very similar. Every man on the clipper ship needs to know exactly what to do at all times. When a storm came upon us, the wind roaring, the waves crashing, it became impossible to hear orders and directions. It was up to each man to know what to do." What Colonel Ames had not learned growing up, he had learned at West Point. "They have to be able to act without hearing. Hell, they need to be able to act without even thinking. Because, when the terror and noise and carnage of the battlefield confront you, then you must not think, only react automatically with those actions that have been ingrained into you by just such mindless repetition as this."

Later, as they studied in the tent, Emmett questioned Chamberlain about what he'd overheard. "But surely the men can't know whether to charge, retreat, or hold fast from their position on the battlefield. An officer must tell them what to do."

"In the heat of battle, it is almost impossible to hear orders. This is why it is all done with bugle calls. One tune is for forward, another for retreat, another for halt, another for rally by fours—the list goes on and on and the men need to learn those. The bugler must stay close to the commanding officer, as must the flag bearer, to display where he is and to lead the men forward and mark where the center of the line is. That is why it is so important to have somebody carry the flag and why replacements must be ready, should the flag bearer fall." To be a flag bearer was an honor, but a dangerous one, as the enemy would target the flag in order to disrupt communications as well as break the spirit of the regiment.

"It is also crucial for the men to understand the order given. If we need to 'refuse' the line because the enemy is attempting to flank us, there isn't time to explain how the men should lengthen the line and bend the far side backward—it must be done immediately or it is already too late and we are flanked, which is the same as to say we've lost."

Although Chamberlain was a professor and used to telling people what to do, he was coming to realize that there was a great deal that he could learn from Colonel Ames. Chamberlain's great-grandfather had fought in the Revolution, and his grandfather in the war of 1812, while his father was a member of the militia. Although his was a military family and he had been instructed in classical military tactics, his knowledge was nothing next to Colonel Ames' wisdom. For the next few months he vowed to listen, to pay attention, to ask questions, all in order to soak up every possible bit of military knowledge from Ames that he could.

"Now back to your lessons," he said. "We've all got new things to learn." Most days when the press of regimental business had slowed and the light waned, Chamberlain found time to continue Emmett's education through a close analysis of "Casey's Infantry Tactics". Though not perhaps the most thrilling of texts, the exercise not only helped Emmett to read and write better, but also familiarized both of them with the detailed role of the soldier in the United States Army. That evening, Chamberlain had asked Emmett to read and paraphrase the "Instruction of the Battalion" concerning when the commander of a battalion might give the signal to fix bayonets.

59. In the movements which require the bayonet to be fixed, the chief of the battalion will cause the signal to fix bayonet, to be sounded; at this signal the men fix bayonets without command, and immediately replace their pieces in the position they were in before the signal.

"Lieutenant Colonel Chamberlain, sah?" Emmett paused as he contemplated why one would fix the bayonet and not just shoot the rifle. "When I was only about eight years old, some friends and me used to go down by the river and play soldier, and every once in a while we would charge, holding our sticks that was supposed to be guns out in front of us, and it always seemed to be a bit scarier having someone running at you than sitting back safe hiding behind trees and rocks."

Chamberlain looked up from the letter he was writing, unaccustomed to such a rush of words from the boy. "Correct, young man. Men charging with cold steel out in front of them can be a terrifying sight, causing even the bravest man to break and run." He twisted his mustache idly, adding, "I used to go down to the river myself when I was a boy and play soldier."

Emmett had a hard time picturing this man as ever having been a boy, much less playing soldier, but the conversation took him back to a happier time. "We would go down past the boatyard in town almost to the woods," he remembered wistfully.

"I know the place well." Chamberlain smiled. "Did you ever manage to walk across the river to Bangor without getting wet?"

"We wasn't supposed to but I did it on a dare once and never told Pa," Emmett said excitedly. It was a rite of passage in Brewer and Bangor to attempt this crossing, as there were times when the river was so busy that one could step from boat to boat and thus 'walk' across the river without getting wet. He never told his parents because, if you slipped and fell into the water, the ships would likely crush you. "It was the only time I ever set foot on a sailing sloop, and that was only for a moment," his voice trailed off. He'd always envied those people sailing by, off to adventures he could only imagine.

"We had a sloop," Chamberlain said, also remembering the happier days of childhood. "And we used to take it down the river almost every weekend in the summer. Us boys used to practice sailing on a ship we built out behind the house in the woods."

"In the woods?"

"When I was a year or two younger than you, I got my brothers John and Horace—Tom was just a baby then—and we cut down a tree and stripped it, making a mast thirty feet high. We put a cross beam on it and then dragged it out into the woods with horses where we dug a hole and put that mast up." Chamberlain felt the pride in the achievement even as he related the story to this boy he'd known less than a week, but for whom he was already feeling a particular fondness. "We attached ropes and sometimes borrowed blankets from the house for sails and we traveled all over the world that summer. At first my mother was worried about us, but by the end of the summer she had us hanging the laundry out on the ratlines."

"I want to sail around the world one day for real." Emmett burst out, a secret that he'd never told anybody.

"I don't know about around the world," Chamberlain replied. "But when this war is over, I will take you to my parent's house and we will sail the sloop down the river and into Penobscot Bay, maybe over to North Haven Island.

"I would like that," Emmett replied.

They sat in silence each lost in their thoughts for several minutes. "You best be getting back to your tent." Chamberlain said finally. "We have another long day ahead of us tomorrow."

Chapter Three

Lawrence, You are in for it. So distinguish yourself as soon as possible and be out of it tis long & sanguinary if we lead, short and bloody if they lead. It has got to be settled in 3 mo (nths) for them or 3 years for us — Shape yourself accordingly. And come home with honor as I know you will if that luckey (sic) star of yours will serve you in this war. We hope to be spared as tis not our war. Take care of Tom, as well as you can by way of easy work until he gets seasoned to the Trenches. Good luck to you. — Letter from Joshua Chamberlain's father[3]

August 30, 1862

Bursting with excitement, Emmett tried to sit still as the officers of the 20th Maine discussed the rumor that they would soon be moving out due to the recent poor showing of the Northern armies. It was late morning on a cloudy day, and Ames had granted a rare break from the maneuvers that they performed endlessly. Although it was not yet noon, they had already been training for seven hours with a long afternoon ahead. It seemed the latest in a long line of Union Army commanders had yet again been embarrassed on the battlefield. In charge for only a few months, General John Pope had blundered into a stunning defeat at the Second Battle of Bull Run as the Confederate General Robert E. Lee and his hard-nosed but brilliant right hand, General Thomas 'Stonewall' Jackson, had churned through the Union soldiers like a plow blade through soft earth. The losses had been horrific — thousands dead and wounded — and new soldiers were desperately needed on the battlefield, whether they were ready or not.

"I heard that Lincoln is putting Little Mac back in charge." Lieutenant William Morrell said to Chamberlain. Like Ellis, Morrell had graduated from Bowdoin College, but a few years later in 1861. He was also a former student of Chamberlain's and most likely one swayed to enlist by his professor's example. Morrell, possessing a keen mind and sharp sense of duty, had been an excellent student, and appeared to be adapting to life as an officer very well, Chamberlain observed.

Emmett knew that 'Little Mac' was actually General George McClellan, a much beloved officer, but also a failed commander whose talents had proven ineffective against the tactical geniuses of the South. All of the men had opinions about who should be in charge, but nobody was more popular than 'Little Mac'. Chamberlain had suggested one night to Emmett that military command should not be a popularity contest run by newspaper men and politicians, a concept Emmett thought on for some time, before concluding that it made a lot of sense.

Ellis Spear shook his head in disgust. "Is President Lincoln going to go with General Pope who obviously has no idea how to run an army, or with General McClellan who is afraid to use the army?"

"That is why we are being called up." Chamberlain replied. "With the army shattered and a lack of confidence in the leadership, they are going to need every available man."

"Hopefully they get us some rifles 'fore they send us in to fight." Atherton 'Pap' Clark said dryly. His demeanor belied his disgust at not yet being armed. Pap had put together Company E and thus been named Captain for his efforts. He was not happy when others didn't do their part, such as supplying rifles.

The men had been issued most of their basic equipment, which included a haversack, blanket, canteen, cartridge box, and bayonet sheath. Very few of the men had received the Enfield rifle that had been promised. This was a weapon highly valued for its accuracy up to 500 yards and because it was less likely to jam than other rifles. Not having a weapon to fight with had been the joke around camp. Now that they had been called to join the Army of the Potomac and fight, it wasn't so funny.

"Do you have anybody coming to see you off, sir?" Captain Spear asked, directing the question to Chamberlain.

"Thank you for the reminder, Ellis. I hope that Fanny will come down with her father, the Reverend Adams, but I must write her a note that our departure is imminent. If you gentlemen will excuse me." Chamberlain raised his eyebrows in apology and went into his tent to get ink and dip pen, pulling loose a piece of the military-issue stationery, his thoughts already turning to what he would say.

My Dearest Fanny, It *has been only a few days since I have seen you but it seems an eternity. Our time together was something I will cherish in my upcoming days in this Great War. I fervently hope that I don't disappoint you in my endeavors as a soldier, for I fear greatly that it will be too steep a leap for me to go from college professor to leader in war, making decisions that determine life and death for men who have families, loved ones, children, etc..... Just yesterday I had a run in with a boy from Castine in Company H. We were 'dressing' the ranks, something that the Colonel has been having us work on for hours every day. When one of the boys sat down, I approached him and asked what the problem was. He told me that he was all set with this particular drill and didn't see any reason to continue doing it, as he was now quite proficient and any more training on this would be a waste of his time. I sympathized with the man, not quite sure that I didn't agree, and that hesitation on my part was all it took for several others to sit down, thinking that they had gotten the best of me. At that point, Colonel Ames rode up on his horse and demanded to know what the.... He was none too pleased and the men couldn't have snapped to attention quicker. I fear that the men see me as a pushover but I have so much to learn before I can give orders without hesitation and without fear that they are wrong. I won't bore you with more of my problems but am hoping that you might come down to see me off, as the word has come down that we will be leaving for Washington D.C. in two days time and then I don't know when I will get a chance to see you again. Bring your father with you and the children if there is no one to leave them with. You ever-loving husband, —L.*

Chamberlain signed his initial, wishing fervently that his plea had been well worded, for he did desperately need to see her one last time before he went off to war. He was wondering how best to get this letter delivered so that Fanny would receive it that day when Emmett stuck his head through the tent door. The familiarity irked Chamberlain, but he checked his emotion, asking, "What is it?"

"Sir, there's a lady here that claims to be your sister." Emmett squinted his eyes in concentration. "But I don't rightly remember you ever saying you had a sister."

"Who," Chamberlain said, the grammarian in him absently correcting the boy's usage. "Who claims, not that claims." Then he chuckled happily at seeing the sibling whom he most easily confided in, for she had a quick wit and a sense of duty and responsibility that matched his own. She had recently given up a job teaching in New York to return home to Brewer, caring for brother Horace who had fallen ill with consumption. Sae, short for Sarah, had spent many sad hours nursing him until his death the previous winter. No sooner had Horace died, an event that had scarred the entire family, than Sae had been called upon to help Fanny, most particularly in caring for the children as Fanny struggled with various illnesses and exhaustion. Throughout all of this, Sae had kept up her own spirits and positive attitude, never complaining, never asking for more. Chamberlain pushed the boy out of the way and exited the tent to find his sister standing there amidst all of the squalor of the camp. A soldier stood next to her, having escorted her to the Lieutenant Colonel's tent, and was about to apologize for breaking the rules when Chamberlain waved him away. "Sae, it is good to see you and your arrival is provident. But what are you doing here?"

"I've brought you a letter from Father as he couldn't come himself, Mother being sick as she is." Sae's blue eyes flashed in the sun peeking out from behind the clouds to mark her visit. No one would ever argue the fact that she was beautiful with her blonde hair and fair skin and a smile that lit up her whole face. "I thought I might get a chance to see you all dressed in uniform and there you are. It is quite fitting for you, dear Brother." She hugged him, Chamberlain awkward and uncomfortable to let down his authority in front of the other men. "I hear that you will be leaving the fair city of Portland behind soon?"

"That is the Providence I speak of, as we leave in two days time, and I just wrote a letter to Fanny asking her to come see me off. Would you be able to deliver it and watch the children so that she might come down? I believe the Reverend Adams will accompany her."

"Of course, dear Brother, of course. I believe I may stay a few days with Fanny upon her return, just until she gets used to you being gone. But you must be careful!" The last was a demand as a cloud passed over her face, and stole away the smile at the thought of her brother in the thick of this war. They walked around camp together and spoke of family as Sae had news of not only their parents whom she was back living with, but also of brother John as well. Joshua told her that Tom was busy drilling at the moment and that he was embracing the life of being a soldier and would certainly be fine. It was a carefree forty-five minutes, rare relief from his duties as an officer, husband, and father—and he relished the brief visit with Sae as always. All too quickly it was time to return to the parade ground, but first he borrowed a horse and wagon to personally deliver Sae to the train, thrusting the letter into her hands and watching her through the window as the train started to move and then gradually picked up speed and disappeared down the track.

*****

"Tarnation, Brown! You're nothing but a lickfinger."

Tom Chamberlain knew that the only possible result of this insult to his newfound friend would be violence, but how had the yen for a tankard of ale in Portland led to this?

It had all started with a rumor that the 20th Maine would be moved out soon, that any day they would board a train bound for Boston and then on to Virginia. When the fanatical Colonel Ames had called a halt to the incessant drilling slightly earlier than normal, Tom had thought of nothing but food and then crawling into his tent to sleep. This plan was disrupted when a fellow soldier he'd become friendly with, John Marshall Brown, had suggested bigger plans for the two of them.

"There will be no sleep for you tonight, Brewer," he had said, using the nickname he'd bestowed upon Tom. "I know you're some kind of lumberjack from up north, but you're in the big town right now, and I could never forgive myself if I didn't provide you a guided tour of my more favorite local establishments." Brown was slightly taller and built a little more solidly than the leaner Tom. His yellow-brown eyes flashed in merriment at the thought of showing this hick the hot spots of Portland.

"I've told you before, I'm not a lumberjack." Tom protested somewhat feebly.

"But Bangor does call itself the Lumberjack Capital of the world, doesn't it?" Brown asked, his eyes dancing mischievously. He cut an impressive figure in his dark blue uniform with the gold bar on his shoulder signifying his rank as a first lieutenant. His face was freckled brown, and, even after a long day of drill, his hair was still neatly combed from the left to the right.

Tom knew better than to bite as the quick wit of John Brown could strike faster than a snake and was just as deadly. "What did you have in mind?"

"Well, my dear sir, in Portland we pride ourselves on having many a drinking establishment. It was right here that the Rum Riot of '55 helped end that unfortunate period of prohibition passed by that ridiculous Neal Dow."

"Will we be allowed to leave camp?"

"Already taken care of, my good man." John Brown smiled broadly.

They had crossed over the Fore River from Cape Elizabeth into Portland and then climbed the hill to the Western Promenade where Brown lived with his parents and sister, Nellie. The house was impressive, rising imposingly on its ten-acre lot facing the White Mountains in the distance and Portland Harbor to the rear. Yet, it was not the size of the house but the detail that truly was astonishing, stained glass windows, rich ornamentation, and even several servants, all hinting at the wealth of the family, for John Brown's father had been tremendously successful in processing molasses and sugar at his factory down on Commercial Street. Tom was introduced to the family, all details lost in a blur as the energetic John Brown grabbed a pair of gloves he'd left behind, answered a quick question or two about the rumor of moving out, assured his mother all would be fine, teased his sister in an affectionate manner and then they were off down the street.

"Is there some thought on food being part of this adventure, or are we to starve?" Tom realized that he'd not eaten for nine hours and his stomach rumbled its protest. "Your family was nice," he added to lessen his complaint.

"The Browns?" The First Lieutenant laughed carelessly. "I suppose they're okay. Did you see my father pull me aside and 'have a word'?" He laughed again, but Tom noticed that this time it was not careless, but forced. "He said he could still get me out of service if I changed my mind, that he had some pull and I could be 'un-mustered'." Brown's eyes flashed with the indignity of the suggestion that his wealth somehow made him too good to fight for his country. "We can start with some food and a drink at Ingersoll & Son's right over on Middle Street, but we will be moving on from there for the real drinking."

An hour later, after bowls of hearty pea bean and ham soup, Tom, wiping the last remnants with the crust of bread, asked, "So your father isn't real happy with you going off to war against the South, mainly because it's going to interfere with his business?"

"He gets his sugar mostly from Cuba, so it shouldn't affect him a whole lot, but he has a number of friends who rely heavily on cotton from the South. If lumber is King in Bangor, cotton makes Portland rich with the export trade, as our ships deliver it to the factories of the world." Brown threw money down on the table and rose to his feet. "Come on, we've a few places to visit yet."

They walked up Pearl Street to Congress and went into the Horse Tavern, ordering more rum. By the time they'd visited several more saloons on Federal Street, Tom was feeling the effects of drink, rum not being part of the Chamberlain upbringing or his Yankee sensibilities. John Brown, on the other hand, obviously had some experience with alcohol, whether it was from living in Portland or having attended various boys' academies, and then Bowdoin College.

Tom was in that invincible stage of drinking when a young man is not all that far from stumbling incoherence, but currently upright and possessed of a grand intelligence.

"No night would be complete without a stop at the Shamrock." John Brown said magnanimously, leading Tom across the street and shouldering the door open. "I could tell you many stories about this place—but most of them would embarrass me!"

The tavern, as its name suggested, was filled with mainly Irish patrons who lived in this section of Portland stretching from the base of Munjoy Hill on the eastern side of town and down along the waterfront to Gorham's Corner over on the western side. They were mostly a rough lot, longshoremen who worked down on the docks, loading and unloading the ships as they came and left port. Many were men who had fled Ireland, first in a trickle beginning with the 1845 potato famine then a flood as word came back that if a man or woman were not afraid to work, then they could make a living and feed their family in Maine.

Stepping in from the quiet streets, the noise that filled the space was loud, joyful, embracing them and pulling them in. Inside, the air was thick with a faint reek of rotting fish and the rank smell of laborers come straight from work with the sweat of the day still on their bodies, this overlaid with the pungent odor of rum seeping from the pores of drunken men—and women. For Tom noticed a few in the crowd, an unusual sight, women out in a drinking establishment. "This is more fun than any military drill!" Tom called to his friend.

Brown caught him eyeing one of the women, a thick lass of middle age, currently draped around a short, thin man who looked as if he might be crushed by her ponderous weight. "We can buy you a girl, if that's what you want," he offered grandly. "But first let us enjoy a drink together."

Tom felt the blush creep up his face, and suddenly felt light-headed and dizzy. "I think there is no place for a woman in the life of a soldier," he slurred.

"Ah, that is where you are wrong, my friend, but I feel no need to drive you away tonight, so perhaps we will remain soldiers for the evening." Brown had noticed Tom's obvious embarrassment, and gracefully switched topics. "Present arms...right shoulder shift...secure arms." As he went through the basic steps, Tom mimicked the motions with the cup of rum he somehow held in his hand.

"How many times must we slog through the steps of loading our weapons?" Tom complained. "We must have repeated the entire process a thousand times today."

"Do we put the powder or the ball in first?" Brown mocked the steps as he swigged his rum. "And how is it that we push it down the barrel again?"

"Don't forget to wad the barrel with the empty cartridge paper and then two taps to make sure the minié ball rests firmly against the powder, and fires cleanly," Tom finished.

"Colonel Ames is a tyrant."

"He's crazy as a loon."

"Somebody should put a stop to his madness."

At that point a rough group of Irish men headed towards the bar stopped, one man gripping Brown's shoulder, "Johnny boy, c'mere, howya doin?"

Brown looked up at him and smiled, "Sean, howya doin?" Tom noticed how easily this well-spoken son of a sugar magnate matched his speech to the Irish brogue in front of him.

"Ah been after workin for ya da down on the wharf." The man tipped precariously back on his heels but luckily was jostled forward by one of his mates. "Is that thahr Bridget with the juicy diddies still after workin at ya hawse?"

John Brown smiled at the image and replied in the affirmative that she was, but the man had been pushed on to the bar and had already forgotten running into them. He turned his attention back to Tom and continued the conversation. "And marching? By column?"

"Company front, attention!"

"Dress the line, Chamberlain." John Brown barked at him. "We were much better off before Ames arrived, back when it was just your brother in charge. Do you think we could put in a complaint and get him removed so things could go back to the way they were?" The alcohol surged like the ocean tides in the young men's blood, stoking their anger and hatred of Colonel Ames at what they thought were senseless drills from dawn to past dark.

"Well, if it isn't little Johnny Brown, soldier boy." Two men, not Irish by the accent, pulled chairs over to the table and sat down as if old friends. Unlike the majority in the bar, they were well dressed, each with a white ruffled shirt, bow tie, vest, and even though it was a warm August night, light overcoat. The speaker had a carefully manicured beard, pointed and shaped like an arrow, while his friend's was thick and wild, better matching his more robust body. "You take the night off from playing soldier to come tarry with the locals?"

John Brown nodded his greeting warily to the two men, his alcoholic cheer suddenly vanishing in the presence of these two weather-beaten men. "Captain Duff, Captain Parker, this is my friend from the 20th Maine, Tom Chamberlain."

Captain Parker glared at Tom. "Chamberlain? Are you the one who's second in command over at Camp Mason?" To emphasize the question, he sent a stream of tobacco spit onto the floor at Tom's feet, a shiny string of the brown spittle catching in his beard.

Tom set his cup carefully down on the table. "That would be my brother, Lieutenant Colonel Joshua Chamberlain, sir." The 'sir' had just slipped out, as if he were talking to a superior officer.

"What brings you to this war, Chamberlain?"

"Love of my country, sir."

"Who gives a bucket of piss what the southerners do with their Negroes?" The captain said vehemently while Tom looked helplessly at his friend, not sure what was going on.

John Brown leaned back in his chair in an exaggerated posture of casualness. "What you don't understand Tom, is that these boys here depend on slave labor as much or more than any southern plantation owner does, because their business is cotton."

"Our business was cotton." Captain Duff leaned into the table, his voice brittle with sudden anger at the reminder of the toll this war had taken on his business. "If I ever get the chance, that Abe Lincoln is a dead man for ruining my business."

"I'm sure his whole purpose was to ruin your business…Charles." John Brown drew out the man's name deliberately, emphasizing the lack of respect.

"My ship hasn't sailed for six months. Money out of my pocket. And for what? To free the darkies? Hell, they ain't got it any worse than the Irish in your Daddy's sugar factory, now do they? At least they get food and a roof over their head and get taken care of when they're sick. Not like the Irish down on the wharf, ain't that right, Johnny Boy?"

John Brown leaned forward until he was in a half-crouch, his face inches from the man he'd called Charles, and stuck his finger out in a threatening gesture. "My father doesn't own any man but pays a decent wage for a decent day's work. You're just het up because you tied your wealth to an institution that was destined to end and you don't like the hard truth of it."

"Tarnation, Brown! You're nothing but a lickfinger."

And there it was.

It was not so much that Tom Chamberlain was afraid. Confused, yes, but not afraid. It was just that he couldn't see the point of antagonizing these two men who conveyed a certain degree of affluence, as well as a hint of menace.

John Brown bared his teeth in what was meant to pass for a smile. "Ah, Captain Duff, I didn't realize you wanted to come to the hoe down and work for my father. Do you want to work in the sugar factory or would you rather work in the house? I think my father could use a butler if you don't mind wearing a top hat?"

With a strangled oath Captain Duff hurled himself over the table, hands grasping for Brown's neck. His weight knocked the table sideways and he ended up on top of him. Tom was shocked at the ferocity of the assault and stared for what proved to be a second too long as a fist crashed into the side of his face.

Lights exploded in his head as he found himself on the floor next to John Brown, who was doing his damndest to wriggle out of the grip of the man on top of him. Instinctively Tom kicked out hard and caught the approaching Captain Parker in the knee, buckling his leg so that he collapsed to the floor with a howl. Having grown up with three older brothers in a town of lumberjacks and bricklayers, this was not Tom Chamberlain's first fight. He rolled over onto Parker who outweighed him by eighty pounds, driving his elbow into the man's throat, a blow blocked by a meaty forearm as thick as a yardarm. Parker's other arm wrapped around the back of his neck and crushed his face to the burly man's chest. Tom squirmed and flailed, trying to gouge the man's eyes, but couldn't get the right angle.

Gasping for oxygen, a desperate Tom opened his mouth and bit into Parker's chest, his teeth sinking into the skin around the man's nipple in a violent seesawing motion. His oppressor roared in pain and pushed Tom away, releasing the death grip on his neck. Tom rolled and came to his feet, the rum slowing his reactions but spurring his anger. He grabbed his overturned chair and smashed it over Parker, who was rising to his feet, missing his head but catching him square on the shoulder, a savage blow that knocked the chair loose from his grip. The Captain fell to the floor, stunned, his one arm twitching in the air while the other lay useless at his side, his eyes glazed with the shock of the blow.

Tom turned to see John Brown still pinned underneath Duff and launched a kick that cracked into the captain's face just below his ear, snapping the man's jaw shut, his clenched teeth biting off the end of his tongue.

Tom pulled Brown to his feet, and they stumbled to the door, escaping into the night. As they went down Middle Street, Tom suddenly had to stop to vomit, the rum burning his throat like acid as it came back up, more painful than the blow to the side of his head from moments earlier.

Brown was exuberant, as the few fights he'd ever been in had been losing affairs, and he now chattered excitedly about how it would be some time before those two cotton kings picked a fight with a soldier. "I'll tell you what, Tom my boy, when we get to the real fighting down in Virginia way I'm going to stay close to you, that's for sure."

*****

Earlier that afternoon, Sae Chamberlain carefully stepped from the train, the 'cars' as they liked to call it around here. She had the letter from her brother tucked firmly into her bag, which was clutched to her chest, as she made sure to not drag her dress on the sooty steps of the train or to brush it against the dirty sides of the door. She was not wearing a hoop as was the fashion, but a simple dress that was functional, if not considered attractive by women of the day. There was no effort to thin her waist, even though she wore a corset underneath, or to pronounce her bosom. She wore her everyday boots—scuffed from travel—but practical and comfortable. Her collar was turned down over the plaid dress, and her hair remained loose on her head. Sae Chamberlain was a pragmatic girl who believed in comfort and who was possessed of a dignity that commanded gentlemanly behavior from the men she passed. It was a short walk to the Chamberlain house and Sae walked it alone, making her way to the familiar landmark of the Church and turning onto Potter Street.

"Mr. Furbish, how excellent to see you," she said to a young man she passed on the street. He replied in kind, smiling pleasantly. It was the middle of the afternoon after all, and Sae did enjoy what little freedom she was given. It seemed that she took care of everybody who she knew, but at the same time they all constantly worried about her.

As she walked down Potter Street, she thought of the wonders of transportation. Only this morning she had boarded the cars here in Brunswick, having spent the night with Fanny and the children, traveled to Portland to visit with her brother and was already back and the sun was still high in the sky! She wished that she could travel like Fanny did, to Boston and New York City, but it was not seen as 'seemly' for a single woman to travel alone. Her thoughts were interrupted by a screech as Daisy spotted her, running from the yard where she had been feeding the chickens. "Auntie Sae, Auntie Sae, you are back already!"

Who needed to travel when one had a niece as beautiful and happy as this one? "Can I help you finish your chores?" Sae asked, beaming broadly at the young girl. "Or do you want to do them all by yourself?"

"Of course I want you to help, silly." Daisy tried to contain herself and be proper but her enthusiastic response was between a shriek and a laugh. It did not take them long to finish feeding the chickens and to collect the few eggs Daisy had missed, and soon they went inside.

"Sae! Good to see you." Fanny Chamberlain set down the book she had been attempting to read while Wyllys took a nap. In truth she had been daydreaming about her life before she was married, before the responsibility of motherhood, when she had spent considerable time in Portland and had been friendly with many artists and musicians. Her memories were not sad, but wistful, a longing for a time that held a promise never realized. "Did you get a chance to see Lawrence?"

"Yes, indeed." Sae replied, bringing the eggs from the parlor to the kitchen. "He was able to walk with me, and we had a very nice conversation. I have a letter for you, somewhere here." Sae fumbled through her bag, finally producing the letter, slightly crumpled but none the worse for wear.

Fanny took the letter from her sister-in-law's hand and, excusing herself politely, retired to her bedroom to quickly read it. It had been but a week since she'd last seen him, but it already seemed an eternity. How would she possibly survive this war apart from him? Perhaps it would be over soon, and Lawrence's absence would be short.

"They are leaving the day after tomorrow." Fanny reported, returning to the parlor a minute later.

"He told me." Sae responded gaily. "Isn't it exciting that your husband and my brother, actually two of my brothers, are going off to help mend this nation of ours and make it a union again?"

Fanny enjoyed the company of Sae, but she reminded her too much of herself, of a young Fanny Chamberlain, a Fanny unburdened, not yet obligated to put on a happy face and keep the home running smoothly while the men went off to earn their glory. "It seems to me that honor would dictate that he should stay home with his wife and two small children," she murmured just loud enough to be heard.

"But what about slavery?" Sae stood up from her seat and went to the window from which one could just see the top of the First Parish Church only about a hundred yards away. "What about the story of Uncle Tom as told by the wonderful Mrs. Stowe? Certainly, we can't let the horrors of slavery continue to exist anywhere in our United States."

"I don't know any slaves, and I am not sure how it is any of my business." Fanny commented, her voice low and controlled.

"But they are being beaten and killed. Surely that must be something worth fighting against?" Sae would have joined the army immediately if it had been fitting and proper for a woman to go fight a war. But, alas, it was not, and so she had to live through the actions of others. Even though she knew that her mother and father opposed her brothers going to war—and now it was obvious that it troubled Fanny as well—she was unable to keep her words to herself. "Surely there must be something more important in life than mere safety?"

Fanny didn't reply for a long moment and, when she did, it was in a whisper that was barely audible. "Is not family more important than duty?" She raised her eyes to meet those of Sae, her meekness giving way to fierceness. "Are we not more important to Lawrence than some idea of union or slavery? We are his family. I am his wife, and I want my husband here with me, helping me to raise our children together. Our children." The air again filled with silence until Fanny's anger faded as quickly as it had come, her body sagging at the thought of the travails to come. "Is life itself not more important than death? I just want my husband to come home, alive, to me and to his children. Is that wrong?"

"I am sure that he will be fine," Sae reassured Fanny. "But I believe that God has a larger plan for us and men have to honor that duty."

Fanny was about to retort when there was a bang from upstairs, Wyllys waking from his nap. Sae jumped up and moved towards the stairs, saying that she would be happy to go check on him, and missing Fanny's final words. "How can a woman without children or husband know what duty a parent and spouse has or does not have?"

*****

Late that night Joshua Chamberlain was disturbed in his study by a commotion outside. He waited for a moment to see if the yelling would subside, but one voice continued to curse in—if possible—an ever-increasing crescendo. Carefully marking his page, Chamberlain pulled on his long boots, before going out into the night to sort out the problem. He followed the noise, wondering who would be up at this time of night after the day's intense training. But then he remembered his youth, before marriage and children, his own mischievous pranks while a student at Bowdoin College. Men would be men, especially when there were no women around to keep them in line.

"What is all the noise about?" Chamberlain asked calmly, directing his question at a soldier who was face to face with another, yelling bloody murder and rousing most of the inhabitants of the camp.

"The problem is...is that this guttersnipe cheated me outta my 'listment bonus, and, and, I want it back." The man was built like an artillery shell, his thick waist rising to thin shoulders and descending to frail legs, giving him a comical look that the men often laughed at. "Nobody's that lucky at cards. Not unless they cheat!" His neck was thin with his Adam's apple bobbing ferociously with every word, spit flying from his mouth as he stumbled to get the words out.

Chamberlain waited, gazing at the man intently, and nodded, listening. As was his way, he first let the man give free rein to his anger, but still did not reply, letting a silence follow the outburst to defuse the awkwardness of the moment. "First of all, private, you'll address me as sir, or as Lieutenant Colonel. What is your name and where are you from, soldier?"

The man took several deep breaths, working hard to regain his composure. "Private Lowell, sah," he finally managed to gasp out.

"And where are you from, Lowell?"

"Houlton, sah."

Chamberlain nodded thoughtfully before turning to the other man. "Private Lunt, isn't it?" He recognized the man as a Brunswick resident, about his own age, with a wife and family and a small place out Maquoit Street, not more than a mile from his own house.

"Yes, sir."

A crowd of about forty men had gathered around, those awakened by the noise, while the majority of the regiment had slept through the commotion. "How much money are we talking about here?"

Private Lowell choked momentarily as he tried to spit out the words. "One hundred dollars," he gasped, and then after a moment added, "Sah."

Chamberlain gave a low whistle. "That is a great deal of money, Lowell. Where did it come from?"

"Up in Houlton they offered the money to 'list with the army, sah, and I just got paid when we was mustered in yesterday." Private Lowell was deflating as he told his story, the fight slowly seeping out of him as he talked. "My Annie was comin to see me off, all the way down from Houlton. You see, I was gonna give it to her to eat whilst I was off to fight the Rebs." He looked around the circle of men gathered in the early morning hours, all of them on the eve of their departure to the battlefields, asking, begging for sympathy.

"I believe that Colonel Ames said there would be no poker for money?" Chamberlain asked, eyebrows lifted. This was indeed true, but certainly not an order followed by very many of the men. They'd bet on how many fleas they'd find in one man's beard, though poker was their favorite. The reality was that most often nobody had enough to lose or win. Still, Ames had known that some of the men had been given enlistment bonuses and that the temptation to gamble was ever present.

"I understand that that is a great deal of money, but we have to face up to the choices that we make, now don't we? The bottom line Lowell is you made a choice, and you must live with it."

Lowell's thin shoulders slumped and he drew one heaving wet breath, but otherwise held his composure. "Yes, sah."

"That being said, Private Lunt," Chamberlain swiveled abruptly to face the other man, his tone changing from gentle to direct. "You have a wife and children at home, I believe?" When Lunt nodded, he continued, "And I'm sure that you're concerned about them and how they're going to get by in your absence?"

"I'm sure the neighbors will help out, sir, and my parents live just down the way from us, but yes sir, I lie awake at night worrying about Caroline. We just had a baby, sir, not yet two months old." Lunt had worked in the huge cotton mill on the Androscoggin River, joining the army when work had dwindled to nothing after the southern blockade had stopped the flow of cotton to the north.

"I believe the people in Brunswick raised $185 for you to enlist, a subscription, wasn't it? And you have given that money to your family to use wisely while you are gone. How do you think Lowell feels having lost all of his money, money meant to help tide his wife and family over?" Chamberlain paused knowing that the next piece of this conversation had to be treated delicately or it would blow up in his face. "You will be fighting side by side with this man for the next three years, protecting the rights of both your families, defending our way of life, preserving the Union. This man made a mistake and now looks for your help, our help. What do you suppose we should do?"

"Sir, I won that money fair and square. If I'd lost, we wouldn't be having this conversation, but now that money is mine."

Chamberlain nodded, letting the silence develop his point, realizing that the group of men surrounding them had not moved, and that at the same time, you could hear a pin drop on this quiet final night of August. "What if you were to give him fifty dollars back for now. You keep fifty and then he pays you back part of it every time the paymaster comes around. Would that answer your needs?"

Around the circle, Chamberlain saw the men slowly nodding their heads in agreement, that this was fair, the best of a difficult situation. Private Lunt, who had worked hard all of his life, and was newly separated from his family, faced his commanding officer. He glanced at Lowell, whose face had lit up with hope to be able to send his Annie home with at least fifty dollars. Lunt, realizing that events were very much overtaking him, listened to the murmurs of approval from the crowd encircling him and resigned himself, nodding his head in agreement. *And what happens, he thought as Lowell reached out his hand, if you are killed next week?*

*****

Emmett was lying on his back in an old hut that had been abandoned long ago. He had taken to coming here when he wanted to be alone. Any day now the 20th Maine would begin their journey to the war, the place that had killed his father. Men would be trying to kill him. The very thought made his stomach tighten into a knot and a light sweat break out on his brow even though it was a cold bitter day with rain and hail being carried on a stiff wind, the weather changing on a whim as only it can in Maine.

"Emmett, is that you in there?" Tom Chamberlain came through the doorway. He shook his head like a wet dog, dousing Emmett. "I thought you might be here."

Emmett hadn't realized that anybody else knew of this old shack, much less that he used it as a retreat. "I just needed a moment to myself," he replied, brushing his eyes with his hand, his voice husky.

Tom nodded his head knowingly, without judgment. "Sometimes, you just need to be alone. Normally, I wouldn't have bothered you, but there are some folks up on the parade ground that are fixing to make a presentation to Lawrence, and I figured you wouldn't want to miss it. So, I said to myself, where would I be on a rainy, dreary day if I was a fourteen-year-old boy...." His voice trailed off, his head pounding from the previous night's drinking and his tongue thick in his dry mouth.

"What sort of presentation?" Emmett raised his eyes to meet Tom's, gasping when he saw a deep, raw-colored bruise spreading in an ugly rainbow over his face. "What...?" Emmett began to ask but caught himself, turning away. It was none of his business, and if Tom wanted to tell him he would.

"I believe they have a gift for him, but that's all I know."

"I reckon we should get on up there." Emmett spoke carelessly, suddenly anxious to be out of the shack. What sort of gift, he wondered idly, would you give a man right before he headed off to war? He shouldered his way out the door, covering up the fact that he'd been caught with tears in his eyes. He paused outside the door with a question on his lips. "Tom, what kind of brother was the Lieutenant Colonel?"

"You mean growing up?"

"Yeah, when you were both kids."

"He was probably more like a father to me than a brother," Tom replied. "Lawrence is thirteen years my elder. But more important is the fact that Lawrence has always been older than his actual years."

"What do you mean?"

"I guess of all of us Chamberlains; old Lawrence is the one who has always been driven, driven to go out in the world and make a mark for himself that history won't soon forget. He was caught between being a minister and a professor, but to see him here and soon to be at war, I reckon that these were just stepping stones." Tom absently twisted a sideburn as he spoke. "What he is really meant to do lies yet ahead. I'm sure he's a great professor and all," the young man continued, "but teaching rhetoric or language to college students is not the greatness that Lawrence has been striving to achieve. This here war, now that might be a different story."

"I don't understand why he changed his name from Lawrence to Joshua." Emmett had been puzzling over this mystery since the argument on the train coming down to Camp Mason.

"Not much of a story there," Tom replied. "He was born Lawrence Joshua Chamberlain, named after a hero of the war of 1812, Captain James Lawrence. About the time that he graduated, my brother decided he wanted to be known as Joshua Lawrence Chamberlain, presumably in honor of our father whose name is also Joshua. That's all there is to it, him being the first born, I reckon he wants to carry on Father's given name."

"I'm the youngest of three boys," Emmett piped up. "Sort of like you."

"I have a sister as well, don't forget Sae." Tom said gaily but then a cloud brushed across his features. "But I did have three brothers until Horace died in December."

Emmett didn't know what to say and merely nodded sympathetically. "I got a letter from my brother, Daniel, a couple of days ago. He said that him and William were fine, but they've been burying a lot of their friends lately."

"Probably a lot of good boys I know from Brewer." Tom stated grimly. "Mother and Father wouldn't hear of me joining up, not until Lawrence was put in command, or next in command I should say, of this regiment. I was going to sign up anyway, but after Horace died I didn't have the heart, not until I heard that Lawrence had joined up, anyways."

Emmett envied the thin young man next to him, envied him for having parents who cared whether he lived or died. "I was always the odd one out in the family, being so much younger than my two brothers."

Tom leveled his gaze at the boy. "I guess maybe you and me are pretty much alike in some ways," he said. "Not only am I the youngest, but I guess you could say I'm the black sheep of the family. I'm not really cut out for an education or becoming a craftsman. Maybe I'll be better suited to soldiering."

With that pronouncement the two young men, or old boys, emerged into the bustle of Camp Mason. There was a ceremony taking place in the middle of the parade ground where a man was speaking before a small crowd, and they got there just in time to see the man hand the reins of a gray horse to Joshua Chamberlain.

Tom leaned over to Emmett and whispered, "That gentleman there is William Field, a friend of Lawrence's from Brunswick."

Chamberlain was making a short speech of gratitude to the Brunswick Women's Auxiliary, which had raised the money to buy the horse, Prince, as a gift for Chamberlain on the eve of his departure for war.

"An officer riding a gray horse into battle?" It was Ellis Spear, whose sudden arrival behind Emmett and Thomas had startled them both. "Might as well put a bull's-eye on his back and have him carry a sign saying 'shoot me'." Spear was not much of a talker, but when he said something, it was almost always worth listening to.

"Is it a bad thing for him to ride a gray horse?" Emmett asked, not quite sure he followed.

Ellis Spear stared intently at the boy. "A Lieutenant Colonel leads the men into battle," he stated bluntly. "The highest ranking officers stay at the back, strategizing and what not, but your man there must be the first into the fray. Now, Johnny Reb knows his best chance to throw a regiment into confusion is to eliminate the leader, so they'll have their sharpshooters looking for the officers as the first targets. It's bad enough to put stars and stripes on a man's uniform, but then set him up there on a gray horse, that is just plain stupid."

"I never thought of that." Emmett hung his head, knowing that there would be a lot of things in the next few months to learn. "Should he just give the horse back?"

"That would be disrespectful to the women of Brunswick." Spear snorted. "We can't have that, now. Besides, he'll be able to ride the horse on marches and the parade ground. He is a fine looking animal."

"Hello, Lawrence!" Tom said loudly, as much in warning as greeting.

Chamberlain had surprised them, appearing with his wife and father-in-law out of the rain. He shot a disapproving glance at his younger brother, who merely grinned at his own breach of military protocol. Ellis Spear and Emmett both snapped a salute, Tom quickly following suit. "At ease, gentlemen." Chamberlain said stiffly. "Ellis, you know my wife, Fanny, and her father, the Reverend Adams?"

The Reverend Adams had a stern look as he greeted Ellis and Tom, a look that chilled Emmett as its focus turned to him. "And who is this young soldier?"

"I am sorry, sir," Joshua Chamberlain apologized. "This is my aide, Emmett Collins."

"I was not aware that Lieutenant Colonels were in the habit of having 'aides'?" The Reverend Adam's eyebrow rose in surprise.

"He is the son of a man I knew in Brewer, a friend." Joshua Chamberlain related. "This Great War has made Emmett an orphan."

"May God be with you, son."

"Thank you, sah." Emmett stuttered back.

By 3 a.m. the next morning, the 20th Maine was breaking camp, crossing over the river to Portland in small groups. A train awaited them at the Great Eastern Depot to transport them to Boston. Joshua Chamberlain stared out the window into the black gloom of the morning as sleet pelted off the glass, musing over the letter Fanny had given him. And then he read the words for the third time.

Dearest Lawrence, I am sure that you will make a wonderful officer and will be a hero to your men and to your country. I am not so sure that I will fare so well here without you. I write this down because I am afraid that I won't be able to tell you my thoughts when I see you, but as Emerson said, "We will walk on our own feet; we will work with our own hands; we will speak our own minds..." and I believe that is what I must do here, that is, to speak my own mind. You know that I took a long time committing myself to the institution of marriage and only did so because I love you so much, but I never expected that the government would take you away from me. I know that if it weren't for the workings of political parties that caused this war that you would never leave my side, but as you are reading this, you must indeed have left my side. And I am not sure that I am cut out to be the happy little helpmeet staying at home and busying myself with the children while my husband is away. It is not who I am because I was meant to walk on my own feet and my feet will not be at home mindlessly, waiting to hear that you have died in the war. But, please, please do not die for I think that if you die, I will die as well and then what of the children? Let me know when I may visit with you and I will be there. Write to me so that I may hear your voice in your words. I believe in you Lawrence, but I cannot believe in a war that has taken you away from me, and so therefore, my obedience is imperfect, but is the most that I can offer. —Your loving wife, Fanny

Chapter Four

It is the discipline, which is the soul of armies, as indeed the soul of power in all intelligence. Other things – moral considerations, impulses of sentiment, and even natural excitement – may lead men to great deeds; but taken in the long run, and in all vicissitudes, an army is effective in proportion to its discipline. – Joshua Lawrence Chamberlain[4]

September 2, 1862

Emmett watched Portland slide away as the train gradually picked up speed on its journey south to Boston. As soon as the city was out of sight, he pulled out the New York newspaper that Chamberlain had given him to read, specifically the article on the Second Battle of Bull Run that had just concluded four days earlier in another Union loss. He carefully spread the newspaper out in front of him, smoothing the crinkled folds into order with his hand, and finally bent to the task of reading.

Pope or McClellan? Disaster Looms for the Union
The latest disaster from the army at the Second Battle of Bull Run puts our nation into a quandary; should President Lincoln continue to split the army into the Army of Virginia and the Army of the Potomac? General McClellan did show his reluctance to use the army in the recent Peninsula Campaign as he refused to attack with superior numbers and retreated after victories, but General Pope has displayed a trait much worse—ineptitude.
Certain that General Thomas Jackson was retreating (perhaps the nickname "Stonewall" should have indicated otherwise), Pope pressed the attack at Manassas, ignoring reports that General Longstreet was approaching with a large force. Jackson was but a bully trap, luring Pope in before pummeling him. As well, Pope communicated poorly with his generals, most notably FitzJohn Porter, giving him ambiguous instructions that left the right flank under General Sigel to take the brunt of the firepower from Jackson, who was not retreating but was, in fact, firmly entrenched on Stony Ridge. His error, indeed, was not one of pusillanimity but hobbled the ability to win the battle nonetheless.

On the third day of fighting, General Pope finally managed to send Porter into the fray where a punishing artillery fire pounded his men as they crossed a large open expanse and then were decimated by a withering volley from the infantry. General Longstreet counterattacked from the left flank driving the Union troops back to Henry House Hill with their tails down, where they finally rallied and held their position long enough to partake in an orderly retreat.

What does this mean for the United States? It means that England is now considering the possibility that the South may actually win this war and could possibly persuade the Brits to throw their hand in with the Confederacy so as to be on the winning side and capitalize on the cotton trade. It means that General Lee now endangers Washington D.C. and that the latest wave of 300,000 recruits that President Lincoln has called for must be thrown into the fire in a desperate attempt to dampen the raging flames that threatens our existence.

As the American Patriot Thomas Paine wrote, these are indeed the times that try men's Souls.

Emmett worried over the report from the battlefield, which he would reach in a few short days, trying to make sense of the impending doom that seemed to loom over the Union war effort. With a sigh, he lay the paper back down and pressed his face to the window. He heard a man in front of him say that they were about to leave Maine behind and pass into New Hampshire. The train came around a bend and Emmett could see a bridge stretching forth in front of them and then the clatter of the train changed as the cars left the firm ground and began to ascend tracks that shook and vibrated unpleasantly as if they were no longer connected to the earth. Outside his window Emmett could see two bridges, one for the train and one for pedestrians, so closely connected that if the window was open, he could reach out and touch the wagons and carriages now passing in either direction. Farm wagons laden with supplies for the people of Portsmouth plodded along, teams of horses pulling their heavy loads into the city, beasts of burden with straining muscles and sweat-flecked withers breathing heavily in the cool September morning. The train was approaching a brougham carrying a man and a woman inside while a coachman sat up front, driving the single light bay in harness, the horse unaccustomed to the smelly, smoky iron beast passing by him, prancing and snorting in fear, desperate to escape. Emmett stared directly into the eyes of the woman as they passed, her parasol held out as if to ward off the train. The coachman was cursing and whipping the horse with a heavy lash to keep him from darting sideways into the wagons coming the other direction, his natural instinct. Then the brick buildings of the city of Portsmouth appeared, the train left the half-mile bridge behind, and Emmett realized that he was no longer in Maine.

"Portsmouth has burned down several times this century, and finally they used bricks from Brewer to build structures that wouldn't burn." Chamberlain remarked, sliding into the vacant seat next to Emmett. "Probably most of these people living here have never heard of Brewer, but they have certainly reaped the benefits of our little town and its brickyards on the Penobscot."

"Up until a couple of weeks ago, I'd never been more than ten miles from home." Emmett responded, returning his gaze to the large factory buildings rising up outside the train window. "And then I took the train to Brunswick, and then on to Portland, and now I'm not even in Maine anymore." Emmett whispered wistfully. "Before I know it, I'll be in Boston, and then Washington, and then somewhere in Maryland, according to this article."

Chamberlain took this as an invitation to discuss the story, first going through the main points and making sure that Emmett had understood what he'd read before proceeding. "You have to understand that the people who write these stories are partisan," he told the boy.

"Why would England join the war?" Emmett asked, puzzled that another country would bother.

"Some people claim England has been hurt by the loss of the cotton trade with the Southern states." Chamberlain said carefully, alluding to the Northern blockade of rebel ports. "But I don't think that it is in their best interest to get involved in our war. They also benefit from the products of the North and wouldn't want to lose this alliance, especially when the North and South eventually reconcile."

"I don't see it being any of their business," Emmett blurted out. "Even if we are losing the war like the newspaper says."

"President Lincoln isn't going to let the North lose the war, Emmett." Chamberlain chided. "The South has won some important victories, but they are a long way from defeating the Union. We have better factories, farms, many more people, and an established government whereas the South must create a country out of whole cloth. We just need to find the right leader for the army, and this is where the newspaper might be right that neither General McClellan nor Pope seems the right man for the job." He pointed out the window. "What do you see out there?" Chamberlain let his words sink in, and then returned to his seat with Colonel Ames.

Emmett stared out the window, seeing nothing, only empty fields. But as he continued to look, he began to see details that he hadn't noticed before. There was a man and his son, about Emmett's age, with two large draft horses in harness, wrestling a boulder from the earth while nearby a half-finished stone wall stood. Farming in New Hampshire had proven to be difficult due to the rocky terrain and the granite that the state was known for. Still, the industrious farmers had spent generations ripping these rocks from the ground, and turning them into stone walls to separate their field from the neighbor's as well as to keep the cattle, sheep, and hogs from the gardens and the grain crops. Just the other side of this was a field of rye, about ready to be harvested and then brought to the grist mill and made into flour, the fields being abundant enough that the excess was probably sold or bartered for items that the family couldn't make or grow on their own, such as the plows used to furrow the ground. Then the farmhouse itself came into view, a modest single-story wooden affair with a solitary chimney rising from the center, dominated by the large barn that housed the grain crops and the hay on the upper level and the dairy cows below. There were five or six cows in sight, and Emmett knew there were probably several more in the barn. The wife would be milking the cows and making cheese and butter from the milk they didn't drink, the surplus being sold or traded as well. A garden plot still growing pumpkins and potatoes was off to the side, carefully protected by another stone wall. The next field was filled with sheep, imported from Spain and supplying wool to the textile mills to weave the cloth for the shirts on the backs of the Union soldiers. Next to the sheep there was a fire burning felled trees, Norway and white pines, to make room for more grazing land—the ash from the burnt wood turned into potash and used in the making of soap and fertilizer. Many of the farmers had left New Hampshire for the more fertile soil of the newly discovered western states, but those who stayed were a hardy lot expecting nothing but what they earned.

A little later, as they left the train in Boston, a city that made Portland seem like a village, Emmett thought back to that New England farmer and his wealth—the cornfields, apple orchards, cattle, sheep, and hogs that he'd seen. That farmer didn't know the meaning of the word quit, and would fight to the death. As well, the food and wool would go a long way in supplying an army for some time to come. As they marched through Boston, there was, at first, not a sound to be heard from the people lining the streets, just the tramping of their feet as they approached the harbor. Then a solitary voice yelled out, "You boys show ole' Johnny Reb what it means to be an American!" And that was all it took to set the spectators to clapping, yelling, and whistling their encouragement. Shivers ran up and down Emmett's spine as the people cheered for him. Ten minutes later they were aboard a steamship, the Merrimac and heading out to sea. Emmett spent most of his first steamship voyage vomiting into a bucket as they moved out into the rough Atlantic Ocean. On the second day he went on deck to find the Merrimac steaming into Chesapeake Bay and then up the Potomac River. Alerted by the captain, the men on board loosed a rousing cheer when they passed Mount Vernon and the house of George Washington. Emmett looked in awe at Washington's home. Now there was a man who had not been afraid to fight for his country. He turned to observe the cheering men, an uncertain smile on his face. He hoped that when the time came, he'd have just as much courage.

Soon after passing Mount Vernon, they arrived in Alexandria, Virginia. After disembarking, Colonel Ames had the 20th Maine brought into marching formation, four abreast, to cross the bridge into Washington. It was aptly named Long Bridge, as it was certainly the longest bridge that Emmett had ever seen, a combination of different spans to reach the far side and the city. The regiment marched quietly, all of them awestruck to finally arrive here on the front lines, ready to defend the nation's capital.

Union soldiers lounged on both sides of the bridge, stopping and searching civilians crossing the bridge, looking for spies or weapons. They were in fact, the last defenders of the nation's capital, and they went about their duties with an insolence that was intimidating to Emmett. They stood aside to let the 20th Maine pass through, a few of them jeering at the amount of equipment carried by many of these green recruits from Maine. Steamships and schooners filled the river, pulling in and out of the wharves that lay at the southern edge of the city. As they reached the halfway point of the bridge, Emmett saw that the river split, the Potomac continuing on to the west and the Eastern Branch wrapping around the other way, nestling the capital in between. Most of the buildings of the city were far from impressive as compared to Boston or Portsmouth or even Portland. Long Bridge led them to Maryland Avenue, which cut up through the heart of the southwest corner of the city known as "The Island", as it was separated from the rest of the city by a canal that connected the Potomac to the Eastern Branch of the river.

Maryland Avenue was a wide street of poorly laid cobblestones, mud from a recent rain oozing up between the cracks. As they marched, Emmett had to adjust his first impressions. If the city of Washington was not that impressive in its buildings and architecture, it more than made up for it in people. They were everywhere—businessmen rushing to appointments, hucksters selling every possible item from combs to coal, politicians ambling along with constituents, freed black men and women, fish and oyster peddlers tooting horns to draw attention, scantily clad prostitutes calling for the men to come pay them a visit, gamblers taking a break—all crammed from one end of the avenue to the other. From the front of a building on Emmett's left, there spilled more black people than he'd seen in his entire life, sullen men and women in tattered clothes, former slaves recently freed under the *Compensated Emancipation Act*, which had finally released the slaves of the capital city from their bondage.

They passed a hotel that had been turned into a hospital, as had so many public buildings in the city in order to accommodate the wounded who streamed steadily in. Out front lounged mostly soldiers on the road to recovery, bandages around heads, arms in slings, men with stubs for arms and others with makeshift crutches to hold themselves up as they grew accustomed to missing a leg. Women and children mixed in with them, having traveled to the capital to nurse their husbands and fathers back to health, most unsmiling, merely staring at these new recruits arriving to plug the breach in Federal ranks. On every corner stood men and sometimes boys with huge baskets of bread for sale. Emmett watched as a boy grabbed a loaf and ran into the crowd with no pursuit. The peddler, who wasn't any older than Emmett, hollered insults at the running figure but was afraid to leave his basket to give chase. Stray hogs and geese foraged underfoot the crowds, escapees from the pens and pastures where they were held in readiness to feed the soldiers and the populace.

Across the street from the hospital was a boarding house with several well-dressed women standing out front, fanning themselves in the afternoon heat, and protecting their skin from the sun with colorful parasols. One of the women couldn't have been that much older than Emmett himself, a blond-haired, fair-skinned beauty he was unable to stop staring at, her hair cascading down and over her shoulders in waves of curls.

"She's some pretty, ain't she?" The soldier next to Emmett muttered. "Not that the likes of you and me could afford the likes of her." Noticing the boy's look, the soldier laughed. "You didn't realize she was a high-brow whore? You need more greenbacks than we make in a year to pay for that strumpet, though."

Still not sure exactly what the appeal of being with a woman was, Emmett, for the first time, wondered if the silver dollars he had stashed in his haversack would allow him to spend some time with this ravishing belle. Emmett struggled with the implication that these women were actually prostitutes working in one of the more affluent brothels in the city, just one of hundreds that had sprung up to meet the demand of the tens of thousands of soldiers who filled the streets on leave, on official business, or recently mustered out.

As they crossed over Virginia Avenue they passed through a large open square. When Emmett looked to his left, he saw the majestic Smithsonian Institute rising up at the edge of the open field, magnificent red towers that awed one with their grandeur, power, and mystery. Beyond the museum lay the Mall, acres of once open green that had largely been turned into a cattle pen and encampment for soldiers. Steer tore up the grass, eating what they could find and churning the rest into mud as they waited their turn for slaughter in the makeshift abattoir there. Hundreds of white tents filled the far side of the Mall, soldiers marching, drilling, and preparing for war. From the middle of the tents rose the tallest structure in the United States, the still unfinished Washington Monument that, at 150 feet, was only a third of the way to its projected height. As Mark Twain had commented, it did indeed merely look like a "hollow, oversized chimney."

As they continued to march into the capital, a new stench overcame the pungent smell of the animals and the slaughterhouse, a rancid reek that made Emmett's toes curl in his boots and sweat break out on his brow. They were approaching the canal built through the center of the city, connecting the Potomac to the Eastern Branch of the river, whose stagnant waters had grown progressively filthier. It had been a concession to the South to move the capital from Philadelphia to the more centrally located Washington D.C., originally an undesirable tract of swamp that nobody wanted. The canal had been designed to bring fresh water to the people of the city, but over time it had become a sewer and then a garbage pit for the disposal of domestic pets. The problem had increased tenfold with the dramatic expansion in population caused by this Great War. They passed over the canal, gagging, and finally coming to the Capitol building itself, an immense building with a huge unfinished dome, recently expanded to house the Congress. The war had interrupted this project as it had many others. President Lincoln had just taken a stand and insisted that this imposing symbol of the United States Government be completed, and work had once again resumed. As of now, the dome rose into the air magnificently, only to terminate in an ugly eyesore that spoke of the inadequacy of the Federal Government.

At the Capitol they turned left onto Pennsylvania Avenue, cutting through the center of the town and its most important street, stretching as it did from the Capitol to the White House, and boasting along its length some of the most prominent hotels and business establishments in the city. The north side of the street had a wide sidewalk and the more impressive buildings and shops, while the south side was dingy and run down, a striking contrast. They passed by the most impressive of the hotels, The Willard, a colossal building of seven stories flew flags, the stars and stripes from each corner. And had become the center of politics in the city, perhaps more important even than the Capitol or the White House. Its 500 rooms were always filled, and it was also the meeting place for every important person in the city. Huge meals were served here up until the final seating, 9:00 p.m. supper, with various meeting rooms and parlors filled by politicians, merchants, army officers, and women come to chat and dance. Some of these women were there to sell their bodies, sometimes for money, sometimes for favors, sometimes for secrets. It seemed that all of the men chewed tobacco or smoked cigars and always had a drink in hand, sometimes two, as they argued, cajoled, fought, laughed, spat, and tried to get an edge.

The street took a ninety-degree turn at the Treasury Department and wrapped around the front of the White House. Emmett found himself staring in awe at the huge white mansion with the six massive columns of the vestibule. There were gravel walkways leading between beds of flowers grown brown in the fall air with shrubs and small trees dotting the large front lawn. Bread ovens had been set up over much of the yard, cooking the rations for the Army of the Potomac. The back of the White House descended to the contaminated canal, its polluted water, some said, having perhaps been the cause of the death of the President's son the previous February. As was custom, the 20th Maine gave three cheers for their commander-in-chief, Abraham Lincoln, as they passed by. Emmett saw a solitary figure on the west side of the White House walking towards the War Department and realized that the tall, gaunt, and bearded man was actually Abraham Lincoln himself. The President paused as the troops cheered, but Emmett was the only one who saw him as he momentarily stared at these fresh recruits, saluting them before continuing on.

The 20th Maine proceeded to the Federal Arsenal where they were finally armed with the Enfield rifle, a single-shot, muzzle-loading weapon. They then bedded down in a tight corner of Washington D.C. to spend a restless night. The next day they woke early and marched back out of the city to Fort Craig.

*****

"Tom, do you know where we're going?" Emmett asked nervously several days later as they marched out of Fort Craig, the rumors flying that the time for fighting was at hand.

"Look's like northwest to me." Tom Chamberlain said, squinting behind him at the sun that was just peeking over the horizon.

"Do you think we will engage in battle today?" Emmett was proud of the word 'engage', a word whose meaning he'd recently learned from Joshua Chamberlain.

"Not today." Chamberlain interjected, having just ridden up behind them. "We have a long day of marching ahead of us. The Confederates under Lee have moved into Maryland and are threatening the Capital as well as Baltimore and points north. We mean to intercept them just over the Blue Ridge Mountains by Sharpsburg." He dismounted and fell into step with Tom and Emmett.

"When will we catch up to the Rebs, sah?" Emmett asked breathlessly.

Chamberlain paused before answering, a habit Emmett was becoming familiar with. Perhaps it was to combat the stutter that Tom had told him Joshua used to have, perhaps it was caring in choosing the right words. "I don't know. All I can say for certain is that today we will need our walking shoes. Battle is only one part of being a soldier."

It was September 12, 1862 and they were just nine days out of Camp Mason in Portland, and now they were marching into the fray. Emmett had spent the time drilling during the day and reading material about the war and military tactics at night by a flickering candle. The orders to assemble to move out had been delivered to the tent this morning while it was still dark. Two hours later the regiment, some in step, most not, moved forward raggedly, spreading out in clumps along the road. As the sun rose in the sky, the day went from merely warm to hot, indeed, Emmett perspiring in his newly issued wool uniform and feeling the burden of all the equipment and rations in his haversack.

He was not carrying the Enfield rifle that the other soldiers had proudly slung over their shoulders. Chamberlain had said he would have no need of it as an aide, and would be kept far from the fighting. But he did carry his rubber blanket, wool blanket, canteen, tin cup, plate, and utensils, three days rations of pork, hardtack, rice, and coffee as well as half of the tent he shared with Tom. The other men also carried forty rounds of ammunition. Many had also brought personal effects—pictures, keepsakes, lucky charms, extra clothes, special food containers, and various other items to bolster their spirits. He thought of the man from Captain Spear's Company who had been proudly showing off a metal vest supposed to protect him from enemy bullets. At the time, he'd envied the man for this curious invention, but was not surprised when, three miles further along he saw the heavy vest lying by the side of the road.

It was not the only item that Emmett saw strewn in the ditches. New recruits often brought too many personal supplies with them. As the reality of marching set in—and the surplus pounds became a burden—the extra blanket and heavy coat, indeed anything non-essential was soon cast aside. Experienced soldiers didn't even carry a haversack but would wrap the bare essentials in a blanket and wrap this around their shoulders like a sling. Some soldiers found even a canteen too cumbersome, keeping just the tin cup to fill up at springs and in camp. It was common for the army to issue three days of rations for soldiers on the move, and many veterans ate them all on the first day rather than carry them.

The combined efforts of the officers were not enough to keep the men together in an orderly fashion. The foot-weary—and those with blistered feet—soon straggled behind, and no amount of urging could convince them to keep up with the main body. The army did not subscribe to the theory that the pace of the march would be set by the slowest soldier, and so moved forward at the clip of a veteran. Colonel Ames appeared disgusted with the efforts of the men from Maine. His face reddened and his voice grew hoarse as he harangued the stragglers, uttering threats of

89

marching practice that he would hold them to in the upcoming months.

Emmett was trudging along when a soldier from another regiment approached General Morrell, who was in charge of the entire division. "General, begging your pardon, sah, but I seem to have lost my regiment. Can you tell me where the 118th Pennsylvania is?"

"Certainly, my man," the General answered with friendly candor. "Everywhere between here and Washington."

After two days of twenty-mile marches, the division bivouacked near Frederick, Maryland on the Monocacy River. Here they could hear the cannon-fire from over South Mountain, an ominous, not-so-distant rumble that made the men grow quiet. "Do you reckon we'll see combat tomorrow, Tom?" Emmett questioned the older man. The two of them had held up rather well on the trek, both being fairly fit and with plenty of experience in walking long distances.

"Hard to say," Tom replied. "Lawrence doesn't think they'll throw a regiment as green as us into the fighting just yet. That is, unless they really need us. Hell, we only got mustered in about two weeks ago and now here we are in Maryland within spitting distance of the Reb army! Some of these boys don't know which end of the gun shoots and which end nestles into your shoulder."

"Don't be too sure of that," Emmett retorted. "Most of the men I know have grown up with a rifle and can bark a squirrel from a hundred yards."

The next day they encountered their first prisoners of war. Emmett, as was his custom, reported to Chamberlain's tent at daybreak but found him already gone. He discovered him meeting with Colonel Ames and Major Gilmore down on the edge of the camp, just as the dawn broke over the horizon. He shuffled his feet and stayed back a few steps so as to not interfere with their meeting.

Colonel Ames was drawing in the dirt at their feet with a stick. "We will march through Frederick, and then travel through South Mountain at this pass." He made an X in the dirt between two triangles that must have represented the mountain pass. "The enemy is west of the mountains in force, and it will be our job to provide support. We will be held in reserve in case of need. I hope to God we are not needed."

Chamberlain turned and looked gravely at Emmett, seeming a bit rattled by his commanding officer's sober words. "We are on the precipice of a cliff now, Emmett. I want you to make sure to stay to the rear when we enter into the skirmish. It is not my desire to explain to your brothers that you were killed while in my charge."

"Should I saddle your horse, sah?"

"I think I will be borrowing a mount from Major Gilmore, one of a darker coat than Prince."

"I will take care of it, sah."

"See to it, then. But to start, I think I will walk with the men for a bit this morning, and take their measure and show my face at the same time."

It was with more precision than the previous days that the 20th Maine marched through Frederick, Maryland, about an hour later. They were not in such a hurry, and the anticipation of battle energized even the weakest of the lot, causing them to appear more professional and self-assured. The townsfolk were out in force, standing outside their houses and storefronts to watch and cheer for the Army of the Potomac. Many of the women handed out slices of bread and ladles of water, some even having milk to share with the men as they paraded through the streets. Among the townspeople, there were very few men, Emmett noticed, other than the very young and the very old, very few of fighting age who dared show their faces at least.

Emmett was again walking with Tom, who was mooning over one of the town's young ladies, a budding beauty who he was certain had given him a special smile as she had handed him a ladle of water. "She had the face of an angel when she smiled at me, the prettiest thing I ever did see," he said for the third time. For the next several hours he went on about the wonders of women and how much they all loved soldiers and how first chance he got, Tom would be coming back to Frederick to pay this lass a visit. Although Emmett wished Tom might change his tune after the first hour, it did help to pass the time.

They had left Frederick far behind and were approaching Middleton, just reaching Turner's Pass through South Mountain,

Emmett having long since stopped listening to Tom's love-struck words when he suddenly grabbed his friend's arm and pointed ahead where a line of men were passing by the 3rd Brigade in the opposite direction. "Who are they?" The men were dirtier, more bedraggled than even the hardiest veterans from the front Emmett had yet seen.

"Looks like prisoners to me." Tom replied, emerging from his dreamland. "If you look close, you can see they're wearing gray uniforms."

"Johnny Rebs?" Emmett breathed in a hushed tone, speechless to see evilness up so close.

"Yep. Looks like maybe we ain't doin so bad up ahead." Tom cracked, smiling broadly.

The prisoners were a motley collection of battle-weary veterans whose clothes were torn and tattered from the elements, time, and brutal conflict, in sharp contrast to the 20th Maine's spanking-new uniforms. The sharpness of their cheekbones spoke of many a missed meal; their chins had not seen a razor for some time, their hair lay greasy and matted upon their heads while their faces were ghoulish, still blackened by the gunpowder of recent battles, making their eyes gleam whitely in their skulls. "They look like devils." Emmett whispered.

Tom looked at Emmett quizzically. "They're men," he said, "just like you and me. Probably some of them work in a grocery same as me and others have lost loved ones same as you. Come on, let's go talk to one of 'em." He pulled Emmett from the ranks and towards the line of prisoners who had paused for a water break, the guards carefully eying the men as they passed a canteen amongst themselves. "Hey, Johnny Reb, have some of mine." Tom said, approaching one of the men, offering up his canteen. The man stared sullenly at the two Union soldiers in their brand new uniforms and spit at their feet, but then he took the canteen and took a long draught, wiping a filthy hand over his face afterwards and handing the canteen to the left. There was no word of gratitude, no words at all, but Tom continued on, asking the man his name and where he was from.

"What do you want, Yank?"

"I'm just making conversation," Tom replied amiably. "What was you doing before the war?"

The prisoner snorted, but finally replied grudgingly. "I was a blacksmith."

"I worked in a grocery store, mostly stocking shelves." Tom said, nodding his head.

"Nothing wrong with good honest labor." The prisoner relented.

"Do you got slaves?"

The prisoner laughed a single crackling chuckle like an explosion. "Now, what would I need a slave for in my forge? I suppose he could blow the bellows, but then I'd have to feed him and give him a place to sleep, and I don't reckon my wife would care for that none at all."

"If you don't got any slaves, why fight to break apart the Union?" Tom tugged at his sideburn in confusion. "No disrespect, but that just don't make no sense."

"What don't make sense is some fellow up in Washington telling me what I can and can't do down in South Carolina. First they'll free the niggers and then next, who knows, maybe they'll tax me and make me pay so the niggers can eat while they sit around doing nothing."

"So South Carolina can do anything it pleases just like that?"

"I'm talking about the guvermint leaving me the devil alone and staying out of my business, is what I'm talking about. I went to the meeting house and they told us all about how you northerners wanted to control us southerners and how you wouldn't be happy until we was your niggers and I signed up right then and there." The prisoner spoke angrily, but then the tension melted from his body. "Of course, I dint reckon being a soldier would be so horrible, sleeping out under the stars, starving all the time, and after awhile even shooting Yanks gets mighty tiresome."

After the prisoners had disappeared behind them, never having returned the canteen, Emmett turned to Tom with a question. "Why did you join up?"

Tom didn't reply for a bit, but finally said, "I think it was more for the adventure than for anything else."

The sun continued to blaze down, a torrid September fire that cooked everything beneath it. After a night near Middleton in Maryland, the 20th Maine advanced into Turner's Gap where they saw the first obvious signs of battle. Two days earlier, the Confederates had tried to hold their positions here as the famous Union "Black Hat" Brigade had attacked and eventually driven them back in fierce fighting. The dead bodies of the Confederate soldiers still lay where they had fallen, baking, and then slowly beginning to swell and bloat and putrefy in the hot sun. As they advanced through the pass, Emmett tried to avert his eyes from the grim spectacle without success, his gaze being drawn back to the grotesque bodies seemingly ready to explode.

Emmett looked to Chamberlain who was walking his horse, Prince, alongside him. "That is the enemy?" He blurted out. "He can't be any older than me." Emmett was pointing at what appeared to have been a boy leaning against a tree with no outward sign of injury, only a puffiness about the face belying his peaceful posture.

Chamberlain looked at the dead Confederate soldier and then stared at Emmett, his face suddenly twisted by some troublesome thought. "You are going to stay in the rear, Mister Collins, when fighting is nigh."

Emmett was in no mood to argue after seeing the swollen corpses littering their path. They continued onward in silence for some time, each lost in their own thoughts. Chamberlain broke the stillness, waving his arm off to their right. "Just down the road that way is Harper's Ferry where John Brown made his statement about the institution of slavery. Did you get through that newspaper story I left out for you the other night?"

Emmett had finished the article and had actually spent much of yesterday thinking about a life that appeared to have been wasted. After killing several pro-slavery men in Kansas, John Brown had fled to the North, where he began plotting an uprising that would end slavery forever. The plan was to attack the arsenal at Harper's Ferry with about twenty men and then distribute the weapons to the surrounding slaves, building an army that would gather momentum and sweep across the South, freeing slaves and killing slave-owners. This outrageous, violent vision was carried out in October of 1859 and was successful at first. Then the townsmen had appeared, pinning John Brown's band in the arsenal until the army was able to arrive. Led, ironically enough, by Robert E. Lee and J.E.B. Stuart, the troops captured the insurgents

___
94

before the weapons could be distributed to rebelling slaves. John Brown was tried, his eloquent defense turning him into a martyr for the Northern cause, a folk hero whose gallant story was told in songs like *John Brown's Truth Goes Marching On*. And then he was hung. Emmett did have one question that had been tearing at him. "Wouldn't lots of innocent people have died if John Brown had been successful?"

"It looks like either way, lots of innocent people are being killed." Chamberlain commented grimly.

Later that day, they passed through the towns of Boonsboro and Keedyville, steadily approaching the battlefront. As they crested the slopes above Antietam Creek, the land as far as the eye could see changed to a darker, shifting color. "What is it?" Emmett gasped to Tom.

Tom smiled at him. "That, my friend, is the Union army!"

And sure enough, it was. Emmett realized that what was before him was a shifting sea of men, the soldiers of the Army of the Potomac. "I never knew there were so many people in the whole world."

As the order came to make camp for the night, they could hear the distant rumble and boom of heavy artillery, signaling movement and combat just to the north. "That would be General Hooker crossing Antietam Creek and getting set to attack Lee in the morning." Chamberlain said as he rode up on the black horse that Major Gilmore had loaned him. Emmett noted the dark horse and nodded grimly to himself. The time for battle was drawing near.

The 20th Maine was up before dawn the following morning ready to move out. In truth, many had never slept, with the sporadic artillery and the sounds of fighting breaking out in the early hours as Hooker advanced just east of the town of Sharpsburg. To add to their discomfort, it had been a wet night, the rain soaking everything in camp. The impending battle would be fought in the mud.

Emmett was waiting beside Chamberlain when Colonel Ames rode up. "Lieutenant Colonel, where is Major Gilmore?"

"He is feeling a touch of the flu, sir, and has remained back at last night's camp until his stomach improves."

Colonel Ames glared at him as if this were his fault but

then relented and swept his hand along the line of trees to one side of Sharpsburg Pike, the road that they were marching on. "Have the men take up positions along here just into the trees. We will be held in reserve to support the main fighting and used where we are most needed."

"Yes, sir." Chamberlain's salute was smarter than usual, his tone a little more clipped. Combat loomed for the first time, and he would soon find out what stuff he was made of in the thick of the battle.

Once the men of the 20th Maine were positioned under cover, Chamberlain motioned for Emmett to follow him. They crossed the road and climbed the ridge, the sounds of battle growing ominously closer as they crept up the slight incline. There was a smattering of officers and soldiers already on the crest, watching the battle unfold in front of them. It reminded Emmett of his boyhood, playing war with a collection of sticks and rocks representing men and weaponry. Except the scene in front of them was real, as they watched tiny figures charge forward, be repelled, only to move forward again. The Union General Burnside fought a relentless battle to gain control of a key bridge and all the while smoke rolled up from the battlefield as if the world were afire. The brightly colored flags of the regiments could be seen moving when a patch of acrid cloud cleared. All of a sudden a cheer rose from the men on the ridge, and Emmett looked over to see a short, stocky man with burning eyes over a bushy mustache ride along the ridge doffing his hat left and right to the men as he rode. It was "Little Mac", Commander-in-Chief of the Army of the Potomac. Though at times excoriated by President Lincoln for his cautious approach to battle, he was loved by the men for that caution, for protecting their very lives.

"Do you think "Little Mac" will press the attack today?" Emmett inquired of Chamberlain.

"Reports seem to indicate that we outnumber the Rebs two to one. They do control the better terrain, set up in the hills across Antietam Creek, but our superior numbers should assure General McClellan in his aggression. Many people have been clamoring for him to bring the attack to the Confederacy. Thus, he has very little choice but to do so, I would presume."

Like a grassfire, word came through to the men that

Burnside had taken one of the bridges over Antietam Creek from the Confederates under hard fighting. That news had hardly been digested when a courier arrived with a message from General Morrell for Colonel Ames; the 20th Maine should immediately be brought forward to support soldiers under General Franklin. As the anticipation rippled through the ranks of men, Emmett noted that many of them thought to take one last piss, some of them too nervous to follow through. Still others tightened their belts and took a drink of water. They were brought into formation and moved to the right several miles in preparation for battle. But as sunset approached, the order came from General McClellan to return to their previous spot, the first of countless false alarms throughout the ensuing action. In a lull towards first light Emmett, half asleep and cold, heard Chamberlain speaking softly to himself, a prayer it seemed. He listened, realizing that it was a prayer and of a very private sort. *Please God, when the time comes for me to face battle, let me do so honorably even if I must die. As long as You do not let me be a coward.*

That night the Army of Northern Virginia disappeared to the south over the Potomac River, General McClellan allowing him to escape, having failed once more to press the advantage. The fighting of that one-day had been fierce, with over 12,000 Union casualties and 10,000 on the Confederate side. A tactical victory for the North, some called it, as the South withdrew and their invasion evaporated.

The next morning, Emmett woke to Tom shaking his arm. "Get up Emmett," he was saying, "today we will fight!"

"What?" In an instant, Emmett came completely awake.

"The 20th Maine has been chosen to support the cavalry in a reconnaissance mission across the Potomac to probe the rear guard of Lee's army."

In what seemed like minutes, Emmett had dressed and packed, making his way to Chamberlain's tent, only to see him disappearing on the black horse that Major Gilmore had loaned to him. Emmett found himself walking with Tom. "Do you think that your brother will allow me to cross the river with the regiment?"

"He won't even notice if you don't show your face and stay to the back." Tom grinned at the boy. "He might be a tad bit busy today. Word is Bobby Lee is in full flight back to Virginia," Tom added. "I guess we're part of the sweeping up crew, making sure none of those Rebs get lost on their way south."

"Ellis Spear said that Little Mac let General Lee get away scot-free."

Tom Chamberlain eyeballed his young companion for a long moment before replying. "I don't envy any of the officers the decisions they have to make. If General McClellan felt that it was unsafe to press the attack, then so be it." At that point, they emerged onto the banks of the Potomac River. Major Gilmore approached on horseback and urged them forward into the flowing water. Before Emmett knew what was happening he was knee-deep in the rushing water, struggling to find his footing on the rocky bottom.

As they struggled out the other side of the Potomac, Chamberlain rode up, reining in his horse and glaring down at Emmett. "What are you doing here?"

"What do you mean, sah?" Emmett replied innocently.

"You were to stay on the far side of the river, where it's safe."

Emmett hung his head and did not reply. Certainly, he wouldn't be sending him back now?

Chamberlain grunted in frustration. "So be it. What is done is done. But you must stay to the rear. I do not want you near the fighting if it should come to pass. Do I make myself clear?"

Emmett nodded his head. At that moment there was rifle fire off to the right, a quick volley and then sporadic cracks, like winter ice breaking up.

Chamberlain dismounted and waved his hat over his head. "Up the bluff, men," he shouted, "to the top of the ridge." The 20th Maine began scrambling up the rocks as Emmett paused, letting Chamberlain get well ahead of him. In the scramble, he lost sight of Tom but found himself next to Major Gilmore, who also seemed to be taking up position to the rear of the regiment.

"Those were the Rebs shooting at us!" Emmett spluttered, his face red with excitement.

"Perhaps." Major Gilmore replied, quick flickering glances to the left and right betraying his nervousness. "I think most of

Lee's army has probably moved south, but there might still be a rear guard left behind. We are not over here in any force capable of engaging the enemy."

At that moment, the first men to reach the top of the hill began shooting, and Major Gilmore grabbed Emmett's arm and stopped him from climbing. "I think perhaps we should stay here," he said, "in case I need to send a message back to General Sykes." Scrub trees clung to the side of the hill, and he pulled Emmett behind their partial cover. The gunfire from the top of the hill was sporadic, random shots at distant targets rather than any real fighting. It was not long before a courier came with a message for the 20th. Major Gilmore read the orders. "We are to pull back." Major Gilmore said to Emmett in relief. "Go find Lieutenant Colonel Chamberlain. Tell him we're to fall back across the Potomac immediately. I will see to establishing order on the far bank."

Chapter Five

Dearest Fanny—It has been three weeks since I last saw you and you sent me on my way with that dreadful letter. When you told me that you would not wait for me, at least not at home, but would travel, most likely to New York City, it pained me deeply. Perchance is that artist Akers, in New York now? The thought of you spending time with him, however innocent the face I put upon it, is almost enough to kill me. You have meant everything to me since the first day I heard you sing and play the organ at the First Parish Church and from that day forward I was smitten with you to the point that I can scarcely breathe. When you finally agreed to marry me, I thought it was the happiest day of my life, but then came our wedding and the births of Daisy and Wyllys and life just got better.... It is enough that I worry about failing my men but now I also have to worry about you. I trust you got my last letter telling you about our brief stay in the capital? It really was quite a disappointing place other than a few magnificent buildings. Please write to tell me that you are home with the children and not doing anything foolish. I need to know that you support me or I don't know if I can go on. Missing you desperately, your loving husband—L

September 20, 1862

Emmett clambered up the rocks like a squirrel climbing a tree, excited to get a glimpse of the enemy. As he neared the top he realized that Chamberlain would be furious with him for being there, even though it was on orders. There was nothing he could do about that though, and once atop the ridge, he had no problem locating the Lieutenant Colonel, who stood calmly at the front of the 20th Maine, all of his attention focused on little puffs of smoke blossoming like deadly flowers from the far trees.

"Sah, I have orders for you to fall back across the Potomac, sah."

The mild eyes of Chamberlain settled on Emmett, who squirmed under the steady gaze. "What are you doing here?"

"I am to tell you that Major Gilmore received orders from the General that we are to immediately fall back across the river." All the while, Emmett was searching the distant woods, eager to catch sight of the enemy. After a few moments, he began to pick out gray figures that were not trees but men just outside of rifle range. This did not stop the occasional soldier from loosing off a shot, usually accompanied by some taunting.

Chamberlain nodded his head, frustrated at being pulled back but understanding the order. "We will fall back then, but I want you to be the first on the other side of the river. Understood?"

Emmett did, and thus, he reluctantly tore his eyes from the enemy in the trees and turned to head back down the hill, moving much more slowly than on his ascent. He was soon followed by men from the 20th Maine who fell back in a sort of orderly fashion, maintaining a presence on the hill-top as long as possible before deserting the high ground. Once he'd regained the far bank, Emmett watched as Chamberlain, now remounted, rode to the center of Shepherdstown Ford and directed men to move on through. He noticed a small splash in the river and then another. *What was this? He wondered.* Glancing up, Emmett saw a scattering of gray uniforms dotting the top of the bluff, rifles to shoulders, firing down the hill at the retreating soldiers. The Confederates were all aiming at the only present officer, mounted and helpless in the middle of the river.

"Sah!" Emmett yelled at the top of his lungs, "Get out of the river!" Chamberlain glanced his way—suddenly jerking from the impact of one of these bullets and collapsing with his horse into the river. Emmett screamed in terror, scrambling down the bank back into the water. At the bottom he slipped and splashed in headlong, then floundered to his feet, sputtering and frantic, just in time to see Chamberlain being dragged to shore by several men.

"Don't worry, boy, your officer will be just fine. Can't say the same for his horse, though." One soldier said, looking back over his shoulder. "Took one right in the noggin, he did." Emmett dragged himself out of the water and followed along behind, relieved to know that Chamberlain was unhurt. Casting a backward glance at the horse, he saw that the corpse had snagged on a rock.

After the bloody battle of Antietam at the end of September, the two armies fell back into defensive positions to lick their wounds and contemplate their next moves. And so began for Emmett what would be six very exciting weeks of military training. Most of the men would have disagreed with him, complaining that it was repetitive, boring, exhausting—and useless in battle—with all blame laid squarely upon the mental imbalance of their Colonel, Adelbert Ames. Training was marked, those first days, by the stench of the dead from the previous fighting on the same terrain, the water in the streams and rivers putrid and undrinkable from the corpses littering the banks. Chamberlain and Colonel Ames took up residence together, sharing a large tent, seven feet tall, ten feet wide, and twelve feet deep, much more spacious than those of the enlisted men.

The officers' shelter allowed them space for their bedroll, but also several tables for eating and planning strategy, along with several canvas folding chairs, and stools for visitors, with light provided by two brass whale-oil lanterns. In the corner they had placed a Sibley, a cone-shaped stove that often filled the tent with smoke.

It was in this tent one evening that Emmett first heard about the Emancipation Proclamation. It was customary for him to come by after supper, Chamberlain setting him to study, usually reading then composing a response to a newspaper article covering some facet of the war. As Emmett arrived, officers were out front arguing about this new proclamation. The boy hoped that he might be able to stay and listen, and maybe even get a break from the schoolwork. Two days earlier he had chosen to linger by the fire with Tom and the other soldiers instead of showing up for his lessons, and Chamberlain had tracked him down for a not-so-gentle word: he would be on the first train back to Brunswick if he was not more diligent with his education.

That night, Chamberlain motioned him into the tent, following Emmett to the small table with a newspaper on it and an oil lamp already burning, even though the last tendrils of light still illuminated the sky. "What are they talkin," Emmett paused at a look from his teacher, correcting his speech. "Er, what are they talking about out there?"

"Interesting that you should ask, as that is tonight's lesson for you. It is a new law being proposed by President Lincoln called the Emancipation Proclamation. Do you know what emancipation means?"

Emmett shrugged. "No, sir."

"Emancipation is the act of freeing or the state of being freed. In this case, it refers to the slave population in the South." He tapped the newspaper. "You read the article, and we will talk about it later tonight or tomorrow." And with that, Chamberlain slipped out of the tent to rejoin the heated conversation.

Emmett sighed and sat down, tired from the day's marching and drills, knowing that he would soon be fighting to keep his eyes open as he worked his way through the dense paragraphs. He tried to listen to the conversation outside the tent, but the men had moved away, and he was only able to catch the occasional word. Finally, in exasperation, he turned to the newspaper on the table and began to read, noting questions as he went.

PRESIDENT LINCOLN'S EMANCIPATION PROCLAMATION;
Mr. President, Is this war about the NEGRO or about secession? Was the South right to leave in the first place?

This Great War has now officially been defined as a war to end slavery. Yesterday, President Lincoln issued his Preliminary Emancipation Proclamation, giving fair warning to the Southern States that are currently in Rebellion against the government that their slaves will be freed, considered men, beginning on January 1, 1863. Many of us are thus asking the question; if the President can so suddenly and seemingly without reason switch horses, do we not have the same right? Can we withdraw from a war we no longer believe in?

This new law applies only to those states that are attempting to secede from the Union, meaning Arkansas, Texas, Louisiana (excluding a few loyal parishes), Mississippi, Alabama, Florida, Georgia, South Carolina, North Carolina and Virginia (excluding the western portion of that state). If any of these states cease their rebellion and rejoin the Union by January 1, they will be exempted.

What does this mean? Some would say it is an empty law that ignores the slave states in the Union, all the while directed at states the law has no control over. Others would say that it changes their perspective of the war and they no longer want to fight against the South, now that the President has clearly named the END of slavery as the goal of the war.

In reality, it is a stroke of political genius at a decisive hour when European Powers, namely Great Britain, are considering entering the war on the side of the South. HOW can they enter into a fray on the Southern side, now that the battle line has been drawn at the institution of slavery, which Europe so soundly denounces? How can Great Britain, which abolished slavery fifty years ago, side with the Southern Institution of Slavery?

Emmett had just finished noting a last question, when Chamberlain came back into the tent. "Well, what do you think, boy?" He asked.

Emmett was exhausted but also curious about what he'd read. "I'm not sure what to think, sir."

Chamberlain took the paper from Emmett and read through it. The two reviewed the grammar, Emmett's mastery of which was improving, if slowly, before turning to the substance of the short editorial itself.

Emmett hesitated only briefly, before asking, "Why doesn't it outlaw slavery everywhere? If it's sayin, I mean saying, slavery is bad, then why is it allowing it to continue in some states?"

"President Lincoln is worried about offending the states still loyal to the Union, but which still have slave owners and slaves. That would be Delaware, Kentucky, Maryland, and Missouri. Congress has already passed a bill saying that slaves who escaped from owners in rebellion against the United States can join the military and won't be forcibly returned." Chamberlain paused, pondering his own questions, the conversation outside with the other officers only having confused the issues. It probably had not helped that he had been persuaded to have a small glass of the scotch General Sykes had brought over. Not being much of a drinker, he found himself a touch light-headed, but liking the relaxing effect it had. "This is just the logical next step to isolate the South and to sow dissension among the Confederate States."

"But, why would some states fight with the Union if they have slaves?" Emmett asked.

"That's a good question—and one with many answers. Missouri? They don't have many slaves to speak of, as there is no real need, as is the case in western Virginia, and to some extent, Maryland and Kentucky. The governor of Delaware claimed that they were the first state to ratify the Constitution and that they will be the last ones to leave it, so I surmise from this that they support the principles of our government and what the Constitution stands for."

Emmett looked down the paper, nodding. "But, what good will it do the slaves in the South to free them? We have no real power to enforce this, so isn't it...meaningless?"

"Right now it is." Chamberlain agreed. "I doubt that any of the slaves in the South will even know that this proclamation has been made. But if the time comes when Southern states fall under Union control, those slaves will be freed and could possibly join the war effort. General Grant is on the verge of driving the Confederates from Tennessee after his victory at Shiloh and this will open the door to legally free the slaves from their plantations."

At that moment Colonel Ames entered, and Chamberlain sent Emmett on his way for the night. The boy returned to the tent that he shared with Tom, only to find a group of soldiers in front of it, still sitting by the fire as it crackled in the dark night. They had received their first pay from the army that morning, making it a very busy day for the Sutler. The army was supposed to pay them every two months, and the 20th Maine was not due their first pay until the end of October, but had been lumped in with the rest of the Army of the Potomac and thus got their first greenbacks after just a month of service. Enlisted men received $13 a month, paid by the official paymaster. Some men had an allotment taken from their pay and sent directly home, but they all looked forward to visiting the Sutler to buy the luxuries so rare in army life. The biggest sellers on payday were whiskey and tobacco, with a few men buying fresh vegetables, candy, tinned meat, fried pies, even newspapers. The men had a complicated relationship with the Sutler, as they badly wanted and appreciated what he sold them, all the while hating him for inflating the prices of often-inferior products.

"Lawrence let you go early tonight." Tom remarked as Emmett sat down on the log next to him, his presence barely noted by the others, more than a little whiskey having made them loud and boisterous.

"Him and the Colonel had some planning to do," Emmett replied. "Did you hear about this Emancipation Proclamation?"

Tom nodded, taking a bottle from the man to his right and swigging. "Its got everybody all worked up, that or the whiskey does, I guess," he added, offering the bottle to Emmett with his eyebrows raised.

Emmett reached for the bottle with bravado. He'd taken a taste of flip before at Christmas, a mixture of beer, rum, and sugar that had gone down easily. "The Lieutenant Colonel had me read an article about it and then we talked it over." He said, tipping the bottle back and taking a mouthful. It burned his throat, and, when he went to swallow, seemed to scald its way down into his stomach. He choked; forcing some of it up through his nose and making his entire head feel as if it were on fire.

Tom laughed and slapped him on the back. "I should've told you to take just a nip."

Luckily none of the other soldiers had even noticed, and Emmett was able to hand the bottle on. "Dang! That'll put a brick in one's hair. It sure ain't nothing like flip."

"Good whiskey's got more bite than flip but this rotgut is the bottom of the barrel." Tom said. "Its probably some cheap moonshine the Sutler made himself with some of his tonics and what-not. No matter. I'll bet after talking to ole' Lawrence you know more about what this whole proclamation is about better than these here windbags."

"Who you calling a windbag?" Sitting back a pace or two away, John Marshall Brown had overheard their whole conversation. "This is the best thing that ole' Abe could have done is to let them southerners know we're after freeing their Negroes."

"Humbug Brown!" A grizzled soldier from across the fire exclaimed, his voice marked by a deep Southern accent. "Once them plantation owners know we're taking their niggers away theys gonna fight fierce, they will."

"Seems to me they're fighting pretty fierce right now," Brown replied. "With or without this proclamation."

"Now, don't get me wrong," the soldier, continued. "I'd be happy as anything to free the niggers and send them back to where they come from, but it sounds like hooey to me. If Abe was to ship them back to Africa or wherever, why I'd go back to Georgia and return to bein a goober farmer." The grizzled soldier's name was Gideon and he'd raised peanuts before slave labor had dropped the price so much that he'd lost what little land he'd owned. He'd been forced to sign on to a ship bound for Portland, where he ended up without a job. With no other prospects, the 20th Maine had seemed his best option. "Hell, I'd go on back to Georgia tomorrah if it weren't for the niggers."

"Well, you're stuck with us for better or worse the next three years whether or not the colored people go away or stay put." Brown said, attempting to keep the smirk off his face. "But it sure does beat all how you lost your land."

Gideon stared balefully at Brown but was handed the bottle at that moment, distracting him from his anger momentarily. A soft-spoken, clean-shaven soldier, a man from Fort Fairfield in far northern Maine, spoke up. "I don't think Abe is planning on sending the Negroes away, just freeing them from servitude." Tim Buck was a staunch abolitionist, having aided many escaped slaves to find their way to Canada over the past several years.

"Course he's gonna send them away." Gideon spluttered, spitting a stream of tobacco juice into the fire. "Y'all don't know what its like to live with them, staring at you with the whites of their eyes, snickering behind your back, lusting after your women. I shore don't agree with slavery, it being wrong according to God, but you're off your rocker if you think that Negroes and whites can jus' live side by side happily ever aftah."

"I did hear that Abe wants to colonize them, maybe down in South America." Tom spoke up, having just taken a healthy drink of the whiskey. "Give them their own place to go and live among themselves."

"But, my friend," Brown said, smiling meanly. "Who will work the cotton and tobacco fields if we send all the Negroes to South America?"

"There seem to be enough Irish in Portland, not to mention Boston and New York City, to fill all the plantations with plenty of workers." Tom retorted, handing the bottle to Emmett, who tipped it to his lips and barely let the liquid scald his tongue before hurriedly handing it on.

"Maybe you and your redneck friends can work the fields." Buck said arrogantly to Gideon.

Gideon lurched up from the stump he sat on. "I've a mind to knock ya into a cocked hat." He staggered slightly, and abruptly sat back down to the jeers of the soldiers, as his legs no longer appeared to support his weight. "I did work the fields," he continued, slurring his words only a little. "All you Yankees like to think that down South we're all rich plantation owners and spend our time sitting on the veranda sipping whiskey on ice. That ain't hardly the truth at all. Most of us couldn't afford a slave if we saved our entire life—and what the hell would I do with one if I could? I've worked hard pickin goobers, I've worked cotton, tobacco, you name it, I ain't afraid to work. Six days a week from sun-up to sun-down, only takin the Sabbath off to go to church."

"It don't appear to make no difference at all anyhow," Tom said, "cuz unless we can defeat the Confederacy, there ain't nobody being freed." This sober statement ended the conversation, as each soldier pondered the reality of defeating the Rebels. Hardly any of them had seen real battle firsthand. But they had seen the horrible carnage after Antietam, and it was these images that flickered through their minds in the firelight. One by one they stood and retired to their tents, until finally only Gideon was left, passed out by the fire. As Emmett drifted off to sleep he wondered, how different were black people from white people?

Reveille sounded the next morning at 6 a.m., rousing the soldiers from their tents, some moving more slowly than normal after the whiskey of the night before. Once the regiment had assembled on the parade ground, the first sergeants took roll call after which Gideon was rustled up from beside the previous night's campfire. Breakfast followed, fresh biscuits with salt pork and hot coffee helping alleviate the cold bite of the fall morning and chasing away the cobwebs from the night's drinking. As soon as the soldiers had eaten, they broke into their day's assignments, some to guard duty, others to work details cutting trees for firewood and digging ditches for latrines, while still others reported to drill. That morning Emmett was attached to Company I with Tom and had been loaned an Enfield rifle for shooting practice.

The drill started with the men going through the motions of loading without actually firing. By the end of the first hour, Emmett felt he could load the weapon in his sleep, first placing it butt down on the ground with top of the bore faced away, removing the cartridge with the powder, twisting and ripping the top, pouring the powder in, removing the minié ball from the cartridge box and pushing it into the barrel with his thumb, taking the rammer and making sure to push the minié ball all the way to the bottom, placing a percussion cap on the nipple below the hammer and then aiming down the barrel. When ready or as ordered, the soldier then squeezed the trigger gently to explode the percussion cap igniting the powder, the resulting explosion propelling the slug of lead out through the rifled grooves. The beauty of the Enfield, the field instructor explained, was that the minié ball was significantly smaller than the bore of the musket, allowing it to be loaded easily even after the build-up of powder inside the barrel from numerous firings during a long battle. Other rifles would jam, and at often crucial moments. The Enfield was also designed so that the base of the minié ball expanded on firing to fit the grooves of the rifled bore, allowing a greater degree of accuracy.

After the endless repetitive practice, the soldiers were finally allowed to fire their weapons, aiming at targets pinned to hay bales set up a hundred yards away, the roar of the volley deafening and the kick of the musket into Emmett's shoulder painful and exhilarating all at the same time. Emmett had fired a gun before, as hunting was how you put food on the table in

Brewer, but never before had he used a rifled bore that actually allowed you to hit a target up to five-hundred yards away, almost as far as he could see. Each soldier got to fire their weapon twenty times, exhausting half the cartridges in their boxes. Emmett's shoulder was bruised and raw by the time they were done, but he felt proud, as he was starting to get a feel for it.

As if the loading drill hadn't been repetitive enough, the rest of the day was spent in mastering the "turning wheel", a maneuver that allowed a company to turn to either flank by having one end or the other begin retreat step—stepping backwards— while the men beside them stayed in formation for a pace before then retreat stepping, causing the entire line of men to swing to the flank like a giant pendulum. Sometimes, when it went well, it was a sight to see. More often, it was a disaster, with men running into and tripping each other.

The regiment might go through maneuvers as a whole, or like that day, drill by company, allowing different companies to work according to their mastery. Firing practice, marching practice, presenting of arms, guard or work details—each drill usually took about two hours, the officers driving them to do five to six different drills a day. The men came to hate these exhausting days, not understanding how marching, maneuvers, and related training would make them more effective against the Confederates. The focus of their anger was Colonel Ames, the West Pointer from Rockland who followed every dictate of the official military doctrine. Emmett enjoyed the entire business, but his favorite was every third day, when Chamberlain was Brigade Field Officer and thus in charge of the entire perimeter of the brigade's encampment. This meant that he had to ride through the countryside for miles and miles, sometimes spending as many as fourteen hours in the saddle, checking the sentry positions and scouting the countryside. After the first such outing, Chamberlain began taking Emmett along, ostensibly to deliver messages, but perhaps as a companion as well. Chamberlain would ride his gray gift horse, Prince, borrowing another mount for Emmett.

The boy wasn't sure what the best part of these days was, as there were so many from first light to dusk. Riding beside Lieutenant Colonel Chamberlain made him feel important as they checked the sentries and cantered past the various regiments of the brigade. Traveling through the Maryland countryside brought new surprises each and every day. The woods were not as thick as in Maine, but in many ways, not all that different. White oaks were common, as were hickory and sycamore trees. Chamberlain would quiz Emmett on the different types of vegetation and birds they saw, and for the first time Emmett became aware of the world around him. He would spot groundhogs and rabbits as well as deer, and before long could tell the difference between a Blue Warbler and an American Goldfinch. They would ride into meadows high up in the hills from which they could see forty miles into Virginia, spying thin tendrils of smoke spiraling lazily into the sky, rising off the campfires of the Confederate army dotting the countryside. Looking east, Emmett could see farmlands stretching into the distance; waiting for spring to flourish and bloom, while in the other direction was the devastated battlefield of Antietam near the town of Sharpsburg.

Though it pleased him to be out in nature, it was also the conversations with Chamberlain that he came to treasure the most during these six weeks of ordered calm before the storm.

"I don't think I will ever be able to go back to the lecture hall." Chamberlain said as honest and plain as the day, early one morning, breaking the silence of those barely risen from sleep. "It's hard to believe that less than six months ago I was teaching rhetoric and oration, and now I am living life as man should." It was true that Chamberlain had flourished in the life of a soldier. His skin had lost the pallor of academia, becoming ruddy and weather-beaten from days spent in the sun, in the fields, with the physical demands making his body strong and lean, his face sharper. As an officer he enjoyed a few luxuries, but rarely made use of them, choosing to suffer the same hardships as his men. He did not require special food and drink, warm blankets, or a soft bed. In his greatcoat and boots, he made quite a commanding figure with his saber and a pistol holstered on either side. Time— and army life—had taken a toll on his uniform however, his cap torn on a reconnaissance mission, trousers worn smooth and patched from so many hours in the saddle.

He had changed as well in his ideas about how to lead his men, interceding with Colonel Ames on their behalf and winning him their respect. Just the previous day, a soldier had gotten news that his son had died of brain fever and had promptly gotten drunk, insulting a lieutenant when confronted. Colonel Ames ordered him to stand on a barrel for an entire day with a placard around his neck that said, "DRUNK". The man had refused the punishment, and it was Chamberlain who interceded, conversing with and discovering the anguish of the man, and coming to a compromise that involved apology but not humiliation.

Deep into the countryside one afternoon, the two had stopped at a stream, letting the horses drink. Chamberlain said, almost as if he were talking to himself. "Do you know that my dearest Fanny sent me a letter? Yes. She wrote that she would like to come and visit me here. Can you imagine my darling Fanny in the same tent with Colonel Ames and myself?" Chamberlain chuckled and shook his head. "Does she think that I am here on sabbatical, staying in some fancy rented house? I know that some officers lodge their wives in nearby towns and then visit them, but when would I get the opportunity? I don't think I could get away more than one day a month, if that." They remounted and continued on, Emmett feeling a sudden pang at the thought of his own family. There had been just the one letter from his brothers since the one telling him his Pa had been killed. It was so short and he'd read the words so many times that he'd memorized it, practically.

Dear Emmett,
We got your letter tellin us you are down here in the army of the Potomac as well. I have been after Lietenant Varny to give us a day to come visit you. We was sad to hear the news bout Mother dyin and all. It ain't easy bein in the war as you will probly come to figure out. Rumor has it there is a big battle comin up soon as I hear we mite go after Richmond agin. Maybe we'll see you there.
William & Daniel

He hadn't shared that letter with anybody, not even Tom, but on this day Emmett found himself confiding in Chamberlain. "Sir, do you mind if I ask you a question?"

They had just come upon one of those high meadows where the whole world stretched out in front of you, it seemed, and they paused, drinking in the view. "What's on your mind, Emmett?"

"I was wondering, I mean, do you know where the 2nd Maine is?"

"I don't know offhand, but I'm sure I could find out for you. Is it your brothers you're thinking of?"

"I got a letter from them saying they was doing okay, but I thought maybe I could visit them if we were ever close by."

Chamberlain continued to stare at the Blue Ridge Mountains in the distance and did not speak for some time. "I'm sure that we can manage that," he finally said. "You must miss them."

"I wasn't all that close to them, being so much younger." Emmett wiped a tear from the corner of his eye. "But they are the only family I got left."

"It must be a terrible thing to lose a mother to consumption and a father to the war, all in three months time," Chamberlain said gently. "The year after Daisy was born we lost a son in childbirth, I never even got to name him. It leaves an emptiness that's hard to fill."

Emmett turned and faced the other way, hiding the tears that now streaked his face. "I mostly feel nothing at all, sir, and I don't think that's right. I should feel something more than nothing."

"I would think that feeling nothing is probably a sight more painful than feeling grief." Chamberlain took his cap off and wiped his brow with his arm. "There isn't a right and wrong way to feel sad, Emmett."

Emmett nodded, and the two of them stared at the Maryland and Virginia landscape, their seemingly peaceful countenances hiding deeper feelings. After a bit, Chamberlain observed the lateness of the hour, and they spurred their horses and rode on.

After six weeks of ceaselessly drilling, the orders came for the 5th Corps to move out. They went south along the Blue Ridge Mountains, crossing the Potomac into Virginia, knowing that somewhere just west of those mountains, Robert E. Lee and the Army of Northern Virginia lurked, waiting to strike.

The popular General McClellan had once again been removed from command of the Army of the Potomac, and Ambrose Burnside put in charge, a duty for which he feared he was ill-prepared. "Old Burn" had come into the war as commander of the Rhode Island militia, working his way up the ladder of command after notable successes at Roanoke Island and New Bern. He had been offered command of the army several times previously but had declined due to his self-professed lack of experience and his loyalty to General McClellan. Finally, however, on November 7th, he had accepted. His plan was to attack Richmond, Virginia by going through Fredericksburg, and to this end he drove the army to the northern bank of the Rappahannock River just across from that city. Unfortunately for him and eventually for many Union soldiers, the pontoons that he planned to use to cross the river were delayed in arriving and the army found itself spending a hungry Thanksgiving fighting the unseasonable cold instead of the enemy.

The morning of December 9th dawned to the discovery that two men of the 20th Maine had frozen to death overnight. The deaths had barely registered when a ripple of excitement and nervousness supplanted it; they were preparing to move out. With an additional three months of training under the tyrannical Colonel Ames, the men from Maine were finally going to be given their opportunity to prove their worth in this long-awaited engagement.

Chamberlain had undergone his own transformation, his former, somewhat aloof and professional bearing having given way to a more confident and assured demeanor, a leader of men whose character would be, like theirs, sorely tested. Yet he went forward with his mind at peace in one respect. The night before, he had received a letter from his wife.

My dearest husband,

I am sorry that I have caused you anguish as that was not my plan. Of course I will be here for you, waiting with the children, for I do love you with all of my heart. I just sometimes get sad and everything seems to be so gloomy. You know that I have not seen Paul in several years, as I know that my friendship with him upsets you. Your sister Sae has been here since you left, helping me with the children and we have had many a wonderful conversation. I know that if you have set your mind to the task at hand, which is this wretched war, you will be successful. I only ask that you also set your mind to LIFE. Your children and I need you to return, so use every caution. Wyllys asks me every morning when he first wakes up if you have returned and Daisy tells everybody she runs into that her father is a General and is going to (per)serve the country. If you could see the looks on peoples' faces you would get quite a laugh. Please let me know if and when I might be able to come and visit with you.

I hope that you rest contented & assured that I am yours,

Your Fanny

Chapter Six

As we advanced over that stricken field, the grave, conglomerate monotone resolved itself into its diverse, several elements: some breathing inarticulate agony; some dear home names; some begging for a drop of water; some for a caring word; some praying God for strength to bear; some for life; some for quick death. We did what we could, but how little it was on a field so boundless for feeble human reach! Our best was but to search the canteens of the dead for a draft of water for the dying; or to ease the posture of a broken limb; or to compress a severed artery of fast-ebbing life that might perhaps be so saved, with what little skill we had been taught by our surgeons early in learning the tactics of saving as well as of destroying men. It was a place and time for farewells. Many a word was taken for faraway homes that otherwise might never have had one token from the field of the lost. It was something even to let the passing spirit know that its worth was not forgotten here. –Joshua Lawrence Chamberlain.[5]

December 10, 1862

The 3rd Brigade, of which the 20th Maine was one small part, moved out for Fredericksburg and two days later, as they approached the Rappahannock, the seething mass of General Hooker's Grand Division of troops came into view. Emmett rode up to the Union Artillery positions on Stafford Heights with Chamberlain and the newly appointed adjutant, John Marshall Brown. Fredericksburg was much like Brunswick, Emmett thought, both towns on the edge of rivers, both with the signature mill surrounded by shops and homes. But where Brunswick was flat, Fredericksburg led upward into a series of small rolling hills.

"What a pretty town." Chamberlain murmured, more to himself than to Emmett. And indeed it was 'pretty as a picture.' Beautiful homes and businesses in typical southern grandeur teased the edges of the river. The far side of town was hugged by those sloping hills, enclosing it snugly in their bosom. Once a slow, pleasant place to live, it was now a place where war loomed, casting on the homes the long shadow of fear.

Colonel Ames overheard Chamberlain's observation and snorted. "It would be a pretty town if we controlled the heights on the other side of it. Now it is nothing but a horror show."

"Is that where the main attack is going to take place?" Chamberlain asked, pointing to the hills behind the town.

"General Franklin will be leading an attack downriver and we will attack here. Hopefully that will cause Lee to split his defenses."

The streets were empty of civilians, but snipers peeked out from windows of homes and lurked around corners, ready to unleash deadly fire into the ordinary soldiers and engineers trying to complete the pontoon bridge ready to be laid across the river for the army to cross. Because the bridges had only just arrived after a delay of several weeks, General Burnside had lost the element of surprise. Now that they were ready to be put into place, the largest impediment was the Rebel snipers from the town who poured volley after murderous volley into them as they attempted to lay the bridge across the river. After the first assault, blue uniforms filled the river, floating face down, bobbing with the current as the river slowly carried them away. A second sortie was mounted, and Emmett watched in horror as waves of soldiers charged out of several boats covered with a makeshift shield of planking, only to be shot down one by one in a matter of minutes.

General Burnside finally decided to change tactics, ordering Brigadier General Henry Hunt to begin an artillery bombardment of the town to dislodge the enemy. At 11 a.m., 150 artillery pieces massed their fire on the quaint village across the river, and it was as if Hell itself had opened up and engulfed it, so tremendous was the noise. For the next two hours the large guns pounded the town with 8,000 projectiles to destroy shielding cover and flush out the snipers. As they watched, the artillery began to find their range, shells bursting all over the town with furious explosions followed by the crackle of flames and the crashing of timbers mixed with the occasional scream of men in mortal agony.

After what seemed an eternity, the artillery barrage ceased, and silence again descended. "That is where we are going?" Emmett said pointing a shaky finger. On the far bank of the river the picture perfect town they had been admiring had been transformed into a scene of carnage and destruction. Smoke billowed into the sky as fire ravaged the buildings, with not a single structure, it seemed, having escaped the devastation.

"It is not the town that I am concerned about, young fellow." Colonel Ames replied. "It is the hills that hide Bobby Lee's army and his guns. That hill there," he said pointing straight across Fredericksburg to a steep incline. "That is Marye's Heights, and General James Longstreet is entrenched just over the crest, waiting to see if we will make the mistake of attacking."

"I've heard that Longstreet is a master tactician, sir." Chamberlain said, looking at the open fields above town, merely waiting to be filled with soldiers. Blue-coated engineers ran to continue the work on the bridge, but amazingly enough, were met with a withering fire from the Confederate snipers still hidden among the rubble and destruction across the river.

"Longstreet might be the best that Lee has for strategy. He seems to see everything three moves ahead of his opponents. I would not want to face him on open ground, but with him commanding those hills? It is suicide."

"I hear that Stonewall Jackson is over there as well, sir?"

"That he is, Lieutenant Colonel. That he is," Colonel Ames sighed.

"Why do they call him Stonewall?" Emmett was embarrassed to know so little, but both Chamberlain and Colonel Ames always appeared to be patient with his ignorance.

"It was at the first Battle of Bull Run, right at the beginning, when events were still looking good for the Union. We were driving the rebels back, pushing them in front of us like cattle, and then we ran into General Thomas Jackson. One of his fellow officers offhandedly said that it was like running into a 'stone wall' when our troops hit him and his men." Chamberlain wiped his eyes with the back of his hand, the smoke from the artillery still blowing past them.

"If there is anybody better at strategy than Longstreet, it would be Jackson." Colonel Ames added grimly.

Volunteers were asked to man the clumsy boats to be used to float the pontoon bridge. The new strategy was to ferry troops across the 400 feet of river to dislodge the enemy snipers. Soon men from New York, Massachusetts, and Michigan had landed on the far side and were forcing the snipers from the town in a deadly game of cat and mouse as they retreated house by house until finally fleeing back up the hills to the safety of the Confederate Army.

As the three of them watched the town of Fredericksburg burn from their perch in the heights, a courier came up requesting Colonel Ames attend a meeting with General Hooker of the Central Grand Division. "Any word on how the Left Grand Division underneath General Franklin is doing?" Chamberlain asked the man.

"They met with little opposition to the building of the other pontoon bridges just down the river a piece and are in the process of crossing now," the courier replied. The battle strategy called for General Franklin to attack about a mile south of town, and when that offensive proved successful, to attack here above Fredericksburg in a two-pronged assault.

"It looks like they're getting this cleaned out, and we won't be far behind them." Chamberlain declared with a wistful expression, staring down at the river where work on the pontoon bridge had resumed.

That night, nervous and cold, thousands of soldiers gathered around campfires along the river where they were bivouacked, attempting to stay warm and keep up good spirits by singing patriotic songs, huddling close to each other. Emmett had never seen a group of men come together as one so quickly; all petty squabbles seemingly laid aside, each and every one of them brothers pulled together to face a threat to hearth and home.

He is coming like the glory of the morning on the wave,
He is wisdom to the mighty, He is honor to the brave;
So the world shall be His footstool, and the soul of wrong His
slave,
Our God is marching on.
Glory! Glory! Hallelujah! Glory! Glory! Hallelujah!
Glory! Glory! Hallelujah! Our God is marching on.

"We're sure going to show them Johnny Rebs a thing or two tomorrow, Tom." John Marshall Brown said, slapping Tom on the back as the lyrics of "The Battle Hymn of the Republic" drew to a close. The men had actually shouted the words at the top of their lungs, and an observer would have been embroidering it a bit where he to call it hymn singing. More than one man would wake up the following day hoarse from song rather than from battle. "The Girl I Left Behind," a haunting lament, began by the fire, many of the men growing quiet and pensive as the words wafted through the air.

I'm lonesome since I crossed the hill
And over the moor that's sedgy
Such lonely thoughts my heart do fill
Since parting with my Betsey
I seek for one as fair and gay
But find none to remind me
How sweet the hours I passed away
With the girl I left behind me

Tom didn't answer his friend, grimacing in the dark and hoping that the firelight did not illuminate his face, for he was afraid. Sure, he was scared of the Confederate Army, and old Bobby Lee, and Longstreet, and Jackson, and all of the soldiers who would be trying to kill him tomorrow. And Marye's Hill, looming ominously across the river and which he would be scaling in the face of Confederate artillery—that was enough to instill fear in any living soul. But these were not the things that terrified him, causing his lips to curl over his teeth, his face drawn, eyes wide, and pupils dilated. It was the thought that these other things had led him to, just in the past hour as they sang song after song. *What if he, Tom Chamberlain, proved to be a coward in battle?* How could he face his brother, how could he ever speak to his father again or ride beside John Marshall Brown, if in the face of battle, he ran away, or cowered in a ditch, or began sobbing as he'd heard of other soldiers doing when confronted by battle?

"What's bothering you?" Brown gave Tom a strange look. "Worried about tomorrow?"

Tom took a deep breath, trying to settle his demons. "I heard some officers complaining earlier," he said finally. "Saying it would be like shooting ducks for the Confederates if we was to try and dislodge them from those hills over there."

Momentary terror aside, Tom was relishing the life of a soldier. He had packed thirty pounds of muscle onto his lean frame over the past three months on rations that most people would think more akin to animal feed, though he had as of yet to see any real action.

"Well, everyone knows that Lincoln is impatient with the efforts of the generals so far." Brown said. "And Burnside boasted that he was going to march the sixty miles to Richmond capturing the capital city and maybe Jefferson Davis along the way. Someone's got to do the fighting, and that's us."

"I know it has got to be done," Tom admitted. "Hell, I guess nobody ever thought I'd amount to much of anything anyway. Mother and Father sent my brothers and sister off to school while I had to get a job cause I wasn't as smart as them."

"We're not all meant for book learning and college." Brown replied. "If I learned one thing on the docks of Portland, it's that there were plenty of good men down there who couldn't read or write a lick, but many of them I am proud to call friend."

"I'm running out of things I can be a success at, is all." Tom shrugged his shoulders. "I'm hoping this soldiering thing works out for me, because I don't got too many chances left."

"Well, as long as you fight like you did back in Portland, why then, I guess we'll be just fine. I've lived my life trying to meet the expectations of my father. But, hell, I joined up because I realized that it is my life to live, not his. Don't live in the shadow of your brother. Best make your own way."

The next morning brought a heavy fog clinging to the ground and wrapping itself thickly along the river valley. The Center Grand Division along with the 20th Maine was being held in reserve and remained on the north side of the river, the soldiers anxiously wondering what was happening. In the late morning the sun burned through the soupy mess, and they could see the Left and Right Grand Divisions, Franklin's men moving in from the left and Sumner's soldiers beginning to move out of Fredericksburg on the right. As Emmett stood and watched with Chamberlain and Colonel Ames, the men marched fearlessly out of town and up Marye's Heights and directly into a hail of bullets and falling artillery that carved swathes through their neat ranks, turning a sea of blue into one tinged with red as the missiles did their deadly work. Bravely, the blue-suited soldiers continued up the hill until finally they hit a small depression, and as one, sank to the ground, just out of sight of the Confederates. From this position, they were unable to retreat or attack without exposing themselves. At this moment the call went out for the 5th Corps to move out. General Hooker would be bringing his men into action. The time had come for the 20th Maine to show what they were made of.

"Steady the bridge! Steady the bridge!" Officers called to the approaching soldiers as they began to cross over under intermittent shelling which mostly missed its mark.

Emmett gritted his teeth and set his feet in motion, moving resolutely forward, determined to show no fear, to give himself no chance of being a coward.

"Best get off your horse, sir." A captain said to his superior officer. "It will help balance things out better and not make you such a target."

Just then, the Confederate artillery began finding the right range for the soldiers crossing the bridge. Shrapnel split the air above their heads with a horrible sound, the detonation seeming to suck the air from the men's lungs. The bridge swayed, horses reared, and the green and untested 20th Maine crossed over, happy to be off the bridge, even if it was escaping the frying pan to be thrown into the fire.

Emmett saw a street sign lying on the ground, Prince Edward Street, as they huddled in loose formation in the middle of the smoldering town, waiting for orders to move forward. The day before, Union soldiers had vandalized the buildings in their rage at the snipers who had used them as cover. Tables, chairs, beds, and even pianos lay broken in the street with smashed mirrors, clothes, and books strewn amongst the mud and crater holes from the shelling two days earlier. The fires had mostly burned out, leaving blackened facades, roofs and walls with gaping holes, the occasional body of a civilian mixed in with the dead soldiers. Here in this charnel house, the 20th Maine waited for orders. This was the worst part, this waiting, but they would not have to endure for long. The bugle call soon came for them to move forward. As dusk began to gather on the edge of town, long shadows from the surrounding hills blackening the terrain, six regiments formed themselves, ready to advance. The 20th Maine was in the front and center, between the 83rd Pennsylvania and the 17th New York, with three more regiments behind them.

"Lieutenant Colonel, you take the right wing, I will lead the men from the middle." Colonel Ames shouted, striding forward, the ground ahead strewn with so many obstacles that horses would be useless. "God help us now."

The men of the 20th Maine moved forward in their blue uniforms, holding tight formation thanks to Colonel Ames' incessant drilling over the previous months. They came to a ditch filled with several feet of icy water, which thoroughly soaked their clothes as they tramped through.

Emmett stayed close to Chamberlain who had unsheathed his sword and led the men forward at a slight jog, moving steadily up the hill. "Sir, where is the regiment from New York?"

Chamberlain looked over at him, and then to the right where New York should have been. "Can't say that I know, Emmett. I suppose there's not much we can do about it now." Ahead, they were confronted by a tall wooden fence blocking their advance as bullets whipped into the ranks from above and from their right side as well, now that they had become the right flank facing the enemy positions.

"Take down the fence!" Rumbled a command from the center of the regiment, but the men paused, hesitating in the face of death.

Chamberlain rushed forward and began tearing at the boards with his bare hands. "Must I do this myself?" He yelled back over his shoulder. "Or will I get some help?" The 20th Maine surged to his side, quickly tearing open large gaps and moving forward.

Up above them, the Confederates waited, at ease and in comfort, ably positioned on the so-called Sunken Road, as years of wagon traffic had worn the road down, a low stone wall running its length further protecting them from Union fire. Meanwhile, the 20th Maine had a half-mile of open expanse to cross, moving uphill, the men stopping to fire a ragged volley, and then continuing forward. But up they went, until they were able to relieve the men who had spent the day at the front, allowing them to fall back into Fredericksburg for the night. They lay no more than one hundred yards from the crest of the hill, clinging to the ground in a shallow depression just out of sight of the Confederate sharpshooters so long as they didn't raise their heads up. Night descended upon them and with it came cold, icy air chilling them further in their wet clothes. It was then that Emmett first began to hear the moans wafting through the heavy black night. As he listened more closely, he could put words to them. Cries for help. Calls for mercy. Screams of agony.

Like ghouls from the darkness these pleas crackled through the air until finally Emmett could take it no longer. "Lieutenant Colonel, isn't there something we can do?"

Chamberlain lay between two dead soldiers killed earlier in the day, not members of his regiment, but Union soldiers nonetheless. The two bodies provided both protection from enemy fire and a semblance of warmth. The regiment's knapsacks, holding overcoats and blankets, had been left back with the quartermaster in town, and with little protection from the cold and no opportunity to build a fire, any source of warmth or shelter, even from a dead body, was better than nothing.

With a sigh, he got onto his knees. "We might as well do what we can until the ambulance crew arrives to bring them to the rear. I don't see getting any rest, and I don't suppose in this darkness the Rebs can see us to shoot us any better than we can see them." With that, Chamberlain began to slither across the ground, careful to keep his head down for fear of a vigilant Confederate marksmen looking for any glint of movement in the moonlight. Emmett followed him, more terrified to be left alone than to crawl through a field of dead and maimed soldiers. A man grasped his hand, the smell of vomit and excrement overwhelming the odor of blood from his mangled stomach, dark slippery pieces falling from his sides as he clutched at Emmett fiercely. Emmett tried to wrench his hand away but was unable, the man clinging to him with a ferocity that was terrifying. The soldier never said a word, and after several minutes, let Emmett loose, presumably to embrace death. The boy scuttled away as fast as he could. A man was screaming for somebody to find his leg, desperate to retrieve this missing body part, and then he too grew quiet.

Somewhere in the middle of that expanse, away from the screams and cries that echoed over the small gentle hill, Emmett sank to his knees, then lay shivering until other figures, the ambulance crew, began to arrive and tend to the wounded. Like angels, they moved among the fallen, shadowy figures plucking the still breathing from the ground and bearing them away. In the early morning hours, Chamberlain found Emmett still trembling and terrified on the ground. Wordlessly he roused him and led him back to their lines that they might attempt a few hours sleep before dawn.

Emmett had barely closed his eyes when the sun began to rise, awakening him far too early. Where the 20th Maine lay, it was impossible to raise one's head more than a foot without drawing a shot. He was happy lying there in the warm sun after the frigid night, drowsing in between moments of alarm. There was some fear the Confederates were going to attempt to shell them out of their thin cover with cannons, but after a brief attempt in which the correct range could not be found, this plan appeared to have been abandoned. Later, several companies of Rebs moved into a new position, one from which they could fire into the Union soldiers. A hastily erected protective wall made of earth, broken fence slats, and dead bodies provided coverage enough until their own rifles drove the Rebs back over the crest of the hill.

"I'm not sure which is worse, the fighting or the boredom." Tom Chamberlain remarked to Emmett, who had crawled the ten yards to where his friend lay.

"I think I have to choose marching up a hill into the blazing guns of the Johnny Rebs as being worse than lying here in the sun," Emmett replied.

"The boys over in the 83rd Pennsylvania are daring each other to run a gauntlet of snipers over that way just to keep the tedium at bay. Each time one of them runs through some low area to get to the other side and draws fire, they roar in laughter."

"I imagine they ain't all right in the head."

"I guess once you live with something long enough and it doesn't drive you insane, well then, you might begin to not fear it so much."

Emmett finally forced out the question he'd wanted to ask all day. "Was you scared yesterday, Tom?"

"To tell you the truth, I was more scared that I would be scared."

"So how did you make the fear go away?"

"I don't guess I know." Tom murmured, and they were both silent.

With the cover of night, they were able to sit up, eat some hardtack, get a drink of water, and stretch their cramped muscles. Soon after darkness came, they were relieved of their position and withdrew back down to the town of Fredericksburg. Before sleep, they first had to bury their dead. They dug the graves in silence with fence slats that then became litters upon which to carry those soldiers of the 20th Maine who had not survived the previous day's fighting. As they picked their way in the dark, tripping and stumbling, suddenly the sky was lit up by an array of lights blooming in the darkness. Emmett stared in amazement as the colors arced from one end of the heavens to another like fireworks—reds, blues, violets, and greens streaking overhead in a breathtaking display. "What is it, sir?"

Chamberlain paused in his gruesome task to stare at the heavens, head raised in awe. "It is the aurora borealis, Emmett. The ancient Roman Goddess of the dawn was Aurora, and it is as if she has come to honor those that we tonight lie to rest." He wiped his brow, his entire being filled with the wonder of this event. "Who would die a nobler death," he quoted, "or dream of a more glorious burial? Dead for their country's honor, and lighted to interment by the meteor splendors of their northern home."

Emmett had no idea what Chamberlain was talking about, and thus kept quiet before finally venturing, "It sort of makes the life of a man to be a small thing." He stared down at the soldier lying in the hastily dug grave, recognizing him as one of the more exuberant singers from two nights before, a man with a quick smile who now lay dead.

"Don't ever underestimate the life of man as he is God's creation and has that divine spark within, each and every one of us." Chamberlain reflected. "It does make me wonder at the ineptitude of our leaders to throw away the lives of so many men in this meaningless way, so many men from Maine, boys...." Chamberlain trailed off, his anger only beginning to smolder as he thought about the previous day's events. "But as it says in Ecclesiastes 3:8, there is a time to love, and a time to hate; a time of war, and a time of peace."

"I have to admit, sir, that until this moment I was overcome by fear of being afraid, being yellow. But I'm not afraid anymore. Tom says maybe you just get used to it. I don't know about that, but I'm not afraid anymore."

"That is good, Emmett. But remember, fear is like humility: it is good to carry a little bit of it no matter where you go." He reached out and laid a hand lightly on the boy's shoulder. "Not that you'll be trying fate again any time soon." He said with a brief smile.

Sleep was again fleeting as the soldiers bivouacked once more on the streets of Fredericksburg, though Emmett was lucky enough to be brought into a house in which Colonel Ames and Joshua Chamberlain had taken up residence. Twice, intense firing from the front caused alarm that the Rebs were sweeping down the hill, attacking under cover of the night. But the morning arrived with no change in position. Emmett helped make a warm breakfast of flapjacks and coffee, perking up everybody's spirits. Most of the men had spent the night camped out on Caroline Street, down in the middle of town, and were intermingled with regiments from all over the North. It was a morning marked by the exuberance of those who had faced death and survived, even the reeking debris-filled streets seeming a safe haven for men who the previous day had lain trembling on the ground, praying and pissing their pants. Now they smiled and laughed, feeling their bravery in the aftermath of battle. Later in the day, they were ordered to the outskirts of town but with no expectation that they would be returning to the fray.

Just before midnight, a courier arrived with a message for Colonel Ames, and Emmett was told to pass the word that the men were to be awakened and to fall in. "What's is going on?" Tom Chamberlain asked him as they stood at ease with the rest of the men in the dark.

"No idea, the Lieutenant Colonel just shook me awake and told me to pass the word."

"Some of the men are saying that we're going to fall back across the river."

Those hopes were dashed when they began to move out, not towards the river but instead back up the hill to Marye's Heights. Just before they set out, Colonel Stockton, commander of the 3rd Brigade had become ill, with Colonel Strong of the 83rd Pennsylvania assuming command of the Brigade, and Colonel Ames moving up the chain to help out. For the first time since Camp Mason in Portland, Joshua Chamberlain was put in command of the 20th Maine. Silently they filed past heaps of dead Union soldiers on their way to the very front lines, relieving the troops there.

Chamberlain looked around the battlefield, its darkness hiding the violence of the day. "To think that it has only been four months," he sighed.

"What has been only four months, sir?" Ellis Spear asked respectfully.

"Four months since my entire life was overturned and shaken up and then put back together again," Chamberlain reminisced.

"The men trust and respect you, sir."

Chamberlain grunted. "Colonel Ames has told me to hold this ground at all hazards and to the last," he paused, chewing over the words carefully. "To the last of what, do you suppose? The last bullet? The last breath of air? The last soldier standing? It is a confusing order, this 'hold to the last' concept. And all hazards?"

Ellis Spear, not given to such speculative flights of fancy or imagination, merely shrugged his shoulders. To him, it was obvious that "the last" meant until they were all dead or the Confederates had stopped attacking, but he sensed that the answer Chamberlain was wrestling with was far deeper, more complicated and profound, and thus remained quiet.

"Go have the officers tell the men to dig in. The word is that in the morning the enemy will have cannons set up to dislodge us from our position here."

"If they are going to shell us tomorrow, it will certainly save others the trouble of digging graves for us if we dig our own." Ellis responded drily, before going off to spread the order.

"Captain Spear always had a dry sense of humor, even when he was a student of mine at Bowdoin College." Chamberlain remarked to Emmett, who had heard the entire exchange. "You stay put here while I go survey our progress."

"Can I come with you, sir?"

Chamberlain looked at the boy and wondered how it was that he had ever allowed him to come to the front, or even come back across the river. Now, there was no time, no good solution. Somehow, he felt that the boy was safer where he could keep an eye on him, and that just happened to be at the front if you were a Lieutenant Colonel. "Come on then." He said finally.

"Throw the dirt to the front, not the sides." Chamberlain whispered to more than one man as they worked their way down the line, keeping their voices low, knowing the enemy was within a hundred yards of their position, and how over the night air a voice could carry. "You are digging a hole to hide in but also a wall to hide behind."

"Who is that digging over there?" Emmett whispered, tugging on Chamberlain's arm and pointing.

"He must be part of C Company," Chamberlain replied. "But that darn fool is throwing the dirt in the wrong direction." They scooted over to the man and Chamberlain whispered, "Throw it the other way, my man. That's where the danger is."

"Golly! Don't ye s'pose I know which side them Yanks is on? They're right onto us now."

Emmett stiffened in shock, realizing they were speaking with a Confederate soldier.

Chamberlain reacted quickly, realizing the danger and thinking on his feet. "Dig away then, but keep a sharp lookout," he said, grabbing Emmett firmly by the collar and scuttling quickly back towards his own Regiment and Army.

As they cautiously made their way back to the Union side, the first two men they came upon were Tom Chamberlain and John Marshall Brown. Chamberlain pulled Brown aside to pass on orders, while Emmett excitedly told Tom about their brush with a Rebel. "We could have climbed right in the hole with him, and he wouldn't have known any different!"

At that moment, a staff officer came bursting in upon them. "Who is the commanding officer here?" He asked loudly.

"That would be me," Chamberlain replied, annoyed by the man's lack of calm.

The man shouted back, "Then get yourself out of this as quick as God will let you. The entire army has crossed back over the river, and you are the only Union soldiers left on this side!"

Emmett was appalled by this, but was even more flabbergasted when Chamberlain retorted, "Steady in your places, my men. This man is a stampeding traitor!" His voice was controlled, but pitched just loud enough for the Confederates to hear. Several officers came to check out what was going on, and Chamberlain continued. "This man is a spy. Arrest him and take him away!" But when the men went to take the staff officer's sidearm, Chamberlain brushed them aside. In a lower voice he told them, "I'll take care of this." He grabbed the man by the arm and pulled him firmly a few steps away from the others closer to Emmett. "What do you think you're doing? Are you trying to tell the enemy that there are only a few men left on this side of the river, and they can capture or kill us at their whim?"

The flustered man gathered himself slightly, a calmer expression settling over his features. "I'm sorry sir, it's just that I've had a dickens of a time finding you as ordered, and I was just about to write you off as lost."

"Can you find your way back down the hill?"

"Yes, sir."

"Then I suggest you do it, and quickly. If you are still in my sight in ten seconds I will have you brought up on charges."

"Yes, sir." And the man was gone.

Chamberlain muttered something about a 'fool' and then beckoned Emmett to come closer. "Go find Colonel Ames, and tell him that we are the only Union soldiers left on this side of the river."

"What are you going to do, sir?"

"I am going to make sure the Confederates know that we're still here and don't plan on leaving any time soon. Now go quickly."

Emmett was back in two minutes with Colonel Ames in tow, Chamberlain confirming the message and the two putting their heads together to come up with a plan of retreat. "I suggest we have the men count off by ones and twos. Then we drop back, first the odd numbers and then the even numbers, staggering the retreat while each line keeps cover. Maybe a hundred yards at a time?"

Colonel Ames agreed to the plan, and they immediately set about communicating it to the officers and the men. They tried to hush the whispered buzz that swept through the ranks, and then the orderly retreat began under cover of a cloudy night sky. The first men rose like dark shadows in the blackness and hurried down the hill with careful steps lest they raise the enemy. The plan worked well until the cloud passed, revealing a moon whose light shone off the muskets of the men, signalling their retreat to the Confederates. A shot rang out, and then another, a ragged volley of bullets whizzing over their heads as the men all dropped to the ground. Over the hill, they could see gray soldiers passing, approaching, searching for them. And then the cloud returned and they resumed the retreat, chased by the dark and the enemy that it cloaked.

Fredericksburg was a ghost town, the doors of the few remaining buildings flapping in the light breeze as they moved through with an invisible enemy on their tail. "Sir, there are wounded soldiers still in some of these houses." Captain Spear reported to Chamberlain.

"Their wounds are so severe that they could not be moved. They will be left to the mercy of the enemy. I believe a few doctors have volunteered to stay and care for them." Chamberlain answered resolutely, his anger already beginning to boil at how the entire operation had been mismanaged. They passed swiftly over the pontoon bridge. No sooner had Chamberlain stepped off, than the army engineers cut the anchoring cables and pulled the bridge ashore to be used elsewhere, ensuring that the Confederates could not cross.

Later, as Emmett sleepily marched with Chamberlain, he posed a question that he would never have had the courage to ask by the light of day or without the dumb bravery conferred by exhaustion. "Do you think we have a chance, Lieutenant Colonel?"

"We have a chance, Emmett, but there is going to have to be better leadership, because these brave lads can't continue to blindly follow orders with no hope of success." At those words, a lone horseman approached, stopping in front of the two.

It was General "Fighting Joe" Hooker, commander of the entire Grand Central Division, of which the 20th Maine was such a small part. "You've had a hard chance of it, Colonel. I'm glad to see you out of it."

The anger that had started to burn as they retreated through Fredericksburg burst from Chamberlain in a terse retort. "And chance it was General. Not much intelligent design there."

"God knows I didn't put you in," the sharp-tongued General Hooker replied.

"That was the trouble, General; you should have put us in. Instead, we were handed in piecemeal, on toasting forks." Chamberlain had been seething at the poor tactics, at how the various regiments had been slowly integrated into the battle and summarily bested one by one, as opposed to one grand attack. The man responsible stood right there in front of him.

On any other day, such blunt words to a Major General would have resulted in disciplinary action. That night, however, General Hooker merely replied, "Perhaps you are right Colonel, not a single day will pass for the rest of my life that I do not think of the events of today and shudder within." It had been another staggering defeat for the Union Army. How many more such defeats could follow, else the entire war be abandoned? The North needed a victory. Desperately.

Chapter Seven

Dear John—I hope that things are fine with you and that Mother and Father are well. I cannot say the same for the war effort. I have seen first hand the type of bungling that has hampered the Northern cause for most of the war. Fredericksburg was a debacle but could have been a glorious victory with the proper leadership. Regiments were thrown in to attack an impregnable Confederate position one by one instead of committing the entire army, but enough of that, I am sure that you have read about it all in the newspaper. It seems that supplying an army this size with rations is no easy matter, but nothing lowers the morale of the men more than going hungry, and that has been happening in a consistent fashion as we sit across the Rappahannock River from the Rebels at Stoneman's Switch in Virginia. It doesn't help that we had fifteen inches of snow the first week of January—a natural event that we men of Maine are better suited for than most. Luckily, Colonel Ames and myself had the men construct huts from what scrub pines and cedar we could find, the walls three feet high with a peaked roof from our canvas tents, chinked with the mud that is everywhere here in Virginia, and most of them have built sod stoves to cook and stay warm by. Unfortunately, we have used most of the nearby wood for building and have to travel miles to find more to burn, but it keeps the men busy. We had a Grand Review, which we all knew to be a precursor to a new campaign, probably a desperate attempt for General Burnside to retain his command. We will never know if the strategy for the new campaign was sound, for on the first day the rain fell, creating a muck that was hard to walk in, much less transport equipment. That first day, the 20th Maine made three miles, and then had to step aside to let the artillery and pontoons struggle past. Two more days of marching bore similar results with wagons and caissons buried in the horrendous mud, some horses had to be abandoned to their death. All the while, the Confederate soldiers jeered at us across from across the river, offering to come lend a hand and mocking our efforts. On the fourth day, the 20th Maine was given the chore of finding lumber to hew and make roads from, not to move forward, but to retreat in humble fashion having accomplished little more than embarrassing ourselves. This was *the final straw for Burnside, as President Lincoln replaced him last week with General "Fighting Joe" Hooker who seems to be committed to raising the morale of the men. Food rations and variety have increased, and winter leaves are being granted in greater numbers. As a result, I have obtained leave for next week to come back to Maine, partially on business to see Governor Coburn about promotions, but I should be able to do some visiting while there. I hope to be able to get to Brewer to see Father and Mother. Give them my best—Your humble brother, Lawrence*

February 8, 1863

Emmett found himself walking up the hill from the train station in Brunswick, struggling to keep up with Chamberlain's long strides, as the man was obviously eager to be home. They passed the First Parish Church, turned onto Potter Street, and within minutes Chamberlain was throwing open the front door of his home, calling out, "Where is everybody?"

A little girl came running to greet him while Emmett stood nervously in the doorway.

"Daddy, is that really you?" Daisy asked.

Swooping the girl off her feet and into a circle around him, Chamberlain—grinning like Emmett had never seen him grin before—replied, "Well, I don't know about that young lady. I do have a little girl, but she is only about half the size of you. She is just six years old."

"I'm six years old," shrieked the little girl.

"My little girl's name is Daisy."

"My name is Daisy," she was now giggling infectiously. Behind her, a small boy had cautiously entered, as uncomfortable as Emmett on the other side of the room.

"Well, you must be <u>my</u> Daisy then." Chamberlain said, hugging her tightly before setting her down. "And who is this young lad here?"

"My name is Wyllys." The boy mumbled, his eyes boring into the floor at his feet.

"Do you have a hug for your father?" Chamberlain opened his arms wide, but Wyllys shook his head no, and when

Chamberlain approached him the boy ran back into the interior of the house.

At that moment, Fanny Chamberlain swept into the room, having snatched Wyllys up on her way. Her beauty stunned Emmett. When he'd first shown up six months earlier, his thoughts had been elsewhere, but now, well.... Perhaps it was the fact that he had matured from a boy to a man in that period. Whatever the case, her beauty now dazzled his eye, rendering him even more hesitant and awkward than he had been. Her medium length dark hair was pulled back into braids, exposing the milky white features that a Maine winter certainly aided. She was thin in a very healthy way, wearing a fashionably dark dress that accented her figure quite favorably.

"Lawrence, what are you doing here?" Her voice was low, breathy, as if she'd been taken totally off-guard.

"My dear little girl, I sent you a letter but probably passed it along the way somewhere. I think only about one in three letters seems to get through in these trying times." Chamberlain said, rapidly closing the distance between them.

"Are you injured?" Fanny asked, a slow flush creeping up her cheeks, having still not moved from her spot.

It was only after enveloping her in his arms and giving her frozen lips a brief kiss that Chamberlain turned and said, "Emmett, come into the house and shut the door. We don't have an entrance hall here."

"We hadn't expected you. I just received a letter from you yesterday, saying that you spent a week marching in the rain and mud only to return to camp." Her eyes were wide and uncomprehending, and it would be several minutes before she could accept the idea that he was home and unhurt.

Chamberlain's eyes blazed in momentary anger at the memory. "I wish I'd come home and avoided that entire 'Mud March'."

They had a light tea, Emmett marveling at its simple magic, how it was possible to sit at a table with a tablecloth, be warm, drink tea, and eat tidbits of food, all the while making civilized conversation. He answered the few questions Fanny posed, but the center of attention for all was certainly husband and father. Young Wyllys had relaxed, and now climbed up and over his father like a little monkey, giggling when tickled, pulling at his father's mustache, and drawing small smiles from Fanny. After some time, Chamberlain suggested that the children take Emmett to feed the chickens and play in the snow. Before long, he joined them, pushing a plow contraption to clear the snow, but which also worked as a sled for the children to ride upon.

Hours later, as soon as supper was finished, Chamberlain allowed that it had been a long day, showing Emmett to his room, kissing his children good night and joining his wife in their bedroom. Used to sleeping in the open or at least, in a cabin with walls like a sieve, the heat from the wood stove felt suffocating to him. Or, he mused, regarding his wife, who stood at the vanity, her hands gripping the sides, shoulders stiff and unapproachable, and emanating a different kind of heat, he considered that it might be her.

"Are you coming to bed, my dear?" Chamberlain turned back the bedcovers, hovering in that delicate space between desire and courtesy.

"I am not cut out to be alone, Lawrence. You of all people should know that." Fanny's voice came out bitter, angrier than she intended.

"I am sorry, my sweet little girl, but there is nothing I can do about that."

"There *is* something you could have done, such as not to volunteer for this war that has nothing to do with us."

"Nothing to do with us?" He looked at her, wondering just how far down this particular road he wanted to go, its end inevitably the death of desire. He replied finally in a compromising tone. "The preservation of the Union? If we will not fight to save our families, our way of life, our government...then who will?"

"Your family is here, Lawrence. This is your place, not out on some battlefield."

"Can we stop this conversation? Over and over we have plowed this field only to find the same stones with each pass of the blades. My place is with the 20th Maine, leading my men, retaining the integrity of the United States of America. Our government is a beacon of light to the rest of the world, and if the Union falls, that light will be snuffed out."

"Noble thoughts, I am sure." She said dismissively. "And now tell me how I am to stay here alone without going crazy."

"You have the children to cheer you up."

"You know that I am not one of those women bred to be a blissful mother and constant bride for you. I need intelligent conversation, art, music, poetry, and good books. I need to visit cities as was my wont before we wed—and to live life as it is meant to be lived."

"And I want to be in the middle of a war, eating terrible food, sleeping under the stars, facing disease, and an enemy who wants to kill me?" Chamberlain retorted, beginning to lose patience.

There was a long pause. "I think you might prefer that to being home with me."

"My dear Fanny, how can you say that? Don't pull away from me, you know that I love you more than anything in the whole world."

"Lawrence, I don't feel like being touched by you right now."

"I know that is not true, my dear. You long for my touch as much as I long for yours. It has been too long, and I am only home for a short time."

"I do not want to carry another baby while you are away at war. I do not want to give birth to a child who has no father. I will not do that."

And then there was silence.

Emmett woke in the morning to the wide blue eyes of four-year-old Wyllys Chamberlain staring at him. "Are you a soldier?" The young boy stood at the foot of Emmett's bed, wearing a dress with a heart pattern, the shoulders ruffled and the material stretching to the floor. It was winter wear, a typical New England style for boys up to school age when they moved to breeches or trousers. His hair hung to either side in what had been braids, but was now only two clumped bands.

Emmett smiled blearily, only half-awake and realizing it was much easier to just agree. "Yes, I am." He noticed a rocking chair in the corner of the room, built for comfort with the rolled edge on the front of the contoured pine seat and the maple arms.

He didn't realize that this room was often the place Fanny Chamberlain came to find solitude from the pressures of everyday life.

"I wanna be a soldier, but my mommy wouldn't let me." Wyllys paused. "Did your mommy say it was okay for you to be a soldier?"

Again, Emmett was perplexed as to how to answer such a young boy, for the truth was not always easy to understand. "Yes. She was fine with it." He lied, climbing out of the bed, noticing for the first time the finely turned posts and carved legs of the frame, all in shining mahogany and the whole much nicer than he had been used to in Brewer.

"My mommy is mad at my daddy 'cause he became a soldier, but he don't have to listen to her cause he's a grown-up."

"Where is your daddy?" Emmett asked finally.

"He left early to go up to see his mother and then to Gusta to see the Gov'ner."

"What?" Emmett gasped, swinging his legs to the floor, the frigid room a shock after the warm comfort of the bed. "Is he gone already?" Thus, Emmett spent the next few days of Chamberlain's absence with the family, playing with the children, helping with chores around the house, and struggling to understand Fanny Chamberlain. She seemed quiet and serious, but one day she played the piano and sang while the children listened raptly, her voice so gay and beautiful that Emmett thought he'd died and gone to heaven. These lighter moments were few and far between, and Emmett chafed, wishing that he could go back to the battlefield, and wondering when his mentor might return from Augusta. The 20th Maine, he realized, had become his home more than any house could be, the hard ground more welcoming than any bed, the men his family. After the horrors witnessed at Fredericksburg, the lives of Fanny Chamberlain and her two innocent children seemed alien to him.

On the third day, Chamberlain finally returned from Augusta. "Emmett," he said almost before he was through the door, "pack your things. We have to start back immediately." He spoke just briefly to Fanny, seemingly irritated in her presence.

"Let me go with you," she pleaded.

"Army life is no place for a lady," he replied brusquely.

"But I would stay in Washington, and you can come to visit me!"

"I have not a minute to myself, much less time to visit you. Besides, the capital is no place for a lady these days."

"I have heard that there were many 'soiled doves' there." Fanny said, her nose wrinkled. "I hope you are not...."

"I would never," he cut in rudely, "but I can't say the same for some of the officers. General Hooker has so many prostitutes hanging around his headquarters that people have taken to calling them 'hookers'."

"Please let me come with you." She paused, as if pained by her thoughts, and then blurted, "I can't stand another day of being trapped in this house, in this weather, alone with the children. Please. Your sister will happily take them for a time...."

Chamberlain would not be convinced, giving her but a peck on the cheek. He kissed and hugged his children, and then they were out the door. Although usually talkative, he barely said a word during the long trip back to Washington.

With the winter had come a lull in fighting, and the commanders knew you didn't just leave a few hundred thousand soldiers idle. General Hooker seemed intent on raising their morale after the last round of defeats. In the army camp various activities had been created to perk up the spirit of the soldiers, and to keep them occupied. Competitions, and particularly, tournaments were held, usually horse racing and jumping, but sometimes marksmanship was tested as well. Grand Reviews were a chance to look one's best, marching in formation past various high-ranking generals.

One day, President Lincoln and his wife arrived in a black barouche, he with his tall top hat and she with a parasol to shade her pale skin from the sun, sitting in the back seats with two serious-faced dignitaries up front. Emmett stole a glance at them as he marched proudly past, the new insignia patch so recently sewn on his hat. The patch was a red Maltese cross, its shape indicating the 5th Corps and its color the 1st Division. He recognized President Lincoln as the man he'd seen between the White House and the War Department building some months earlier, but today Honest Abe did not look quite so gaunt or tired. He sat with a military bearing, straight in his seat, saluting each regiment as it strutted past. His face was long with a wide forehead, all of his hair pushed back and off his face, tucked under the brim of his top-hat, his eyes sad and friendly all at the same time. His body seemed to be mostly composed of elbows and knees, which jutted at prominent angles from his body, his ears threatening to burst from the captivity of the hat. But it was Mrs. Lincoln who intrigued Emmett, causing him to lose his cadence; bringing a blush to his face so certain he was that he'd made a fool of himself. Mrs. Lincoln's face looked as if it had been pushed together, her features crowding her distinct nose, itself wrinkled in distaste and the eyebrows drawn together as if she were suffering a splitting headache that caused her eyes to dull with the pain of it.

All the men looked forward to "Ladies Day", another morale raiser instituted by General Hooker when women of impeccable character would visit the officers in camp in beautiful hooped dresses of dazzling colors for tea and gentle conversation. For many of the men it was their first chance to speak with a woman in months.

Perhaps the best new policy adopted by the army was a system of furloughs over the winter break in fighting, when one man from every company was granted a ten-day liberty as necessary. John Marshall Brown and Tom Chamberlain asked for, and were granted their liberty request, planning to go into Washington, with four months pay jingling in their pockets. After Chamberlain signed their furlough papers, he asked that they check the city's military bookstores to see if they could find some manuals to be used in the new officer training that he had started— as a student, not an instructor. He'd convinced a few of the younger graduates of West Point to fill some of the long winter nights with classes for the volunteer officers, such as himself, and was now trying to find more material for them to use. Impatient to get started with these new books, he ordered Emmett to go with them, spend the night, and then return the following day.

They journeyed first by train, the cars full of other soldiers on furlough and also with the sick. It was a short hop of thirteen miles before they arrived at 8 a.m. at Aquia Creek Landing. This was a bustling wharf town that had sprung up to service the Union Army in their winter headquarters in Falmouth, a transfer station between the train and the steamer that would take them on the next

142

leg of the journey forty-five miles up the Potomac River. The soldiers disembarked from the train, and, immediately a crew of burly teamsters began to pack it with supplies and rations to return to Falmouth. There were saloons and taverns littering the street of the small community, but the men hastily boarded the steamship for the capital.

Ever since he'd learned that he would be accompanying Tom Chamberlain and John Marshall Brown, Emmett had not been able to banish from his mind the image of the young woman he'd seen on the September march through the city, the woman who a soldier had suggested was a prostitute. Emmett at times imagined himself tracking her down, and discovering that she was not a prostitute at all. No, she was really an orphaned girl living with her aunt and helping tend the wounded in one of the many hospitals, a young lady with whom he would strike up a friendship. He had imagined the letters they would share through the course of the war, and then their eventual heartfelt reunion when the war was finally over. Other times, his mind traveled to the other possibility—that she was indeed a prostitute, forced into the occupation by circumstance, and selling the only thing she could offer. In his dream, he might pay her for such a visit, but the rest of the fantasy played out much like the first, with a mutual friendship springing up, letters throughout the war, and him returning to be her savior at the conclusion of the war.

"What are you mooning about?" Tom asked, sidling up next to him on deck of the steamer as the capital city came into view.

"Nothing." Emmett felt his cheeks grow red and turned away as if inspecting the approaching wharf.

"You haven't said two words since we left." Tom replied, his face aglow with the excitement of ten days furlough in the lively city. "So what's eating you?"

"I was wondering where we'd spend the night." Emmett said to cover, but then his face colored as he thought of spending the night with the girl.

"We'll stay in a boarding house, probably down in the Island, as I hear its cheaper there than up by the Avenue." Tom had not noticed the quaver in Emmett's voice.

They docked at the 6th Street Wharf, watching first the exodus of soldiers from the steamer, and then they were conscripted to help carry the sick to the waiting ambulances. There were very few wounded, as there had been little to no conflict recently. But camp fevers like typhoid and malaria had recently been a problem, ravaging the army, with the worst cases being sent to the capital for better treatment. The ambulances were mostly boxy, open wagons drawn by teams of four horses. As Emmett, Tom Chamberlain, and John Marshall Brown strolled up 6th Street, they saw many of these ambulances as well as other hacks and carriages, all stuck in the mud. It had been a particularly cold and snowy winter in Washington, and a late February storm had dumped more than a foot of snow, now melted and mixed with spring rains to create a deep muck in the streets, rendering them all but impassable.

The first order of business was to visit the military bookstore to which Chamberlain had directed them, Phillip & Solomon's Booksellers & Army Stationers. This was not official army business, and he had been forced to take up a collection to pay for them. The list had them ordering five copies each of "Wilson's Tactics with Questions" for $1.50 apiece and "U.S. Infantry Tactics" for $1.25 apiece. They also picked up single copies of "New Army Resolutions for 1863", "Schalk's Art of War", and "Gillmore's Siege and Reduction of Fort Pulaski". Tom paid the clerk, and they loaded the books into an empty haversack, Brown making a crack about how if they ran across the enemy in the capital, they could just throw books at them, such was their weight.

They had been recommended to stay at Mrs. Springer's Boarding House back down by the Potomac, and they went there next to drop off their bags. Louise Springer was a sprightly grandmother who was raising her granddaughter in the bustling Island section of Washington D.C., no easy feat during a time of war. She had shrewd eyes, and at first told them she was full and had no rooms to rent. When John Marshall Brown produced a letter from Captain Murphy of the New York Regiment, however, her eyes turned friendly and she beckoned them in. The three of them squeezed into a tiny room, but Emmett would only be there the one night. Mrs. Springer told them that supper would be at five o'clock if they were interested in eating, and then left them alone.

"What should we do now?" Tom asked, sitting on one of the two beds, arms stretched back over his head as he acclimated to the fact that they were now in Washington D.C. with their first free time in six months. Train, steamer, capital—and they had not yet eaten supper. Just this morning they'd awakened in a tent in the raw Virginia countryside, and now they only had to look out the window to see signs of vibrant life everywhere.

Brown held up a flier he'd picked up from the street. "There is a show tonight at Varieties on the Avenue," he said casually.

"What sort of show?" Tom asked, curious.

"It says here that it is a night of 'Music, Songs, Farces, Fun & Frivolity'," Brown replied with a gleam in his eyes.

"Perhaps a stop first at the Willard Hotel?" Tom had been told that no visit to Washington would be complete without a drink at the Willard, a place famous for the politicians and powerful men who frequented its bar and restaurant.

The evening became a blur for Emmett, as they first traveled up the busy Maryland Avenue with street trolleys splashing mud on the multitudes crowding the sidewalks and spilling into the streets. Prostitutes kept approaching the three soldiers, offering their wares and promising a good time for cheap prices. Newspaper boys waved copies of the *Weekly National Republican*, spouting out the headlines about the failed Mud March and rumors that the Confederates were going to attack the capital, burn Baltimore, and invade the North. The rumors were rampant, but they all had two things in common, betraying a deep fear of Robert E. Lee and his right-hand man, the religious fanatic Thomas "Stonewall" Jackson.

They entered the impressive lobby of the Willard Hotel and were immediately accosted by several bootblacks vying to scrape the mud off their boots and shine them. Emmett let himself be persuaded to take a seat along with Tom and Brown, all having their boots cleaned and buffed. The black youth about Emmett's own age worked energetically to remove the caked mud, all the while keeping up a conversation without ever lifting his head.

"First time to the Willard, sah?" Without waiting for a reply, he continued, "I can tell by the way you'se lookin around that you ain't been here before, eyes all round in your head. Well, this is where it all happens, every big decision gets made here at the Willard, yes sah, it surely does. See that man over to your right there?" The bootblack jerked his head towards the far end of the room, where men gathered in small groups at the entrance of a dark bar. "The man with no hair on his head, none at all but a bit of white fringe around the sides, more like scruff than anything else. He's got a face to break down doors? That there is Mr. Salmon Chase, Secretary of the Treasury. The man across from him with the long thin face with a mop of hair dropped on his head, and a mouth that always looks like he is sad? That's Mr. William Seward, Secretary of State. The other gentlemen there? He owns the Willard. That is Captain Joseph Willard."

Willard was a strikingly handsome man, about forty years old with sandy blonde hair, thick and rich, and combed carefully to the side, a striking contrast to the two men he conversed with. Thin side burns trailed from his ears to his chin, but the rest of his face was clean-shaven. His Union uniform was immaculately pressed with the gold buttons polished and gleaming, a saber at his side and a drink in his hand. "Don't tell anybody where you heard it, but rumor has it that Masta Willard has fallen in love with a Confederate spy, which wouldn't be a problem if he weren't a Union Officer and already married to Mrs. Willard." He chuckled, and Emmett grinned at the casual way in which this boy shared rumors of monumental proportion.

"That'll do you, sah." The bootblack said, giving a final snap of the towel and straightening up so that Emmett could see his face, glistening with exertion, black as coal, his eyes sparkling with a lively intelligence, and his lips parted in a knowing smile.

"Give him a nickel," Brown told Emmett, who was at a loss as to what the next step was.

"We are the only three in here without a drink in our hands," Tom observed, leading them to the bar. "Whiskey for everybody?"

Emmett shook his head, remembering the burning liquid by the fire a few months earlier, but not wanting to appear too childlike, he suggested a beer or cider, what they drank up in Brewer when they drank at all. Drinks in hand, they wandered into the grand ballroom, 150 feet across with chandeliers whose intricate crystal and ornate detail flickered in the gaslight. The walls were adorned with portraits of George Washington and Queen Victoria and immense gleaming mirrors. It was too early yet for the dancers who would grace the floor later in the evening, and they went back into the main lobby, returning to the bar for a second drink. Emmett could feel his head buzzing slightly from the alcohol, a pleasant feeling that massaged the chaos of the capital from his system. "Is that General Sickles over there?" Emmett asked Tom, tugging on his arm, but Tom was busy talking with a robust woman in a hoop skirt who was smoking a cigar.

The man next to Emmett had heard the question, however, glancing over and nodding that it was indeed he, correcting the rank slightly. "That is MAJOR General Sickles," he said. "Or so I believe the promotion has just been approved. One of our most famous citizens, he is."

"I guess generals are certainly important people." Emmett mumbled, staring at the man who commanded the Third Corps of the Army of the Potomac. He was puffing on a huge cigar, waving his whiskey glass animatedly as he spoke, an audience of men and woman gathered around him and listening raptly.

"You could throw a stick in here and hit six generals at once," the plump man in a suit, vest, and bow tie replied. "But General Sickles is a celebrity. He makes the news about every week with one thing or another, ever since he shot his wife's lover in Lafayette Square right across from the White House." The man paused to take a deep drink from his glass, and Emmett realized the man wasn't just unsteady on his feet, but dead drunk. "That's what you get when you marry a woman eighteen years younger than you, I guess. Not that General Sickles didn't have his own affairs," he continued, speaking carefully so as to not slur his words. "Even went so far as to bring a whore to meet Queen Victoria in England and presented her using the alias of a political opponent of his in New York. Left his wife pregnant at home while doing it, but it sure makes for a good story. Can't hardly blame her for beginning an affair with that man Key, who was district attorney here in the capital at the time. But when Sickles caught them in intimate conversation right here at the Willard, he was furious. Shot the man the next night and pleaded insanity. Unfortunate way for the son of Francis Scott Key to die, but I guess he dallied with the wrong man's wife."

"Did he go to jail?" Emmett was entranced by the story as he stared at the charismatic Major General Sickles holding court.

"See the man to his right? That's Edwin Stanton, Secretary of War and his good friend, *and* legal counsel. Helped defend him and they pled temporary insanity. They leaked the whole sordid affair to the newspapers, and after that there wasn't a court in the land that was going to convict a man for shooting the rogue who had taken advantage of his young bride. Now he's out in Falmouth with his good friend General Hooker, and I hear there are more whores and whiskey there than in all of Washington D.C."

Emmett's mind turned unbidden to the beautiful young girl of his fantasies, but he was quickly pulled from his thoughts as Tom grabbed hold of him, urging him to finish his beer as it was time to go to the show. Varieties was just down the Avenue from the Willard, and before Emmett knew it he had paid fifty cents for an orchestra seat and was sharing a silver flask of whiskey that Brown had smuggled into the performance. After two beers, the whiskey did not seem to have the same sting as before, or perhaps the quality was better. The stage dominated the room, but it was the box seats that ringed the audience that most amazed Emmett— and the very rowdiness of the crowd crammed into the space. A piano with several banjos accompanying greeted them as they arrived, playing "Ole Dan Tucker", with many of the patrons singing along.

I come to town de udder night,
I hear de noise an saw de fight,
De watchman was a runnin roun,
Cryin Old Dan Tucker's come to town.

So get out de way! Get out de way!
Get out de way! Old Dan Tucker.
You're too late to come to supper.

Tucker was a hardened sinner,
He nebber said his grace at dinner;
De ole sow squeel, de pigs did squall
He 'hole hog wid de tail and all.

148

After the song, the show began with a banjo player by the name of George Dobson who could play anything asked of him, from opera tunes to popular ballads and all of which had the crowd singing mightily along. A strikingly beautiful woman billed as M'lle Lizetta who fluttered around the stage like a tiny bird followed him. It was so quiet as she ran and leapt and twirled that it was as if the entire room dared not take a breath. When she was done tremendous applause rang out. Then Fred May sang Irish Ballads such as "Pat Murphy of Meagher's Brigade".

'Twas the night before battle and, gathered in groups,
The soldiers lay close at their quarters,
A-thinking, no doubt, of their loved ones at home
Of mothers, wives, sweethearts and daughters.
With a pipe in his mouth sat a handsome young blade,
And a song he was singing so gaily,
His name was Pat Murphy of Meagher's Brigade
And he sang of the land of Shillelagh.
Said Pat to his comrades, it looks quare to see
Brothers fighting in such a strange manner;
But I'll fight 'til I die, If I never get killed
For America's bright starry banner.

Emmett remembered his father humming Irish ballads in the house while he was working, sometimes mouthing a line or two softly. By the time the song concluded, there was not a dry eye in the house, Irish or not.

The day after battle, the dead lay in heaps
And Paddy lay bleeding and gory,
With a hole in his breast where some enemy's ball
Had ended his passion for glory,
No more in the camps will his letters be read
Nor his voice be heard singing so gaily
For he died far away from the friends that he loved
And far from the land of Shillelagh

When Miss Nella Richings came out to sing, Emmett's head had began to swirl so badly from the whiskey that he never heard a word, but just stared open-mouthed at her beauty, the sound caressing his ears as gentle waves rather than as words with any particular meaning. Then the show was over and they were spilling out onto the Avenue with hundreds of others, Emmett trying to hide the tears that streamed down his face, John Marshall Brown and Tom Chamberlain chattering excitedly about the next stop, which turned out to be a saloon just off the Avenue on 12th street.

"I've never seen anything like it." Tom chattered, flush with excitement. "That Fred May sure can play and sing."

"It's been quite some time since I've seen so many pretty girls." Brown rejoined, drinking heartily from his glass.

"What was your favorite part?" Tom asked Emmett, swinging around to face him.

"I'm not sure." Emmett mumbled, thinking again of the fair-haired beauty from the fall.

"Hey, what's eating away at you?"

"I was thinking of a girl I saw here when we marched through in September," he answered with drunken candor.

"Aha! That's my boy. Did you hear that Brown? Emmett has a girl on his mind. I don't think we'll ever find her in this city unless you somehow got her address?" Tom joked happily.

"I think I know where she works...." Emmett trailed off, thinking of her profession.

"Works? What does she do?" Brown joined the conversation, intrigued.

Emmett hesitated only momentarily before blurting out, "She's a prostitute."

Tom and Brown, half-drunk, cackled with sheer joy, much to Emmett's distress. It was immediately decided that they must go in search of this young lass, for Emmett's sake, wherever it led them. The three finished their drinks and proceeded to Maryland Avenue, and after stumbling around for a bit, Emmett finally spotted the building in front of which he'd first glimpsed her. The three soldiers marched to the door, but paused upon reaching it, with Brown finally knocking. An elegant woman answered the door, dressed in a dark silk dress, her hair graying but still very much possessing the looks of a beautiful woman.

"Yes?"

Emmett's first inclination was to flee. It looked as if Tom may have shared this notion, but both froze as Brown replied with a question. "My young friend here was searching for a young lady, blond hair, tall and thin, who he saw outside this address several months ago. Is this, perchance the right establishment?"

The elegant woman smiled in a friendly manner. "It is possible. What is it that you want of her?"

This, flustered even the glib-tongued Brown, who stuttered out, "Maybe just...perhaps we could...do you mind if my friend were to have a word with her."

Why don't you gentlemen step in for a moment?" She suggested, still smiling. "Would you like a glass of champagne?" A house servant appeared with a tray and handed each of them a glass. "You know that you are in a brothel?" She spoke candidly, embarrassing the three of them to their very toes. "A very expensive house at that, and the kind of place where a gentleman needs to make an appointment weeks in advance. I am Mary Anne Hall. And the girl you speak of is Susannah, I believe. But she is currently busy, and unfortunately, not to be indelicate, but a visit with her would be far beyond your means even if she was available. May I suggest a house in Murder Bay? A very nice Madame named Eliza Thomas has an establishment on Ohio Avenue that I think would suit your purse." As graciously as they had been greeted they were ushered back out the door.

"Well, we tried, anyway." Tom draped his arm over Emmett's shoulder. "What should we do now?"

"Do now?" Brown looked incredulously at Tom and Emmett. "We are going to take the advice of that very nice Madame and we are going to Ohio Avenue to look up this Miss Eliza Thomas and then, what will be will be, naturally."

*****

Emmett groaned as he rolled over, his head aching as if a mule had kicked him. The sun was blinding as it slashed through the window, making him face the wall. Slowly, the fact that the sun was high in the sky filtered into his addled brain, and he rolled over with a jolt that caused shooting pains in his head, and a momentary urge to vomit. He opened his eyes carefully, and sat up slowly. Tom Chamberlain lay snoring in the other bed, but John Marshall Brown was nowhere to be seen. Emmett remembered, groaning aloud, that he was to have been up at dawn and aboard a steamer back to Aquia Creek Landing. Carefully he stood, fighting the nausea and dizziness, desperate for water. There was a pitcher on the table, filled, and he poured a glass and greedily drank. But the water was raw in his throat, and he set it back down after two gulps. He pulled his boots on, taking a moment to lie back on the bed for a single comforting minute, before rousing himself, for he knew that he had to go. Chamberlain would be expecting him back that day with these books. He grabbed the haversack and reached down to shake Tom's shoulder. "I'm leaving." He said, getting no response other than a murmur that might have been goodbye.

He arrived at the dock after a fast walk, luckily to find a steamer about to head for Aquia Creek Landing with supplies for the soldiers and was able to get a spot aboard her. It was not until they passed by Alexandria that Emmett began to piece together the previous evening. They had indeed proceeded to a brothel run by Miss Eliza Thomas. Three girls had been procured for their pleasure and Tom and Brown had disappeared. Emmett had been taken to a room by a girl named Nellie, hardly older than himself, but he'd been too shy to do more than just talk, paying her $3 for the conversation, telling her his whole life story before Tom came and dragged him away. Brown waved them away when they finally found him in one of the rooms, choosing to stay the night.

*****

Life returned to normal in Falmouth, normal in that it was a time of drills and endless marching in preparation for the spring campaign that everybody knew was steadily approaching closer each day. About a week after Tom Chamberlain had returned from his furlough, Chamberlain beckoned his aide. "Emmett, go and see if Tom is available to come over to my tent."

He found Tom in his tent, playing cards with several other soldiers among them John Marshall Brown. Fifteen minutes later, they were back to find Chamberlain shaving, all the while whistling. "Lieutenant, I have a request of you. I need a personal leave pass to visit the capital, perhaps even to go to Baltimore." Tom Chamberlain had become the adjutant as well as a lieutenant, which made him responsible for paperwork such as this.

"Not a problem, Lieutenant Colonel." Tom replied,

following proper military protocol, if with a soupçon of mockery. "What for?"

"Fanny has come to pay a visit. She is currently at a hotel in Washington."

"Is everything all right?"

"It would seem to be more than alright." Chamberlain said, smiling through his thick mustache, eyes dancing with an inner light.

Emmett picked up the message from the table and read it idly, wondering at the strangeness of the situation. After all, he'd been present six weeks earlier when Chamberlain had sternly told his wife that she could not come to visit him as it was no place for a lady, yet now he was excited at her arrival? "Lieutenant Colonel, will you be needing a companion?" He asked.

"No, Emmett, this trip I will take alone. You stay here and keep an eye on Tom."

"I would think that there is more need of somebody to keep an eye on you, Lawrence." Tom retorted, teasing.

"Oh, I have somebody watching over me," Chamberlain replied. "And don't call me Lawrence." With that, he mounted his horse and rode off, whistling.

Chapter Eight

In April of 1861, the eleven companies of the 6th Massachusetts Volunteer Regiment travelled 300 miles from their homes through jubilant cheering crowds on their way to join the Army of the Potomac to preserve the Union. As they neared Baltimore, the officers warned the men that their reception would become more sour as there was a strong rebel sympathy in that city, the third largest in the United States and a southern city at that. The 700 soldiers were issued twenty rounds of ball cartridges for their Springfield rifles, and told that they were to fire only if ordered or if in peril for their lives. By city wartime ordinance, no trains were allowed to travel through the city limits, and thus, the Philadelphia, Wilmington & Baltimore train only went so far as Presidential Street Station in the northeast corner of the city, at which point teams of bay mares were hooked to the cars to pull them down Pratt Street to Camden Station on the other edge of the city, where they would board another line for the trip to Washington D.C. The first seven companies made it safely to Camden Station, but the last four found the tracks blocked by an anchor and cartloads of sand, forcing them to disembark and march through the narrow cobblestone streets. The pro-southern citizens began to accost these Union soldiers, throwing bricks, rocks, brickbats, and other objects from upper story windows. Men in the streets lunged at them, trying to grab their rifles, canteens, any sort of souvenir possible. When the streets became impassible, the officers ordered the men to fire. Twelve citizens and four soldiers were killed in the melee, setting the stage for the imposition of martial law in the city of Baltimore, a coercion that would endure for the rest of the Civil War.

April 4, 1863

Joshua and Fanny Chamberlain arrived in Baltimore at Camden Station on the afternoon of April 4th. Chamberlain had gone to Washington, only to find Fanny disgusted with the Capital. Between the smell and the ubiquitous prostitutes serving the soldiers seemingly from every other house, she had been only too happy to take the forty-mile train ride to Baltimore. The journey had been spent in catching up on news of the children, who, in Fanny's absence, were being cared for by Sae. Wyllys had had a bad cold soon after Joshua had left in February, but was now better, and Daisy was proving to be quite the reader. He, in turn, filled Fanny in on the improved morale under General Hooker's regime of better food, more free time, and organized entertainment for the ranks. Eventually, the train pulled into the station with a screech of brakes and a hiss of steam, smoke from the engine stacks billowing backwards and into the windows, blackening everything in its path. The wise traveller took a minute before disembarking, allowing the coal smuts to settle and the air to clear.

Taking Joshua's proffered hand, Fanny stepped from the train, careful not to brush against the filthy door, her eyes sparkling and happy. "And now, dear husband, we have addressed the items we had to, and we will discuss them no more for the next three days. No talk of children, no talk of war, just romantic words between man and wife."

"And you no longer despise me?" Joshua teased her with a mischievous smile lifting the corners of his mouth.

"I told you I am sorry for how I behaved when last you visited Brunswick." Fanny replied pertly. "It was just that you surprised me, and I was angry at being left alone with the children, and the winter. But as soon as you left, I cried my eyes silly. And then it hit me that I loved my husband and the last thing I wanted to do was drive him away. So I began planning my visit then and there, and here I am! But," Fanny raised her eyebrows in a mocking manner, "Perhaps you would rather I return home?"

"Not for the life of me," Joshua chuckled.

"Then take me to our hotel."

"That my fair Queen, sounds like a capital idea." Joshua replied, his smile stretching from ear to ear. He hailed a brougham, two horses pulling a large carriage with a rack in the rear to accommodate Fanny's large trunk and two smaller bags, as well as his own haversack.

"Where to, Colonel?" The coachman asked, promoting Chamberlain either erroneously or to stroke his ego in search of a bigger tip.

"The Rinn Hotel on Pratt Street, do you know it?"

"I know the house well, and may I add, a wonderful choice for you and the missus. Will you be staying in Baltimore long, Colonel?"

"I have but three days before I must return to the army."

"Are you with General Hooker, Colonel?"

"That I am, my good man, that I am."

"I don't envy you that, Colonel, I certainly don't." With that the coachman flicked his short whip, and the horse team set off down Pratt Street.

"And what would my beautiful wife like to do during her stay in Baltimore?" Joshua inquired as the brougham rumbled over the cobblestone street.

"Shop for dresses and bonnets and listen to music and eat in wonderful restaurants if there be such." Fanny said breathlessly, the warm April sun bringing color to her pale cheeks.

"And we shall do all of that, my dear, all of that and more. We shall buy you jewelry, and books, and shoes, and explore the city." Joshua said grandiosely. "I believe that Baltimore Avenue has many interesting shops, as does the street we are now on."

"If I may interrupt, Colonel," the coachman turned his meaty shoulder to address the Chamberlains. "If you are looking for fine dining, you will get none better than right there," he gestured with his right hand that held the whip. "The *Beacon Light* is run by a fine gentleman by the name of Henry Luck, and if you're looking for fresh oysters you won't find any better."

Soon after, they arrived at the hotel, a nondescript brick building with an awning in front, RINN HOTEL painted onto a sign over the door. A young black boy ran out and asked if they were staying. At Chamberlain's nod, the boy tugged the large trunk down and wrestled it in through the front door.

"Is he a slave?" Fanny wondered aloud, knowing that Maryland was indeed a slave owning state.

"Not many slaves in Baltimore, Ma'am." The coachman said, handing the other bags to Chamberlain. "Most of the Negroes you see around are freed, as it don't pay to keep them slaves. Not that they are good for much other than carrying bags and manual labor."

The proprietor was a heavy man with a thick German accent, welcoming them to his hotel, and showing them to their room. There was a moment of awkwardness once in the room, as each looked at the bed, and then away again, both remembering the sting of their last parting. "Should we take a walk before supper?" Joshua inquired of his wife to break the moment.

"That would be delightful," Fanny replied. "Just give me a moment to wash after that filthy train."

Before long they were back in the April sunshine, Fanny with a bonnet firmly tied upon her head, and a parasol to protect from the sun, Joshua in his full dress uniform, strolling down Pratt Street without a thought of children or war. "Perhaps tomorrow we might do some shopping?" Fanny wondered, not wanting to be bothered with that now, as she just wanted to experience Baltimore.

"Today we will see the sights, tomorrow we shall shop, and the next day, we will wait and see." Joshua replied magnanimously. The cobblestone street was narrow, with brick buildings rising four and five stories on either side, the sun behind them as they walked east. As they passed Gay Street, Joshua Chamberlain pointed out that it was here that the citizens had blocked the cars filled with Union soldiers, forcing them to disembark, some to kill, some to be killed.

"No talk of war, Lawrence." Fanny cautioned.

A group of young men turned as they passed, and then, following them down the street, one finally got up the courage to accost them. "Hey Lieutenant, is it true that all you Northerners are nigger lovers?"

Fanny tightened her grip on Joshua's arm. "Is he speaking to you?"

"Just ignore them, dear."

"Or maybe you just want to tell me what I can and can't do in my own home? Well, I'm right here, so go ahead and give it a go."

"What is he going on about?" Fanny was perplexed, verging on anger.

"Many people in Baltimore resent the Northern intrusion and sympathize with the South. He's trying to pick a fight with me, but I imagine he'll grow tired of baiting me soon enough if we just ignore him." Joshua spoke in a low growl, restraining himself because of Fanny's presence. At the next corner, a group of Union soldiers lounged, smoking cigars, and the Chamberlains paused, the young rowdies behind them continuing on their way.

They walked as far as the harbor, known locally as "The Basin", but here turned back and retraced their steps to the Beacon Light, having decided to follow the coachman's recommendation for supper. The white tablecloth and fine china distinguished it as a higher-class establishment than many of the other saloons, taverns, and restaurants they'd seen on their walk. "To love and marriage." Joshua said, raising his glass of wine.

Fanny raised her glass. "To life," she rejoined.

Joshua hesitated, but decided to pass on the undercurrent of the toast, and they both drank. The black waiter, an elderly gentleman with graying hair, brought them dodger and stew to begin, the small loaf of corn bread for sopping up the last bits in the bowl. "Is that a new dress you are wearing?" Chamberlain asked.

Fanny smiled, happy that her husband had noticed. "According to *Godey's*, it is the latest fashion, and I made the paletot myself from their design."

"Did they also have a new song for all of the fashionable wives to learn on the piano?" Joshua asked, beaming at her, impressed that this fine embroidered coat was of her own hand. He reached out and stroked her sleeve, wondering at this burst of domesticity. Fanny, he knew, would read the magazines and popular novels, but it was rare for her to depart from the purely practical when it came to fashion.

"'*The Old and the Gray*', but I found it rather depressing." Fanny remarked grimly. "So I only played it the one time for the children, and then put it away."

"No talk of children, Fanny." Joshua chided gently.

"Oysters, sir?" The waiter approached the table with a bowl of fried oysters, a staple in the south but not so widely prevalent in the north, where they preferred their shellfish in chowders and stews.

"Yes, set them down." Joshua waited for the waiter to leave before reaching across the table to tuck a loose wisp of hair behind Fanny's ear, wondering how he could have forgotten her beauty.

They finished the oysters and a main course each before agreeing to share a slice of pumpkin pie. All the while, they talked pleasantly of books and music, before returning to their hotel room for a night of tender love, a return to a time before the cares of children and the worries of war.

*****

Back at the camp, the days passed slowly for Emmett, as the men of the 20th Maine performed seemingly endless drills, a daily slog met with much less grumbling since their recent noteworthy involvement in the battle of Fredericksburg. The general consensus was that the intense drilling that Colonel Ames had put them through had been extremely beneficial—a key component of their conduct in the battle, which in turn led to respect from the ranks of other regiments and praise from many officers throughout the army. The battle had been a Union loss, but the men from Maine had earned a reputation as a strong regiment to be reckoned with. Emmett was surprised one night at suppertime by his two brothers, William and Daniel, who had gotten permission to pay a visit, and the three of them had stayed up far into the night catching up.

Late in the afternoon on the fourth day, Chamberlain rode back into camp and up to his tent, dropping from his mount with a flourish, and handing the reins to a waiting Emmett. "Squire, take my horse," he said with a smile.

Squire? Had Lieutenant Colonel Chamberlain lost his mind? "Sir?" Emmett looked at him oddly.

"Emmett, you are like a squire to me. In the Middle Ages, knights were the warriors who fought for honor, for glory, and for the love of women. Each knight would have an apprentice learning the art of war who would act as his assistant. I am a knight in this war, seeking glory and honor, and just returned from my reward of four days with my lovely wife, and thus, you are my squire."

"Reward, sir?"

"My fair and lovely wife does indeed love me, and that is all the reward that any knight could wish for, that, and the recognition of honor earned on the battlefield by the King, I suppose." Chamberlain's blue eyes sparkled merrily as he went on, talking more to himself than to Emmett.

"Did you enjoy a show like the one I went to with Tom and John Marshall Brown?"

"Well, my boy, there were too many soldiers in the capital, too much hustle and bustle, so we took the cars over to Baltimore to escape the war zone, so to speak. There, we had sumptuous dinners, followed by lovely walks along Baltimore Avenue and Pratt Street and down to The Basin. We talked like we haven't talked since before the children were born, and we fell in love all over again." He began humming a tune, walking with Emmett to stable the horse for the night, and then even sang a few words of, "Sleeping, I Dream of Love."

Chamberlain's overflowing happiness was not destined to last long as some men of the regiment came down with the smallpox shortly thereafter. It appeared that a defective batch of the inoculation had found its way into their camp, infecting enough soldiers with the virus that the entire regiment was put into quarantine, their confinement to endure for at least two weeks. Chamberlain was incensed, for he knew a fresh battle loomed on the horizon, and he did not want to be left back in 'sick camp'.

Sure enough, on April 27th the order came for the Army of the Potomac to move out, and the 20th Maine was marooned on Quarantine Hill. Emmett was making the rounds of the camp with Chamberlain when Colonel Ames rode up to them with the news that the army was on the move.

"There must be something that we can do, Colonel? We can't just be stuck on this hill while the rest of the army goes into combat." Chamberlain's blue eyes flashed with a steeliness far different from the love struck knight of a few days before.

"There is something I have to tell you as well, Lieutenant Colonel." Colonel Ames replied carefully, knowing that Chamberlain would be even more annoyed. "I have obtained a position on General Meade's staff for the upcoming engagement, and thus, you will remain here in charge of the 20th Maine in my absence."

The only visible sign of displeasure Chamberlain exhibited was a slight flaring of his nostrils. "I, too, have tried to seek placement with a regiment that is moving forward, but to no avail. It is like I am talking to myself, it is all so very frustrating."

Colonel Ames nodded, mentioning idly, "I wonder if

perhaps there are plans for the 20th Maine, and that is why you're needed to stay behind?"

"I hope you are right, sir."

But it did not appear that this was true, as they remained quarantined, while the rest of the Army of the Potomac moved forward. Chamberlain became so unbearable in his ire at being marooned that Emmett took any chance he could to escape him. Finally, one day after the light midday meal, Chamberlain could take it no more. "Emmett, get Prince saddled for me and see if you can't borrow a horse from Major Gilmore for yourself."

"Where are we going, sir?" Emmett asked distractedly, watching an enormous observation balloon, this one with a huge portrait of George Washington on its side, bouncing gently in the light breeze of the day, several hundred feet off the ground. This was an innovation that fascinated Emmett almost as much as the six barrels of the Gatling Gun that could fire 350 rounds a minute, a weapon that a salesman had demonstrated in camp a few weeks earlier. Every day the balloon went up to spy upon the fortifications in Fredericksburg, sending messages back down the trailing telegraph wire.

"We are going to visit General Butterfield to see if we can't get involved in whatever is happening in the wilderness by Chancellorsville. Now let's go! No time to waste."

Formerly the commander of their Corps before his promotion, General Butterfield was now Chief-of-Staff for General Hooker. He had been left to the rear of the fighting with orders to relay information, while General Hooker had gone ahead to set up his command post at the Chancellor Mansion. It was only three miles to his headquarters, and before Emmett knew it they were pushing by blustering orderlies with Chamberlain demanding to see the General.

Unfortunately, General Butterfield was less than helpful. "We can't afford to put you into battle," he said. "You have over eighty confirmed cases of the small pox in your regiment. If that spreads to the rest of the army, consider the consequences! We'd be annihilated by the Rebs."

"Isn't there some duty to occupy us that wouldn't contaminate the rest of the army?" Chamberlain asked, his frustration simmering at a low boil.

"Lieutenant Colonel Chamberlain, I admire your zeal and have heard nothing but positive comments about your conduct. However, I am going to have to decline your services at this time. Will that be all?"

It was obvious that this was a dismissal rather than a question, but Chamberlain was unable to contain himself. "If you put us in sir, we could at least give the small pox to the enemy." But it was to no avail.

"It is as if I'm being punished for having done no wrong," Chamberlain grumbled to Emmett later as they rode back to camp. "There is nothing to do but sit on our rear ends, and wait for news from the battlefield to trickle back to us. Doesn't a single one of those nincompoops realize we are being wasted, that there are plenty of healthy men in the 20th Maine? At the very least, Major Gilmore is perfectly capable of being in charge of a 'pest' house." He ranted peevishly on and on all the way back, with Emmett offering no more than an occasional grunt of confirmation, wise enough to know that no real comment was needed.

It was after midnight that Emmett was awakened by an excited Chamberlain tugging at his arm. "What is it, sir?" Emmett muttered sleepily.

"We have been given orders!"

"Orders for what?"

Chamberlain grunted and made a face. "We have been assigned the task of guarding the telegraph wires against saboteurs. Not much of an assignment I grant you, but better than sitting around on Quarantine Hill." He shrugged his shoulders before telling Emmett to have Major Gilmore and the company officers come to his tent to be filled in on the details.

In the two days prior, 50,000 soldiers of the Army of the Potomac had secretly marched west to cross the Rappahannock River, and then the Rapidan River with the intention of flanking the Confederates at the tiny town of Chancellorsville. Another 30,000 soldiers had crossed at various spots up and down the river, effectively surprising the Confederates with their boldness. The remaining soldiers under Generals Sedgwick and Reynolds were to attack the Rebels at Fredericksburg, creating a diversion.

Spies and sympathetic Confederate civilians had been sabotaging the telegraph lines that allowed the commander of these massive, and far flung, troop movements to be kept informed and to coordinate their attacks. General Butterfield had determined that the 20th Maine could be used to protect these crucial lines of communication. As soon as Chamberlain was given the orders, he began mapping the lines, assigning each of his companies a section of the line to patrol. The orders called for immediate action, the men moving out as soon as their orders had been transmitted.

It was a fifteen-mile ride to the river crossing called the U.S. Ford, Emmett accompanying Chamberlain, John Marshall Brown, and the new adjutant, Tom Chamberlain, on horseback in advance of Companies A and B, which had been assigned the forward section of the line. The bulk of the army under Generals Howard, Slocum, and Meade had crossed two days earlier in a lightning flanking movement some fifteen miles further west at Kelly's Ford with almost 50,000 soldiers who had taken the Confederates completely by surprise. Just the day before, General Couch had crossed the Rappahannock there at the U.S. Ford, with General Sickles following with his Corps. They had immediately established a telegraph line between Chancellorsville and the Falmouth headquarters to help coordinate this complicated dance with so many partners.

Every effort had been made to keep Couch and Sickle's flanking movement a secret until the last minute, and many of the Virginia citizens in the surrounding towns and villages near the points of departure had been rounded up and watched closely to prevent them from spreading the word. Now, however, the secret was out, and the Virginians sympathetic to the South had been given their liberty. Some, inevitably, had resorted to sabotage. Upon reaching the ford, Chamberlain directed Brown to wait for A and B companies to arrive, and have them cross the river and patrol the telegraph line between the river and the Chancellorsville command headquarters. Chamberlain led Tom and Emmett onward, crossing over the pontoon bridge that had been set in place the previous day, following the wires towards the command center.

The three of them trotted into Chancellorsville, which mainly consisted of one large house, owned by the Chancellor family, a mansion requisitioned by the generals of the five corps who had already arrived at the scene of the battle. Chamberlain had hoped to report for duty to Hooker in person, but that general, who had just arrived, was busy meeting with his commanders, and so the newly-minted telegraph rider had to settle for one of his juniors. The place was milling with officers and their aides, messengers coming and going, all mixed in with the Chancellor family, whose six beautiful daughters had every soldier in the area looking for an excuse to pay a visit to the house. Had any such dared to report for this duty, they would have found their reception sorely lacking in warmth. Like many Virginians, the Chancellors were anti-Union to their very bones and made no effort to hide their dislike of this army that had taken over their home.

Chamberlain and Emmett spent the rest of the day riding the telegraph lines and making sure that one company from the 20th Maine guarded each section, establishing a rotation of duty. It was almost midnight before Chamberlain felt comfortable with the arrangements, and finally he and Emmett started back for camp for some much-needed shut-eye.

They had just crossed over the pontoon bridge at U.S. Ford when Chamberlain paused, holding up his hand for Emmett to be quiet, even though the boy had been on the verge of falling asleep in his saddle.

Emmett looked around, trying to get his bearings, desperately searching for the danger that Chamberlain had sensed. After a moment, he discerned shadowy figures by the telegraph lines, mysterious shapes shifting in the dark night, men too silent to be up to any good.

Chamberlain pulled his Enfield rifle free, cocking it with a loud click that rang out into the still night. "Who goes there?"

The three shadows froze, and it was then that Emmett saw a fourth form off to the side and away from the others. *Should he warn Chamberlain?* If he only had a rifle, he could help cover the men.

"Identify yourselves," Chamberlain walked Prince forward as he spoke.

A sudden flash from the fourth man followed by the stinging crack of the bullet split the air, Chamberlain's horse began to rear and scream, and then more shots rent the darkness, the muzzle flashes like orange tongues of flame. Emmett was motionless, unsure what to do, weaponless. Prince toppled sideways, apparently having been struck by one of the shots, and Chamberlain was flung from the saddle, crashing to the ground with a dull thump.

Emmett cried out in helpless rage, his every instinct telling him to turn and flee for his life. But he would never leave Chamberlain, and so he jumped to the ground, scuttling sideways to the inert form of his mentor. Another shot pierced the air, and this time Emmett felt the lead slug whistle past his ear. He dove in a heap next to Chamberlain, Prince having struggled back to his feet and run off, leaving his rider unconscious on the ground.

"Did you get him, Abner?" A voice asked after several minutes had passed.

"I think so." Came the response. "He went down, anyways."

"Chester, go see if he's dead."

"*You* go see if he's dead."

They hadn't seen him in the darkness! Emmett felt around and found the barrel of the Enfield poking out from underneath Chamberlain's body. Pulling the rifle free, he realized the barrel was still cool and had not yet been fired. He aimed the weapon at where the voices had come from, searching for the outlines of bodies against the dim night sky, all the while wondering what was he going to do against four of them? He might get off one shot, but then they would be on him before he could reload. He picked out a patch that was darker than the rest of the surrounding gloom and realized a man was creeping slowly forward. *Chamberlain's pistol!* Emmett reached his hand out, finding the Lieutenant Colonel's leg, and then the holster. He grasped the walnut handle and pulled the Colt Army Model free. He set it down next to the Enfield, again picking up the rifle and siting down the barrel at the approaching man. He could not afford to give warning, but could he kill a man? He could now see the glint on the barrel of the rifle as the man inched forward. Emmett closed his eyes and squeezed the trigger. The Enfield jerked into his shoulder, bruising the flesh, the powder stinging his face, and the flash temporarily blinding him. Emmett couldn't worry about this, and he dropped the rifle to pick up the Colt. There was a startled yelp and then a rush of men charging, and he was pulling the trigger of the revolver again and again, screaming in anger and fear as he did so.

A man was yelling in pain, feet scurried away, followed by the rattling of a horse's bit chains and hoof beats retreating into the darkness. Emmett sighed, his entire body shaking, tears streaming down his face.

He looked over to see the befuddled eyes of Chamberlain coming into focus, first noting the boy's face, and the Colt still smoking in his hand. "Are they gone?" He mumbled.

Emmett nodded.

"Prince?"

"He ran off, too."

Chamberlain nodded again, happy that the horse was alive. He rolled to his knees and then to his feet, his saber twisted at his side. "Can I have my revolver back, please?"

Emmett handed him the pistol, his hand shaking, embarrassing him. Chamberlain appeared not to notice, carefully loading six cartridges into the pistol, and then holstering the weapon at his side. Emmett picked up the Enfield to hand it too back to Chamberlain, but the older man made no effort to take it.

"You keep it."

"Sir?"

"You earned it. I can get another tomorrow for myself."

The two men walked into the darkness, searching for their horses.

Chapter Nine

National Republican Extra   May 7, 1863

Latest from Hooker's Army

———

GENERAL HOOKER HAS CHANGED HIS BASE

Capture of Nine of the Enemy's Guns, a Large Number of Rebel Battle Flags, and 10,000 Rebel Prisoners.

———

FIFTEEN THOUSAND REBELS KILLED AND WOUNDED

There are all sorts of rumors in town to-day, and among them is one that Hooker's army was whipped and driven back across the Rappahannock by the rebel Lee. There is not one word of truth in this report. For sound military reasons, Gen. Hooker changed his base yesterday; not in consequence of any demonstration by, or fear of, the enemy, but for reasons which in due time will be made known.

A gentleman who left Gen. Hooker's headquarters last night and arrived here this morning states that he was in the best of spirits; that he had captured nine of the enemy's guns, a large number of rebel battle flags, not less than ten thousand prisoners, and had killed and wounded at least fifteen thousand rebels.

Suffice it to say that Gen. Hooker has not been whipped during the late five days battles. The worst treatment any of his men received was on Saturday, when the enemy massed its strength against a single corps, and we have the authority of a general who participated in that fight that the German troops behaved as well as men could under the circumstances.

———

Emmett set the newspaper carefully on the ground next to him as he sat with his back against a tree, enjoying the shade after yet another strenuous day's march. They had broken camp guarding the Rappahannock fords three days earlier, this followed by three days of hot, dusty, and exhausting marching as they followed the movements of Lee's Army of Northern Virginia. That army had left camp ten days earlier, and later reports had it now moving north on the west side of the Blue Ridge Mountains. The Union Army was traveling only about twelve miles each day, that day reaching a bivouac near Manassas Junction where the two battles of Bull Run had taken place. There had been no sense of urgency to start off the morning, the officers allowing them a leisurely breakfast and plenty of time to gather their kits. Even during the march, they were given a ten-minute break every hour and halted to set up camp when the afternoon sun was still high in the sky. But still, that sun was hot, and the dust from the road got into their mouths and eyes and noses. The pack, rifle, and equipment became almost unbearably heavy as the hours wore on.

Chamberlain rode up on Prince, who had indeed survived the slight wound he'd received outside of Chancellorsville. He had walked with the men during the day, making his way up and down the lines to share in their travail. Now he was riding the rounds to make sure the work details and pickets had been established correctly. "You look mighty tuckered out for a lad of fifteen years." Chamberlain said, stepping nimbly down from his saddle, the reins grasped lightly in his gloved hand.

"Not so much tired, sir, but confused." Emmett replied, making a motion to rise, but Chamberlain gestured for him to remain seated.

Chamberlain tugged the end of his mustache. "Confused? About what?"

"I've been reading the National Republican you gave me, and there's a report that General Hooker did not lose the battle at Chancellorsville. But if that is the case, sir, why did we retreat?"

"That's a mighty good question, Emmett, a mighty good question." Chamberlain replied, looping the reins over a tree branch and squatting down on his heels beside the young man.

"I've told you that newspapers are partisan, just the opinions of like-minded individuals who can write whatever they want. And they're living, breathing men just like you and me. So you have to be careful what you read."

"Yes, sir."

"Where do you suppose the National Republican got the information about the battle of Chancellorsville for their story?" Chamberlain asked, very much the professor.

Though Emmett felt odd sitting with his back comfortably to a tree while speaking with his commanding officer, as he'd been told to stay put, he felt that he shouldn't get up. "I guess they must get their information from people that were there, else how would they know what happened?"

"Exactly, my boy. Do you think that they got that information from Lee or Jackson or any other Confederate soldier?"

Emmett laughed, thinking of Thomas Jackson sharing information with a Northern newspaper. "I reckon not."

"Then it stands to reason that the National Republican got their information from General Hooker, or from the Secretary of War Stanton, or even from the President himself?" Chamberlain swatted at the flies swirling around his head.

"I guess so, sir."

"And do you think the Government wants the people to think we're being whipped? That General Hooker is going to admit to having been thoroughly thrashed and thus defeated?"

"So the truth is, we *were* whipped?"

Chamberlain grimaced, wrestling with how to answer the question. "I talked to some officers. They did tell me the corps commanders took a vote on the last day across the river whether to stay and fight or to retreat. Well, they voted to stay and fight, because they felt they were holding their own, and could win the battle. General Hooker saw it differently—and ordered a retreat."

Emmett nodded. "So we held our own, but got scared and backed away?"

"General Hooker had an outstanding strategy, and then executed the strategy perfectly, surprising the Confederates. And yet then he froze, and didn't change the plan as the battle shifted, instead letting Lee and Jackson isolate segments of our army to their numerical superiority. Some people were very upset by his passivity. General Couch has resigned his commission in disgust that we did not pursue the attack on May 1st when we had the Confederates outnumbered and out of position."

"Was General Hooker scared?"

"No. No, I don't think so." Chamberlain knew firsthand that commanding a regiment of almost 1,000 men was difficult. But being in charge of an army of 130,000 men? That must be a monumentally more complicated and burdensome task. From reading his military manuals, he'd come to understand that preparation and strategy were only the first part of being a successful leader. "He didn't react to the favorable situation on May 1st," he continued, "and then he was shocked by Jackson's flanking movement on the second. By the time the Confederates controlled the heights on the fourth, allowing their artillery to dominate the field, the decision was probably a good one to withdraw back across the Rappahannock."

"Are we ever going to be able to defeat them Rebs?" Emmett spoke with the concern of one who had yet to see any sort of decisive Union victory in the field.

"Not until we find a Commander-in-Chief with a sound strategy, the ability to implement that strategy, and the cleverness to adapt to the ebb and flow of the battle." Chamberlain said grimly. "Not until our leadership matches that of the South," he added reflectively, thinking back to a month earlier when protecting telegraph lines they'd exchanged gunshots with saboteurs, only to watch as the Army of the Potomac retreated back across the river two days later. In the few short weeks since their withdrawal from Chancellorsville, Chamberlain had learned a few things about leadership. For one, that it was a post with no fixed hours or duties, and with sometimes-terrible decisions to make.

Almost four weeks earlier, he had become the acting Colonel, taking the reins from Ames who had been promoted to general. At the ceremony, he had cause to reflect on what he had learned from his commanding officer, never the easiest of men. "It has been a pleasure serving under you, sir." Chamberlain had said, shaking the hand of Adelbert Ames. "You certainly deserve the promotion. At the same time, the boys will miss you."

Brigadier General Ames had smiled wryly. "I don't know if the boys will miss me, truly, Lieutenant Colonel," he had said with a knowing smile. "But I appreciate your sentiments."

"They understand that it is due in large part to your diligence that they have become the efficient regiment that they are." Chamberlain insisted.

"I have never strived to be liked by the men, but rather to prepare them the best I could for battle—to keep them alive. I hope that you are right, that I have indeed earned their respect. Now it is up to you to continue to lead them."

Chamberlain had only been in charge of the regiment for four days when a detail of men from the 118th Pennsylvania escorted a group of 120 ragged-looking soldiers lacking rifles and kits into their camp. The captain in charge of the detail came swaggering up to Chamberlain's tent, where Emmett had been lounging. "You, boy! Is this the 20th Maine?"

"It sure is, sir." Emmett replied, scrambling to his feet and saluting, knowing that Chamberlain, a stickler for detail and discipline, was probably listening if not observing.

"I have a present for whoever is in command here," the captain sneered. "As well as a message from General Meade. Be a good lad and fetch him for me."

Emmett did not like the Captain's manner, but a message from General Meade could not be ignored. Chamberlain was inside the tent in conversation with Major Gilmore and appeared annoyed by the interruption, but followed Emmett out. Upon emerging, Emmett noticed that the Captain had been joined by a large group of gaunt and dirty men, surrounded by what appeared to be armed guards.

"What can I do for you, Captain?" Chamberlain asked, looking puzzled at the intrusion.

"Sir, I have some deserters that General Barnes requested I bring to you, and a message from General Meade in regards to the situation."

"I am afraid I don't understand, Captain." Chamberlain replied, looking quizzically at the tattered soldiers. "I am not in charge of deserters or prisoners. Why me?"

"The deserters are from Maine."

"Who are they?"

"The 2nd Regiment of Maine."

Emmett felt the blood drain from his face at the news. As if in a fog, he heard the voices continue to speak. "General Meade says that you can do whatever you want with these men. If they refuse to serve, you may shoot them."

It was hard to say whose shock was greater, Emmett's or Chamberlain's, at this fresh, horrific revelation. "I will take it from here. That will be all, Captain."

"Did you hear me—General Meade says to shoot them if you need to?" The Captain repeated, mockery in his tone.

While Chamberlain was a mild man, Emmett had too often experienced the smoldering intensity just below the surface. "My rank, Captain," Chamberlain said coldly and at his most formal, "is Lieutenant Colonel, and would that you address me thus."

The captain suddenly realized how thin was the ice upon which he tread, and snapped to attention. "Yes sir, Lieutenant Colonel."

"I do not believe that we will have to shoot anybody, Captain, do you understand?"

"Yes sir, Lieutenant Colonel."

"You may collect your men and leave now, Captain. Do you understand?"

The Captain squirmed for just a moment, aching to tell the Lieutenant Colonel that he best replace his own men with armed guards before leaving a group of 120 deserters lounging around camp, but thought better of it. "Yes, sir." And then he was gone, along with his guard. The prisoners, exhausted and hungry, had already sat down where they were.

"I must talk to them." Chamberlain murmured to Emmett. "Not that I know what I will say." He stood outside the tent, reflecting on the strange quirks of life and war. "Please have Captain Spear put together a picket to keep an eye on them until we can figure out what sort of mess we have."

"Lieutenant Colonel? Sir?" Emmett's pleading tone caught Chamberlain's ear, as the boy almost never asked for anything. "My brothers, sir, my brothers belong to the 2nd Maine."

Chamberlain surfaced from his own problems to fix Emmett with a compassionate stare; strange quirks indeed. "Of course, Emmett. Go see what you can find out. I will talk to Ellis myself."

Emmett walked slowly towards the ragged bunch of soldiers—some already fast asleep—others staring angrily at him as he approached. There was no guard, no protection, just he and a group of wrathful, hungry men.

"What do you want, boy?" One of them asked belligerently, the question more a challenge than a request.

"I reckon I'm looking for William and Daniel Collins," Emmett murmured. "Do you know them?"

The man stepped closer. "What's a guttersnipe like ya want with them?"

Emmett held his ground. "I am their brother."

The man paused at the unexpected words, and a change came over him. "You're the brothah of William and Daniel Collins?" He asked suspiciously. "No bull?"

"I am Emmett Collins," he replied, sticking out his hand, "their kid brother come to see the elephant."

The man took the proffered hand, at first tentatively, then firmly. "Little Emmett. I haven't seen you since you were knee high to a mosquito. You're all grown up now, though, aren't ya? I knew your father. God rest his soul. I am David Garrick who lives just down the road from ya."

Emmett did not remember the man. "Mr. Garrick, it is good to see you again. But what of my brothers?"

Garrick's eyes clouded momentarily. "Daniel is right around here somewhere." He said, putting his burly arm around Emmett's shoulder and steering him into the center of the men from Maine. As they were weaving their way through the throngs of soldiers, Emmett wondered what had become of the brave 2nd Maine, known throughout the army for their valor and daring. "Daniel Collins, where are you?" David Garrick bellowed.

With that, a lanky young man rose from the patch of ground, tufts of red hair poking out from underneath his soldier's cap. "Emmett," he said, eyes widening. "I've been meaning to pay ya a visit but things got complicated." He took two long strides and hugged Emmett fiercely, and then stepped back, embarrassed, both the Collin's boys turning away to wipe their eyes.

Daniel was gaunt from hunger, but his shoulders had broadened in the two years he'd been with the army, and over his youthful cheeks and chin now bristled a reddish, curly, and substantial beard. His devilish eyes, always filled with jokes and pranks, had grown harder from the violence of the battlefield. Emmett saw little resemblance to the spindly teenager who had proudly marched out of Bangor with the local men in May of 1861.

"Where's William at?"

A long pause grew to a painful silence punctuated only by the scuffing of Daniel's feet. "Them Rebs got him over in the Wilderness outside of Chancellorsville." Daniel's words came harshly, the pain and anger still raw in his being. "Shot him in the stomach. I found him afterwards, still alive, on the battlefield. I carried him to a farmhouse where the doctors had set up, but they told me there was nothing they could do. I sat with him through the night, out behind the barn. He was crazy as a loon with the pain, and there was nothing I could do for him." Daniel bowed his head. "He passed just as the sun came up the next day, and I buried him right there, out behind the barn of the McDonald's farm, so we can go back and visit him after this thing is over."

Emmett was too overcome to speak for a time. "We will visit him together." He said finally, grasping his brother's shoulder firmly. A sudden inspiration came to him, and he reached for his hip where his cartridge box was, lifting the leather flap and digging his hand through the twenty rounds that he carried. His hand grasped the ornate case that he'd carried since Brewer. "I brought this from home, and a few months ago the hinge busted on it, and now I reckon it broke for a reason." He gently took the two sides of the case and pried them apart, showing the two daguerreotypes to his brother. His right hand held a living image of the three Collins brothers, Emmett four, Daniel ten, and William twelve. "Why don't you take this?" Emmett offered the Sheffield Plate with the image to his brother. His other hand held the daguerreotype of his Mother and Father.

For the next hour, the two shared memories of their brother, vowing to visit his grave at the end of this war. Finally, Emmett looked at the men around them, then to his brother, shrugging and lifting one brow. Then Daniel spoke hotly, and quite a bit, his anger and frustration evident in every hard word. When it was done, Emmett told him that he needed to share this information with Colonel Chamberlain. They found him, finally, just returning from General Meade's headquarters. Even though he'd obviously been riding hard and was in a hurry, he agreed to listen, but not before he gestured for Ellis Spear to join them. "Ellis, I want you to make a plan to split the new men up among the companies evenly. Once that is all arranged, have the 2nd Maine assembled so I can talk to them."

"Yes sir, Colonel." Ellis had taken to calling Chamberlain Colonel even though the orders had not yet come through; it appeared to be only a matter of time until the promotion became effective.

Chamberlain took a second glance, and then shrugging his shoulders imperceptibly, he turned to Daniel Collins. "You are Emmett's brother?"

"That I am, sah. I am Daniel."

"Emmett has been indispensable to me. You should be proud of him. He even saved my life two weeks ago." Chamberlain spoke in a calm and measured tone. "What can I do for you?"

"It's about how we we're being treated, sah, like we was the enemy or somethin. The 2nd of Maine doesn't have a single coward in the whole regiment. It ain't that we're afraid to fight, sah."

"I didn't say that you were Daniel."

"No disrespect, Colonel, but people have been saying all kinds of gull about us. I swear we just want what's right done by us."

"Why don't you tell me what the problem is, and then I'll see what I can do."

"It was that, that high falutin man from the recruitment office who lied to us. Most of the men were all signed up for two-year hitches back in May of 1861 and that's what this gent told us. None of us thought to read the paper and see that we was actually signing up for a three-year hitch, didn't bother at all because he told us that it was for two years, and we trusted him. After all, we was volunteering to help, wasn't we?"

Chamberlain nodded his head, whether in agreement or merely in understanding, it was hard to tell as he absently twirled his mustache with his thumb and forefinger. "Go on."

"Nobody knew nothin about any of this two and three year thing. So when the two years was up, we all thought we'd be goin home. But when the men were mustered out, there was a group of us left out. When we complained, that's when we learned we had another year to go according to the contract. We had to sit and watch the rest of the regiment pack up and go on back home to Maine. Well, some of us decided that it ain't right to make a man fight if he don't want to. They cussed us out good, threatened us, haven't fed us for days—but we haven't broke. Not by a long sight. We just want what is right done by us, nothing more."

Again, Chamberlain nodded his head. "I make no promises. For now, come with me, I have something to say to all the men of the 2nd Maine. No sense repeating myself." And he strode away rapidly, Emmett jogging to keep up with him, Daniel not far behind.

Even though he walked with purpose, his mind was yet in turmoil over what to say, what to do, how to handle these unhappy men. He'd spoken with General Meade, but that hadn't helped. Like a good professor—or good military commander—he was just going to have to think on his feet, and hope to God his instincts were true.

Ellis Spear met them as they approached, the congregation of men rousted to their feet and gathered together. "The men of the 2nd Maine are assembled and ready for you, sir. I have a list of which company each will be joining." He paused, looking away. "I will execute that order when desired, sir, but I don't think they're going to go for it."

"Go on, Captain Spear, why do you think that?" He asked. Inwardly, he cringed at Spear's use of the word 'execute'.

"I've spoken with a few of them, and they are angry, sir. They've gotten stubborn and set their feet like a mule, and aren't willing to budge. I've known a few people from up Bangor and Brewer way, sir. Once they make up their minds, well, there's no changing it."

Chamberlain smiled wryly, but a smile barely making it to the corners of his mouth. "Don't forget that I'm from Brewer myself."

"I know that, sir, and there sure isn't much changing your mind once you have it set, that is a fact."

"Well, let's see what we can do." Chamberlain replied, turning and facing the men of the 2nd Maine. "Gather around me, men, so you can hear what I have to say without me having to shout it out to all the hills around." He stood among the men, casually waiting for them to draw closer to him as if he didn't have a care in the world. He could have been calling them over to tell them a joke, were it not for the rigidity of his shoulders, and a stiffness to his neck betraying great tension. They might refuse to listen to him. They might insist on going back to Maine. In any case, he knew he couldn't, wouldn't, shoot them. Not and ever return to the state of Maine. The men of the 2nd Maine shifted and slouched their way closer, and eventually Chamberlain determined it was time to speak.

"Now, you men listen and hear what I have to say. I am not going to lie to you. I understand that there was some fierce conflict about the enlistment time. Maybe some lies and deception. I will see what I can do to answer your charges. But it will ultimately not be my decision, and I don't know what the final determination will be. The fact of the matter is, you men signed papers enlisting you for three years in this wretched war."

"We've done our part, Lieutenant Colonel." Came a call from the crowd. "We've done our share of fighting."

Chamberlain's eyes finally settled on the speaker and fixed the man with a stare. "And you are?"

"The men chose me to do the speaking for us all," he said. "We've been in eleven battles so far, sir. How many battles have you been in?"

"Not that many," Chamberlain admitted. "But that doesn't matter right now. What matters is what we're going to do about this mess. The captain who brought you to me gave me the authorization to shoot the lot of you if you did not obey. Well, I'm not going to do that. I just rode over to speak with General Meade and asked permission to handle this situation however I see fit. He agreed. I've assigned all of you to different companies in the regiment and will see that you are issued rifles. I will see that you are fed, and in the meantime I will see if I can do anything about your enlistment tenure. But I make no promises."

"Why should we?" The anonymous spokesman demanded. "We've done our part and now we want to go home."

Chamberlain took two steps toward him. "Where are you from?"

"I'm from Milo, just outside of Brewer."

"I'm from Brewer myself; I *know* many of you, and if not you, your fathers and mothers and sons. I know that you have homes and families to get back to. Mouths to feed, roofs to fix, planting to be done. I know that. But why did you join up in the first place?" Chamberlain paused briefly, not expecting a reply. "I watched the 2nd Maine Regiment march off to war in May of 1861, and along with the rest of Maine, I cheered for you. Don't tell me you signed up for the money. That might be true for some of the Irish out of New York, but that's not true for you. Don't tell me you did it for glory, because I know better. Men in Brewer don't go looking for glory. They just do what needs to be done. Stop me if I'm wrong," he said, spreading his arms to his sides, palms up. "You joined up in May of '61 because it was the right thing to do. You joined up because you believe that this country will only be half as great if we let the South break away. You joined up because you wanted to defend the country that allows you the freedom to not have to bow down to anybody, and allows you to walk like a man, and to be the king of your own castle." Around him, Chamberlain could see men nodding their heads.

"Well, let me tell you something. Very soon now the Spring Campaign will begin, and it is going to determine whether or not we continue to be the United States of America or two different, weaker countries. It is my belief that Bobby Lee is going to bring the war to the North. And we are going to meet him along the way. And there is going to be a battle that will make everything that's happened so far look like child's play. If we lose that battle...well, let's just say that we cannot lose that battle, for I'm afraid if we do, then the war may be lost."

"Is Lee really going to head north?" A man called out from the middle of the pack.

Chamberlain nodded. "I'd bank on it. What other choice

does he have? He needs to convince Great Britain he can defeat us, else, sooner or later, he's going to run out of manpower and supplies. There is only one way for him to gain victory, and that road lies to the north."

"But can we beat him?" Another man challenged.

"I think we can beat him." Chamberlain said. "But to do so, we need every healthy man holding a rifle and doing their part. We can't beat him unless we are totally committed, each and every one of us working together." Chamberlain let his eyes travel around the men, taking in the skeletal faces, the clothing falling to bits, and dirty faces that could not hide the intensity of the souls that burned within. "Now I must go. But if you'd like to help out in this fight we got coming, you see Captain Spear here and he'll tell you what company you're in and get you a rifle. If you still refuse to help, well, we'll put you under guard, and you can await the decision as to your fate. Regardless, you will all eat." With that, Chamberlain turned on his heel and walked away with Emmett in tow. When they were fifty feet from the men, he asked Emmett, "What are they doing?"

Emmett stole a glance over his shoulder. "Nothing, sir, they haven't moved at all."

At seventy-five feet Chamberlain wanted to ask again, but Major Gilmore came upon them. "We've been given orders to move up to U.S. Ford picket duty, sir." This would mean moving camp seven miles from their present bivouac at Bank's Ford.

"Very well, assemble the men. Tell them that they have one hour to break down camp, and we will be moving out. Emmett, get my horse." Later that night Chamberlain learned from Ellis Spear that all but four of the 120 men had decided to join the 20th Maine, bolstering ranks much depleted by illness and battle.

It was also not until that night that he got a chance to open the letter that had arrived from his sister, Sae, earlier in the day.

Lawrence—It was good to hear from you and know that you are well. The newspaper suggested that the battle of Chancellorsville was a terrible nightmare, and many good men and boys died. I have to admit that I do not know where Fanny is, but suspect that she is in New York. I have been staying at the house with the children, and have been helped out by Deborah Folsom. They are both doing wonderful, but little Wyllys did ask the other day, "Where does Mama live now?" On the brighter side, brother John will be coming to visit with you on official business. He has signed up with the Christian Commission to help tend to the physical and spiritual needs of the wounded. It is a six-week engagement, and pays his way to visit with you and Tom, as well as see the war, and maybe even do some good along the way. He should be there sometime in the middle of June, so make sure you keep an eye out for him. I have not seen Mother or Father as I've been here in Brunswick. It was good to hear from you that Tom is doing so well as a soldier as he needed something like this in his life.

Take care of yourself and BOTH brothers, Your favorite sister, Sae

Chapter Ten

My lovely Lizzie,
It pains me to miss you as much as I do. I was happy as a duck in water to hear that our son was born. I can't say that I'm overly happy to call him Melville, but will allow you the decision in this matter. I don't know when I will get home to see you, if ever, as a battle looms with that old dog Lee, and it don't appear we can beat him. We been trailing after him since he whipped us down in Chancellorsville, and I don't rightly know if we want to catch him or not. So many men have fallen out in the last few days hard marching that it seems as if half of the 20th is missing. Some men just can't stand up to the pace (we went thirty-one miles yesterday), but others have fallen out as the reward to sticking the course is to face them Rebs, and we ain't done so well with them thus far. I have to confess to a bad feeling, as if my time is up, and that the Creator will be coming to claim my soul in this upcoming fight. If I fall in battle, I hope that it helps in some way protect this great country of ours, but fear that it will not, and that all is lost. I have to go now as we are moving out, even though it is late at night and we have been marching all day. There is talk that Lee has been confronted in a place called Gettysburg in Pennsylvania, and every available regiment must hurry to get there.
I love and miss you, my butterfly, remember that always,
Llewellyn Jenkins
20th Maine
United States Army

July 1, 1863

Emmett Collins had been put on latrine duty, and thus was digging trenches at the end of a day that had started thirty-one miles to the south. The past few weeks had seen the Army of the Potomac mirroring the Confederate army's movements as they moved up the west side of the Blue Ridge Mountains into Pennsylvania. Much had happened in that time, Chamberlain's promotion to Colonel, Charles Gilmore becoming Lieutenant Colonel, while Adelbert Ames had moved on to command another brigade.

A third Chamberlain now rode with the regiment, as brother John had finally caught up with them after spending several weeks in Falmouth tending to sick and wounded Maine soldiers, some from the 20th. When these soldiers had realized that John was Joshua's brother, they had become very excited and profuse in their praise. As John had later related to Joshua, it was enough to make his ears burn. *He treats men like men and not like dogs as Ames used to, and he don't say go boys, but come, follow me. If a hole needs to be dug, he grabs a shovel, and if we have to charge a passel of Rebs, you can be sure he is out front. We got the best damn Colonel in the whole army, we do.*

Earlier that day they had crossed into Pennsylvania, happy to be back on northern soil after having spent the last nine months in the hostile state of Virginia. The brigade, now commanded by Colonel Vincent Strong, had unfurled its banners, showcasing the new division flag with its Maltese Cross. It was the flag adopted by the regiment to represent them, originally used in the First Crusade. The band had struck up "Yankee Doodle", and the men had put a snap into their weary steps as crowds poured out to cheer on their own, soldiers no longer attacking but defending their very homes. Civilians came out in droves to show their support, encouraging the men on. This rare and heartfelt reminder of the importance of what they were doing straightened their backs and tightened their cadence. They were still flushed with pride as they wearily stacked their rifles to prepare for supper and camp for the night. The foraging wagons had procured fresh pork and vegetables from the local farms, and the men crowded around to get their share.

Into this jubilant and exhausted bivouac came a hard-riding courier from General Meade, who now commanded the Army of the Potomac. General Barnes, Colonel Vincent, Colonel Rice, and Colonel Chamberlain were gathered in front of Barnes' tent as the man rode into the camp, his horse frothing white at the mouth. Dropping the reins, the courier sprang from the saddle as the horse staggered, and then stood with its head drooped almost to the ground, panting. "Message from General Meade via General Sykes for General Barnes, sir."

"What is it?" General Barnes demanded impatiently.

"The enemy has been confronted about sixteen miles from

here, in a small town called Gettysburg, sir. There was fierce fighting today, and our boys managed to hold their positions. The ground is very favorable, but we need to get every able body up into position, or we will certainly be driven from the field."

"Was it a skirmish with cavalry or the real thing?"

"Scouts report that General Lee has amassed his entire army in the area, and it is believed that it is through there that they plan to attack the capital." The courier was starting to regain his breath from the wild ride.

"And you said the field of combat was to our advantage?" General Barnes had graduated fifth in his class from the military academy the same year as Robert E. Lee, who had graduated first and certainly knew a thing or two about the importance of the terrain in dominating an opponent.

"Yes, sir. According to General Hancock, it is the finest he has ever had the pleasure to command."

"This is it, then." General Barnes said decisively. "Is there any more news?"

The courier dropped his eyes and shifted his feet. "General Reynolds was the first on the scene to support the cavalry and was killed on the battlefield." General John Reynolds was one of the brightest stars of the Union forces, a military man through and through, respected by his own men, President Lincoln, and the enemy alike.

"May God have mercy on his soul. Tell General Sykes we will be along shortly." General Barnes said dismissing the courier. "Colonel Chamberlain, make sure this man has a fresh mount. Pass the word along that we will move out in thirty minutes."

There was little grumbling as the men reformed ranks to resume the march. As the moon, full and bright, rose over the horizon, they unfurled their banners, and the band struck up lively marching music. This was no longer a fight about secession and slavery; it was now about protecting their homes. As they were passing farms and towns, families came out wishing them well, most of them women, all made beautiful by the gentle light of the full moon. These were the ones who the men were fighting for— the women, children, and those unable to protect themselves—and each and every man felt lighter in spirit. At one point, a false rumor swept through the ranks that the popular General McClellan had been again put in command, and some even claimed that George Washington had been seen riding the hills.

Some time after midnight a halt was finally called, and the men sank to the ground where they stopped, falling immediately asleep, their hunger ignored in the face of sheer exhaustion. It seemed that Emmett had barely touched the ground when Chamberlain nudged him awake. "Emmett, time to move out." All around, there was a rustling in that dark hour of night just before sunrise.

Everyone somehow sensed the imminent clash of forces, their bodies pumping with adrenalin. Some were quiet, lost in their own thoughts, while others were chattering away as if they hadn't a care in the world. Emmett kept close to Colonel Chamberlain, ready to deliver messages to the company captains as needed. The sun came up, and with its arrival, Emmett realized they had reached the battlefield, or at least, its very edge. There was a hustle and bustle of activity as men under orders rushed into position, while others loitered in preparation for what was to come.

Colonel Vincent, the new commander of the 3rd Brigade and quite resplendent in his uniform, trotted his horse over to them. "Colonel Chamberlain, we will rest here, but make sure that the men are prepared to fight. We may be put in at any moment."

"Yes, sir," Chamberlain replied. "The situation is propitious?"

Colonel Vincent pointed to the west. "Our troops hold a defensive position on the high ground that stretches that way just over the Taneytown Road, and then wraps this way in a fish-hook to where we are, on the far right flank. It is good terrain. As good or better than what the Confederates had at Fredericksburg."

"General Buford did a great thing yesterday, holding this ground," Colonel Chamberlain agreed.

Colonel Vincent snorted. "General Buford is a saint for what he did yesterday. With ground like this, ole' Bobby Lee is going to get himself whipped today."

"Let's hope that General Meade is ready to fully commit to this battle." Colonel Chamberlain replied.

"He showed courage during the Peninsula Campaign though he was wounded. He did a right fine job making a stand at the Second Battle of Bull Run, and proved his mettle at

---

186

Fredericksburg. Let's hope he has the grit to command the whole dang army." Colonel Vincent did not have to mention how that terrible burden of responsibility had already proved too much for Generals McDowell, McClellan, Burnsides, Pope, and most recently, Hooker.

"Let us hope, then. Let us hope." Chamberlain, not yet a year into the war, had already grown cynical of the leadership. With a shake of his head, he banished ill thoughts from his mind and returned to the business at hand. "Emmett, spread the word that the men are to rest, but be kept ready to move at any moment. Have each soldier issued twenty extra rounds for their rifles."

"Yessir." Emmett dashed away, the excitement of the officers rubbing off on him. The decisive moment of the war, or so it seemed, had arrived, to be decided here, maybe even today, and they held the high ground. For once, the advantage was theirs, and all present could almost sense the tipping of the scales in their favor. They would not be charging uphill into entrenched enemy gunfire as at Fredericksburg. Rather, they would be entrenched and with the superior position. An hour later, with no sign of action, that excitement began to ebb, and Emmett nodded off to sleep with his back to a tree, only to be wakened as the regiment was moved slightly to the west. Again, no new orders materialized, and they began to doze in the warm Pennsylvania sun. They were moved several more times, always towards the left flank, while guns boomed somewhere in the distance, with sporadic rifle fire puncturing the day. The battle, it seemed, was close but not yet upon them.

Finally, in the late afternoon, a courier came bursting into their midst looking for General Barnes. "He is not here presently. You may give me the message." Colonel Vincent was itching to get into the fight and do his part.

"The message is for General Barnes only." The courier snapped brusquely.

"You are wasting my time." Vincent barked at him, his smooth-shaven face and slicked back hair making him look more like a Greek statue than a Union soldier. "General Barnes is away from the command, and I speak for him. What is the message?"

The courier shuffled his feet but could not withstand the intensity of the man in front of him. "General Warren has realized that our left flank is unprotected, and he believes the enemy is massing for an attack at that very spot. He needs somebody to take up position on that hill." He pointed to a barren hill to the west, apparently empty of men. It was immediately obvious, even to Emmett, that this hill commanded the battlefield, and whoever held this position held the upper hand.

"Tell General Warren that the 3rd Brigade will occupy that hill. What is it called?"

"Little Round Top, sir."

"Colonel Rice?" Colonel Vincent swung away from the orderly. "See that the 3rd Brigade follows me to Little Round Top. I will go ahead and scout the position." He turned to his private orderly. "Norton, you come with me."

Restless and impatient, the men were quick to assemble, at the point where even fighting was better than waiting. It was not the battle that the men feared most, but rather the slow agony leading up to it. The 3rd Brigade moved out at double-time, crossing a small creek, following Colonel Vincent. Emmett was riding along with Tom and Joshua Chamberlain when their middle brother, John, temporarily attached to the field hospital of the 20th Maine, came galloping up on his horse. His face was flushed with excitement, this being his first brush with battle. The four of them walked their horses, leading the 20th Maine towards the hill called Little Round Top.

"This certainly gets the blood flowing." John Chamberlain yelled.

Joshua Chamberlain had only been present fully in one conflict so far. In comparison to his brother, however, he was a veteran of the carnage that he knew was about to descend upon them. "The blood will certainly flow today, dear brother, and you will be kept busy in the field hospital tending to the wounded."

As the four of them were pondering this grim prognosis, there was a sudden noise that reminded Emmett of the whoosh of an owl's wings directly over his head one night when he was out hunting possum. This innocuous sound, however, was almost immediately followed by the booming crash of a tree not ten feet from them, which exploded in a shower of splinters. The Rebel Artillery had spotted the movement of troops, and was very close to finding their range.

"I think we should separate." Joshua Chamberlain said in his understated manner. "Another such shot as that will make it rather hard on Mother."

"I need to report back to the field hospital anyway." John replied, his face ashen at this brush with death. Joshua and Tom had barely flinched, while Emmett had jumped but then quickly recovered his composure.

"Tom, you bring up the rear of the regiment." Colonel Chamberlain ordered.

"I don't want to go to the back and miss everything." Tom argued, upset at being treated like a little brother.

"One of us has to lead and that burden would fall on my shoulders. What would the men think if I was leading from the rear?"

"They would have no faith in you at all and wouldn't follow orders." Tom confessed.

"I am sure that before long you will get an opportunity to show your mettle. As a matter of fact, I can almost guarantee that before the day is over, you will be in the thick of the fray." Chamberlain looked almost hungrily into the clear blue sky, twirling his mustache with his pinkie. "This spot right up here is where it's all going to happen. I can feel it in my bones."

"Good luck, brother." Tom said, turning his horse and riding off.

Upon reaching the crest of Little Round Top, they had a sweeping view to the north. In the distance they could see wheat fields shimmering golden. A little to the west was a peach orchard and then closer to them, a huge jumble of broken rocks—many the sizes of houses—tossed and turned and littering the ground. There was something incredibly powerful and intimidating about these rocks, so out of place in the fields and woods of the area, as if they were the debris left behind after some terrible Armageddon. The very rawness of the terrain had given it the nickname Devil's Den, for it certainly appeared to be a place in which Satan himself might feel at home. As Emmett stared in awe at these massive rocks, he realized that there were tiny creatures scurrying around and between them, creatures that he soon realized were Rebel soldiers moving steadily in their direction. Artillery shells whizzed above them, the booms only coming after the passage of the shells.

Where they stood, the ground was brown as if grass knew better than to grow here, a few scrubby bushes protruding from the boulder-strewn terrain. On the very top of the hill grew a scattering of trees, mostly bare of leaves, their branches wavering eerily in the light breeze of the day. It was an ugly little hill; an appropriate spot for killing, and the men of the 20th Maine marked it in respectful silence.

When they caught up with Colonel Vincent and his orderly, Private Norton, they found the Colonel radiant with the knowledge that battle was imminent, and also that his quick action in rushing to this flank had saved certain defeat. "Colonel Chamberlain, have your regiment take up position on the southern slope of the hill. Leave the high ground for the artillery so we can pepper them Rebs with shells if they try to flank us."

"Yes, sir."

"Colonel, do you understand that your regiment will be the extreme left flank of the entire line?"

"Yes, sir."

"If the enemy is able to overrun you, they will roll right down the entire line and smash our defenses in front of them."

"Yes, sir."

"Colonel, you must hold this ground at every hazard."

Chamberlain looked at his commanding officer and friend, giving him a thin smile. "Yes. At every hazard." He nodded, pondering the words, words that would forever haunt him, Vincent's last to him in this world on that sunny day soon to explode into a fiery Hell. There could be no failure here. Death was not an option, for this position must be held at every hazard, and death would merely be another kind of failure. The 20th Maine could not, would not, fail.

"Captain Spear, we will place the men by 'right by file into line'. Company A will end up here and so on down the line. We will skip Company B, as we will have them protect the open air on our flank. Emmett, go get Captain Morrill for me." This maneuver would allow the men on the right to face the enemy, while helping to get the regiment into the proper positioning to defend the flank of the Union Army on top of Little Round Top.

"Yessir." Both Emmett and Captain Spear replied in unison, rushing off to their respective duties. Emmett saw no signs of the exhaustion that by all rights, the men should be feeling in their weary bones, for the excitement of impending battle was animating them, filling them with a brimming energy. As Emmett returned with Captain Morrill, he saw the beginning of the maneuver that would place the companies in position just below the crest of the hill that was Little Round Top, facing the larger hill to the west that was called, simply, Round Top. The men in the rear two columns marched in place, allowing the front two ranks to move into their position as a single line of men, and once in place, the rear ranks followed suit. As Emmett watched, a single line of defense spread across Little Round Top in an efficient manner, ready to defend the ground. "Do you think that this is where the Rebs are gonna attack, Captain Morrill?"

"You can bet your boots on it, Emmett." Captain Morrill replied candidly as Chamberlain came to meet them.

"Captain Morrill, I'm worried about those woods." Colonel Chamberlain said, pointing across the way, in the direction of Round Top, a much larger hill with less strategic value because its slopes were so heavily timbered. "If the Confederates get around us into those woods and attack from our rear, we will be terribly exposed. Bring your company out there and dissuade any sort of Southern presence."

"Yes, sir." Captain Morrill saluted, immediately rushing back to Company B.

Chamberlain had dismounted some time earlier, sending his horse to the rear. He now walked down the line of the 20th Maine inspecting the men's positions. His orders had been followed to the letter, and the regiment was now spread across the southern slopes of Little Round Top in a line. Some men lay on the ground, using rocks, roots of trees, dips in the ground, or whatever was available for cover. This posed a problem in reloading, which was far easier to do while standing, just more dangerous. Others, here and there, stood or knelt, shielded by young oaks and pines that dotted the side of the hill. As he went, he dropped a word here, a handshake there, and a smile to another. "Don't forget to breathe before you squeeze the trigger. Stay behind the cover of the tree." His calm presence among them seemed to focus their energy and concentration on the impending clash. Even as they had maneuvered into position, the air had filled with the deafening noise of the Confederate artillery bombarding the Union forces. The battle raged off to their right as the Rebels pressed the attack from the peach orchard, close enough so that the horrible screech of the Rebel yell echoed through the air and deep into the bones of the Union soldiers.

"Emmett, once the fighting begins you will have to help tend to the injured, bring them water, bind wounds, whatever you can do until they can be transported to the surgeons."

"Yessir." Emmett replied, his breath catching in his lungs at the memory of his last experience with the wounded and dying.

"Captain Clark, do you see that scattering of trees?" Chamberlain pointed to the west. "I think they will come through there first. Have the men hold their fire until they pass by that large oak there," he said jabbing his finger at one of the few trees of any girth within sight.

"I see it." Captain Clark was in charge of the right side of the 20th Maine, and thus, the link tying the regiment to the brigade via the 83rd Pennsylvania, and the rest of the Union army sprawling for miles to the north and east, 90,000 men versus Lee's 70,000.

"What is that?" Emmett suddenly gasped. It was not something he'd seen or heard, but rather the abrupt lack of noise that garnered his attention.

Chamberlain looked around at his regiment dug into the hillside, the late afternoon sun bathing them in light and warmth, a light breeze blowing the few, sparse leaves. "Their artillery has stopped," he said coolly. "Get ready boys, they will be coming now." No artillery meant only one thing—that an assault was imminent. With the words of Chamberlain still hanging in the air, a rustling in the scattered trees below gave away the presence of the Rebels, a shadow here, movement there, as they slithered through the woods like beasts come to devour their prey. Suddenly a deer burst from the rocks below, charging across the front of the 20th Maine, a nervous soldier shooting and missing to the jeers of the rest of the men.

The attack came rolling up on them, striking a glancing blow to the 83rd Pennsylvania to their right, and then barreling into the flank of the 20th Maine. The Confederates emerged from the rocks and scrub brush, unloosing a fusillade above their heads, the minié balls breaking branches, which rained down on the men from Maine. Henry Sidelinger was commanding Company E on the right, a hefty assignment for a nineteen year-old farm boy from Maine. At a distance of no more than four rods he ordered his men to fire, the withering volley dropping many of the Confederates in their tracks, the smoke washing back and through the regiment, the soot clinging to the sweat that the heat and stress of the day had produced. "Fire at will boys," he called out, aghast at the knowledge that he'd just killed a man. An accomplished soldier could load and fire three times a minute, but the nerves of actual battle caused the men to hurry, spill the powder, drop the cartridge, or worse, forget to remove the rammer from the barrel in their haste to fire their weapons.

Lieutenant James Nichols came rushing to the center of the line to find Chamberlain. "Sir, there is a lot movement to the left. I think they're trying to flank us." Chamberlain clambered up a large rock that he'd been using for shelter just a moment earlier, peering in the direction that Lieutenant Nichols had indicated, with Emmett pleading for him to get down from his perilous perch. Finally, he nimbly leaped down, much to the boy's relief.

"You are right, Lieutenant. It looks like there is a whole regiment swinging to our flank under cover of those trees. Pass the word along that we will refuse the line. Emmett, have the color guard move the flag to the far left, by the stump of that rotted tree and behind the rock ledge," he said pointing. "That will be the new center. We will move to the left and backwards, at intervals when possible, until our far left is bent back and around, facing almost south." Chamberlain moved quickly down the line to the spot that would be the new center, where he found Captain Spear commanding the left wing of the regiment. "Ellis, our new line will stretch to that point there," he said, again pointing to their left. "I think this is where the focus of their attack is going to come. The rest has been just a diversion. You know how important it is that we hold this ground." The maneuver to stretch their line to double its original length, changing the center to the far left flank was made seamlessly, the officers and men moving together in unison. The men on the far left had to stretch back around the spur of the ridge to create a new line of defense against attack. Where the men had originally been elbow to elbow, there was now a space of about a yard between each of them, extending the entire line with the same number of soldiers, thus, thinning the ranks to a dangerous degree.

It was hard to believe that less than a year earlier, almost all of them had had different jobs, from lumberjack to professor, and now they were executing a military maneuver that would have made many a career soldier jealous. "Thank god for Adelbert Ames." Chamberlain said to Captain Clark as the final steps of the move were completed, both of them staring in awe at the new positioning of the regiment.

"Last September," Captain Clark murmured, "I contemplated killing him in his sleep. I'm sure glad I didn't follow through."

It was not a moment too soon; for out of the woods burst the 15th Alabama, a battle-hardened regiment sure that it had the element of surprise on its side. Instead, a withering fire met them, as the left flank of the 20th Maine under the direction of Captain Spear laid into them with a vengeance. The 15th Regiment from Alabama fell in droves under that initial barrage and those left standing froze for a moment, shocked at the deadly fire. Recovering from their surprise, the Alabamians began returning fire, the men from Maine taking cover any way they could as they hastened to reload. After the initial attack, the sides exchanged steady fire, men from Maine rising up to fire only to have their brains spilled over the barren earth. Steadily, the men from Alabama moved forward.

Their momentum carried them within ten feet of the 20th Maine line, where Ellis Spear had readied his company. On his command, they stood as one unit and fired, decimating the Confederates, the two groups staring at each other eyeball to eyeball before the Alabamans broke and retreated. Their officers rallied them, and soon they returned to the fray, again pushing back the far left of the line. Captain Charles Billing urged his men to stand and return the fire, but a chunk of lead tore a hole in his thigh, dropping him to the ground, white-faced and writhing. Emmett was now helping injured soldiers move from the front line to the rear where they were collected by the ambulance crews and taken to the field hospital. He ran to Billing's side, tearing a piece of cloth from his tunic and tying it tightly above the wound to cut off the blood flow. Billing's swallowed and gasped, "I never thought it would hurt so bad."

Emmett scurried to pull wounded soldiers to safety in lulls sometimes lasting no more than seconds. Precious seconds allowing the soldiers to catch their breath and drink, load their weapons, first running a bristle brush down the rifle barrel to clean out the gunpowder remnants. At one point, a minié ball stuck a tree near Emmett's head, its sharp fragments slashing his cheek like angry bees, the pain almost immediately forgotten in the terror of conflict. He was still picking the splinters from his face when he happened upon Tom, who was methodically loading his rifle and firing—loading and firing—a look of fierce determination on his powder-blackened face. Several bullets struck the tree behind which he stood, and he sunk to the ground for protection, Emmett diving in beside him.

"How we doing?" Tom yelled, knowing that the boy had been up and down the line.

"We're holding our own so far, but we're down some men." Emmett tried to be matter of fact about the dead and injured.

"You've got blood on your cheek."

"How come it's not getting dark yet?" He hollered the question at Tom, wondering why the sun had barely moved in the sky.

Tom looked at his pocket watch, shook it once, and then grinned. "Less than an hour since they attacked is why."

Emmett shook his head in disbelief, and then scooted out from behind the tree and back down the line. He saw tongues of smoke and flames leaping from the barrels of the Enfield rifles, the faces of the men like coal miners from the black powder that blew back with every shot, and all the while the steady booming of cannons as the Northern Artillery tried to punish the Confederate Infantry as it moved forward to attack the high ground. "Emmett!" Chamberlain barked, striding over to him. "Go over to the 83rd Pennsylvania and see if they can spare any men. Tell them that our lines are perilously thin. Go!" Emmett went running along the ridge behind the 20th Maine, catching a glimpse of the regiment flag barely visible through the smoke, held firmly in the crook of the color guard's arm as the man loaded and fired a musket he'd picked from the ground. The men were stretched sparsely to begin with, and now the wounded and dead left huge gaps in the line, gaps through which the Confederates were sure to pour before long.

Emmett soon found the color guard of the 83rd Pennsylvania and its commanding officer, Captain Woodward. "Sir," he panted. "Colonel Chamberlain was wondering if you could spare any men as we are stretched awful thin."

"Tell Colonel Chamberlain that we have none to spare, and are busy with a bunch of Texans ourselves. We could stretch to the left a mite so that that you can condense your line." Captain Orpheus Woodward, newly promoted, was handling himself well after Colonel Vincent's rise to the brigade commander.

Emmett thanked him and hurried back to pass the information on to Chamberlain, who seemed pleased to be at least able to concentrate his men slightly.

Tom Chamberlain approached with a look of concern on his face. "Lawrence," he said, "we are almost all out of ammunition."

"Tell the men to scavenge from the dead and wounded for the time being." Colonel Chamberlain retorted grimly.

"They already have," came the reply, but it was drowned out by that horrendous rebel yell, and then the gray uniforms again surged up the hill to be met by a ragged volley from the Union troops.

Still the Confederates pressed on, urged on by their officers with threats and pleas, the men from Alabama climbing the hill once again until they were upon the 20th Maine, and the battle turned into a brawl, soldiers swinging rifles, stabbing with bayonets, throwing rocks, punches, kicking, gouging at eyes, tearing at hair, anything for an advantage. There was no more order or discipline, just men fighting for their lives. Private George Washington Buck swung his rifle, knocking a Confederate Corporal to the ground, and losing his grip on the weapon, he ran leaping astride him while picking up a rock, clubbing the man in the side of the head. With horror he stood, looking down upon the mangled mess of a face left below him, just as a gray-coated captain pressed a Navy Colt against his shoulder and pulled the trigger, the lead splintering his bones and rending his flesh.

Finally, the Confederates broke and retreated back down the hill.

Chamberlain arrived on the scene as the fighting waned, a few soldiers firing at the retreating Rebels, but most pausing to catch their breath, and gulp the last of the water from their canteens. He went immediately to Buck, kneeling by the potato farmer from Lineus, a small town in northern Maine. "You turned the tide and saved the line, Buck."

"I killed a man with a rock." Buck gasped, the shock and horror of the fighting as painful as the wound.

"You did what you had to do to save the line, and with it the flank. God will understand that it was necessary."

"Colonel, am I going to die?" His right shoulder was soaked, white bone chips flecking the dark red blood.

"You'll be fine." Chamberlain lied. And then he thought better of it, not wanting that lie to follow Buck to his grave, and linger in his own conscience. "I don't know, son. I don't know."

"Colonel," Private Buck whispered, motioning Chamberlain down. "Tell my mother that I didn't die a coward."

"I will Buck, and I will also tell her you died a sergeant, for I am promoting you now to that title for your heroism."

Two men came over, pulling Buck to his feet, and hauling him behind the line to await help from the medical staff. A man stood pissing against a tree, while another massaged his shoulder, sore from the recoil of the rifle. Several soldiers exchanged their Enfield's for the enemy's Springfield rifles, thinking them a better model. A man from Alabama bleeding to death on the ground asked for a drink, and was given one by the man who had shot him, the two exchanging names in the process.

It was not long before the Confederates had regrouped, and again were moving up the hill with deliberate steps, intent on evicting the 20th Maine from Little Round Top. As they neared, it was hard to tell the screams of the attackers from the screams of the wounded. Chamberlain strode up and down the line, in plain sight of the enemy, as casually as if he were giving a lecture on rhetoric. "Fire low, boys! They're downhill, so you're going to tend to shoot too high." A minié ball hit a hunk of granite at his feet, fragments piercing his boot and slicing open his foot. He limped on, not stopping long enough even to examine the wound. Another flying piece of lead flattened itself against the scabbard of his sword, mangling the steel and leaving an ugly bruise on his hip, but at no point did he lose his composure.

In the middle of the line Chamberlain could see the color guard, Andrew Tozier, one of the men from the 2nd Maine, holding the Maltese Cross in the crook of his arm while he fired an Enfield he'd taken from a wounded soldier. The center had been taking fire from three sides for more than two hours, and now was rent with gaping holes, the dead and wounded scattered over the ground where they had fallen. "Tom!" He yelled to his brother, waving. The younger Chamberlain looked up, then immediately crossed over the thirty feet of ground. "Go help out in the center by the color guard. See if you can't shore things up, perhaps pull them back a tad to help close some of the holes in the ranks." Chamberlain winced as he gave the order, regretting sending his brother into this terrible situation, but he must hold the ground at every hazard.

Tom nodded his head, striding forward into the very gates of Hell. The Confederates had come within twenty feet of the Union line, with men on both sides hurrying to reload, nervously glancing at the enemy to see how quickly their death would come. A rammer flew past Tom's head as he approached, a Rebel soldier having forgotten to remove it before he shot. An Alabaman let loose a guttural yell and came charging the short distance between the two armies, aiming for Tozier and the fluttering flag that had been torn by numerous bullets. The man held his rifle with bayonet fixed meaning to spear the color guard through the chest. Tom flung his empty rifle, butt first, its ten pounds catching the man a glancing blow to the shoulder. It was enough to deflect the blade, which sliced the sleeve of the guard's coat instead, leaving just a scratch on his arm. Tom grabbed the man's rifle, and the two of them twirled as if dancing, fighting for control of the weapon. The man was larger than Tom and flung him violently from side to side. But Tom hung on grimly, knowing that to let go would mean receiving the business end of the bayonet in his chest. He managed to hook his foot behind the man's ankle, toppling them both to the ground, the gun clattering away. Tom rolled and jabbed a punch into the man's face, his opponent's hands in turn grasping either side of Tom's head. Then he was on top of him gouging Tom's eyes with his thumbs. A gun boomed, and the

Rebel's eyes widened as he struggled to say something, and then slumped forward. Andrew Tozier stood behind him grinning, wide legged, the battle flag and the still smoking Enfield splayed to either side.

"We need to pull the center back and close down the ranks." Tom stumbled to his feet, wiping the blood from his face.

Tozier nodded, falling back about twelve paces while Tom directed the men on either side to also fall back, thus tightening the line. For the time being the Confederates fell back as well. One soldier was stuffing moss from his cartridge case into a bullet wound in his forearm, wrapping a piece of his ripped shirt around the injury, and then tying it off with his one good arm and teeth.

Emmett's world had evolved into two simple chores. First he pulled the wounded from the field and, second, he gathered the ammunition of the dead and those whose wounds had taken them out of the fight. Emmett traveled up and down the line, sometimes crawling, other times hunched over scrabbling on all fours. He crawled behind a ledge and found his brother, Daniel, loading his rifle from his knees, keeping his head low while ramming the cartridge onto the powder below.

"How are you holding up for rounds?" Emmett posed the question to his brother.

"I've only got about five left." Daniel said grimly, his eyes shining white in his soot-blackened face.

"There's about ten more in here." Emmett handed Daniel a cartridge belt still stained with the blood of a dead soldier.

"This is as good ground as Malvern Hill, but there we were able to pound them better with the artillery." A minié ball clipped the ledge showering them both with granite chips. "Is there no end to these Seceshers?" Daniel stood and fired at a moving target, dropping back down beside Emmett to reload.

"How was it that Pa died?"

Daniel paused in reloading, pondering the question that Emmett had not asked until now. "A stray bullet went through his eye. Killed him instantly." He leaned around the rock, firing from his knees before ducking back.

Emmett had gotten kind of used to having his brother around, and secretly hoped that Daniel wouldn't be mustered out of service, but would stay with the 20th Maine for another year.

Daniel finished priming the weapon, and struggling to his feet, he aimed the rifle at a Confederate just ten feet away, the Rebels eyes brown and wide as he pulled the trigger. Daniel sat back down without firing, almost as if remembering something he wanted to say, and then Emmett saw the blood cascading down his face.

"No!" Emmett screamed, just as the Confederate soldier peered over the ledge. Without thinking, Emmett pointed his rifle at the man and pulled the trigger. The minié ball struck the man in the throat, tearing through the soft flesh and partially severing the spine, so that his head toppled obscenely to the side. He fell slowly backward, dead before he hit the ground. Emmett looked up to see a swirl of gray coats as the Confederates crested the spur on the Southeastern corner of Little Round Top. Emmett pulled Daniel's rifle free and fired, and then stood and began swinging the rifle over his head, one part of a life and death struggle between a regiment from Maine and a regiment from Alabama, struggling for control of an ugly little hill outside the inconsequential town of Gettysburg, Pennsylvania. At one point, Captain Spear and Captain Land had to beat the men forward with the flats of their swords so they wouldn't retreat. And then it was over, for the time being, the Confederates falling back and melting into the scrub brush down below.

Chapter Eleven

Ground on which we can only be saved from destruction by fighting without delay, is desperate ground. –Sun Tzu, 'The Art of War'

July 2, 1863

This Great War had taken his entire family. Emmett left his brother where he had fallen, covering his face with his forage cap. He would come back and make sure that Daniel had a proper burial if he could. Taking the rifle numbly with him, he made his way back to Colonel Chamberlain to see where he was needed. He was ready to do more than just carry messages and tend the wounded.

Though the Confederates had again been repulsed, however momentarily, there was a stirring below in the trees as if they were preparing for one final furious thrust to pierce the thin and weary defense, and thus flank the Union Army. Chamberlain stared at the sun peeking through the clouds off behind the enemy, wondering how it could still be so high in the sky. It must be about 6:30 in the evening or so, he judged, though it had already seemed an eternity. Their part in the battle had only lasted two hours up to this point. Men reached for canteens that were empty, the heat of the Pennsylvania summer and the acrid taste of gunpowder parching their throats. A crow was cawing from off to their left, drawn to this place of death by the promise of a feast. A faint breeze rippled up the hill, clearing the smoke away and exposing the Confederates gathering themselves below.

Tom scrambled half bent over across the ridge and joined them with bad news. "Lawrence," he said panting. "The right wing is out of ammunition. I don't think we hold more than twenty rounds between all of us combined."

None of them had noticed the approach of Captain Land from the opposite direction. "That is twenty rounds more than the left wing has," he added drily.

The smoke rose from the ground and worked skyward like spirits returning home as the sun descended in a fiery ball of red.

A silence enveloped the ridge as all eyes turned on Chamberlain, awaiting his orders.

At every hazard....

A man so covered in dirt and sweat, his uniform so rent and gray from the sun that he could only be identified as a captain from the insignia on his shoulder barged in on them. "We have to fall back," he pleaded. "We have no ammunition left and them Reb's are all fer chargin us again!"

"Ammunition!" Another officer shouted. "I don't have any men left, much less ammunition. We have no chance; we must fall back and save ourselves."

Chamberlain searched his mind for the solution, thinking of his many conversations with Ames, the manuals he'd pored over late at night, the West Point officers' teachings in tactics. He looked around at the men staring at him, knowing the balance of their lives was in his hands, that to do anything but fall back might be a death sentence for them all. What could be done with no ammunition? With no support? There was only one possible conclusion.

A third officer, braver than the first two, or perhaps more foolhardy, came up and saluted, "Permission to go forward to help some of the wounded, sir?" All eyes stared at Chamberlain, and Emmett heard him utter the words, "At every hazard...."

Chamberlain shook his head as if in wonder, a small smile lifting the corners of his mouth. "We will fix bayonets." He said decisively. "We are going to charge them. Tom, pass the word to Captain Clark on the right that we will execute a spinning wheel charge. He will be the anchor upon which we spin. Captain Land, the left side will sweep down to the south, turning gradually until you are sweeping to the west and north. You will have to make sure the boys on the far left are really moving out. Lieutenant Melcher, we will *all* go forward to aide in the recovery of our wounded, and drive the Confederates before us like cattle." Lieutenant Melcher whooped in joy and ran back to his company. Soon, all along the line the word was passed that they were going to give the Rebs the cold steel.

"Bayonets!" Chamberlain yelled at the top of his lungs, and the cry went all down the line, followed closely by the clanging of bayonets being fixed, snapping into place and

202

transforming the rifles into deadly spears with seventeen inches of razor-sharp blade glinting evilly in the bright sun. With more accurate, longer-ranged rifles and more precise artillery, the bayonet charge was something many soldiers had never met in this war. There was a primitive ferocity to it, an effectiveness too, in that being rushed by hundreds of points of steel tended to loosen the bowels and provoke the urge to flee in the enemy.

Chamberlain raised his sword high over his head. "Forward!" He called, but the word was lost in the roar of 400 screaming men. The left flank had to move fast so the entire line could swing like the hand of a clock, from south to west and then north. The far right flank was the pivot point upon which the wheel turned, while the center with Colonel Chamberlain and the color guard set the pace, jogging down the hill into the Rebel army.

Down at the bottom of the hill, Colonel William Oates, the commander of the 15th Alabama Regiment, was considering his options. The men were dangerously low on ammunition, his younger brother John had just been killed, and he was afraid that unseen forces had enveloped his line. His orders had been to damage the enemy to the best of their ability, and that they had done. He knew that if they could just take that damn little rocky hill, well then, the Confederate army could roll down the flank and whip the Yankees good. But where were Bulger and the 47th Alabama? And who were the soldiers firing on them from the woods on Round Top? He couldn't get the image of his brother's dead body with its gaping bloody bullet wounds out of his mind, and the hellish landscape around him only reinforced the horror. Everywhere he looked, men had fallen in grotesque poses of death, their blood puddled between the rocks as if pools of rainwater. He looked again at the hillside in front of him. There were only two choices: to make one last valiant onslaught upon the rocky spur above and surely die, or to retreat and succumb to the pesky Union regiment above. Sudden screaming interrupted his contemplation. Looking up, Oates saw a wall of blue descending from Little Round Top with bayonets thrust in front of them, careening down the hill in a vicious charge.

Ellis Spear led the charge of the left flank as they burst from cover behind the boulders and trees with their flashing blades leading the way. At first, they jogged slowly, but then a strange competitive spirit swept through the men, and they ran as if possessed. Fearful of lagging, the hindmost pressed forward until they were all at a full sprint, leaping rocks and scrambling over the rough terrain. Ellis found himself yelling along with the rest, an animalistic roar striking dread in their enemy. They split to pass a huge boulder, finding seven or eight Confederate soldiers behind it in various stages of dropping their weapons. One of the Maine men smashed his gun butt into a soldier cowering on his knees, but Ellis could not pause for prisoners or reprimands as their momentum drove them on.

The Rebels had not counted on being met with a horde of crazy men charging down the hill, steel daggers plunging in front of them. It was much easier to face the sting of invisible bullets than to face a wave of keening beasts with blades intent on ripping their flesh and carving their bodies into pieces. Emmett looked to the left where he saw the blue uniforms under the command of Ellis Spear hurtling themselves down the slope, momentum and adrenalin combining to create a flash flood of humanity crushing everything in its path. The men of the 15th Alabama, it seemed, were dropping their weapons and surrendering immediately, the more cowardly breaking and running like stampeding cattle, panicking and out of control. From the woods over by Round Top came a crashing volley of fire. Next to him, Chamberlain shook his head and made to slow their progress. "I forgot all about Captain Morrill and B Company over there," he said. "Looks like those Rebels running away just ran smack dab into the middle of them."

Captain Morrill and B Company had indeed been isolated from much of the battle up to this moment, having taken up a forward position at the base of the larger Round Top to prevent any sort of flanking motion by the enemy. Cut off from the rest of the regiment, they had watched most of the battle from the protection of a stone wall in the rear of the 15th Alabama. As the charge broke the ranks of the Confederates, scores of them retreated towards the safety of the trees filling the larger hill. "Hold your fire, men, steady, wait for them." Morrill calmed the soldiers, waiting until the panic-stricken Rebels were right upon them. The opening fusillade took a murderous toll, the minié balls horribly accurate from such a short distance, tearing gaping holes in arms, legs, and cleaving chunks of bone from skulls. Men screamed and fell to the ground, the survivors freezing in shock, teetering on tipped toes, caught between the terror behind and the death in front. "Charge!" Morrill yelled, and the forty men of B Company scrambled over the wall and into the assorted gray uniforms who were raising their arms in surrender as fast as possible.

On the upper slope of Little Round Top, Chamberlain had once again urged his men on. Now he jogged down the hill, happy to be released from the moment of decision and transported into action. He was at the center of the line, holding out his slightly curved saber as much in defiance as to point the direction for the men to follow. A distant image, a snippet of a memory of fencing with his father slid through his mind. The color guard kept pace with him, the left flank swinging on their point like the spokes of a wagon wheel. A lone gray uniform stood in his path, evidently choosing to not flee, but to merely stare at the onrushing horde, open-mouthed. As they closed the ground to within ten feet, the soldier, now identifiable as a lieutenant by the bar on his shoulder, suddenly raised a pistol. The Navy Colt revolver's barrel gaped as wide as a Parrot Cannon at this distance, and Chamberlain braced for the impact he was sure would follow. The hammer fell, and the shot rang out, but he felt nothing at all. The man had missed! Chamberlain took two more steps and flicked the point of his blade to the man's throat. "Sergeant," he called over his shoulder. "Take this officer as a prisoner, here, take his sword, I may still have use of the pistol."

James Rice, formerly a New York lawyer, currently a Colonel in the Union Army and now commander of the 3rd Brigade after Strong Vincent had fallen, stood with a spyglass on the heights of Little Round Top surveying the enemy. The men called him "Old Crazy" for his violent temper and peculiar habits. If ever there were a time to pull a rabbit from a hat, it was now, he thought. He'd been watching the ebb and flow of the battle most of the afternoon, the seemingly invincible, unstoppable waves of truculent rebels repulsed, repelled, beaten off. Now, with both the iron will—and the black powder and shot—in short supply, the prospects certainly looked dim. Aides were pestering him with requests from the regiments under his command for support, for ammunition, for any sort of help. He could see the Confederates massing down in the low shrubbery, preparing for another assault on the left flank, an offensive he just couldn't see how to combat. His high forehead was blackened with soot and furrowed with concern, his eyes a manic white in the wide dark expanse. Several staff officers stood by, impatient for orders, but knowing better than to interrupt his thoughts unless they wanted to face his wrath. But one brave officer did suddenly interrupt, actually having the nerve to tug on his sleeve, pointing off to the left. With exasperation, he swung his attention in that direction in time to see a wave of blue uniforms come charging down the hill, sweeping from left to right. The noise of their yelling rose faintly up to where they stood, rising in crescendo in step with their velocity. The last sun of the day flashed off their bayonets as they came, crushing the assorted blobs of gray in front of them, wiping out everything in their path. "Thank God for Maine." Rice muttered, as if his silent prayers had been answered. The blue wave scattered the first regiment they came to, driving the 15th Alabama in every possible direction. The 47th Alabama was behind them, bracing for the impact, the shock seeming to shake the ground upon which Rice stood.

Emmett had not yet had an opportunity to use his bayonet as the enemy had surrendered, or fled, before the need had presented itself. And then they crashed into the 47th Alabama, who, rallied temporarily by their officers, were like a sandbar in the face of the tide. Emmett crested a rock to find a rebel hastily attempting to reload his rifle. The man looked up, his shaking hands trying to put the cartridge in the breech of his Sharps, making no attempt to surrender. Emmett drew back his rifle to thrust the man through with the bayonet, but could not bring himself to do so. He quickly reversed the weapon and struck him in the side of the head with the gun butt, knocking him to the ground where he lay still, either unconscious or happy to feign such. Emmett continued on, trying desperately to keep pace with Chamberlain, who was now firing his newly obtained Navy Colt with one hand while waving them on with the saber in the other.

Tom had lost any thought of concern for his own safety, leaping from rock to rock, slashing, and marauding, bayonet-first into clumps of resisters. Anyone observing would have had a hard time imagining him as a store clerk. Black sheep he may have once been, but here on the field of battle, he had found his true calling as a warrior. There were only gray coats and the steel blade in front of him. He felt the angry hiss of lead past his ear. Vaulting a fallen tree he came upon a Rebel who had just slipped the percussion cap onto the nipple, the rifle already at half cock. With a howl, Tom flung his rifle and bayonet like a spear, the blade piercing the man's shoulder. The weapon discharged, exploding a small rock at Tom's feet, splattering him with sharp stone fragments. Tom, still howling, wrenched the rifle from the Rebel's shoulder, preparing for the final deathblow. The man fumbled a dagger from his belt, an eight-inch Bowie, and Tom had no choice but to lunge forward with the bayonet. He aimed for the stomach, but the bayonet glanced off the Rebels chest and up into his throat, blood spewing forth to shower them both in a red haze.

"Halt the charge!" Chamberlain yelled, his voice being swallowed by the battlefield. "Halt the charge!" The Confederates had been swept from the field and were in full retreat, but Chamberlain knew that further on were more regiments from Alabama and Texas, and that his men were now exposed and in disarray. As well, the orders were to hold the left flank of Little Round Top, and currently it stood empty. He grabbed Sergeant Tozier, the man holding the regiment colors, by the arm, stopping him from moving any farther forward. "Emmett, pass the word to halt the charge."

Emmett bounded off to communicate with the officers and men who had lost sight of the colors in their mad dash down the hill. Calls of, "On to Richmond," filled the air as the rare occurrence of the Confederate Army fleeing inspired the men to visions of grandeur. Stopping the men of the 20th Maine was like reining in a wild stallion, but stop they eventually did, coming right up to the 5th Texas Regiment, having cleared the field of two southern regiments already. They had passed by the front of the 83rd Pennsylvania and were now in front of the 44th New York. Scattered behind them were hundreds of Confederate prisoners while many more had escaped into the hills.

"Colonel Chamberlain, what are your orders, sir?" Ellis Spear gasped, coming up to his superior. He was the first captain to report in.

"Fall back to our original position, Ellis. We have cleared the field, but now we need to return, for Little Round Top is undefended. We are still the sole protectors of the left flank."

"Very good sir, what about the prisoners?" Captain Spear was flush with excitement.

"Put together a detail to have them escorted to the rear."

"Excellent show, sir, excellent show." Captain "Pap" Clark said, beaming as he checked in for orders a few moments later, having performed admirably in charge of the right flank of the 20th. "A right wheel—outstanding decision, sir."

"Captain Clark, put together a detail of men to help the drummer boys with the wounded, both ours and theirs." Chamberlain replied, looking down and absently noting that he still held a sword in one hand and a revolver in the other. He tucked them both into his belt. "Emmett, stay with me," he said, limping back the way they'd come.

"Colonel Chamberlain, were you hit?" Emmett questioned, noting the bloody boot.

"Not enough to mention." Chamberlain responded without slowing his pace.

Chamberlain's injury caused Emmett to think about Daniel, lying dead on the hill above with a smashed skull. The adrenalin of battle had flushed the image of his brother's bloody face from his mind temporarily, but now the pain came flooding back. "Sir, permission to tend to my brother, Daniel." Emmett said.

Chamberlain paused in the middle of the carnage and looked at Emmett with concern. "Was he injured?"

"He was killed, sir."

"I am sorry to hear that." Chamberlain said, putting a hand on the boy's shoulder and patting it awkwardly. "I am very sorry to hear that. We will make sure that he is given a proper burial. Go to him."

Emmett picked his way back through the butchery all around, the dead splayed in every imaginable pose, many shot in the back. The wounded, Union and Confederate alike, called for help, begging for water, screaming in agony. He found his brother sitting up, part of his tunic ripped into a strip tied around his head, his eyes wiped clear of the caked blood. "You're alive?" Emmett was incredulous. He wondered if this were some trick of his imagination, and wiped at his own eyes as if to clear them.

"It would seem so," Daniel croaked. "Do you have any water?"

Emmett fumbled with his canteen, holding out the container. His brother's hands, brown with more dried blood, shook as he hurried the canteen to his mouth, gulping such that his brother reached out. "Slowly," he said, "Or you'll be sick." He drew back, and Daniel smiled. "You were shot in the head." Emmett said finally.

"You don't need to tell me that."

"Can you walk?" Emmett roused himself to action, realizing that his brother was indeed alive, but badly wounded. "We need to get you back to the hospital."

"I can try." Daniel stood shakily, leaning his weight on his younger brother. They took two tottering steps, Emmett barely able to hold the weight, making him realize that they would need help at this rate. Suddenly, another soldier pulled Daniel's right arm around his own shoulders and lightened the burden. It was Tom Chamberlain. They went about fifty yards, finally waving down two members of the ambulance crew carrying a stretcher.

Emmett followed along with them, sitting with him until a doctor had a chance to unwrap the makeshift bandage and clean out the wound. "You're one lucky soldier."

"How so?" Daniel was not quite sure how being shot in the head was lucky.

"You have a hard head." The doctor said. "Your skull deflected the bullet along the side, tearing a gash the length of your noggin, and knocking you senseless. But other than a few stitches and the need for some red meat to replace the blood loss, you're going to be fine."

Emmett left his brother with the doctor's assurance that everything would be fine, returning to the 20th Maine who had been allowed to fall back slightly, ceding their place to the Pennsylvania Reserve. Many of the men were sleeping, having sunk to the ground immediately upon moving back, lying in repose almost as the dead upon the field had looked, a steady snoring and twitching of arms and legs the only indication they actually lived. Some were heating coffee over fires, unable to sleep, the horror of the day returning in vivid images to their minds, just as silent or more so than the snoring men beside them. A few crunched on the hardtack in their kits, pensively staring into the flickering flames of the fire.

Colonel Chamberlain was in conversation with several officers from his own regiment, as well as those of the Pennsylvania Reserve, when Emmett approached, but looking up he interrupted the meeting. "Tom told me you found your brother?"

"He was alive, sir." He said, his voice hollow, so deep the exhaustion coupled with relief. "He was shot in the head, but will be back on his feet soon."

"I am glad for you." Chamberlain's eyes found those of his brother, who was drinking coffee by the fire. The two exchanged small, fleeting smiles. "I couldn't imagine the horror of losing one brother, much less two."

They were interrupted by the arrival of Colonel Rice, who talked of the wound Strong Vincent had sustained that day. "He was with the 16th Michigan when they were overrun by the enemy, and he jumped into the breach to rally the troops. In the process, a bullet mangled his thigh leaving a horrible mess for the surgeons to deal with. I doubt that there is much they will be able to do for him."

"He will be missed," Chamberlain agreed. "Men of his valor are not made every day."

"It will be a sad passing," observed Colonel Joseph Fisher, leader of the Pennsylvanians.

"For the moment, I will take charge of the 3rd Brigade," Colonel Rice continued. "Thanks to your efforts, things appear to be in order here. The Pennsylvania Reserve is here to bolster your position. Continue to see to the wounded and prisoners."

Before he had left, however, a messenger arrived, handing a note to Colonel Rice. He read it carefully, and then read it again before looking up. "Apparently General Sykes does not share my view. He is worried about the Confederates massing on the larger hill, Round Top, and then flanking our position from there. We must take Round Top, post haste and by night. Does anybody know what sort of presence the enemy holds there?"

Chamberlain shook his head wearily. "I know that the 15th Alabama came through that way to attack our left flank earlier. After we routed them, many fled in that direction. I would think that, at the least, they would have reassembled there. Other than that, I don't know."

Colonel Rice swung his attention to one of the other officers. "Colonel Fisher, do you think you and your boys from Pennsylvania can occupy that hill?"

Although almost fifty years of age, Joseph Fisher looked like a schoolboy who had pasted a thick black, bushy mustache to his thin, fresh face. He hesitated at this request. "We have just arrived on the scene and do not know the terrain, sir. It is black as Sam Hill out there. I fear we would be bumping into things and alert the Rebs to our presence. We would be happy to support another regiment that knows where they are going." As if to refute his argument, the full moon emerged from behind a passing cloud, bathing them all in its soft white glow.

"I don't have anybody else, Colonel. That is why I'm asking you." Colonel Rice spat out the words, slowly and one by one, underlining his impatience.

"Again sir," Fisher wheedled, not wanting to lead his men into a Confederate ambush. "I would plead ignorance of the terrain, which might leave us wandering in the dark. Perhaps we could support Colonel Chamberlain and the men from Maine in this endeavor?"

Colonel Rice shook his head snorting, disgusted with the passive nature of the man, but at the same time, wanting to send a warrior and not a follower. "Colonel Chamberlain?" He said wearily, his eyes on the flickering fire, not daring to look the exhausted soldier in the eye.

Chamberlain looked around the camp at his men, all but a few of who now slept soundly in the dark shadows. They had been 400 strong at the beginning of the day, but that number was now roughly half. Of those still present, almost every single one of them had some kind of wound or injury, clumsy bandages wrapping arms, legs, hands, necks, and every conceivable body part. Water had arrived, and after slaking their thirst, some of the men had made vague attempts to wash the grime from their faces.

Deep snoring rent the night air, the noise of exhausted men. They were men who knew fatigue, men who worked hard, long hours, men whose livelihoods held ordinary danger, but was this not too much? So many of these men from Maine who had been entrusted to him for safekeeping had already fallen, and now he was being asked to endanger those who had survived today's ordeal?

"Colonel Chamberlain?"

"The 20th Maine will be happy to defend Pennsylvania if Colonel Fisher decides they would rather not." Chamberlain replied doggedly.

The bitter words hung in the still air, the three colonels and various officers silenced by the simple rebuke. Finally, Fisher opened his mouth as if to reply, but then thought better of it, saying nothing.

"Very well then," Colonel Rice finally said. "See to it."

Emmett did as asked, his body screaming at the thought of returning to fight their way up an unknown tree-covered hill in the darkness. It took ten minutes for the officers to pull the men of the 20th Maine from their deep slumber and back to the reality of their duty as defenders of the extreme left flank of the Union Army. Slowly, they began to gather around Chamberlain, who stood next to the regimental colors.

"Gentlemen," Chamberlain began, pausing and looking around at the worn faces. "Friends. Neighbors. You accomplished a great feat today. *We* met the gray tide and turned it back. There were no officers and soldiers today, just us men doing the job we were asked. I saw Corporal Livermore over there putting his farming skills to work as he plowed down the hill, tilling the land of Confederates with his bayonet. You made the people of Milo proud today, son, because you had a job, and you got it done." Various men nodded their agreement, while those around Livermore punched and pushed him. "Lieutenant Melcher...Holman, you nigh on made me cry when you came to me today and asked if you could advance to help the wounded, as it was you that made me see clearly what needed to be done. If you ever want to cross the river from Topsham and become a college teacher, I will help you in any way I can, after we finish this here job of work before us."

"What job is that?" The voice came from beyond the fire,

the words hurried together and anxious, shot through with their speaker's anxiety that their task was not yet complete.

Chamberlain looked around at their gaunt faces, eyes shining in the moonlight, grizzled, hard men, and seasoned men, his men. "We whipped the Confederates real good today, but now we have to finish the job so we can all go home."

"That can wait until tomorrow, can't it?"

Chamberlain shook his head and then raised it skyward, a look of pain flitting briefly across his face. "Colonel Rice has come to me with a request from central command. They have asked us to seize control of the summit of Round Top over to the southwest. I cannot order any of you to come with me after what you have been through these past few hours." Chamberlain paused, thinking of how a year before he'd just finished the spring semester, sending his students home for the summer, and now many of those students stood around him, soldiers he was asking to go far above and beyond their duty. "I'd sure enjoy some company."

"Why can't somebody else go? We've had a hell of a day."

Chamberlain contemplated this, listening to the hum of insects in the air, the crackle of a nearby fire. "I reckon if you want to get the job done, you get men from Maine to do it, is all."

"I'd be proud to go with you, sir." Lieutenant Melcher spoke, still flush with the pride of being singled out by Chamberlain.

"Personally," Sergeant Tozier commented, a wry grin breaking out on his face. "I was staring at the hill over there all day thinking it sure would be a nice place for a midnight picnic. I guess I'm in."

The men of the 20th Maine grunted their assent, many adding their own comments about paying back the Reb who had shot at them today, or remarking on how they'd dropped their watch out that way earlier and would like to take a look for it.

"Very well then. Fix your bayonets if you bothered removing them. We must go quietly, so there will be no firing of weapons, none at all. If the enemy realizes that we are but 200 men, all will be lost. Loose formation as there will be many obstacles in our path to navigate, but keep the man on your left and right in sight so we don't get too separated."

Soon Emmett was jogging to keep up with the long strides of Chamberlain, who seemed to glide over the rocks and roots and around the trees that blocked their path. "Sir," he asked quietly, "how many Rebs are up there?"

"I have no idea, Emmett."

Many more questions hovered on Emmett's lips, but he managed to contain himself. The moon kept dancing behind the clouds. When it burst through, however, it did so with a blast of light illuminating the regiment all around, then disappearing just as capriciously and returning them to their isolation. It reminded Emmett of the summer when he was eight, the first time he was allowed to go possum and coon hunting with Daniel and William. Their old hound dog would lead them through the moonlight, searching for these nocturnal animals. William would carry the only gun, Daniel and Emmett being armed with crude spears that were effective only if they cornered the beasts. There would be frogs croaking, as near the ponds was always a good place to find possum and coon. It wasn't all that different slipping through the Pennsylvanian woods, except for the simple fact that they were now hunting men, men who, unlike game, could and would fight back, and ferociously.

Round Top was different terrain, more heavily forested, and they spread out in a rough skirmish line, picking their way through and around and all the while constantly climbing. A burst of rifle shots abruptly marred the dark and silent night, shots that appeared to have been fired wildly and in panic. The 20th Maine pressed on, and a breathless message was delivered to Chamberlain that ten Confederates had been captured. They were part of the 15th Alabama, a badly decimated regiment, found sleeping and exhausted without even a picket set for watch.

As they flitted through the shadows near the summit, Emmett became aware that they were moving in and among shapes of men who he realized were not of their regiment. Momentary terror overtook him, but before the Southerners knew what was happening, the men from Maine had surrounded them, bayonets pressed to their throats, not a word being spoken as one by one the Rebels dropped their weapons. A few questions revealed that they were a forward detail sent by General Hood to reconnoiter the hill in preparation for his division to occupy it. The 20th Maine had arrived just in time to command Round Top.

It was quiet on the hill, almost serene, and one could start to disbelieve the events of the previous day. Emmett closed his eyes, sleeping as peacefully as he had in some time.

Around midmorning of July 3rd, the regiment was relieved and allowed to retire from the field for some much needed rest. They passed by their previous day's defensive position atop Little Round Top, continuing on to the center of the entire Union Army. They were positioned safely behind the front line for what promised to be a day of rest. They had no sooner settled in than the calm air of hills and valleys was rent by a mighty thundering of hundreds of cannons, as the Confederate Army began a new offensive. Most of the men, dog-tired, slept on, huddled like corpses behind a stone wall, their snoring made mute by the unending barrage.

An urgent tugging on his arm woke Emmett from a deep sleep. "What is it?" He opened his eyes to see Chamberlain standing over him.

"I am going forward to view the upcoming battle. Come along in case I need to send a message." Chamberlain spoke impatiently, ready to be on the way.

Emmett noticed that the Union Artillery had ceased, the oppressive silence an indicator that the infantry battle was ready to begin. With a groan, he rolled to his feet.

"I brought your rifle in case we're needed. Don't forget your cartridge case." Chamberlain held out the Enfield for Emmett to take. "Follow me." And with that, they moved from the safety of the rear to the front and center, the very place that General Meade had predicted the attack would come. They took up an observation point just behind the 19th Maine, Chamberlain being an acquaintance of its commander, Colonel Heath.

There was a copse of trees, seven or eight of them, just out in front to one side, and further north ran a stone wall at an angle. The day was as hot as it had been all summer, the sun scorching through the scattered clouds, the air still and deathly. As Emmett watched, a mile across the open fields to the west a line of gray appeared fanning out until it covered an expanse a mile across. The soldiers were so far away that he could barely tell they were moving until he then saw more waves emerging from the distant cover and realized they were marching steadily forward. The attack was beginning. As if to mark the momentous occasion, the Union Artillery resumed its grisly work, sending shells screaming through the air, some finding their target and tearing great holes in the enemy lines, but many overshooting or falling short at that great distance. Still, the gray soldiers marched onward. After a few minutes, the smoke from the barrage cloaked the Confederates in a protective haze, hiding them from view. Soon, they began to materialize at a distance of about 400 yards, and the infantry began to fire, their rifles adding to the carnage of the cannons. Emmett heard Chamberlain murmur that they'd doubled up the canister shot, the effect murderous to the Confederates at this close distance. They still presented a solid line of gray, but stretched only half as far as they had at the start, filling the holes by tightening the lines.

The goal seemed to be the copse of trees, and towards that effort the Rebels now broke into a jog, volleys of lead from cannon and rifle cutting them down until Emmett could barely continue watching. "Why don't they go back?" He muttered in vexation. Still, they came on, with the soldiers on their left curving and crossing over in front as they aimed for the very center of the line.

"Those are Pickett's men crossing over." Chamberlain said, recognizing their uniforms and hats. "Old Pete must be in command of this attack." This, Emmett knew, was General James Longstreet, the right hand and warhorse of Robert E. Lee.

From the angled stone wall a group of blue uniforms now retreated in the face of the Confederate onslaught, and the 19th Maine was called in to support. Other Union regiments moved forward, and the last momentum of the Rebels was halted. Finally, a ragged retreat began, the Rebels struggling to pick their way back across the field around their numerous fallen comrades, some dead, many gravely wounded.

"That should crush their spirit." Chamberlain said, as appalled at the senseless slaughter as Emmett. "We best be getting back to the regiment in case we are called to action."

Late that afternoon, a note arrived from Brigadier General Adelbert Ames, the former Colonel of the 20th Maine. Chamberlain read part of it to the men as they waited for further orders. *"I am very proud of the 20th and its present Colonel. I did*

216

want to be with you and see your splendid conduct in the field. God bless you and the dear old regiment...My love to the officers and men.'' The men waved their hats and gave their former colonel three cheers, all well aware that his harsh discipline and dedication to drilling had been a major factor in their exemplary conduct in battle the day before.

Chapter Twelve

July 18, 1863

My dear Fanny,
We are on the pursuit—5th Corps in the advance—Griffin's Division leading of course—and the casualties of the service have brought me in command of the famous old "Third Brigade" now more famous still from its heroic conduct at Gettysburg....
You are witnessing some rather unpleasant scenes in the city now I judge. I am sorry you happened to be there. Don't you think you are staying away rather too long from home? I should imagine you should wish to see the children. Lord knows I miss them dearly.
You can do as you choose about going home. I had a note from Father saying that Cousin D. was failing and that you had better go home. But do as you wish. What in the world can you have been doing in New York? Not writing me letters that much I know!
-L^6

August 10, 1863

Emmett glanced out the window of the train car as they passed Portsmouth, New Hampshire, heading north. It was hard to believe that just a year earlier he had been crossing this same bridge heading south, a mere boy from Brewer who had never been out of the state before. He had grown taller in that time, becoming sturdier of build and more muscular. There was an almost invisible reddish fuzz over his upper lip and on his chin, and his voice had grown deeper. An observer might look on the pleasant features and broad shoulders and see a fine young man, wondering perhaps at the serious expression and at the deep shadows under the green eyes. These physical changes were nothing compared to his growing intellectual and emotional maturity. Under the tutelage of Chamberlain, Emmett was becoming better spoken, better read—and more importantly, thoughtful and curious. A year earlier he had shown up on Chamberlain's doorstep a frightened orphan, but the battlefield had forced him to become decisive, organized, and confident. He had metamorphosed into a soldier, growing up quickly, his only choice in order to survive.

"Looks like this war is finally starting to go our way." Daniel commented, laying down the newspaper that Emmett had shared with him. The two were traveling with Colonel Chamberlain, but planned on spending only a night in Brunswick before continuing up to Brewer, the hometown neither had seen in some time.

"Quite something about Grant capturing Vicksburg the same day we beat ole Bobby Lee." Emmett turned to his brother, noting the bandage still wrapped around his head. Daniel had been given leave for two weeks to further recover from his head injury, and then would continue on with his enlistment.

"Thirty thousand prisoners? What are they gonna do with all of them, do you suppose?"

Emmett shook his head to show he had no idea. "I can't even imagine what that many men would look like."

"There was almost twice that dead and wounded at Gettysburg by the time we were all done there, if you include the Rebs with our own." Daniel had been spared many of the horrors of the aftermath of the battlefield, but had experienced his own gruesomeness in the hospital.

"To think that both victories came on July 4th? Independence Day? It must be some kind of sign." Emmett was well aware of the superstitions of soldiers who believed in omens and carried talismans, and sometimes visited the Gypsy fortunetellers who followed every army.

"We shouldn't have let Lee get away with his army. We should have trapped them before they could cross the river. Then it would have been a real victory." Daniel seemed personally affronted that the Army of the Potomac had let the Army of Northern Virginia escape back across the Potomac to fight another day. "If we'd just given chase, we coulda trapped them right up against the river and finished the job."

"I don't know that we were in any position to chase anybody." Emmett said. He was remembering the aftermath of the battle, the days after Gettysburg as they attempted to bury the dead in the pouring rain. There had been almost as many horses and mules killed as soldiers, with many of the presumed dead discovered to be still alive, and many of the wounded carried off to the makeshift field hospitals, dying quicker than they could be buried. Sometimes he thought he could still smell the putrid reek of decaying human flesh, still hear the moaning and wailing of the wounded.

"I bet 'Unconditional Surrender' Grant would have gone after them scalawags." Daniel quipped.

"He sure does seem to be whipping them Rebels good out West," Emmett agreed.

An hour later they were approaching Brunswick, Emmett waking Chamberlain who'd been sleeping several rows back. He had come down with malaria in late July, having fought the symptoms for several weeks after the battle of Gettysburg as they pursued Lee's army back to Virginia but finally succumbing to the disease when the action had come to a standstill. As their leave had been granted with unusual dispatch, they fully expected to surprise Fanny who had only recently returned from New York City.

Emmett breathed in deeply as he stepped off the train in this small town he was coming to know in all its seasons. He had forgotten how clear the air in Maine could be. He had become used to the mugginess that gathered in the Maryland and Virginia valleys and bottomlands, the air so thick that the act of breathing was like chewing molasses. They had stepped off the train to a shining bright day, the sky just as blue as it could be, not a hint of a cloud, not a shred of humidity.

"What's town like?" Daniel wondered, nodding his head down Main Street, a wide, dirt road to the north. They could see several church spires rising high into the sky, and a huge redbrick mill dominated the far end of the street where it crossed the Androscoggin River.

"I haven't been down that way once, the two times I been here," Emmett confessed.

"We might need to get a hack." Chamberlain spoke for the first time since waking up, his skin pale from the battle with exhaustion and malaria.

"Colonel Chamberlain!" A bookish young man of mid-twenties strode towards them. "What a pleasure to have you home. Especially after your stunning exploits at Gettysburg." The news had come home to Brunswick first in a trickle, and then in a rush, of the victory of their very own at Little Round Top.

"John Furbish. It is good to see you as well." Chamberlain nodded weakly, taking the offered hand. "This is my aide, Emmett Collins, and his brother, Daniel."

"What brings you home from the war? You're not wounded, are you?" Furbish asked, noting the pale demeanor, as well as the bandage wrapped around Daniel's head.

"A touch of malaria," Chamberlain confessed. "Also, I am the executor of Captain Badger's estate, so I thought I could kill two birds with one stone, so to speak."

"Shame about poor Joseph, but he had a full life." The young man's eyes clouded momentarily in pain.

"Well, here is Professor Chamberlain, back from saving the niggers." They all turned at the cantankerous words spoken by a mean-looking older man with unruly hair and a mustache that curled up on either side of his face like a handlebar. He was apparently on the platform to catch the train as it continued north. "How many men did you kill in Gettysburg to give freedom to the darkies?"

"Leave it alone, Gleason." Furbish tried to intervene between them. "Don't you worry about him, Colonel Chamberlain. He's just one of the copperheads, making a lot of noise around town, all the while doing nothing."

"Don't you care a whit about your country?" Daniel spat hotly at the man. "I got shot in the head at Gettysburg trying to protect it while you were safely here in Maine complaining."

"By protect, you mean killing your fellow countrymen?" The man cackled, as if this were somehow funny.

Furbish took Chamberlain's arm and guided him off the platform, while Emmett grabbed his brother and dragged him behind, glaring back at the man who spit tobacco juice at them as they walked away.

"My wagon is right outside if you want a ride home, Colonel?"

"That would be greatly appreciated." Chamberlain walked slowly, his breath ragged. Furbish seemed to be bursting with questions, but, seeing this hometown hero's obvious weakness, had the courtesy to refrain from asking them. He did go on with local news and gossip, that Leonard Townsend had been elected town clerk, and that they had had their first military draft looking for fifty soldiers. Thirty-five of those chosen had some sort of disability, while twenty-six men had chosen to pay for a substitute to go in their place, happily handing over the $300 to be able to stay home and tend business. "They even drafted a colored boy, Isaiah Freeman, from up the road." They had been sufficiently brought up to date in the short time it took for the wagon to take them up the hill to the Chamberlain house on Potter Street.

Wyllys was marching about with a stick, playing a game that appeared to have something to do with the military as they clambered out of the wagon. He shielded his eyes to better glimpse who was here, hurriedly dropping the stick, and running down to greet them. "Father," he squealed in joy, grasping onto Chamberlain's leg with a hug. He had grown bigger and more confidant since the last time Emmett had seen him.

"Little Wyllys, you are not quite so little any more, are you?" Chamberlain was unable to pick his son up in his weakened condition, and thus, bent awkwardly to return the hug. "You are practically a man, you've grown so much since I last saw you."

"Will you take me on a pony ride?"

"All in good time, little rascal." Chamberlain tousled the boy's long hair with his hand. "Let me find your mother and sister first."

"You are Emmett." Emmett was surprised by the small girl who appeared as if out of nowhere, his attention having been on the reunion of father and son in front of him. "And who is that with you?"

Emmett nodded his head in agreement, his tongue thick in his mouth. "This is my brother, Daniel."

"I remember you visiting last winter, but you look different. Older."

"So do you," Emmett muttered.

"I am Daisy." The little girl said very matter-of-factly. "That is my father," she added, pointing a thin finger at Chamberlain. "I hear that you have been off fighting the Rebels with him?" It was more a question than a statement, and from a small child who did not really understand what Rebels were, or what war was, only that adults talked in tones either hushed or very loud indeed when discussing these two things.

Emmett again nodded his head mutely.

"Have you killed any men?" She asked, obviously repeating words she'd heard from an adult spoken to a returning soldier.

"There is my beautiful Daisy!" Chamberlain called out to his baby girl, saving Emmett a reply. "That is the prettiest dress I have ever seen." He exclaimed, limping to her side. "Your mother must have just purchased that in New York City."

Emmett couldn't stop thinking about Daisy's question regarding the men he'd tried to kill. First was when they'd been ambushed on the telegraph line, and then again when he thought his brother had been cut down on Little Round Top. He was pretty sure the man on the other side of that stone wall had gone to his Maker.

"Will you play a game with me, Father?" Daisy asked in the same serious manner.

"Not yet," Wyllys lectured. "Let him say hello to Momma first, and then he needs to take me for a pony ride, and THEN he can play a game with you."

"I want to go for a pony ride, too," Daisy whined.

Fanny stood in the doorway of the house, watching the domestic reunion unfold in front of her and not feeling quite a part of it. She was completely surprised by this visit, having just recently heard of her husband's huge success at Gettysburg, and his blossoming reputation. Fanny was not quite sure how she felt about being married to a hero, a man already idolized by her neighbors, when she also felt deserted and neglected by this hero. She was angry with him for his obvious weakened state, knowing that he must be injured in some way, as he moved stiffly and had made no move to pick up either child. This anger was mixed with love, sympathy, and concern, and she was not sure how strong she could be.

"You are a sight for sore eyes," breathed Chamberlain, transfixed, as always after an absence, by his wife's beauty, her vitality. "Come out here, my lady, so that this brave knight and his squire might have a chance to view your grandeur."

"Why are you home?" Fanny asked, afraid to cross the threshold of the doorway, fearful to come out, terrified that once she did she would discover her husband had been maimed in some horrible way.

Chamberlain chuckled. "I would venture to guess that means you have not gotten my letters. I was sending them here, and then heard you were in New York City and sent letters there. Finally, I learned you were home again. You are one difficult lady to find!" He wagged a finger in mock chastisement. "But then just a few days ago I received a two-week pass to come home, and here you are."

"Have you been wounded?" Fanny asked, noting the paleness of his skin and his slightly stooped carriage.

"Just a touch of malaria, my dear." Chamberlain again chuckled. "Nothing that your cooking won't fix right up. Although I am sure that the process could be sped up if you would deign to give your loving husband a hug and kiss?"

"You are too weak even to pick up your children." She chided him, relenting slightly.

"I will pick them both up at once if that will earn me a kiss."

"I went down to New York City hoping to see you, thinking that maybe you would be able to get away and come for a visit, but then I got caught up in the most dreadful riots." Fanny had still not moved an inch, remaining aloof, wanting to defend her absence, share the fears that she had to live with every day. "I don't know that I am really cut out to be the wife of a soldier."

Chamberlain decided to ignore the last remark, instead, clucking his tongue. "Oh, you poor girl. You were staying at the St. Germaine Hotel?"

"Yes, and the most horrible people were outside protesting the draft. I was afraid to leave the building when it became violent. They finally called in the army to break things up, and there was a melee, shooting and killing. We weren't allowed to go anywhere at that point. We couldn't even get a letter out, not until just a few days ago, so you should have one waiting for you back at your regiment." Her rambling words trailed off, and she took a hesitant step towards her husband, eyes downcast.

That was all he needed, as he pulled her into a lingering embrace that attempted to do away with all of the lonely nights, missed conversations, the fear and longing, the unfulfilled desire.

After a moment, suddenly conscious of their audience, the two broke apart. "Your husband, my dear lady, has been put in charge of the 3rd Brigade as of late, and there is even talk of promoting him to Brigadier General." Chamberlain boasted. "Daisy, will you and Wyllys take Emmett and Daniel up to the spare room?"

"I know the way, sir." Emmett reminded Chamberlain. "After we drop our bags we might take a walk in town, if you won't be needing me for anything?"

"That would be fine." Chamberlain dismissed the boy. When the children had disappeared up the stairs with the men, he turned back to his wife. "My dear sweet girl," he said. "I am so sorry that this troubles you so, but it is also a sore trial for me. To go to bed at night without your warmth next to me, to wake alone in the morning, to not hear your voice speaking or singing is of the most incredible difficulty. Without your presence my days are dismal and bleak even when the sun is shining. Sometimes I can conjure an image of you or a memory will flit through my mind, and my spirit will temporarily brighten, but all too often it is like those three long years we spent apart before we married." Chamberlain spoke into the top of her head as she had now pressed her face into his chest, inhaling deeply the aroma of her husband's body.

"I will try harder to be a good wife," Fanny whispered. "Or at least to hold my tongue."

Chamberlain brushed a curl sideways from her upturned face and bent slightly to kiss her.

Daniel had suggested that they take the children for a pony ride, to give Joshua and Fanny some time alone, and Emmett agreed enthusiastically, telling the Chamberlains they'd welcome a chance to stretch their legs after the long train ride.

"Hector is still the king rooster, but he's being challenged by Achilles who we might have to sell now that he's gettin older, that's what Mamma Deb said anyways." Wyllys rambled as they crossed the backyard to saddle the pony. Mamma Deb was his aunt who had been watching them while his father was at war and mother in New York City. "Victoria, Anne, and Elizabeth are still layin the most eggs, but Hester, Gladys, and Abigail have been helpin out quite some bit as of late."

Emmett and Daniel put both children up on the pony together, solving the problem of who got to go first. They walked the children across the Bowdoin campus, wondering which building Chamberlain had worked in, but the children were too young to be of any help in that regard. They circled around the backside of the First Parish Church, traveling down Park Row behind the Mall, a grassy flat space in the middle of town. They went into the Lufkin store and Daniel and Emmett bought some penny candy, which they happily shared with Daisy and Wyllys. There seemed to be just about anything you could want here, walls of high shelves filled with tins containing herbs, medicines, cigars, coffee, and a variety of other supplies. There was a coffee grinder on a table by the counter, with more dry goods scattered over tables in the center of the room. Everything was carefully marked with name and price on stiff bright paper tags. They walked by another store called Furbish's, connecting the name to the man they'd seen on the train platform who had given them a lift. It appeared to be new, the gleaming-red brick building in stark contrast to many of the worn wooden structures around it. Daniel's eyes lit up when they came to the boarding house with a tavern on the corner of Pleasant and Main Street, but he made no mention to Emmett, knowing that there would be no opportunity for a drink during their one day stay in Brunswick. Finally, as the shadows lengthened, they went back up Main Street, returning to the Chamberlain home.

"Thank you for the pony ride." Daisy said in her grave, grown-up, seven-year-old voice.

"Father used to take us for pony rides all the time," Wyllys chimed in. "But he ain't been around much."

Emmett realized that these children had lost their father to the war, the same as him, if only for a time at least. The difference was that their father made the occasional brief visit home, and would return for good at the conclusion of the war. "You both are excellent riders," he told the children, missing his father, who had, a lifetime ago it seemed, paraded a young Emmett around town proudly on horseback.

"Can you stay here when Father has to go back to the war?" Wyllys asked.

*****

The next morning, as Emmett and Daniel rode the train to Brewer, he felt an odd sense of dislocation, and finally posed the question that had been nagging at him. "Do you think you'll come back to Brewer after the war is over?"

"I reckon so," Daniel replied. "Don't rightly know what else I would do."

"I don't imagine I will." Emmett said quietly, already feeling like he no longer belonged, and he wasn't even there yet.

"What will you do?"

"I don't know."

The first order of business upon arrival was to deliver a letter from a nineteen-year-old Brewer boy who had been mortally wounded at Gettysburg. Emerson Bradford had spent the last two days of his life on a cot beside Daniel in the hospital, dictating a letter to his father, begging Daniel to personally bring the note to his family if possible, and to tell them he had died bravely. The Bradford's were a seafaring family who lived on the Penobscot River, only a few miles from the Collins homestead. Daniel had known him growing up, although they had never seen much of each other, Daniel working in the brickyards and Emerson working for his father on the river. The house was a grand white building in the Federal style, Captain Ezra Bradford having become quite wealthy shipping lumber. It was an imposing two-story house with an open porch at the front held up by four thin pillars with ornate detail. The door had an elliptical fanlight, an intricate pattern depicting a sailing ship.

There was a doorknocker, and Daniel lifted the iron ring, giving two solid thumps. They could hear footsteps, and then a well-dressed man of about forty-five opened the door, his suit jacket barely able to contain his prodigious body.

"Captain Bradford?

"Yes." The man raised one furry eyebrow, snow white on his weather-beaten face. "Are you lads soldiers?"

"Yes, sir. My name is Daniel Collins, and this is my brother Emmett. Our father was John Collins, from down the Post Road here."

"Did you know my boy?"

"I was in the hospital with Emerson after he was wounded at Gettysburg."

Captain Bradford stepped to the side, gesturing them in. "Please, come in. We were about to have tea. You will join us."

A woman came from the rear of the home into the large semi-circular parlor carrying a tray with a teapot, as well as some cheese and bread and butter, some teacakes. She was dressed in a plaid hoop dress that dwarfed her thin body, her fragility in stark contrast to that of her husband's mountainous frame. She froze, shooting a fleeting glance at Captain Bradford. "You're the Collins boys aren't you, fresh from the war?"

"Yes, ma'am. We are both, I mean we are, I am Daniel Collins, and this is my brother, Emmett. We got a two-week furlough from the 20th Maine." Daniel was flustered, suddenly realizing the enormity of his task. Bringing a deathbed letter to the parents had seemed noble at the time. Now, it only seemed dirty, in a petty little way, and he wished that he could just run back out the door.

"Please, sit down." Mrs. Bradford gestured towards two armchairs, European in style, made of mahogany, embroidered with cushions of green silk. "I will bring two more cups."

She returned almost immediately, pouring tea for them, making them each take two sugar cubes, as well as a pastry and a thick slice of bread slathered with butter. Emmett and Daniel ate and drank, the food lying heavier in their bellies at each bite.

"The papers would have us believe every battle is a victory, but it appears as if this may truly have been the case at Gettysburg?" Captain Bradford inquired, awkward and out of place in his own home, his voice booming in the prim parlor.

"We gave them Rebs hell, excuse me, ma'am," Daniel blushed red to the roots of his hair. "We sure beat them real good, sir, that we did. We had the high ground, and they just kept coming at us, and we kept beating them back. It was a close call for awhile on Little Round Top, but Colonel Chamberlain led us in a charge that could be a poem, it was so beautiful."

"The Chamberlains are a good family." Captain Bradford attested, nodding his head sagely. "Your Colonel Chamberlain has made them right proud."

"I brought a letter from your son, sir, that he wrote in the hospital." Daniel reached into his haversack, pulling the crumpled envelope out.

Mrs. Bradford made a move to rise, but Captain Bradford, proving quite agile for his size, beat her to it.

"Does it say when he's coming home?" Mrs. Bradford asked in a thin voice, her hand trembling as it held the teacup.

Captain Bradford stepped to his wife's chair, resting his hand gently, but firmly, on her shoulder. "Gladys, you know that Emerson isn't coming home."

"Not until after the war, you mean?" Her hand shook and tea spilled onto the Oriental rug under their feet.

"Darling, he is dead. Emerson is dead. He died in Gettysburg, Pennsylvania on July 7th." Captain Bradford spoke patiently, but his frustration was obvious.

The cup dropped from her hand, spilling down over her dress, bouncing on the rug, unbroken until she stepped on it rushing from the room.

"I am sorry about this lads, but if you will excuse me?" Captain Bradford put the letter into his pocket to be forgotten—never to be opened—never read, the last words of their son too bitter a pill for them to swallow. He followed his wife out of the room, asking the Collins to show themselves out.

"You reckon we should go visit the cemetery?" Emmett asked his brother as they walked down the road, both lost in thought over what had just transpired.

"This war sure affects more people than just soldiers, don't it?" Daniel said, thinking that the only person to care if he died was walking next to him right now.

"It certainly is a strange thing," Emmett agreed. "How about we just go to the house, and then visit Ma in the morning."

As they approached their childhood home, they could see a broken window, Emmett not having thought to close the shutters before leaving the previous summer. Snow and rain had been driven into the parlor, soaking the cushions of several chairs, pooling on the hardwood floor, causing the boards to buckle and crack. Mold clung to the damp stuffing, peppering the wet wood, and causing Daniel to begin sneezing violently. Dust coated everything in a fine layer, tiny footprints trailing through the rooms. A family of raccoons had taken up residence in one of the bedrooms, their pungent smell filling the small house. Daniel walked to the tintypes, wiping the front of one clean with his sleeve, and then setting it back down.

"This isn't really our home anymore, is it?"

"That's how I felt when I left last year," Emmett agreed. "Without Ma and Pa, it's not the same, sort of like visiting neighbors."

"You suppose there's a train going south tonight?"

Emmett shook his head. "I think we done missed the last one. Beside, we need to visit Ma in the cemetery."

They built a fire in the back yard, warming the corned beef, beans, and apple dumpling that Fanny had packed for them to take. As they lounged by the fire, they began sharing childhood memories, until they fell asleep under the stars, a bed more comfortable to them now than what lay just inside. In the morning they picked wildflowers, leaving them at the cemetery, bidding their mother and Brewer goodbye.

They had several hours to wait at the depot for the next southbound train, Emmett buying a copy of *The Whig & Courier*, the local newspaper. He was reading accounts of the pursuit of the Army of Northern Virginia, the campaign he'd just recently been a part of, when a boy interrupted him by clearing his throat.

"You're Emmett Collins, ain't ya?" The boy was taller than Emmett, his body thin and angular, and his skin soft. Carefully combed brown hair topped his head, with blue eyes that were curious. "Are you really a soldier?"

"I am part of Colonel Chamberlain's staff, yes."

"You ain't but fifteen years old. I was in school with you back a few years. Elias Bickmore, you remember me?"

Emmett suddenly realized that this boy who looked still wet behind the ears was his peer, that they were the same age. "I remember you. We went fishing together a few times."

"If you're part of Chamberlain's staff, you must've been at Gettysburg. Did you fight?"

Emmett thought about firing to kill when he believed Daniel to be dead, he remembered running down the rocky slopes and clubbing a man in the head with his gun butt. The smell of the dead drifted to his nostrils, the screeching of the wounded pierced his ears, and the fear clenched his bowels tight. "Yeah, I saw some fighting."

"If you're with the Colonel, you probably have the best

view in the house." The boy said excitedly.

Emmett thought about his place at Chamberlain's side, a view not from the top of some hill or from the rear of the lines, but up close and personal as they led the regiment into the fray. "We generally get to see the action up pretty close."

"My Pa won't let me sign up, says I'm not old enough yet. How'd you get your Pa to let you join up?"

Emmett thought about his father dying in Virginia and about his mother's gravestone in the cemetery. "My Pa didn't have much to say about it." Emmett was proud to be a soldier, but he couldn't even begin to explain what it was like, not to this boy who hadn't ever come close to seeing real death and misery. He would never understand what it was like to try to kill somebody, to watch a friend die, to feel the terror of impending fighting.

Chapter Thirteen

January 29, 1864

Dear Fanny,
I am very anxious to hear from you. In fact I am becoming nervous about it.
Please write to me at this address until I notify you of some change. At present I am in the Hospital at Georgetown but shall probably soon be transferred to the city. I want to know if you mean or wish to come and spend a month or two with me. I think I shall be here that length of time as the court I am on is ordered by Sec. of War and I cannot easily be relieved even after I fully recover.
I would like more than I can tell to have you with me and do not you think of the expense for I am sure I can afford to have my own darling with me. And you know I have now over $100 a month extra pay.
At all events do let me hear from you. If you come the sooner the better. The weather is marvelous. How you would enjoy it. If you wish you could bring Daisy.
I can find some good healthy place for you no doubt. But Washington I confess is not particularly distinguished for such places.
But I miss you and could be well content to be here if you were here.
Please write and tell me about it.
In haste
your loving[7]

February 2, 1864

Emmett walked wearily back to his room at 402 13th Street in Washington. The streets were muddy, as the spring rains had come strong, deluges, which pooled in the dirt roads crisscrossing the national capital. Before the rainwater could drain away, passing wagons, troops of soldiers, caissons, and livestock churned the mixture into a thick muck that often mired wagons up to the hub, as if holding them for ransom. He had been here off and on since Chamberlain had again fallen ill with malaria in November. The relapse had necessitated a long recovery and light duties with the consequence that Emmett found himself living alone, with time on his hands, a young man out and about—and very quickly at home in the hustle and bustle that was Washington. The houses of prostitution continued to titillate his imagination, a strange, deep yearning calling to him, but thus far he'd refrained, hearing too many tales of thievery and disease. He did occasionally go to the Willard, nursing a beer at the bar while watching all the powerful people interact around him.

With so much time on his hands, Emmett had taken to volunteering at the Armory Square Hospital, wanting to separate himself from the Georgetown Hospital that Chamberlain was in, so as to not live in his shadow. The hospital had been set up in the old armory on the Mall, just up 7th Avenue from the steamship wharves and the Washington & Alexandria Train Depot. Situated so close to the river and railhead, it welcomed the worst cases of sickness, the most badly injured, as it was closest from the front lines. The final push that made him leave Chamberlain's side was his mentor's developing relationship with a woman who had arrived just in time to share the last few days of her husband's life. As the man had passed in and out of consciousness, Chamberlain shared many conversations with the woman, Mrs. Robinson, supporting her as she faced her husband's death. She was to Chamberlain the female company that he craved, for he had not heard from Fanny even after sending off a multitude of letters begging her to come and visit.

At the hospital, Emmett was given the job of running errands, cleaning, and disposing of bandages and amputated body parts, as well as other menial tasks. There was a muskiness to the ward, the heavy odor of men crammed together, as well as blood and medicine. At first, it had been harder to bear than the aftermath of Gettysburg, but over time Emmett came to not even notice the fetidness. The patients were more comfortable with him than the other nurses and workers, once they realized he was also a soldier, had seen the elephant and that he understood the awfulness of the battlefield. This day he had worked with another volunteer, a fascinating man by the name of Walt Whitman. Whitman had come from Brooklyn to search for his brother, George, whom he'd heard had been badly injured at the battle of Fredericksburg in December of 1862. George had proved to be perfectly healthy, but Walt had since stayed on in Washington, working as an army paymaster and volunteering his time in the area hospitals.

Emmett was holding a damp cloth to the forehead of a feverish soldier from Michigan who had recently had his leg amputated, and as a result, was currently fighting an infection. He watched another volunteer working his way down the long line of cots towards him, moving from patient to patient, handing out pieces of hard candy, taking letters to mail, jotting notes, giving the comfort of touch and talk to the sad, lonely, and often, mortally wounded.

"Hello, son." The man said, approaching. He was burly; with white, unruly hair and a matching beard so generous it could house a family of sparrows. "Is he your kin?" He nodded at the wounded soldier Emmett was tending.

"No, sir." Emmett replied. "I'm just helping out where I'm able. I mop floors. I fetch tobacco and write letters. Mostly, they just want to talk, it seems." He finished with a small shrug of his shoulders.

The man's eyes were tired and drooping, his long forehead lined, the deep sockets of his eyes dwarfing his small nose, all contributing to a kind and tender demeanor. "The same as me, dear boy. My name is Whitman, by the way, Walt."

"Emmett Collins, sir."

"Call me Walt."

"Yes, sir, I mean Walt."

"You are a soldier?" Whitman noted Emmett's uniform.

"I am with the 3rd Brigade, aide to Colonel Chamberlain, recently put in command of the brigade."

"What brings you into the city?" Whitman offered a piece of slightly bitter horehound candy to Emmett, who hesitated, and then took it.

"Colonel Chamberlain has been struggling with fever, and I am along to help him however I can." Before Emmett knew it, he had told Whitman about the death of his parents and brother, his relationship with Chamberlain, including his discomfort around Chamberlain now that he'd befriended the new widow. Whitman just listened, nodding from time to time, seeming to understand that, just like those he tended, the boy had no one to talk to.

The next day dawned bright and hard, a crisp clear day at the end of January, making for a cold walk to the Georgetown Hospital in which Chamberlain had spent the last few weeks recovering. Today he would be leaving the hospital, and Emmett had woken early to make sure that the rooms they were renting downtown were prepared for his arrival. A wagon had been arranged to transport the still-weak Chamberlain to his new residence. The following day he would begin light desk duties handling the backlog of court martials that had accumulated as the war had dragged on. More and more, disgruntled soldiers were attempting to desert, refusing to fight, or plundering property. Mrs. Robinson was already at the hospital when Emmett arrived, having offered to help get Chamberlain settled. When he entered the room, Emmett felt as if he had interrupted a private conversation. To fill the awkward silence, he mentioned his new acquaintance, Walt Whitman.

"Walt Whitman, the poet?" Mrs. Robinson said breathily, eyes raised in either mock horror or disdain.

"He mentioned he'd written some poetry before the war started. He said he's been too busy working at the Army Paymaster Office and volunteering at local hospitals to do much writing lately. Do you know him?" It was Emmett's turn to be surprised that the large, bearded, and genial man he'd met the day before was a famous poet.

"I should say not." Mrs. Robinson said thinly, raising her chin ever so slightly to look down her nose at Emmett.

Chamberlain chuckled. *"The bodies of men and women engirth me, and I engirth them,"* he said, filling the suddenly tense air. *"They will not let me off nor I them till I go with them and respond to them and love them."*

"Don't be so terrible," Mrs. Robinson said, glaring at him. "Those poems are not fit conversation for a lady, or a gentleman for that matter."

"Yet you know what I was quoting," Chamberlain chided, a hidden smile lurking in the corners of his eyes. "Meaning that you have read the works of Mr. Whitman?"

"Of course not." She blustered, realizing that her recognition made clear her lie, but not knowing what else she could say.

Chamberlain let her off the hook, sliding his eyes away from her to Emmett. "Your new friend published a book of poetry a few years back. It was called *Leaves of Grass* and many considered it scandalous in its analysis of men and women. Still, the work is a rather genius bit of writing, as even Ralph Waldo Emerson has attested to."

"He seems to be generous and friendly with the men at the hospital," Emmett murmured, thinking that he would need to read this collection of poems, but knowing better to say that in the present company.

It was only after that they'd settled into their residence, and Mrs. Robinson had excused herself to run some errands before meeting the both of them for dinner, that Chamberlain approached Emmett with a sheet of paper. "I'm sure that you are burning with curiosity about your new friend's poems. I'm sorry to say that I only have this one he wrote about the onset of the war, but I found it very true at its essence. You may not understand its every nuance, but read it over a time or two, and then maybe we will talk about it more. Mr. Whitman is an absolute genius with the pen, whether or not his writing is considered 'appropriate' for polite society."

Emmett took the paper from him with red ears, embarrassed that Chamberlain had been cognizant of his curiosity about the scandalous poems. He sat at the table by the window, reading by the afternoon sunlight streaming through, while Chamberlain retired to his bed to rest from the exertion of the day, his strength still far from returning.

Beat! Beat! Drums! By Walt Whitman

BEAT! beat! drums!—Blow! bugles! blow!
Through the windows—through doors—burst like a ruthless <u>force</u>
Into the solemn church, and scatter the congregation,
Into the school where the scholar is studying,

Leave not the bridegroom quiet—no happiness must he have now
with his bride,
Nor the peaceful farmer any peace, ploughing his field or
gathering his grain,
So fierce you whirr and pound you drums—so shrill you bugles
blow.

Beat! beat! drums!—blow! bugles! blow!
Over the traffic of cities—over the rumble of wheels in the streets;
Are beds prepared for sleepers at night in the houses? no sleepers
must sleep in those beds,
No bargainers' bargains by day—no brokers or speculators—
would they continue?
Would the talkers be talking? would the singer attempt to sing?
Would the lawyer rise in the court to state his case before the
judge?
Then rattle quicker, heavier drums—you bugles wilder blow.

Beat! beat! drums!—blow! bugles! blow!
Make no parley—stop for no expostulation,
Mind not the timid—mind not the weeper or prayer,
Mind not the old man beseeching the young man,
Let not the child's voice be heard, nor the mother's entreaties,
Make even the trestles to shake the dead where they lie awaiting
the hearses,
So strong you thump O terrible drums—so loud you bugles blow.

The great force of the lines was like a river rushing down
the mountain, stopping for no stone or tree, nor the deaths of
Emmett's mother, father, his brother, nor his anguished late night
cries, causing not the merest pause or ripple, drowned out by its
thundering progress, the words stopping the very breath in his
throat. He didn't quite understand what it was saying, but the
sheer power of the words struck him like a blow, leaving him sad,
thrilled, excited, and frustrated all at once. Emmett read the poem
over and over, marveling at the power each word held, and it was
in this moment that he knew that he wanted to be a writer, to grasp
and wield a power which took an innocent form, incarnating and
bringing forth ideas and sentiments so visceral and atavistic that

the ordinary man had no voice to express them.

*****

Several weeks later Whitman invited Emmett out to an evening show at Canterbury Hall. At first, Emmett declined the offer, for no apparent reason that he could think of. The two had seen each other daily at the hospital, chatting idly as they worked, easing the suffering of the patients. "If you've never taken in a variety show, you really should give it a go," Whitman cajoled him.

"I've been." Emmett snapped, not sure why he was upset. "I went to one last year when I was in the city for the first time." He remembered how much fun he'd had, and wondered why he'd declined the offer.

Whitman smiled broadly at him, folding his arms across his chest. "Well then, you know how amusing they are. I won't take no for an answer. Perhaps we should meet at the Metropolitan Hotel, in the lobby at, shall we say, seven p.m.?"

The show was like the one that Emmett had seen at Varieties the previous year, but with more of an Irish theme. There was a juggler with the unusual moniker of Martini Chiriski who amazed, a banjo player, an Irish comedian, and to end, a farce called "The Irish Tutor" that left Emmett laughing uncontrollably in his seat. Just before the farce came a ballet troupe with its famous Bouquet of Beauties, nine stunning ballerinas fluttering around the stage entrancing him with their long legs and revealing costumes.

"Perhaps a drink?" Whitman asked after the show was over. Emmett agreed, and the two of them wandered into the bar at the Metropolitan Hotel just down the street.

"I find it necessary to escape the pain and suffering in the hospitals every once in a while." Whitman said once they were seated, he with a scotch and Emmett with a hard cider.

"Mr. Scott died this afternoon." Emmett said, thinking sadly of a soldier who had spent the last few months fighting an infection from a wound to his thigh.

"It is hard to believe that just a few miles away, hundreds of thousands of soldiers are preparing to wreak mayhem upon each other, and all the while, tens of thousands more struggle for their lives in various hospitals. Yet, men go each night to productions like the one we just attended, as if none of the rest were reality."

"It sure takes you away from the war for a little bit." Emmett said, fondly thinking of the ballerinas floating on their long legs.

"What did you enjoy the most, my boy?" Whitman set his empty glass down, gesturing to the barkeep for it to be refilled.

Emmett colored, claiming the skill of the juggler—five flaming torches in the air! —most impressed him.

"It seems to me that you were entranced by the "Bouquet of Beauties", but perchance I could be wrong." Whitman smiled broadly, and took a mouthful of the scotch, a bit of it dribbling down his chin into the tangled beard below. "It seems that a young man such as yourself would have a girl somewhere, someone to write letters to and what not. Do you have a sweetheart back home?"

"I didn't even know any girls back in Brewer." Emmett stammered. "Didn't even notice them when I was in school, and then there weren't much call to talk to any of them once I was working in the brickyard."

"How about when you went to church on Sunday? Surely you must have seen some pretty girls then?"

"No sir, not that I can remember. It was hard to tell what was there, with all the hoops, dresses, and material. I don't imagine I ever even looked at them."

"So, there is no girl that you dream of?"

Emmett blushed, thinking back to the young prostitute with the honey-colored hair who he still thought about daily, from just the one glimpse on his first time through the capital city. "There is a girl that I think of, but I never met her, and only seen her the once. She's a prostitute named Susannah, over on Maryland Avenue by the Mall. She works for Mary Hall." Emmett blurted out the story while Whitman just nodded his head comfortingly, never once smiling or judging or commenting on the source of his affection.

"She sounds ravishing, one might even say a 'Bouquet of Beauty'." Whitman smiled. "Maybe you should pay her a visit?"

Emmett shook his head in dejection, never thinking he would get up that amount of courage, and Whitman turned the conversation back to the show.

While Emmett and Whitman made small talk over the various acts, Chamberlain was having dinner with Jennie Robinson at the Reynolds House, just a few streets away.

"How is your tripe?" Jennie asked, looking over the small table at the man who had been constantly at her side since her husband's passing only nine days before.

"It is far better than camp food, that I can tell you." Chamberlain replied, smiling across the table at her, the ache at missing his wife somewhat appeased by conversation and a meal with this attractive woman. "How are your rock oysters?"

"Well, as my cousin Sally in Texas would say, it's a 'huckleberry above a persimmon'. We don't have these in New York, not at least inland where I live. Do you have oysters in Maine?"

"Poor man's food, more than anything else." Chamberlain wiped his mustache with the linen provided, taking a careful sip of the red wine in his goblet.

"Have you heard from your wife?"

"Not a word since before I was in the hospital." Chamberlain answered, squirming uncomfortably in his chair. "The mail is so unpredictable. When do you plan on returning home to New York?"

"I have some things to take care of here first," Jennie said with a small smile.

"If I can be of help in settling your affairs, I would be more than happy to do so." The words came out easily from a man who was used to helping others.

The server came and took their plates away, Jennie deciding to have ice cream while Chamberlain had a cup of coffee. The restaurant was crowded with patrons, many single men getting a meal at the end of the day, trekking in before a night on the town, with just a few couples at the tables. "I greatly appreciate all that you have done for me," she said after a few moments of silence, "and couldn't even begin to ask you for more."

Chamberlain appraised the widow over the rim of his coffee cup, watching her eat, the tip of her pink tongue licking dabs of ice cream from the spoon. She smiled at him between each tiny bite, her teeth pearly white and delicate in her mouth. Her eyelashes fluttered when she looked at him, peeking glances as she enjoyed the dessert. He knew that his flirtations with this woman bordered on the inappropriate, that Fanny would be devastated if she witnessed their coy conversations, and that the late Mr. Robinson would turn over in his grave if he were privy to his wife's actions so soon after his death. "You know, Mrs. Robinson, that I am a happily married man."

"Yet you spend your time with me."

"I enjoy your conversation. I enjoy your company. Is it so wrong, I ask myself, for a man and woman to be friends?"

She shook her head, no, and turned abruptly away, her eyes filled with unshed tears. "Death brings people together in strange ways." She said finally.

"And then sends them apart." Chamberlain replied, idly stirring his coffee. "You should go home, Jennie. There is truly nothing more for you here but memories of your husband's passing." He had unthinkingly stretched out a hand toward her own, and then drew it back.

*****

The following evening, Emmett was washing up from a day in the hospital when there was a knock at the door. He pulled his shirt on, and, opening the door, was shocked to find Fanny Chamberlain with two soldiers who had carried her bags. "Mrs. Chamberlain?"

"Don't just stand there, Emmett, let us in. I am sure these gentlemen have something more important to do. Is Lawrence here?"

"He's not back quite yet, but I expect him any moment," Emmett said finally.

"I was surprised that he was not waiting for me at the train station, but these soldiers came to my aid. I suppose this means he didn't get my letter?" Fanny breezed into the room. "Thank you boys, you can leave the bags here." She pulled out a purse and tucked a fifty-cent piece into each palm with a warm smile. She inspected the wallpaper and furniture as the two soldiers pulled the door closed behind them. "What a dismal town this Washington D.C. is," Fanny chattered on. "What have the two of you been doing with yourselves in this dreadful place?"

Emmett mumbled something about being busy volunteering at the hospital, but Fanny appeared to need no reply.

"One would think that the capital of our country would be a little bit grander, but I'm sure we can find something to do. Have you found time to get out into town and enjoy yourselves?"

Emmett was saved a reply as the door opened to reveal a very surprised Joshua Chamberlain frozen in the entryway. "Fanny! How did you get here?" It was a very rare occurrence to see Chamberlain at a loss for words, for he was indeed astonished.

"By train, of course," she said laughing gaily, happy to have stunned him so.

"Well, of course, by train, but...." Chamberlain stammered, stepping forward and wrapping her into his arms, staring intensely down into her eyes. "I guess you did get my letter. I wasn't sure as I hadn't heard back."

"Of course I replied, but I guess somebody sent my letter to the wrong man, and now I suppose some other Colonel is anxiously awaiting the arrival of some woman named Fanny, wondering all the same who she is." Fanny tittered, almost giggling.

"Let me take your bags into our room," Chamberlain interrupted, "and you can unpack while I clean up."

"I am absolutely famished. Please don't take long getting ready, as you need to take your wife out to a nice restaurant in this dingy city. Have you had a chance to eat out or have you been too busy with your work?"

"I know of a wonderful place we can go. As a matter of fact, I was going to have supper there tonight with a friend, sort of a send-off."

"I am sure he will understand if you cancel as your wife has shown up in town." Fanny said flirtatiously.

"Actually, it is a she, Jennie Robinson; surely I wrote and told you about her?"

Fanny paused momentarily but continued gamely on, "No, I don't believe you have. Who is this Jennie Robinson?"

"I was in the hospital with her husband." His voice grew solemn. "John Robinson was an assistant surgeon for the cavalry before he was wounded. He passed away, but over the course of his decline, I got to know her. She is a lovely woman."

"Pretty, you mean?"

"Can't hold a candle to my wife, no." Chamberlain murmured.

"Do you suppose that she would mind if I had my husband to myself for supper tonight, and perhaps we can meet another time?" Fanny had lost her playful tone, and with it most of her gaiety.

Emmett tried to relieve the tension by chiming in, "They eat together almost every night, so I'm sure that won't be a problem."

Chamberlain looked at Emmett, a flash of anger crossing his face at the same time a flush crept up from his collar. Time froze for just a moment, the air seemingly too thick to breathe, before Fanny broke the silence. "Perhaps we should have supper with her tonight after all."

"No, no." Chamberlain said stiffly. "She is returning home in a day or so and will understand that your arrival must change any plans."

Although an early thaw brought balmy breezes and sun-splashed days to Washington D.C., the house on 13th Street was increasingly uncomfortable for Emmett. Two days after Fanny's arrival, Emmett found himself escorting Mrs. Robinson to the train station, from where she would travel north to her family, leaving behind this in-between life and embarking upon a new chapter. Emmett was not sure if the initial tension between Fanny and Joshua had been worse, in his mind, than the rekindling of their passion for each other as the days of February wore on. The couple behaved like young lovers, once again with no children underfoot, as they had been left home with Sae Chamberlain. Off in a strange city, and with few cares and fewer real duties, they enjoyed days upon days of escape from responsibility and the reality of war. Whispering to each other, giggling like small children, holding hands, brushing against each other in passing, and worst of all, just staring at each other open-mouthed and googly-eyed—it was enough to send Emmett out onto the streets most evenings in search of respite from the spectacle.

One day in early March, Walt Whitman approached Emmett at the Armory Square Hospital with a beaming smile. "I have a bit of an eye opener for you today, Emmett my boy."

"What's that?" Emmett was busy changing bedsheets, one

of the many jobs in a hospital otherwise bustling with surgeons, physicians, nurses, chaplains, gravediggers, cooks—many of whom it was Emmett's job to assist in one way or another.

"I have set you up with a...rendezvous." Whitman could not contain his excitement.

"A rendezvous?" Emmett had no idea what the man was talking about.

"Remember a few weeks back when we relished the performance at Canterbury Hall, and I noticed your fascination with the young beauties?" Whitman took his time, finally having garnered Emmett's full attention. "Afterwards, over a nip, you let on that you sometimes had 'thoughts' about a lovely young lady, a working girl named Susannah?"

Emmett found his face hot and uncomfortable all of a sudden, ducking his head to his work as if he were disinterested in the conversation.

"Well, I made inquiries of the Madam, one Mary Hall as you said, and have arranged for you to have tea with this young lass."

"Tea?" Emmett finally looked up from his work.

Whitman laughed, a booming cannonade that echoed down the long hall of the hospital ward. "I am sure that more can be arranged, if that is what you want."

"What will we talk about? What will I say?" He spluttered.

"You will be fine, my boy, just fine. Tell her about yourself. Tell her about your Colonel Chamberlain. Tell her anything you want."

Later the next afternoon, Emmett found himself sitting nervously at a table in a tavern on Maryland Avenue, caught between anxiously awaiting the young woman, and hoping that she didn't show up. He had arrived twenty minutes early, and had worked himself up into such a state that he was about ready to walk out when she swept into the room at the appointed time. He took in her features once again, the milky white skin glowing like the fresh face of the new moon, a delicate, up-turned nose, and deep blue eyes that twinkled with defiance. He focused on a dimple in her left cheek as he stood awkwardly to pull back her chair. She leaned her parasol against the side of the table, arranging her layered dress carefully as she sat down, a teasing smile on her face.

"I assume you are Emmett?" Her voice was child-like, not the seductive purr that he expected from this beautiful woman of the world.

"Emmett." He said stupidly, confirming his identity before blundering on. "And must you, eh, you must be Susannah?"

She laughed then, an infectious giggle that made Emmett smile instead of feeling like an imbecile. "I am Susannah Smith."

"Would you like some tea?" He asked. They talked, and Emmett hewed to Whitman's advice, telling her all about his father and brothers leaving for the war, the loneliness of them gone, the adventures he had found at Chamberlain's side. "And what about yourself?" He finished, realizing he'd been jabbering on for almost a half an hour.

"Do you mean how did I become a 'soiled dove'?"

Emmett blushed, shaking his head no. "But you must have family?" He was having difficulty ignoring the sweet fragrance emanating from across the table, an intoxicating smell that made his stomach tighten and his fists clench.

"My father is a minister just across the river in Maryland, and I have three sisters. I was supposed to marry a member of my father's congregation, an older man of considerable wealth." She looked at the table, reaching out to swipe up a bit of spilt sugar with the tip of her finger. "But I loved another, a boy that I grew up with." The only person she'd shared her story with was the Madam, Mary Hall, and the words started slowly, but then came rushing out. "My sweet, unlucky Rufus." She looked up at Emmett and smiled painfully. "So we ran away together and got married. My husband found employment here in the city as a tanner, and we took a room in a tenement in Murder Bay. I was sixteen years old."

"What happened?" The noise of the room seemed to fall away, and Emmett listened intently to the girl's tale.

"The war came. My husband went to fight for his country. He died at the First Battle of Bull Run almost three years ago now."

"Did you write to your father? Your sisters? Surely someone would take you in?"

"Father is too proud a man to take me back, that I knew. I tried to find work, but there wasn't much I was good at, and eventually I was thrown out of the tenement building. That is when Mary Hall found me walking the streets and starving. I have been a prostitute ever since." She finished simply.

"Is it difficult?" Emmett blurted, then clapped a hand to his mouth, aghast at what he'd said.

"You are a soldier?" Susannah asked, her eyes flat and hard, the mettle of the woman showing through for the first time. Emmett nodded that he was, and she continued, "Is it hard to kill a man?"

"I'm sorry." Emmett apologized, afraid that he'd ruined the tea. "This war touches everyone and has brought tough times on us all." He paused, then because the words seemed so right, he began to recite Whitman's poem from memory. "Beat! beat! drums!--blow! bugles! blow!...." He began softly, then seeing her eyes widen and her head dip in a brief nod, continued with more confidence through the final lines. "That's a poem by a friend of mine, Walt Whitman, and somehow to me it is the war, my war, but in words."

"That it is." Susannah answered. "*No happiness must he have now with his bride.* Indeed!" She became lost for a moment, searching for a long buried memory, before continuing, "Tell me about your brother, Daniel."

They spent another half-hour sharing stories and laughing. For Susannah, it was a welcome respite to converse with a male with no further expectations. For Emmett, well, he was in love. They promised to exchange letters, and then Susannah had to go. Emmett walked all the way back to the town house, his head in the clouds, looking around his room and not remembering how he'd gotten there.

After supper that night, Chamberlain took Emmett aside. "I have contacted General Warren on your behalf," he said, "to see if he could use an aide at the 5th Corps. At least until I can get myself reinstated to active duty. He would be more than happy to have you until I can break away from this infernal court martial duty."

"Will I be able to visit with Tom and the other men of the 20th?"

"I'm sure there will be plenty of time for a visit. Until the ground dries out and the rivers drop, the war will not resume. Hopefully, I will be back by then."

"Sir, will you be Brigade Commander or will you be back with the 20th?"

"It looks like General Bartlett will be getting command of the brigade. So it is the 20th for me once again." Chamberlain said with resignation, both frustrated to be passed over for promotion, and at the same time happy to return to his beloved regiment from Maine. "You leave in the morning, so best make an early night of it and get your things together."

Chapter Fourteen

National Republican   June 15, 1864

A Change in Command

___

<u>Commander-in-Chief Ulysses S. Grant Begins Overland Campaign</u>

On March 2nd of this past year, Ulysses S. Grant was approved by Congress as the Lieutenant General of the United States Army, effectively making him the General-In-Chief. Grant, if you remember, was the General who whipped the Rebels in Vicksburg on July 4th of last year, and then drove the Confederates out of Tennessee with his victory at Chattanooga. The 5'2", 117 pound Grant is not a large man, but instills fear into the hearts of the enemy. Grant earned his nickname "Unconditional Surrender" when the Confederate General Buckner asked to negotiate the terms of surrender of Fort Donelson, to which Grant replied, "No terms except unconditional and immediate surrender". He is a West Point graduate who fought in the Mexican-American War, and, with his aggressive strategy and seeming lack of fear, could be just the leader that the Union Army has been looking for. Since taking command of the war effort, Grant has masterminded a strategy of aggression from all facets of the army. General Tecumseh Sherman has been pursuing General Johnston from Tennessee all the way to Georgia, cutting off valuable supply lines for the Army of Northern Virginia. General Meade and the Army of the Potomac, under the close supervision of General Grant, have begun the Overland Campaign whose first battle was fought in early May in the Wilderness by Chancellorsville. When the Army of the Potomac met with stiff Confederate resistance, Grant tried flanking them by moving south. Battles at Spotsylvania Courthouse, Santa Anna River, and the disastrous Cold Harbor followed, with the army moving constantly south in an attempt to get around the Rebels and move on the southern capital. The army *is now poised to strike Petersburg, a major supply link for Richmond, and a break-through here would probably mean the capital city of the Confederacy would fall.*

June 18, 1864

"That," Chamberlain was saying to his officers, "is Rives Salient." He pointed toward the protruding angle of the Confederate defense, just outside the city of Petersburg. The Confederate lines ringed the city in a semi-circle, except for this one angle that jutted out from the lines by several hundred yards. "That is where we will be called upon to attack." Earlier that morning, a planned assault had stalled when the Union sortie discovered that the Confederates had fallen back from their position to the more easily defended salient. The newly created 1st Brigade with Chamberlain in command had been given what is sometimes the most difficult of orders—to wait, the impending battle nearing with each passing moment. The small city of Petersburg was key to the defense of Richmond, itself the gateway to the South's heartland. The men seemed to sense that a victory here would be a big step towards ending this war.

"They appear to be well dug in, sir." Emmett responded after the other men had drifted away. His voice was now deeper, his body filling out and growing so much that he'd been obliged to pay the Sutler for a new uniform.

"Hopefully headquarters will throw the entire might of the army into the attack." Chamberlain said wistfully, knowing full well that indecision, rather than bold action, characterized the Union command, an indecision that did not plague their Confederate foe.

"They say of General Grant that he doesn't do anything half way." Emmett replied with the ardor of a young man who desperately wanted to believe in a hero.

Chamberlain nodded his head but spoke more cautiously. "The papers try to sell copies, and the President tries to sell optimism. I hope that General Grant is our savior, but he will have to prove it to me first."

"The new regiment looked mighty queasy coming up this morning." Emmett noted grimly, not one to laugh at death. While five of the Pennsylvania regiments in the 1st Brigade were battle-hardened veterans, the sixth was made up of newly formed, raw recruits, who had not yet witnessed the carnage of battle. Their path this morning had been particularly bad, still littered with bodies after an ill-considered charge the day before. He remembered, a small shiver running down his spine, the first bloated bodies he'd seen approaching the battle of Antietam, and then the mangled corpses in the killing fields below Marye's Heights. Worst of all had been burying the sodden and putrefying remains of the tens of thousands of fallen in mass graves after Gettysburg.

"They will adapt quick enough, I imagine." Chamberlain was looking at the enemy lines through his field glasses.

"I reckon they won't have much choice."

"General Grant is of the opinion that there are more people in the North than there are in the South." Chamberlain said, lowering the field glasses as an artillery shell exploded about fifty feet in front of them, neither man wincing at the impact. "Every time one of our soldiers dies, we can replace him. Every time a Reb dies, the Confederacy has one less soldier to fight for them."

Emmett spit onto the ground. "Well, war ain't quite what I thought it was going to be."

Chamberlain pondered the boy's words, realizing that he had indeed made the hard passage to manhood in the two years that he'd known him. He had shot up in height, and was long limbed, well muscled, and graceful such that his Enfield rifle seemed just an extension of his arm. His shoulders no longer hunched forward, but were thrust back as he held his head high. "It is exactly what I thought it would be." Chamberlain finally replied. "'To be ambitious of true honor, of the true glory and perfection of our natures, is the very principle and incentive of virtue.'"

"Sounds like a poet wrote that, because it sure ain't like the battlefields we've been on, sir." Emmett spoke cautiously, thinking as the words emerged that it was what Tom might say if he were here, and not back with the 20th Maine about a mile or so behind them.

Chamberlain turned to face Emmett with a surprised look on his face. "I suppose you are right. Perhaps the sentiment of Sir

Walter Scott has no place in this cynical Great War of ours."

"What do you suppose is the purpose of us all standing here in range of their artillery?" Emmett asked. "I could see if we were attacking, but just standing here?" He was not complaining, so much as trying to understand the minds that controlled their movements.

"What do you think would be the point?" Chamberlain had a way of always turning Emmett's questions around, making him think instead of speaking without reflection.

After a bit, Emmett ventured an opinion that he didn't necessarily hope was correct. "The artillery is being set up behind us, which is what makes me think we will be attacking here. My guess would be that we are providing a diversion so that the Confederates don't realize the artillery is setting up."

"I think you are exactly right." Chamberlain said drily, his expression caught between a grimace and a grin. It was rather unfortunate to be a mere distraction to the enemy, but he was proud of the military wisdom that Emmett was coming to possess.

"Two days ago, they might have had no idea of the plan, but I'm pretty sure ole' Bobby Lee knows where we are now." Emmett observed, grinning wearily.

Chamberlain nodded his agreement. "I don't think there will any surprises today, either, Emmett. That is why I have a favor to ask of you."

"You name it, sir, and I will do it." This was not a casual statement. The man had given so much to Emmett, bringing him along as an aide, reuniting him with his brother Daniel. When they had changed brigades, he'd had Daniel transferred to keep the two Collins together. He'd been Emmett's tutor for the past two years as well, helping a small, scared boy grow into a confident and mature young man under the most difficult of circumstances.

"If I fall today, will you make sure my wife gets this letter?" Chamberlain had often commented that he assumed he would get wounded at some point. This was the first time he'd written such a letter, causing Emmett to look at the older man closely. So far he had weathered several minor wounds and numerous close calls, but nothing serious.

"You are not going to fall today." Emmett said desperately, as if saying it would make it so.

"I've had a feeling for a couple of days that I would be shot in the abdomen." Chamberlain said, holding the letter away from his side as if it was poison. "It is not the worst thing to be killed in the defense of one's country."

Emmett tried to laugh it off. "As far as I can tell, soldiers are the most superstitious bunch I've ever seen, worse than my grandmother and her cronies thinking they can talk to the spirits. It seems to me that God doesn't favor the ones with a rabbit's foot or the ones carrying a picture of their special girl close to their heart. He doesn't take you cuz you think you're going to die and leave the damn fools who think they'll live forever. It just kinda happens." He shut up then, realizing he'd perhaps trod roughly over delicate ground.

"You may be right, Emmett, but I would feel better knowing this letter will find my wife and children if I die. Will you do that for me?"

"Perhaps you should stay to the rear for a change, sir, now that you command an entire brigade." Emmett suggested, pocketing the letter.

"Would you have me send the men into battle," he scoffed, "while I watched safely from the rear? God has a plan for each of us, and he will take me when the time comes, hopefully leading the men forward." Chamberlain fixed his field glasses on an approaching group of Union officers, marking that it was General Warren and his staff, flags flowing gloriously behind.

"Just do as I ask." He said without another glance at Emmett, the words more harsh than he intended.

Confederate shells from Napoleon twelve-pounders were exploding around the brigade, occasionally striking the dug-in infantry and sending bodies and body parts flying through the air. This did not appear to bother General Warren in the slightest as he rode through the bursting shells without looking left or right, pulling up his horse in front of Chamberlain and Emmett. The rebel battery had been set up a half-mile in front of their defensive position, in order to be able to reach the Union soldiers. And it was this battery that held his attention. "Colonel Chamberlain, I find that Rebel artillery to be fairly annoying." General Warren was a master of the understatement.

"Yes sir, I would agree that they are being irksome to the

mood of the men," Chamberlain concurred.

"Do you think that you might silence them?" General Warren posed the question almost as if it were a philosophical inquiry.

"I believe my men would be up to the task," the Colonel countered.

Warren nodded, putting his own spyglass away. "See to it then." And he rode off without another word.

"Emmett, gather my officers. It looks like the wait is over."

The 1st Brigade was soon marching forward in orderly precision, using what little cover there was until the final assault would be made. The battery continued to boom, shells exploding on the ground in front of the men, nothing but their momentum and solidarity driving them forward into this rain of death from above. The veteran units did not falter in the slightest when the whoosh of the projectile went by, knowing that the sound meant they were safe. A shell exploded in the rear of the brigade, its metal shrapnel slicing through three men of the newly formed 187th Pennsylvania, one man dropping to his knees to apply pressure to a dead man's throat. Several others hesitated, but ultimately decided it was better to continue forward than to retreat and leave themselves at the mercy of the cannon fire.

As they approached the final field to cross, Chamberlain maneuvered the regiments so that the three veteran groups led with three more in support, including the newly formed 187th. He and his officers rode between them. Emmett, two other aides, three lieutenants, a bugler, the color bearer, and several orderlies comprised Chamberlain's retinue. They drew closer to the enemy, the infantry walking steadily forward, closing ranks when holes were ripped in the lines as men were picked off by the Rebel sharpshooters. Emmett could hear officers yelling for the men to remain steady, to move forward, to stay tight.

"Spread the word that we will begin the charge at that small alder tree." Chamberlain directed, his staff spreading the command to the six regimental commanders. As the front men reached the designated tree, he motioned for the bugler, urging him to "Sound the charge." The brash notes filled the air, urging the brigade forward into its first action as a group, sending them sweeping across the open ground with a roaring vengeance.

"Look at them go." Chamberlain said to Emmett proudly as they trotted along in the middle of the charging brigade. Bayonets had been fixed, as they were only facing the one regiment of infantry protecting the artillery. As soon as they were close enough, they would stop and fire a volley, and then charge behind their steel blades.

"It is a thing of beauty," Emmett replied, barely finishing his sentence when a load of canister shot came ricocheting off the ground, tearing a wide swath through the center of the brigade, and into Chamberlain's staff as well. Men and horses toppled like dominos, Emmett himself pinned momentarily under his horse, which lay without moving. Another horse was screaming in pain, a shrill shriek, the noise piercing and disorienting. With the dull roar from the explosion still echoing in his ears, Emmett pulled himself from underneath the dead animal, which was missing both of its front legs entirely. Next to him an orderly gasped huge gulps of air, his hand trying to prod his eye back into the socket from which it hung by some invisible thread. Each time he pushed it in with his thumb, it slipped back out.

Emmett looked around bleakly for Chamberlain, noticing a lieutenant on the ground laughing at his shattered hand, whether in shock or with the knowledge that he would not be able to fight any longer, it was hard to say. He noticed Chamberlain's horse, Charlemagne, still lay kicking on the ground. Attempting to orient himself, he next saw the Colonel staggering forward, having picked up the color guard's flag, the bearer lying either dead or unconscious on the ground. Emmett ran to catch up and the two of them chased the brigade across the field, the colors streaming behind them, the pole cracked, but still holding firm. They caught up just as the men had paused to fire a ragged volley at the artillery, felling roughly one-third of the men of the battery with their withering fire. The survivors were busy hooking the limbers and caissons to the horse teams that had not fallen from the barrage, turning the Napoleon cannons and fleeing as fast as they could.

The Confederate infantry protecting the artillery battery had no desire to face the charge of a brigade, and they too fled their positions back to Rives Salient, giving the 1st Brigade the field. Surveying the land, Chamberlain had the men fall back slightly to take cover under the crest of a hill. They now lay within rifle range of the outer defenses of the city of Petersburg, well in advance of the rest of the Union Army. Chamberlain set the men to the hard task of digging themselves in, mounting primitive earthworks and preparing artillery placements. Luckily, it was not long before reinforcements came up to strengthen their position. They all knew that a brutal attack loomed. If rumors about General Grant were true, he would attack no matter the cost in men and material. So far on the Overland Campaign his inclination had been to attack, attack, attack, and then attack some more. The Confederates lay well entrenched on the high ground encircling the city, with several forts protecting their position. They had wrested rocks from the ground to create fortifications and erected wood breastworks whose sharp ends faced out, one more barrier for any would-be attacker. Emmett thought back to the battle at Fredericksburg, and the assault on Marye's Heights. It was not going to be a very pleasant day he concluded, but one did what one had to do.

"Message for Colonel Chamberlain," yelled a staff officer, riding up hard to the Maltese Cross, the Corps flag, set in the middle of the Union lines of the 1st Brigade.

Chamberlain stood and walked over to the man, taking the hand-written note and scanning it. "Will we be supported in this attack?"

"I don't believe so, sir, I think you are to be the entire offensive at this point."

"Does General Meade know the force and position of the enemy that we will be attacking?"

"I don't know, sir."

"Wait here. I have a message for him." The Colonel replied, taking out his field book and pencil and spending several minutes scrawling out a detailed outline of the situation.

Chamberlain asked Emmett to assemble the officers, and in a few minutes, each of the six regimental commanders had gathered around the Colonel, most of them bending their head to remain out of sight of snipers, while others walked straight up, almost daring a shot. Chamberlain wasted no time filling them in on the situation. "We have orders to attack at Rives Salient by heading up the Jerusalem Plank Road."

"Alone?" Major George Merrick queried with eyebrows raised.

"I hope not. I have sent a message requesting more information. I expect we will hear back before very long."

"This is it then." Major Horatio Warren said quietly. "We drive the Rebs out of Petersburg, and Richmond is ours. It is up to us to break the Confederate lines."

They made small talk, waiting for the reply from central command. A few minutes later, it came, directly from General Warren. It would indeed be an assault by the entire army but spearheaded by the 1st Brigade. "Gentlemen, we will be commencing the action at precisely 3:00." Chamberlain said brightly to the assembled officers. "We will form a skirmish line before crossing the creek here." He said, diagramming the plan for his officers in the dirt with a stick. "And then begin to move to the left of their position as we ascend the hill. This will avoid the direct fire of their gun placements here." He said making another x on the ground. He looked up to see nodding faces, and moments later the officers hurried off to their duties as Chamberlain turned to Emmett. "Let's take a walk and say hello to the boys." With that, he led the way to the front line, strolling along as if he were walking the Bowdoin campus, chatting with this man and that man. He even invited them to approach the crest of the hill, to show them the fortifications they were facing, and what they were expected to do and why.

One man, his cheeks bulging with a wad of tobacco, looked at Chamberlain in amazement, "You ain't much like other officers, are you, sir?"

"What do you mean?"

"Well," the soldier continued, "they don't usually tell us why we're doing what we're doing. They just tell us to do it, and then follow along behind to make sure we don't stop doing it 'til it's done!" The man had a bloody bandage wrapped around his forearm where fragments of canister had ripped away chunks of flesh, and his clothes were filthy from digging and marching. His eyes were red from lack of sleep, but they shone forth confidently. "I heard about you at Gettysburg, and that charge of yours. I spoke with some boys who said you led them, you didn't just send them."

"It is hard to lead from the rear." Chamberlain confessed. "I guess if I knew how to do that, I might. But I haven't figured that one out yet, so today, you will just have to follow me."

When the time was upon them, Colonel Chamberlain strode to the front, giving the commands. "Attention! Trail Arms! Double-quick! March!" Thus began the attack on Rives Salient, the forward protruding point in the defense of Petersburg, the brigade hoping to open a breach in the lines that the Army of the Potomac would be able to exploit. As the bugle sounded the notes of the charge, the brigade poured over the crest of the hill in a line over a quarter mile long, the men jogging steadily down towards the stream.

Chamberlain ran in the lead, his saber pointed forward, yelling, "Follow me, boys!" The entire lot of them erupted in a scream that made the Rebel yell seem weak tea indeed. Down the hill to Poor Creek, a minor stream, they raced as one, following their commander, Colonel Chamberlain, as all around them the Union cannons thundered, the barrage meant to protect their advance by softening the defense.

The Confederates were intent on mowing them down like wheat in a field with their own artillery, firing shells and canister into the midst of the advancing troops. A fort on the far left began to lay down enfilade fire, which meant that they were taking fire head on and from one side. Thousands of Confederate soldiers fired volley after murderous volley, while the Union soldiers held off until they were closer. Surging to the fore, led by Horatio Warren, were two 'Bucktail' units on the left, nicknamed thus for the deer tails that hung from their hats. A shell passed through a man on Emmett's right, leaving a gaping hole in his middle, his feet continuing to carry him down the slope for several more feet until the body collapsed in pieces on the ground. Another man tripped, his fixed bayonet plunging into the calf of the man on his right. He rose wordlessly, and continued running, leaving the other man writhing on the ground in pain.

"Stay with me, Emmett!" Chamberlain gasped, splashing through the shallow creek. "We need to make sure that the men begin moving to the left towards the Salient on the other side of the water." To slow down or pause now meant certain death, the only hope for survival was to reach the incline close enough to the

Confederate lines that their cannon barrels could not be lowered enough to fire effectively.

They clambered up the far bank of the creek and then to the rim of the larger ravine through which it ran before pausing to direct the men. Chamberlain's intent was to move the attack to the left behind a small knoll that would protect them from fire from that ill-placed fort. That way, they would only be facing the still fierce and commanding guns of Rives Salient. Chamberlain was waving his sword over his head in a windmill fashion, urging the men on to some shelter, "To the left men, to the left."

It was then that Emmett saw Chamberlain suddenly rising up on his toes and moving forward in some weird, distorted dance, staggering several feet sideways to the left, and then back to the right as if on a ship in a storm. He stopped abruptly, jamming his sword firmly into the ground to steady himself. From this position he continued to wave the men forward and to the left with blood spraying out from his hip, showering the passing men in a fine mist of red. The mass of men prevented Emmett from getting to his side for many long seconds. By the time he had, Chamberlain was completely covered in his own blood from the waist down to his boots. Once by his side, Emmett stood next to his mentor, unsure of what to do next. So Emmett merely stood there as the 1st Brigade passed them by in their attempt to take Rives Salient. As the last man passed, Chamberlain seemed to look fondly after the charging brigade, and then twisted and slowly toppled to the ground, first coming to rest on one knee, and then to both knees, before finally landing on his back.

"Emmett, there your are," Chamberlain murmured, staring straight up into Emmett's face, the boy hovering anxiously over him. "I believe I have been shot, but can't feel a thing. Do I still have my legs?" He tried to raise his head frantically, Emmett soothing him as best he could.

"I was shot in the side as I motioned the men forward. I was not shot in the back." Chamberlain gasped desperately.

"I know sir, I saw the whole thing." Emmett had ripped part of his shirt off and was attempting to staunch the flow of blood. "You were directing the men forward when you were hit."

Two lieutenants, Funk and Walters, ran up then, and the three of them grabbed Chamberlain, pulling him back down behind the better cover of the river bank. His face was white with the pain, the initial numbness apparently going away. He tried to speak but vomited instead, green bile spilling from his mouth and dribbling down the front of his blue army coat. He hacked to clear the acidic liquid from his mouth, spitting, but the very effort causing him to cry out in pain. After a bit, he managed to croak out orders. "Funk, see that Irwin knows that I am down, and that he is now in charge of the brigade."

"Yes, sir." Lieutenant Funk replied, pausing momentarily, unsure of whether to leave the wounded man's side, but then being waved off.

Their position was now only slightly better than before, with some shelter from the bullets and artillery shells flying through the air all around them. Emmett knew that there was no way of moving the wounded Chamberlain any further without a stretcher to aid them. "I will go find an ambulance to come and take you out." Emmett blurted finally, unable to watch any longer without doing something. Before he could be refused, he was off. As he ran crouching toward the rear, he met up with other men heading in the same direction, and realized that they were members of the unseasoned 187th Regiment of Pennsylvania. It did not bode well for the attack or the honor of the 1st Brigade to have one of its regiments fleeing to safety.

On the hill a captain of the artillery was attempting to rally the retreating troops, and Emmett ran up to him. "Captain, Colonel Chamberlain is down. I need a stretcher to move him back from the battle."

Captain Bigelow of the 9th Massachusetts instantly called four of his cannoneers over. "Follow this soldier and do what he says. Find a stretcher so we can get Colonel Chamberlain out of there as quickly as can be."

Emmett immediately began jogging back towards where he'd left Chamberlain with Lieutenant Walters. Men, in retreat, floated by, detached from their regiments with no officers to rally them, all the while heavy artillery continuing to boom, rifles clattering and yells splitting the air in one colossal clamor. Emmett splashed back through Poor Creek, his eyes scanning the far side as he went, looking for Chamberlain amidst the other downed soldiers and rough terrain. "This way," Emmett grunted, finally spotting the inert form.

As the five of them rushed to his side with the stretcher, Chamberlain didn't even look up, his face ashen, his forehead streaked with sweat, his breathing ragged and hoarse.

"Colonel Chamberlain, sir?" Emmett was afraid that he was dying, but at his words, Chamberlain's eyes fluttered open.

Taking in the men and the stretcher, Chamberlain winced, shaking his head to the negative. "I'm all done." He grunted, his voice cracking as he spoke. "Give me a drink and then go save somebody who has a chance at living."

"My captain told us to bring you back, sir," one of the soldiers said as they laid the stretcher down next to Chamberlain, "and that is what we plan to do."

"I am a Colonel, and I say I will die here." Chamberlain panted in ragged gasps, ripples of pain choking his body, causing him to jerk spastically as he spoke.

"I will not disobey my commanding officer, sir." The soldier replied as he ignored the order to leave. "So you will be coming with us. Now brace yourself. We need to lift you onto the stretcher." Two men took his shoulders, and two his feet, lifting him screaming in pain, spittle flying from his mouth, his arms flailing to strike out, anything to stop the excruciating agony.

The men began to move back across the creek, half-crouching, bullets and shells whizzing all about them. They had just reached the far side when an artillery shell exploded mere feet away, sending them all toppling to the ground like toy soldiers, Chamberlain falling from the stretcher like a sack of potatoes. The pain forced him into unconsciousness, a blessing in disguise, allowing the men to roughly pull him back onto the stretcher and continue on their way. They reached the crest of hill from which the charge had originated, placing him gingerly down on the far side, and thus out of harm's way.

"We have to get back to our regiment," one of the soldiers told Emmett. "We'll let the ambulance crew know where he is for when it gets dark."

Emmett sat with the unconscious Chamberlain for an hour, but after a bit, he crept to a vantage point to watch the battle, which had shuddered to a standstill. A good number of the 1st Brigade had managed to get within fifty yards of the Confederates, but they had gone to ground, unable to overrun the breastworks without support. Perhaps the 187th Pennsylvania would have been enough help to carry the fortifications, but now they were stranded, unable to go forward or back, at least until dark came to hide their retreat. Dead men littered the ground in increasing numbers the further forward they were.

Below him, Chamberlain stirred, groaning as he rolled onto his wounded side. As far as Emmett could see, the minié ball had gone into his right hip, tearing through the center of his body before finally coming to rest just under the skin of his left hip, ugly purple swollen flesh marking where it lay. Emmett, along with Funk and Walters, had managed to plug the external wounds with rags to slow the bleeding, but it was obvious that surgeons were needed quickly or his life would be forfeit. "Are you awake, sir?"

Chamberlain's eyes focused on Emmett's face, recognition gradually dawning, and then confusion. "Where am I?"

"We are back behind the hill we attacked from this afternoon, sir." Emmett uncapped his canteen, tipping it forward to let a few drops trickle down Chamberlain's throat. He didn't have enough to wet a rag and wipe his brow, and he regretted not asking any of the cannoneers if they had extra water to leave with him. "You've been wounded in your hip."

Chamberlain's hand reached claw-like for the wound, just the touch enough to make him gasp in pain. "How is the attack going?"

"It doesn't look good. General Cutler's brigade didn't attack right at three, which left our boys pretty exposed. Most of them are pinned up on the hill just below the Rebs. The new regiment broke and ran; I saw a bunch of them as I was searching for help for you, sir."

"That blamed Cutler." Emmett drew back, this being the first time he had ever heard Chamberlain swear. "I tried to speak with him before the attack, but he got all uppity and thought I was ordering him around."

"I don't know anything for sure, but I can tell you I never saw his brigade. And they're nowhere in sight now."

"Are you sure the new regiment broke or was it only a few of them?" Chamberlain coughed, his body wracking in suffering.

Emmett opened his mouth then closed it, thinking of what

he'd seen before answering. "I think it was most of them I saw skittering back up the hill, but I can't say for certain."

"It's a hard thing to throw men into battle as fierce as this with no real training, no knowledge of anything except how to earn a decent living in the civilian world." With this comment went the last of his strength, and he seemed to lapse into unconsciousness. Emmett knelt by him as his face grew rigid and his eyes glassy, a bit of spittle escaping his mouth and dotting his chin and mustache. His eyes ceased looking out, their focus instead on some distant place, and Emmett was convinced that he was watching his mentor die.

When the long shadows of night began crawling up the hill on which they lay, motion from the rear began, a bustle of men out with stretchers, hurrying along like busy ants with a job to do. Chamberlain was quickly plucked from the brow of the hill, the ambulance crew efficiently shuttling him to a field hospital a few miles to the rear of the fighting. The hospital, which filled a small clearing and looked as if a gypsy caravan had set up camp, was merely a series of tents with tables for operating on the injured. He was put into the care of a surgeon named Everett who gave him ether to ease the pain, and then began to cut away the blood-soaked clothes.

"Sir, will he live?" Emmett demanded.

"It does not look good," the surgeon replied, shrugging. "The bullet passed through the middle of his body, and he has lost a great deal of blood. I will know more shortly." Emmett stood by while the surgeon removed the lead—a flat, ugly, vicious looking hunk of misshapen metal—from Chamberlain's left hip. After fifteen minutes, he looked at Emmett. "The minié ball has mangled too many organs. It's just not possible to repair them, and certainly not here. I'm sorry. There is nothing I can do for him."

"No," Emmett said, shaking his head violently from side to side. "He is going to be okay. He has to be okay. He is still talking. He can't die." He stumbled from the tent in shock and denial. He had to find Tom Chamberlain. Tom would know what to do, how to fix the situation. He grabbed the first soldier he saw and asked him if he knew the whereabouts of the 20th Maine. He did not, and Emmett ran off into the dark, running for help, running from pain, running because to stop was to stop hoping. Finally he happened upon a man who pointed him in the right direction.

Tom was sitting by the fire, discussing the rumors of the events of the day with the men around him, when he saw Emmett approaching through the tents. He instantly realized from Emmett's face, from his hair matted with sweat and clothes splattered with blood that this was not a social visit, but rather another grim tiding of war, and took his friend aside. "Tom," a wild-eyed Emmett spluttered, "your brother has been shot."

"Is he alive?" Tom asked, his voice cracking, the calm night broken into pieces. He turned toward the fire, where the others had frozen at the news, Chamberlain being one of them, an officer true, but a Maine man first, and a man of honor and valor second.

"Yes, but he's in a bad way."

"Where?"

"The field hospital about two miles east of here."

"I have to tell Captain Spear I am going. Emmett, see if you can get Doctor Shaw to go with us. He's back by his tent." Surgeon Abner Shaw was the regiment's doctor and had proven his worth on numerous occasions. More importantly, he was a close friend of Chamberlain. Emmett found him in his tent reading, and they left camp minutes later, joined by Morris Townsend, surgeon for the 44th New York, who had heard the news and came to offer his services.

They found Chamberlain lying just outside of the tent on a blanket, hovering between consciousness and oblivion. Moaning seemed to indicate that he was unconscious, and a grinding of the teeth meant he was awake and in severe pain. Soldiers with no hope for recovery were removed from the tent and left nearby, usually in a field where they lay together, dying one by one. It was only in deference to his rank and reputation that the other surgeons had left Chamberlain there.

Tom charged into the tent, but was forced to wait while the surgeon finished sawing off the leg of a man with a handsaw, the shattered limb being deposited out back in an ever-growing pile. When he was done, Tom pulled him from the tent where Emmett and the two surgeons waited to hear the prognosis.

"It appears that the bullet ricocheted from the ground, flattening out and tearing a wider swath as it traversed his body." The surgeon said wearily. "The ball bounced its way through his body, smashing bones and nerves as it went, severing the urethra entirely and slicing the bladder. We removed the lead from his left hip where it ended up. Actually, I have it here in my pocket," he said, dropping the flattened lead into Tom's hand. "I'm sorry. There is nothing we can do to save his life, but those lives in *there* may still have some hope." The physician nodded his head at the tent, and then went back in.

"What does that all mean?" Tom asked, looking to Shaw.

Shaw sighed heavily, rubbing his temple with his thumbs. "The bladder and urethra are the problem. The bladder is the sac that collects urine, and the urethra is the tube that runs from the bladder out the length of the penis for him to be able to piss. Otherwise, the urine leaks into the stomach cavity, and that leads to infection and death."

"Can't they be repaired?" Emmett filled the void, each of them cringing inwardly at what the bullet had done.

"Tom, is that you?" Chamberlain had awakened and heard their voices across the front of the tent.

Tom went to his side with Emmett following, giving Shaw and Townsend a chance to discuss what they might possibly do. "Lawrence," Tom said, grasping his brother's hand in a firm clasp. "I am here."

"Thank you for coming. Make sure to tell Mother that I love her."

"I will Lawrence, I will, but save your voice to tell her yourself."

Chamberlain mumbled something unintelligible, and Tom leaned closer. "And don't call me Lawrence." He was grinning, a ghastly toothy smile that made Tom chuckle weakly in return.

Shaw and Townsend had decided that their only hope was to try a procedure that had never been attempted before as far as they knew. The four of them carried Chamberlain back into the tent, laying him on the table, the surgeon happy enough to take a break from his duties. They had brought much of what they needed and set out their instruments, including several doses of morphine. Chloroform and ether were often the drugs of choice, but morphine was more effective, even if more expensive and harder to come by. They injected a dose using the recently invented hypodermic needle, and Chamberlain dropped off to sleep.

There was not much they could do for the smashed pelvis, other than to scrape out the bone fragments by the flickering oil lamps, Emmett and Tom doing their best to supply the requested tools, occasionally restraining the patient as he drifted in and out of a drug-induced sleep. Several arteries had been severed, and these Shaw and Townsend had to tie off to prevent further blood loss. Finally came the injury that had caused the original surgeon to pass a death sentence on Chamberlain. How to repair his bladder and urethra? They carefully inserted a metal catheter the length of his penis and connected it to the bladder so that the urine would have a path to leave the body. They attempted to sew up the urethra, a mangled mess, as best they could, with little hope that it would heal well enough to one day remove the catheter.

At one point, with Chamberlain's insides laid open and his heartbeat failing, they paused to confer as to whether or not there was any reason to continue. Chamberlain roused himself long enough to urge them on, his voice bleary and harsh, stating his intention to live.

When they finally finished hours later, the Colonel was moved to a tent for those recovering from surgery. Visitors stepped in, and they were numerous. Ellis Spear had journeyed over from the 20th Maine to pay his respects to his former professor and commanding officer. He would go back to tell the men of the 20th Maine that Chamberlain had been awake, and that he had been wounded in the groin. Generals Warren and Griffin both stopped in, letting him know that they were recommending him for the long overdue promotion to Brigadier General, news that trickled through the veil of morphine to temporarily perk up his spirits. And yet, as the dawn of a new day came, it looked increasingly as if the wounds incurred at Rives Salient would certainly kill him. Emmett allowed himself, finally, to nap by his commanding officer, his dreams plagued by horrific scenes of grief as he passed Chamberlain's family the dread news that their son, husband, and father was dead.

Chapter fifteen

June 18, 1864
Special Order #39
Colonel Joshua L. Chamberlain...is for meritorious and efficient services on the field of battle, and especially for gallant conduct in leading his Brigade against the enemy at Petersburg, Virginia...appointed Brigadier General of Volunteers, to rank as such from the 18th of June, 1864.   General U.S. Grant[8]

June 20, 1864

The Connecticut steamed into Annapolis Harbor late on the night of June 20th. Just beyond the wharves a vast sea of hospital tents had grown up where once the U.S. Navy had been housed. Emmett aided a stretcher bearer in moving Chamberlain from the interior of the ship to the dock alongside 600 other wounded soldiers, many just arriving from the devastation at Cold Harbor, but some, such as Chamberlain, having fallen at the Battle of Petersburg. All around, delirious men cried and moaned, an unceasing cacophony that unsettled Emmett to his very core. The hospital was lit brightly for the new arrivals, long tent structures housing the thirty-eight wards that had been created at the beginning of the war. These wards were nestled in the center of a bustling town originally grown up around supplying the Navy, but now booming with the business of caring for a steady influx of wounded and sick.

A host of male nurses acting as stretcher-bearers came charging from the buildings to move patients from the wharf and into the hospital. It had been a difficult journey, and Chamberlain was pale, the heavy sedation of morphine barely keeping the pain at bay.

"Will you be all right while I find somebody to help get you inside?" Emmett asked the barely-conscious man.

"I don't need any special treatment." Chamberlain replied blearily, slightly revived by the fresh night air, a definite improvement over the steamer's stuffiness. "Let these other fellows be treated first." His voice was weak from the wound, and the travel, and a nasty experience aboard the ship.

"I'll be back shortly." Emmett ignored Chamberlain's noble statements, having come to realize that the Professor's ideas of valor came more from books than real life, and that even these most recent bloody, harrowing travails couldn't quite change them. He tried to attract the attention of two stretcher-bearers, but they were oblivious, bent on routine that could not vary, picking up an unconscious man who was missing a leg. Emmett spotted a man of authority weaving his way through the injured, and hurrying to his side, he requested help.

"What can I do for you, young man?" He was dressed in a dark jacket buttoned high around his neck, clean-shaven with eyes that shone bright.

"I am here looking after Colonel Chamberlain who was badly wounded at Petersburg." Emmett said desperately. "I need to get him off the wharf and into the hospital to be treated. It was a very difficult trip, and I fear that the good work of the field surgeons may have been undone by one of the doctors aboard the ship."

"I think that we should be able to do something about that." The man said brightly. He held his arm out, stopping two nurses passing by with an empty stretcher. "Bob, do you mind if the young lad and I borrow this for just a moment?"

"Not a problem, Father," the nurse replied.

They carried Chamberlain into the Middle Department of the hospital reserved for officers, Emmett suddenly nervous about interrupting a chaplain in his duties. "Thank you for taking the time to help us, Father."

"That is what I do." The chaplain said plainly, walking in front of Emmett with his back to him, his step energetic, Emmett having to scurry to keep up. "What is your name, lad?"

"Emmett Collins, sir, I mean, Father."

"I am the Reverend Henries, the head chaplain here at Annapolis. We have services on the Sabbath at two and seven. I'll expect to see you there."

Emmett mumbled something to the effect that he would certainly try. They found a bed open in the long room that ran the length of each hospital ward, and Henries found a surgeon who promised to attend to Chamberlain as soon as he had finished with his current case. Emmett pulled a chair up to the bed, intent on staying awake until Chamberlain had been treated, but found his head nodding, too heavy for his neck. Several times he jerked awake, but slowly the exhaustion of the past several days caught up with him, and his chin came to rest on his chest.

In his troubled sleep, Emmett found himself back in Virginia, with the grievously wounded Colonel floating in and out of consciousness and sometimes shrieking with pain. There were eight soldiers carrying his stretcher, almost as if pall bearers, transferring the Colonel from the field hospital to City Point where he could be loaded onto the Connecticut, a steamer bound for Annapolis. The stars were hard in the night sky, and not a man said a word as they grimly marched to the river. What had been a dull hum on the night breeze slowly rose in volume until, at the vessel's side; Emmett realized it was the agonized screeching of the wounded, the drugged, and the dying.

A large smokestack thrust up from the center of the ship, smoke curling out of it as the fire was stoked to make the steam to turn the large wheel to the rear. Two masts rose fore and aft, for the ship harnessed the wind too, whenever possible. Because of his rank Chamberlain had a cabin of his own, but most of the wounded lay on litters scattered haphazardly all over the deck. The pallbearers, having deposited their cargo on a dirty cot against one wall, immediately left to return to the battlefield. Chamberlain was delirious, calling out to Fanny, demanding to know where she was. Emmett was afraid to leave him, attempting to keep his brow cool with a rag and water that had been left on a small table, the only other furnishing in the room. The rocking motion of the boat was making Emmett queasy, and it was a relief when a man stumbled into the room with a doctor's bag in hand.

"Who do we have here?" The man, a bloodstained and befouled apron covering his corpulent body, demanded loudly.

"This is Colonel Joshua Chamberlain." Emmett replied, reassured that all would be okay now.

"And you are?" The man asked, taking a large flask from his coat pocket and swigging generously from it.

"Emmett Collins, sir. I am Colonel Chamberlain's aide."

"What's the matter with him?" The boat shifted, causing the man to keel sideways, only stopping himself by grasping Chamberlain's leg, the feverish man groaning and opening his eyes to look wildly round the darkened space.

"He was shot in the hip, sir. Tore through the middle of him pretty good."

The man tipped the flask to his lips again. "This war sure is hell, son. It don't take no pity on anybody." He began to pull at the bandages with shaky hands, causing Chamberlain to grit his teeth, a hiss escaping through his compressed lips. "You just sit still there, Colonel, and let me take a look at what's going on."

Emmett stood at the man's side, the sharp odor of whiskey washing over him like foul rain. The doctor's eyes were rimmed red, stubble dotted his mottled face, and his chin and neck were thick and puffy. "Are you sure you know what you're doing?" Emmett asked.

The man cackled, drinking again. "I'm a surgeon, and I have seen more wounds than anybody should ever have to. I think I know what I'm doing."

Emmett now recognized from the slurred speech and unsteady hand that the man was dead drunk. "I think we will wait for another physician, if it's all the same to you." He said, moving to put himself between Chamberlain and the doctor.

"Don't think I'm good enough to treat a Colonel?" The man said accusingly, glaring at the boy, anger boiling over into a rage. "Get the hell out of this room and let me do my job, you little bastard!" The man held a straight razor in one hand, reaching out his other arm to grasp Emmett's shoulder, shaking him violently.

"Get out!" Emmett shouted, coming out of the chair where he had fallen asleep, his fists cocked and ready to fight.

"Settle down, soldier, I didn't mean to startle you." Emmett looked around uncomprehendingly, and then shook himself awake, looking at a nurse who had backed a pace away, but showed no sign of fear. She was a slight figure with a square face, her hair black as coal under a white scarf that matched her white apron. "You're in a ward at the General Hospital in Annapolis, in case you're wondering." She said with a reassuring smile. "I was wondering if you might be able to share some information about our friend here?" Chamberlain's uniform had been cut away during the procedure to save his life two nights earlier, and thus, there was no way to determine his rank.

"Sorry, ma'am. I was having a strange dream, but it weren't no dream at all." Emmett drew his hand across his brow, trying to scatter the cobwebs from his brain.

"What was your dream about?"

"On the steamship coming here there was a drunken doctor trying to tend to Colonel Chamberlain, and I had to stop him. The man could barely stand, and refused to leave, so I had to give him the butt of my gun into his gut, which was a mistake because he vomited all over the place, and then I had to drag him out by his foot while he lay there sobbing and retching. I found a surgeon on board, who, as luck would have it, was a former student of the Colonel's, Doctor Moses, who was of immense help."

"Sounds like a nightmare." The nurse said, her head nodding sympathetically, imagining the ordeal aboard the ship. "So this is Joshua Chamberlain, college professor turned hero of Gettysburg? I thought he would be taller."

"He's looked better." Emmett admitted.

"I'm sure he has." The nurse giggled. "We don't usually get to see the soldiers at their best in here. My name is Mary Clark, by the way. Where are my manners?"

"Good to meet you, ma'am. I'm Emmett Collins."

"Can you tell me anything about the Colonel's wound?" And so Emmett told her everything he knew, from the time when he was shot, to the operating table, and eventually how they had ended up here against all odds.

As Chamberlain was getting much-needed attention and Emmett was scrounging for supper and a room, 500 miles north Fanny Chamberlain was opening a letter that her husband had written the day after being wounded, Emmett having lost his original letter in the heat of battle and its terrible aftermath.

My darling wife I am lying mortally wounded the doctors think, but my mind & heart are at peace. Jesus Christ is my all-sufficient savior. I go to him. God bless & keep & comfort you, precious one, you have been a precious wife to me. To know & love you make life & death beautiful. Cherish the darlings & give my love to all the dear ones Do not grieve too much for me. We shall all soon meet Live for the children Give my dearest love to Father & Mother Sae & John Oh, how happy to feel yourself forgiven God

bless you ever-more precious precious one.
  Ever yours Lawrence⁹

No sooner had she read its contents then she set about preparing for a long trip south, her deliberate actions and calm demeanor hinting that she had contemplated this moment for some time, indeed prepared for it. The next day she was aboard the train, leaving the children behind with Cousin Deb Folsom. She arrived in the afternoon, bursting into the hospital tent like a whirlwind, full of purpose and worry all mixed together. She ran and knelt by his bedside, resting her head on his chest. "Lawrence, you are so thin and pale, but at least you are alive."

Chamberlain was astounded to see his wife, having to shake his head twice to make sure she was not some drug-induced hallucination. "Thanks to Abner Shaw who put me back together, and the grace of God, I am still alive. And Nurse Clark here, has been helping me regain some strength." Mary nodded and greeted Fanny, then discreetly withdrew, fluffing the sheets of an empty bed ten feet down the corridor.

"Your letter arrived telling of a mortal wound." Fanny continued, pressing his large hand between her own. "And then a telegraph from the army saying the same thing, and I had to get here in time to tell you to not leave me, but then on the train I read in the paper that you had died, and I thought I would die too, but here you are."

"I am so sorry for that, my darling." Chamberlain murmured, stroking her hair. "But it appears that I must yet have some purpose on this earth. I guess you're stuck with me."

"Thank God." She replied. "I will have to write Cousin Deborah and your sister Sae to spread the word that you are alive and well, maybe not exactly well, but well enough." She finished her words in a muddle.

Chamberlain grinned at her with cloudy eyes, fighting to stay awake. "You are like an angel come down from heaven."

"But tell me what happened, and what you shall need to do to recover." When there was no response, Fanny picked her head off his chest, realizing that her husband had fallen fast asleep.

"The doctors tell me that it is a miracle that your husband survived." Mary Clark whispered, having observed the scene.

Fanny turned her head, taking in the woman dressed in black with a white apron and hat, the light behind her making her features indistinguishable.

"I have been at your husband's side since his arrival, and he seems a remarkable man. Also, everyone calls me Mary, and I am from Boston, although I sometimes summer in Maine. You are the Fanny the Colonel has talked so much about." She pulled a chair from against the wall, offering it to Fanny, and then found a second chair from the next bed and sat down beside her.

"Tell me about his wound." Fanny beseeched the nurse, having had almost no details other than he was badly injured.

"They'd left him for dead when his brother, Tom, arrived with a Doctor Shaw, and he and another doctor labored to treat his wounds all that night. The bullet entered his hip here," she said, standing and pointing. " And then lodged itself here."

Fanny choked back a sob at the awful words, but nodded her head and waited for Mary to resume.

"Emmett said that blood was spraying from both sides of him, showering his men as they passed by to lead the assault on the Confederates at Petersburg, even though the bullet didn't exit. Doctor Vanderkirf, the head surgeon here, thinks that bone fragments may have been pushed out from his left hip. Doctor Shaw repaired the arteries as best he could to stop the blood loss, and scraped out bone fragments and other debris from the wound, but it was the injury to his bladder and urethra that posed the biggest problems. Doctor Shaw was forced to put a steel catheter into his penis so that his urine wouldn't leak into other body parts. They are hoping to be able to remove this in a few weeks time, as it is only a temporary solution."

Fanny sat still for a long time, staring at her husband sleeping in the bed, thinking how pale he was. Finally, she ventured the thought that stuck in her mind like an unwanted visitor. "They put a steel catheter into his penis?"

"The urethra is the tube that carries urine from the bladder out through the penis, and it was shredded, so this was necessary for the time being while they try to repair the tube."

"Will we...." Fanny blushed, but continued on. "Will we be able to ever again be intimate as husband and wife?"

Mary Clark looked sympathetically at this woman from

Maine who was so lucky not to be a widow. "That is not for me to say." She replied finally.

"Please." Fanny asked softly.

"I don't think so, but you never know." Mary Clark said with her head bowed.

Fanny nodded her head almost imperceptibly. "I am pregnant." The words emerged without adornment, a simple statement.

"Does Joshua know?"

"You are the first person I've told." Fanny replied forlornly.

"Joshua tells me you have two wonderful children already."

Fanny noted the familiarity, but chose to see it just as part of the nurse's plainspoken manner. "Two children who may never see their father again, and one on the way who may never even know him at all."

"You have to look on the bright side. Your husband is going to live, and will come home to you, to your children, and he will be a wonderful father. Perhaps best think of what you have been blessed with already."

Suddenly undone by the exhaustion of accumulated worry and then this ghastly news, she began to talk, hearing the words tumble out and yet unable to stop. "At one point I thought I would never marry—that I didn't want to attach myself to another being who would be the master of me. I wanted to be a musician, free and able to live life without the care of a family to hold me back."

"Life has a way of interfering with the best laid plans, and here you are with a wonderful family, married to a dashingly handsome war hero. I would say that things have worked out well for you."

"He was just so persistent." Fanny said, laying a cool washcloth on her husband's feverish brow. "I rejected his advances numerous times, and told him no over and over when he proposed marriage, but he just kept at it, until finally I gave in and agreed to marry him." Fanny's thoughts had drifted back to a time before the war, a smile flitting across her lips. "He wrote the most beautiful letters to me when we were apart, and he said the most romantic things when we were together. I knew I had made the right choice. And then Daisy was born, and I discovered that children were a blessed event in a marriage, even though her birth almost killed me."

"You are a lucky woman." Mary Clark marveled that so much happiness could come to one person.

"And then the war came." Fanny continued, her soft eyes changing to flint. "And now I am pregnant with a third child, sitting in a suffocating tent beside my husband, hoping beyond all hope that he survives. And yet, too," and here she smiled bitterly, "that his health does not improve so dramatically that he will return to this pointless war."

"Pregnant?" Chamberlain exclaimed, stirring in his bed, his eyes focusing on his wife, a dim memory of her arrival coming to his addled brain. "You are pregnant?"

Fanny nodded, tears beginning to course down her cheeks.

"How?"

Fanny laughed awkwardly. "I would imagine it was from our time in Washington D.C. this past spring."

Chamberlain's pale face colored slightly; shifting his eyes to Mary Clark, but then again back to his wife. "That is wonderful news."

Two weeks later more good news arrived in the unlikely form of Major Gilmore. He had been serving desk duty in Washington due to an old injury known infamously in the regiment for appearing to flare up whenever battles were imminent. Emmett had been taking his customary walks every day around the community of Annapolis, and so happened to discover Gilmore disembarking from a steamer. The Major came striding down the gangplank of the ship with a steady step that suggested he was healthier than he claimed. His eyes were searching the buildings just off the wharf to get his bearings, trying to pick out the hospital amidst the town surrounding it.

"Major Gilmore? Is that you, sir?"

"Emmett? Well, that certainly is a piece of good luck to run into you. Perhaps you can bring me to Chamberlain?" He deliberately left off the rank, which Emmett thought odd.

"Right this way, sir." Emmett led him from the wharf through the scattered town to the hospital tents. "But what are you doing here?" They made small talk with news of the 20th Maine, of which there was little, as the Union had laid siege to Petersburg, both sides digging in with little engagement. They found Fanny at her usual place, sitting beside her husband, who was propped up in his hospital bed.

"Good afternoon, Mrs. Chamberlain, it is a true pleasure to see you." Gilmore said, his attention briefly caught by her beauty.

Fanny had heard in numerous letters from her husband how Gilmore found every possible excuse to miss battles, and replied somewhat coolly with just a slight nod of her head. "Mr. Gilmore."

Chamberlain interrupted their exchange, rasping from his bed. "Major Gilmore, good to see you," each word dry and clipped.

"General Chamberlain." Major Gilmore said, saluting, a slight smile crinkling the corners of his mouth.

"General Chamberlain?" Emmett gasped, the first to respond to this fortuitous news. Chamberlain remained silent on his cot, but his eyes held the same question.

"Yes, sir." Major Gilmore said. "Generals Griffin and Warren both recommended you for promotion immediately after you fell at Rives Salient, and this was passed on to General Meade, and then to General Grant who made you a full Brigadier General. The Senate has just now approved it, and so you are now General Chamberlain."

"Thank you," Chamberlain whispered, and Emmett noticed his eyes welling up slightly. "I will be making my own recommendations for promotions, and sending them off to the Governor once I am able to sit up and write."

"Should you make it back to the field as General Chamberlain," Gilmore began, turning away from Chamberlain.

"Oh, I will be back." Chamberlain interrupted. "Of that you can be sure."

Fanny remained quiet as the two men exchanged news. As he had dropped these five little words, she had seen her husband's face, recognizing from his look of fierce determination that there was nothing she could do to keep him away. As soon as he was able, he would be back to the front, leaving her and his children behind. Yes, she thought, there were times when she wished she'd never married. And yet, she continued to love him, an emotion that she could not control.

Emmett had been exchanging letters with Susannah in Washington ever since they'd shared tea together in the city. His last letter had expressed his boredom, as his purpose here was uncertain with both Fanny Chamberlain and Mary Clark caring for Chamberlain. Emmett had written, telling Susannah that he was considering returning to the battlefield as perhaps an aide to one of the other generals. In mid-July, a letter arrived at the hospital from Susannah, urging him to visit her instead. She suggested in the letter that she had nobody to talk to in the city, and that she desperately needed a friend, and wondered if Emmett might be that friend. He was not sure that friend was quite what he wanted, but it would certainly do. General Chamberlain was only too happy to write him a general leave for seven days, and Emmett soon found himself aboard a steamship on his way to a week in the city.

Washington was now a familiar place, he reflected as he walked comfortably up Maryland Avenue to his first stop at the Armory Square Hospital to pay a visit to Walt Whitman. The city was far different than the late winter, early spring times that he was used to. The streets were dry and dusty, the passing wagons, horses, and people raising a stifling grit into the air that along with the heat created a dull haze. The stench was far worse as the temperature baked the open sewerage, the animal carcasses, and the rotting food, the acrid pong mixing with the dust and muggy weather to make breathing difficult. The poet-turned-nurse was happy to see him, and happier yet when Emmett told him the purpose of his visit. "Where are you staying?" He asked.

"I don't know yet," Emmett admitted. "I but got the letter yesterday, and here I am today."

"I know a Senator who has a standing room at the Willard, a very good friend who owes me a favor. He happens to be leaving tomorrow for a visit home. Let me see if you can borrow his room while he is away."

Emmett protested, but weakly, for he could already see himself hobnobbing in the lobby, puffing on a cigar with a drink in his hand, and a beautiful woman on his arm, an eager crowd hanging on his every word.

"Tell you what, I will meet you at the Willard, in the lobby later tonight. Should we say around eight? You must have a few errands to run." Whitman winked at Emmett. "Such as a haircut, and a new uniform. You might even be due a shave and a bath? There's one right around the corner, Johnson's Bath House Number One."

"Bathhouse?" Emmett had never heard of any such thing.

"Ah, yes, I forget you are a country boy. It is a new concept from Europe that has taken hold mostly in the larger cities. There is a boiler that heats water, so that people can pay for a hot bath to clean themselves up."

There were twelve partitioned sections at the bathhouse, but still Emmett had to wait for a tub to open up. He took the time to write a note to Susannah, letting her know that he was in the city. Before he could find somebody to deliver it, a man summoned him, bringing him to his tub and handing him a rough towel, pulling the curtain behind him. Emmett took off his clothes, twice checking to make sure the curtain was securely closed, and then climbed into the steaming water. There was a huge bar of Grandma's Lye Soap, which he used to scrub the sweat and grime from his body. He then lay back in the soapy water, dozing until it actually became chilly, before climbing out of the tub. He picked up his clothes, hesitant to put them back on his now-clean body, but had no choice, eventually dressing and leaving the bathhouse.

On his way towards Pennsylvania Avenue he came upon a barbershop. There was a chair open, and Emmett slid in as the white-haired Negro tucked an apron under his chin. "What we want today, soldjah?" The man had a wide grin, his teeth square and blocky in his mouth.

"I am meeting a beautiful woman today." Emmett had never been to a barbershop before, and was not sure what to say. "Can you just trim me up and make me look better."

"I can do that, yes I can."

"Is there somebody here can deliver a note for me?"

The black barber hollered, and a boy looking to be about nine or ten years old slunk his way into the shop from a back room. "My boy, Joseph, can take it for you."

Emmett handed the boy the note for Susannah, giving careful instructions as to where it should be delivered, giving him a half dime and promising another when he came back. The Negro first cut his hair, then stropped his thin razor carefully before shaving the fuzz from his lip and chin without commenting on its scarcity. The boy returned with a message from Susannah that she was busy that night, but would meet him for a late breakfast in the morning. Emmett emerged onto the street more uncomfortable than before in his shabby uniform, its bloodstains and tears all the more obvious to him now that he was freshly groomed.

He found a tailor on Pennsylvania Avenue who catered to military and civilians alike. The man wouldn't be able to make Emmett a new uniform for several days, as he was busy. Luckily, he had one that had been ordered but never picked up, and it was therefore cheap. It may have been just a tad large, but at least it had no rips or stains. Just down the street, Emmett went into Griffin & Brothers, buying a pair of ankle jacks that were far more comfortable than the Army-issued boots. At 8 p.m. he walked into the Willard a new man.

"Emmett? Emmett Collins?" Walt Whitman stood with an expression of feigned astonishment on his face. "You look like a young Lieutenant from the gentry, my fine young friend. I see that you have been lavish with your money."

Emmett tried to ignore the comment, but his face was crimson. "The army has been paying me the past two years, and truth be told, I haven't ever had a thing to spend it on before. I thought I'd save it up for after the war, but it seems like a good time to let some of it go."

"Well, you are a most handsome young man. You will be glad to know that I have acquired you a room free of charge, and the best part is that my Senator just left for home, so you may begin your stay tonight."

Emmett had never slept in a bed with cotton stuffing before, but he imagined that it was the next best thing to sleeping on a cloud. He woke in the morning, taking a bath in the tub in the corner of the room, all the while wondering that such luxuries existed in the world. For the past two years, washing up meant a refreshing stream in the summer hoping there were no snipers on the opposite bank, or in the winter, quickly dousing oneself with freezing water and hoping one didn't catch cold.

On the street he bought a bouquet of flowers from a tiny black girl who could have been no more than seven, flowers having been the recommendation of Walt Whitman. They were yellow marigolds tinted with red, fresh from the countryside and not yet withered by the heat of the city. He knocked on the brothel door, bouquet in hand, but his ability to speak left him when Susannah Smith opened it, flooding the street with her beauty. She wore a low-cut bodice of a light green, a crinoline giving substance to the bottom portion of the dress. She had a paisley shawl wrapped around her neck, her hair in a chignon, her tightly curled blonde locks rolled and braided at the back of her head. Emmett's eyes were drawn to her creamy skin, eyelashes fluttering around a sparsely-freckled, pert nose.

"Are those for me?" Susannah clapped her hands, taking the flowers from Emmett's stiff fingers. "Thank you. They're beautiful."

"As are you," Emmett mumbled.

"And look at you! I almost didn't recognize the dusty soldier I had tea with in the spring." Susannah looked him up and down, taking in the carefully combed hair, scrubbed cheeks, pristine uniform and shiny boots. "You clean up nice, Emmett Collins," she nodded, approvingly.

Emmett found himself unable to reply to this, the silence lengthening awkwardly around them.

"I'm famished," Susannah said lightly. "Do you mind if we go right off to eat?"

When Susannah heard that Emmett was staying at the Willard, she insisted they return there to eat. They had buckwheat pancakes with Vermont maple syrup, and different kinds of sausages, cheeses, and potatoes. "How long are you here?" There was a tiny drop of syrup on the corner of her lip that she flicked with her tongue, relishing the sweetness.

"Um, I have leave for a week." Emmett replied, his eyes unable to leave her mouth.

"I am so happy you came to call on me. Miss Hall said that she needs me to work for the next three nights, but then I could have two nights off." Susannah said, waving her arms excitedly, not used to be given such freedom.

They strolled through the streets of Washington, she at times holding onto Emmett's arm, creating a sensation in Emmett so strong that he was fearful of passing out, as her scent wafted past him and her arm and body brushed against his. They walked down Pennsylvania Avenue and circled the White House before heading northeast on New York Avenue. They came to Northern Market Space, a large square that served as a produce market for the nearby inhabitants. Emmett noticed there was far more Negros than further downtown, not just working, but buying as well.

"That's because Nigger Hill is right up there," Susannah told him, pointing north to the heights.

"I've never really known any black people, but they don't seem all that different from me," Emmett commented as they sat in a small shop eating doughnuts and drinking cider.

"They're people, same as you and me, doing what they can to survive." Susannah had grown up around slaves, but hadn't appreciated their plight until she'd become a soiled dove, a slave of a different sort.

A boy came up trying to sell them flowers, but Susannah claimed that she already had the prettiest bouquet in the world, and didn't need any more. "Does that mean you're against slavery?"

Susannah wrinkled her nose. "I don't know that slavery is all that bad, but I am against mistreating people, no matter their color."

Emmett let his glance travel around the crowds of people filling the market, fascinated with how many different people there were in the world. "I'm pretty sure I killed a man. I thought he'd killed my brother, and I shot him." Susannah kept quiet, letting Emmett talk. "I sometimes wake up in the middle of the night, and wonder about his family. I imagine what his life was like."

"We do what we have to in this world." Susannah whispered, grabbing his hand over the table and holding it firmly.

"Sometimes I think this war is terrible, but other times I wonder what I'll do when it ends."

They walked southeast on Massachusetts Avenue, stepping into shops to look at hats, books, shoes, and anything else that sparked their interest.

For the next three days, this is how Emmett passed the pleasant hours from late morning through the early afternoon, thinking that he had never been so happy in his entire life.

The fourth day when Emmett went to call upon her, Susannah opened the door with a caba in her hand. Emmett offered to carry the satchel for her, his curiosity getting the better of him, he asked, "What do you have in here?"

Susannah wrinkled her nose at Emmett. "You can't expect a girl to spend the night out without a few personal items, can you?"

Spend the night out? At first Emmett was horrified thinking he'd uttered these words aloud, covering his confusion by asking, "Are you hungry?"

"Let's drop my caba off at your room, and then let's get some ice cream. Do you mind? It has been forever since I've had ice cream."

"Can we eat it on our way?" Emmett asked mysteriously.

"On our way where?" Susannah paused, only to be urged along by Emmett, who couldn't contain his secret any longer.

"We are taking the Phoenix, a steamer from the 7th Street wharf, along with a brass band, to a picnic site for the day."

"A picnic? And a band? I could fall in love with you, Emmett Collins." Susannah hugged him tightly, and then began skipping down the street so that he had to run to keep up.

The day held many firsts for Emmett, as Susannah insisted that they dance to the band, held his hand everywhere they went, and kissed him first on the cheek, and then later on the lips. The steamer arrived back at the wharf in the early evening, Emmett suggesting that they could go to Ford's Theater where there were several comedians.

"I'm afraid I'm tired. Is it okay if we just go back to your room at the Willard?" Susannah asked, raising her eyebrows.

The night held another first for Emmett, one that he would never forget.

*****

The summer had passed with ups and downs in Chamberlain's health, one moment on the road to recovery, and the next relapsing and hanging onto life by a thread. One such relapse was grave enough for his brother, John, to come down from Maine to pay his last respects. And then, the next day he was sitting up in bed talking about a return to active duty. His 36th birthday came on September 8th, Fanny making a cake and holding a small celebration in the hospital. Mary Clark and some of the other 'sunbeams' attended, sunbeams being the nickname that the men had bestowed upon these women who brought such warmth and light to the drab hospital ward. The best birthday present he received was the news that General William T. Sherman had captured Atlanta, effectively cutting off a source of supplies for General Lee, the first undeniable harbinger that this Great War was now in its final stages.

Finally, in mid-September, Chamberlain was allowed to return home as the healing process continued. It was a brutally hard trip as he lay over the backs of several train seats on a stretcher, the bumps and jolts of the two-day trip exhausting what little strength that he possessed. Fanny was at his side the entire time with a cool cloth, medicine, and words of support. The college had arranged for a hack to be waiting for them, but Emmett had to beg a ride from a passing buckboard, for Chamberlain could not sit upright.

"Is that Colonel Chamberlain?" The driver of the buckboard asked Emmett as they went up Main Street.

"It is General Chamberlain." Emmett's thoughts were back in Washington D.C. with the fair-haired beauty of his dreams.

"Yes, I heard about the promotion, but I thought he'd died at Petersburg?"

"He just about did." Emmett replied brusquely. "But its gonna take more than a Reb bullet to take his life, that I can tell you for sure."

"I don't get to town much," the driver admitted. "Guess I should try to keep up with what's going on down there in Virginia. But it don't make much sense to me." He pulled the team up in front of the Chamberlain home, graciously offering to help carry the General in. They brought him straight to the bedroom, past his wide-eyed children and Cousin Deborah.

"Mama, can we say hello to Father?" Daisy inquired when she realized that he would not be immediately re-emerging from the bedroom.

"Not now." Fanny replied distractedly, the two days with an invalid having taken a toll on her as well.

"Please." Daisy whined.

"Your father is not feeling very well." Fanny snapped, wishing that she could let him deal with the children so that she could sleep.

The buckboard driver came out of the bedroom, tipping his

hat to Fanny and Deborah, and then letting himself out. Emmett was on his heels with a message for Fanny. "He was wondering if Daisy and Wyllys would be able to come in and say hello?"

"Of course he would," she said wearily. "Go ahead in children." They eased into the room half-excited, half-terrified of this much-changed man who was their father.

Wyllys tried to climb onto the bed, but Deborah Folsom pulled him back, having followed them into the room to see the man as well. Wyllys fought, pulling to get loose, but her hand was like a talon on his shoulder. Finally he stood still, asking, "Can you come out and play with me later?"

"Hello, son." Chamberlain murmured, summoning the last of his energy. "Maybe tomorrow I will be able to, but today I need to rest." This small lie was enough to appease Wyllys, who began to squirm, wanting to escape the stuffy room.

Deborah gave him a nod towards the door. "You may go outside, but don't leave the yard."

Daisy stood by her father with eyes round like saucers. "Does it hurt horribly?"

Chamberlain gave her an attempt at a smile that more resembled a ghastly grin than anything else. "No, it doesn't hurt, my sweet Daisy."

She could see the lie in his eyes, and ran sobbing from the room, with Fanny following.

"Hello, Deborah," Chamberlain said.

"You look terrible." Deborah Folsom had never been one to mince words.

"I am sure that I look no worse than I feel." Chamberlain retorted with candor, and just a glimpse of spirit. Aunt Deb was a plain woman who saw any luxury in life as unnecessary and frivolous. She could be a terrible headache to have around, spending most of her time scolding Joshua and Fanny as much as the children, but she did care for them all deeply.

For the next four weeks an uneasy truce rippled just below the surface calm they all tried to present. Fanny was now in her sixth month of pregnancy, a time that had always proven difficult for her physically, but was now complicated by her concerns for her husband and their future as well. At the same time, it would most assuredly be their last child as it was becoming ever plainer that their sexual life was now over. The damage from the minié ball that had ripped through her husband's body simply could not be repaired, with scar tissue from operation after operation only complicating the healing.

After that first week of recuperation in which he never left the bed, Chamberlain beckoned Emmett one morning to help him move to his study. Once there, he began to write the first of what would become an endless stream of letters over the next few weeks. Among the letters he sent was one to Adelbert Ames, his former commander, assuring him that he would be coming back to active duty soon. He had left the unfinished letter on his desk that night, and Fanny happened on it in the morning, bringing her fears to fruition. Her husband was determined to return to the ranks. This fear and anger overflowed one afternoon when Emmett had taken the children fishing down on the Androscoggin after school.

"Fanny," Chamberlain called from his office. "I have letters that need to be mailed." Every day there was a new stack of stiff, buff envelopes. Confined to his desk, with only short trips outside the home, Chamberlain sent letters to many, many people—letters to Governor Coburn, Generals Grant, Meade, Warren, Griffin, as well as Tom, Sae, and John, his mother and father, and his Bowdoin students gone to war, like Ellis and Doctor Moses.

"What are all these letters for? What could be so important about your life in Brunswick, Maine that General Grant would need an update each and every day?" Fanny asked. She had bided her time for this confrontation, and the time was now.

"I am asking to be reinstated to a field position with my brigade." Chamberlain spoke honestly, knowing that this was the first salvo of what could become a long engagement indeed.

"Your place is here with your wife and children."

"My destiny lies with the Union Army."

"Your *destiny* is growing inside of me, and wants to know her father as a man, a whole man, and not a vague memory as she looks at a tintype of somebody in a uniform who died during the war." Fanny spoke sharply, angry that he was willing to throw away so much.

"My darling wife, when have you ever known me to start something, and then not finish it?" Her husband asked patiently.

"You've given enough to your country. Two years of our life together for an ideal that does not affect us in any way. Two years in which I have had no husband, and the children have had no father. I have stood by silently for *two years* while you have fulfilled what you determined through some false sense of honor to be your duty. But now that your body has been maimed, and our lives are forever changed, I can no longer keep my silence. Your place is here with me, with your children."

Chamberlain chose his words carefully before replying. "I hope that my body continues to heal so that my recovery is complete in every way, but there is yet unfinished business to take care of back in Virginia." He paused and looked into those brown eyes he loved so, hoping to see in them understanding rather than anger. "That is a call that I can't ignore."

"And the unfinished business of raising your children?"

"Now that I am a general, it is no longer my role to lead the men into battle, but to stay safely to the rear directing the action. I will come home to my family."

"What good will you be there?" Fanny demanded of him. "You can barely walk from bedroom to study, yet you are going to return to battle?"

"There is more for me to do. I can feel it in my heart."

"When news came that you were wounded and expected to die, when I read in the New York newspaper that you had died, I rushed to your side. When I found you alive, I nursed you back to health, never expecting that I was doing this merely as preparation for your return to the slaughter." Fanny was now quietly crying, little gasps between her words giving away her tears.

"I have no choice." Chamberlain said softly, throwing up his shoulders as if in despair. "Would you have me shirk my duty? The last two years have tested me, and the experience has changed me. I am no longer an academic. I can no longer take the path of the professor. I need to finish what I started, to find out who I am."

"Do not expect me to come rushing to your side again," Fanny said coldly. "For I cannot watch you die. If you must, return to the battlefield, but wish your children and this yet unborn baby a careful goodbye, for they are what you are sacrificing." She left the room, sobbing. He made no move to follow her, but sat with his head bowed.

Several days later, he beckoned Emmett into the parlor where he sat working at his desk. "Tomorrow, we go back to Washington. Arrange for a wagon to take us to the train station in the morning."

Orders had come from General Meade to report to headquarters for assignment to active duty. This was no callousness on the part of the war machine, but a result of the endless correspondence Chamberlain had been sending to every person imaginable, letters pleading for just this result. For General Joshua Chamberlain realized that the war was coming to a close, and he was not ready to be on the sidelines for that conclusion. No, he felt the overwhelming need to finish his part on the front lines, as a soldier, as a man. It was less than five months after the injury that had left him for dead at Rives Salient. He was not yet capable of walking even the quarter of a mile to the train station, yet he was returning to the battlefield against the wishes of his wife and children, for the war beckoned, and he could not refuse.

Chapter Sixteen

National Republican　　　　　**November 15, 1864**

The Siege of Petersburg

The Noose Tightens Around the City of Petersburg and Robert E. Lee

The stranglehold continues to tighten on the Army of Northern Virginia in the city of Petersburg. The siege didn't start well, with the debacle of the 'Disaster at the Crater' on July 30th of this year in which a Union demolition team tunneled under Confederate lines, exploding several large bombs. This initially was successful, opening a breach in the Rebel lines, but the ensuing infantry attack charged down into the crater, and were not able to get back out, allowing the enemy from the south to shoot them 'like fish in a barrel'. General Grant was further embarrassed by the 'Beefsteak Raid', in which a contingent of Rebels stole over two thousand head of good beef cattle, helping to alleviate the hunger of the besieged. Nonetheless, the Army of the Potomac has now stretched itself three quarters of the way around the city of Petersburg, cutting the Rebels off from access to supplies. At Globe Tavern, the Union Army captured thirty miles of the important Weldon Railroad, forcing the enemy now to bring supplies by wagon from Stony Creek. General Sherman has captured Atlanta, and appears to be in control of the southern states. Some people are starting to whisper that the end of this Great War is in sight.

December 7, 1864

Emmett rode alongside Chamberlain as the 5th Corps moved out on a raid to destroy more of the Weldon Railroad tracks. Cutting this means of supply had been determined to be of the utmost urgency in the war effort. In the months that

Chamberlain had spent recovering, the Union Army had fought minor skirmishes to expand the area they controlled to the south and west of Petersburg. As fast as they were dismantling the South's key railroads, they were laying track to make sure the Union lines were well supplied, creating a rail system from City Point on the James River running thirty miles inland. Chamberlain had been put back in charge of the 1st Brigade, but other changes had also occurred, the brigade now being comprised of just two regiments, the 185th New York and the oversized 198th Pennsylvania, which brought together fourteen companies.

"Here comes your brother." Emmett commented, pointing to their left where Tom Chamberlain was approaching on horseback.

"He rides mighty fine." Chamberlain spoke almost as if a proud parent.

Tom galloped his black gelding right at them, only slowing at the last moment, reining the animal in beside them as they walked along. "You look like hell, Lawrence." Tom laughed, happy to be on the move, in action, on horseback. "How you stay on that horse, I do not know. One would think that those frail limbs of yours wouldn't have the strength to hold you upright."

"General Chamberlain, or sir, would be what I should expect from a captain addressing his superior." Chamberlain said this with a straight face, knowing full well that Tom had recently been promoted to provost marshal of the 1st Division.

"You might outrank me brother, but I can lock you up if I deem it necessary, so you'd best watch your mouth."

Chamberlain shook his head in feigned disgust, a smile forming on his lips. "What has it been? Two weeks on duty, and already abusing your power? It is true that power corrupts, at least in your case."

Tom laughed, happy that his brother had kept his sharp wit, even though his appearance truly was appalling. His arms and legs were like brittle sticks poking out from a shrunken body, his cheeks sunken into his skull, and his skin still pale as the cotton blooms that would be blanketing the land all around them come summer. The past two weeks back in the field had returned a hint of his former ruddy complexion, and being away from hospitals and doctors, even the cares of family life, seemed to breathe new life into him, hastening his recovery. "I reckon it's all relative, as you look better than the last time I saw you in that tent after you were shot at Rives Salient."

"I'd have to say I feel better as well."

Tom switched his attention to Emmett. "I heard from a friend that you paid a visit to a particular young lady in Washington. Is that true?"

Emmett blushed deeply, avoiding the searching glance of Joshua Chamberlain, to whom he'd never revealed the purpose of that visit. "I have no idea what you're talking about," he grunted.

Tom shook his head in wonder. "You will have to introduce me some time."

They marched twenty miles that day through southern Virginia, country controlled by the Union Army but sympathetic to the Confederacy. New recruits not used to hard marching straggled behind, unable to keep up with the pace set by officers and the veterans, but no one came out of their houses to offer food or water. The second day, they came to Stony Creek, engaging a single brigade of the Army of Northern Virginia protecting the railhead. It was here that the supply trains arrived, unloading their provisions into wagons, which were then smuggled through and around the lines to sustain the besieged soldiers and citizens of Petersburg. The Rebels at Stony Creek had no chance against the superior numbers of the Yankees, retreating to safety, while the 5th Corps let them go.

They were not here to engage the enemy but to destroy another twenty miles of train tracks all the way to Hicksford on the Meherrin River, near the North Carolina border. They started at the end of the tracks, ripping the rails up, attached ties and all. They then flipped the rails over to wrest the sleeper ties loose. They made a bonfire with the ties, stacking the rails on top. The heated steel became malleable, allowing the soldiers to bend and twist them, ensuring they could never be used as tracks again. Some men wrapped the pliant tracks around trees, calling them Sherman's neckties in recognition of General Sherman who, just recently in Georgia, had made this kind of wholesale rail destruction famous. Some innovative soldiers even created a Maltese Cross, the emblem of the 5th Corps, out of one section, leaving it as a reminder of who had come and done this.

After three days of destroying rails, the 5th Corps, its objective realized, made their final camp before starting on their return journey. It was a bitterly cold night, the temperature hovering around freezing, with a dampness in the air that, along with a stiff wind, made the cold all the more penetrating.

"I thought it was supposed to be warm down south." Tom said, huddled by a smoldering fire burning weakly against the cold.

"If we was up in Brewer, we'd be sitting in about two feet of snow right about now." Emmett replied, holding his hands over the thick smoke from the wet wood.

"At least we have food and this here applejack to keep us warm." Daniel held up his tin cup, half-filled with the brandy that had been 'requisitioned' that day from the local homes, along with salt pork and real bread, instead of the insect-infested hardtack they were used to.

"Who let you out to play?" Tom directed the question at Emmett. "I thought Lawrence would be keeping you busy making sure the camp was secure."

"He went to bed early. He won't say, but I think his wound is acting up something terrible. He was barely able to get off the horse on his own today, and then I thought his legs were gonna just give out, but he managed to crawl into the tent on his own."

"It sure is something that he's back at all." Daniel said with astonishment. "Less than six months ago the surgeons gave up on him as not worth their time, and here he is on a raid tearing up tracks in an ice storm."

"Lawrence always was a stubborn cuss." Tom agreed. "Once he sets his mind to doing something there ain't no stopping him, that's for sure."

A horse nosed its way up to the fire, a cold and wet lieutenant on General Griffin's staff astride him. "Provost Marshal Chamberlain?"

"That's me, Lieutenant." Tom remained sitting beside the fire. "What can I do for you?"

"I've had a dickens of a time finding you." The man slid to the ground, walking to the fire to warm his hands. "General Griffin was wondering what you were doing about the applejack problem."

Daniel's hand holding the tin cup froze halfway to his lips.

"What applejack problem?"

"It seems that in today's requisitioning of supplies from the locals, many barrels of apple brandy were liberated as well."

"The men deserve a warm drink on a cold night, especially after their hard work." Tom shrugged his shoulders. "I don't see the problem."

"Many of the men have become downright raucous." The lieutenant was not beyond a nip or two himself, but he'd just come from General Griffin who was furious at the men's antics. "Some have filled their canteens and are drinking it like water." Almost as if on cue, loud laughter came spilling across the way.

"I will look into it." Tom said, and stood reluctantly.

Daniel discreetly dumped his tin cup to the ground. "Need a hand?"

The lieutenant went to report back to General Griffin while the three men from Maine walked in the direction of the rowdiest noise. General Chamberlain, oblivious, slept hard in his tent, worn out, weakened, not quite up to the task of being in the field just yet.

The next morning came too early for many of the revelers of the night before. Tom and the provost guards had barely slept, having gone from regiment to regiment breaking up good times, all the while staving in barrels and barrels of the brandy. Fifty-eight men of the 1st Division were unable to be roused at all and were left behind to face the cold—and maurading Rebel guerrilla's—on their own. The 1st Brigade fared better than others, not leaving a soul behind, and it was with pride that Chamberlain was able to report that all of his men were accounted for. Deep down, however, he knew it was not due to his leadership, but to Tom's attention and just blind luck. The General himself had slept through most of the debauchery.

Emmett was riding beside Chamberlain when they discovered the first dead body. The man had been stripped naked; his throat slit from ear to ear, and his body was encased in a layer of ice from the sleet of the night before. It was one of the new recruits who had straggled on the way south, falling behind. Unable to keep up, he'd been caught by bushwhackers sympathetic to the South. There were dozens more of these corpses, all naked, all with their throats cut, left in the middle of the road as a warning to the Northern soldiers.

A soldier in the 3rd Brigade could be heard swearing obscenely, angrily, urging the men in his company to retaliate. Suddenly, a small group of men veered out of column and into the yard of a house. They burst through the door, dragging a family—mother, grandmother, and three young children—from the house. Then Emmett saw the smoke curling out through the broken windows, and realized they had set fire to it.

"What are we going to do?" Emmett was disgusted, unable to take his eyes off the smallest of the children, a boy of no more than five years old, screaming in terror as his home burned before his eyes.

"I don't know." Chamberlain replied weakly, his eyes looking back down the line of the 5th Corps, the news of the dead bodies having traveled quickly, fresh fires licking the sky from other homes down the road. "The men are angry, and I can't rightly see stopping them now. Better just keep moving best we can."

Emmett had never seen Chamberlain at a loss, unable to do the right thing, and for the first time was disappointed with his mentor. It was one thing to destroy property that helped the Confederacy, like their railroads, or to take the supplies from homes to feed the army. But it was another thing entirely to make families homeless, families with no men to help, nowhere to go, in the bitter cold of winter.

*****

Three months later, Emmett was huddled by a fire before the sun had risen, clutching a cup of coffee in his hand. It was March 29th and the massive mobilization to dislodge Robert E. Lee and the Army of Northern Virginia from their defensive positions in Petersburg was to start this day. Chamberlain was studying a map across the fire from Emmett. Soon after the raid on the Weldon Railroad the previous December, he had succumbed to his injuries, returning to Philadelphia in January for surgery to ease the pain, followed by further recuperation in Brunswick. This time Emmett had stayed with the 5th Corps, acting as a courier for General Warren.

A sudden commotion disturbed the darkness, and General Griffin emerged from the blackness astride a handsome chestnut mare. He swung down lightly while his retinue remained in their saddles. "Welcome back, General Chamberlain." He said. "You look much better."

"General Griffin. Good to see you." Chamberlain replied, rising to his feet.

"I believe this time we may finally flush the Confederates from Petersburg. I am glad that you made it back to be part of it." General Griffin, commander of the 1st Division of the 5th Corps, was Chamberlain's immediate superior. "Your brigade will lead us out this morning at sunrise. Do you have any questions?"

"None, sir." General Griffin walked to his horse, putting his boot into the stirrup he slid nimbly into the saddle. "Let's get it done then." He half-turned his mount, then stopped, looking back. "Is your health up to the task?" He asked.

"I've never felt better, sir." Chamberlain replied, thinking of the letter he'd written his sister recently.

March 9th, 1865
My dear Sae,

I have been back about ten days now, and find the change very agreeable so far as my health is concerned....

You cannot imagine how favorable this kind of life is to my health. One would not think me fit to walk a half mile if I was at home; but here I ride as fast + far as the best, and ask no favors. I have no doubt that my recovery will be greatly promoted by my return to the field, and I do not in the least regret my choice. I shall not feel obliged to lead any more charges, unless it becomes necessary, and hope to escape any further injuries. I have no insane desire to deprive my little family of my protection + support I assure you. No man's ever was dearer or more blest. And to no man could it be a greater sacrifice to leave them far away and face the dangers, which in threatening me threaten them tenfold. Still let me say the course I take is not only which honor + manliness prompt, but the one which will prove best for them + for all who belong to me or to whom I belong....
Your ft. Brother,
Lawrence[9]

*****

As the sun crept over the horizon, the 1st Brigade led the 5th Corps on what many hoped would be the final campaign of the war. The battle-weary soldiers marched quietly, at first to the south but then swinging around to the west via the Stage and Vaughn Roads, and then back to the north up the Quaker Road. Major General Sherman had carved a path of destruction from Atlanta to Savannah, Georgia the previous November and December that had left the rebel Army of Northern Virginia low on supplies and its soldiers fearing for the safety of their families back home. Sherman had prosecuted a policy of total war in which his army had not only burnt farms and supplies, but wrecked any infrastructure—bridges, railheads, dams, train tracks, even ferries and wagons—necessary to support the war. He was now moving north to help surround Lee and his army. The Army of Northern Virginia, now almost starving, had also begun to suffer widespread desertions seriously depleting the ranks and severely limiting its options.

"Are you so sure that ole' Bobby Lee will run?" Emmett could not remember him ever retreating from battle, except maybe after Gettysburg.

"He has no choice." Chamberlain answered.

"It seems that we've thought we had him before—and then ended up with our nose bloodied for the effort." Emmett had never been one to count his chickens before they were hatched.

"We will soon dislodge the old fox from his hiding place. The trick will be in whether we have him well enough surrounded or leave a gap through which he is able to slip away." Chamberlain still rode the horse with some discomfort, it being obvious to all that his wounds caused his stiff posture in the saddle.

Each man had been issued seventy cartridges for their rifles, a certain indicator that battle loomed. As he turned his gaze to the spring countryside, Emmett saw violets blooming in the fields, as were the peach trees in their orchards. It reminded him of the picnic the previous summer he had shared with Susannah. At first, she had written him as regularly as he wrote her, but there had been no word from her for several months now. He was jolted back to the present when a staff officer rode up.

"General, sir, there is a creek ahead with Rebs dug in on

the other side. It looks like they destroyed the bridge and now are waiting for us."

"Let's have a look," Chamberlain said, urging his horse forward. From a small knoll he assessed the situation with a spyglass, taking no more than a few minutes to make a decision. "Emmett, take this note to Colonel Sickel of the 198th, directing him to split his regiment and set up a covering fire from down below, there," he said pointing, "while we cross the creek there."

His horse at a canter, General Griffin came up the knoll with his staff trailing just behind him. "What's the situation, General Chamberlain?"

"We are going to have six companies under Major Glenn cause a demonstration on the right, diverting their attention from the rest of the brigade crossing the creek on the left. What's the name of this place, sir?"

"Gravelly Run." Griffin replied, looking to an aide, who nodded confirmation. "Go to it then."

Daniel Collins heard the rifle fire begin over on the right side, and a minute later the order was given to charge. He clambered down the bank with his new regiment, the 185th New York, the men hitting the waist deep water as fast as they could, knowing that crossing over before the Confederates realized they were coming was the best hope of survival. The first of the men were climbing the shallow bank on the far side when a light volley hit them, several men dropping in their tracks, and then they were upon the enemy, fighting hand to hand. Daniel found himself locked in the embrace of a short barrel of a man with long hair matching his thick beard. Latching his right hand into the man's hairy face, Daniel grabbed a firm handhold of the facial hair, while punching overhand to connect with his cheekbone. The man tightened his thick arms around Daniel, his breath sour. Daniel struggled to get loose, and when unable, drew his head back and then snapped it forward into the man's nose, smashing it in a shower of blood. The man released him, bellowing in pain and falling to the ground.

Emmett stayed by Chamberlain's side. Barely two months after his latest surgery, and less than a year after being left for dead on the battlefield, here he was again surging into battle without any apparent fear. They did follow the men over the creek instead of leading the charge, but that was the role of a general, who was supposed to stay 150 yards to the rear until battle commenced, and then was permitted to go wherever he thought best. The Confederates had turned their attention to their right flank to meet this charge, thus giving Major Glenn an opportunity to surge across the water on the left. They harried the Confederates for the better part of a mile, steadily pressing forward through the woods, a mass of men rolling forward unchecked.

Daniel was out of breath from the chase, dodging trees and leaping rocks, all the while expecting a gray uniform to suddenly materialize from behind a tree to thrust a bayonet into his guts. He emerged from the woods into a clearing, seeing a farmhouse ahead with several outbuildings behind which the Confederates had taken up defensive positions.

"Forward! Drive them out of there!" The call went up and down the line, and Daniel burst forth from the woods, part of a blue wave streaming across several hundred yards of open ground leading up to the farm. The Confederates fired a ragged volley, and then broke in the face of the approaching storm, fleeing their positions to cross a road into more woods. The Union soldiers paused when they reached the buildings, gasping for air, taking the opportunity to drink from their canteens. Those who had bothered to fire their rifles reloaded, all of them wondering if the advance would continue.

Daniel took a long swig from his canteen, looking around to get his bearings. The cleared area of the farm was a large square, each edge being about a half-mile in length. The Quaker Road ran through the middle of this clearing, with a farmhouse, barn, toolshed, and outhouse on the right side of road. The Rebel soldiers had fallen back to the far tree line. On the right corner of the clearing was a five-foot-tall sawdust pile that stretched about 200 feet from a mill on the edge of a small stream. He felt bad for the owners of this home, thinking of his own house in Brewer, wondering how he would feel if a battle raged around it. The family had evacuated the premises, but he imagined them as a grandmother, mother, two young girls and a boy barely able to walk, the husband and father might very well be hunkering down behind the sawdust pile at the far end of the clearing, hoping beyond hope that his family had gotten out. Chickens ran squawking around the yard, and a cow mooed from the barn. It was the milk and eggs that probably allowed the family to survive, Daniel knew, and he also knew that when the Union Army moved on there would be no more cow and no more chickens. He watched as General Chamberlain and his staff rode up to the main house, his younger brother Emmett riding confidently by his side, and a flush of pride swept through Daniel to realize his kid brother held such a prominent position in the army.

"General, they are well dug in on the other side of the road." A staff officer reported to Chamberlain. "They have breastworks built from logs and earth, and what seems to be a brigade manning their positions."

"Have the men take up defensive positions, and we will wait for reinforcements." Chamberlain made his decision quickly. "We could use a breather anyway."

Chamberlain sent Emmett to gather the officers in the main house of what they now knew was called the Lewis Farm. "And make sure that a regiment takes up position by that sawdust pile," he said, pointing to where the steam wood mill had left huge mounds of shavings, the dense piles of wood particles making for an effective defensive breastwork.

"That is the center of the Rebs defense, sir. They are nestled in on the far side of the pile as we speak." One of the staff officers interrupted.

"Well, we will need to push them out of there eventually, but not now."

General Griffin arrived as they were waiting for Colonel Sniper and General Sickel. "Chamberlain. What's the hold up?" He asked.

"The enemy is in force down the road there. Their center appears to be that sawdust pile, and they are well dug in and have erected a solid breastwork. Prisoners suggest that reinforcements are on the way to drive us back from our position here."

"That is exactly why we must attack now, before they can be supported." Griffin replied, unfolding a map on the table in the farmhouse. "If we can control the Quaker Road, we have a wedge with which to dislodge them." The Quaker Road led directly towards the center of the Confederate strength.

"Yes, sir." Chamberlain turned to Sickel and Sniper who had arrived in the meantime. "General Sickel, you will command the right side in the advance here, and Colonel Sniper, you will command the left side, while I will lead the attack from the center, right up the road. We will move together as one unit. Understood?" Chamberlain snapped out the orders with a false bravado, wondering if he was up to the task. He still had nightmares of being shot, terrifying images that left him dripping wet with sweat, gritting his teeth ferociously to keep from screaming out in the middle of the night. He knew that physically he was not the man he'd been a year earlier at Gettysburg. There was little chance that he could march, much less charge into the enemy on foot, and fear churned his guts as he thought of charging his way up the Quaker Road on horseback into the very teeth of the enemy.

Moments later, Emmett walked his horse alongside Chamberlain as the center of the brigade moved down the Quaker Road. As they approached the site of the mill, bullets began to come at them like angry bees. "Save your fire men, we will give them the steel today." Chamberlain ordered.

Emmett holstered his rifle in the scabbard, pulling the revolver, which Chamberlain had given him as a more practical weapon from horseback. He was doubly proud of it, coming, as it had from the General's own belt. He could feel the heat of the sun on his back, faintly recognizing that the Rebels would have that sun in their eyes. Dust rose into the air from the trampling of a thousand feet as the men began to jog. They were now only about 200 yards from the sawdust pile and woods that protected their enemy. To the right and left of the road men in blue moved forward with deadly intent. To Emmett's left, a man who he merely knew as Abraham took a bullet to the face, his features collapsing into blood and bone. Emmett forced himself to look away, all the while pressing forward. And then they were upon the Confederates, bayonets flashing in the late afternoon sun, stabbing, piercing, and thrusting into the enemy.

Emmett took careful aim at a soldier and fired his Colt Revolver. His horse danced sideways just as he pulled the trigger however, and the bullet went whizzing harmlessly into the sky. The man grabbed his reins and tried to wrestle his horse to the ground. Emmett sighted along the barrel and shot him in the chest. He coughed, his eyes widening as he realized he was dying, and then fell to the ground.

Under this ruthless onslaught, the Rebels momentarily fell back from the sawdust pile. Then reinforcements came to their aid, and they surged forward, clashing again with the Union troops of the 1st Brigade, stalling their advance. In the midst of the battle lines, Chamberlain rode to rally his men, waving his saber over his head, Charlemagne rearing underneath him.

As Emmett watched, the general suddenly slumped forward over the horse's neck, blood covering both of them. Lieutenant Vogel toppled from his horse at the same time. Emmett grabbed the reins of Charlemagne, leading him backwards to let the infantry pass by. "General? Can you hear me?"

General Griffin approached, having witnessed the incident from the rear. "My dear General, you are gone." He said, wrapping his arm around the fallen man's waist to keep the body from plunging into the dirt.

"No!" Emmett yelled, grabbing at Chamberlain's limp arm. Blood covered his face and chest, as he lay collapsed over his favorite mount. It seemed a cruel fate to return to duty only to be killed during the final moments of the war.

Then, just as suddenly as he had fallen, Chamberlain picked his head up from Charlemagne's neck and straightened, his face and body covered in blood, hat gone from his head, his hair matted and wild. As the others stood silently in shock, he shook his head and wiped blood from his eyes with his sleeve, regarding the situation all around them. Even in this state, he recognized the danger on the right where some soldiers were falling back, for he had thought that Griffin's words referred to the battle and not to his life. "You are right General, I am gone." He said to General Griffin, ripping the reins from Emmett's hands, riding hard to stem the breach on the right, the insanity of the ancient warrior evident in his narrowed eyes and strange smile, in his first words to the retreating soldiers. "Kill those bastards!" He screamed. "Turn and fight."

General Griffin shook his head in wonder and looked at Emmett. "Stay with him, Collins. And when he falls, as he surely will, make sure you bring him back." Emmett was already turning and racing after Chamberlain almost before the words had left the general's mouth.

"Turn and face the enemy!" Chamberlain exhorted the fleeing Union soldiers of the 198th Pennsylvania. He brandished his saber above his head, looking like death unleashed, a terrifying apparition from hell who inspired more fear in the soldiers than the Confederate Army at their backs. Emmett shrugged his shoulders, joining in, blocking the way of the retreating soldiers with his horse, pulling his new pistol out, whether to threaten the fleeing Union soldiers or the charging Confederates, he was not sure.

"Do not," Chamberlain yelled, "let the message to your mothers be that you were shot in the back while running away!" Chamberlain had now stopped the flight, and was regrouping the men to counter-charge. Off to the right Emmett saw General Sickel tumble to the ground, a horde of gray overrunning his position. "Follow me to glory, men!" Chamberlain yelled, a guttural roar evoking man's basest instincts, the savagery necessary to fight, to survive.

As he galloped down the road, Chamberlain suddenly realized that he was completely covered in blood, as was his horse. Its coppery scent seemed to tinge the dreamlike scene before him. He could somehow see the men following behind him, careening crazily into a horde of gray uniforms. He watched the scene unfold below as if from the perspective of a hawk floating on the wind, seeing himself cantering between the two lines, one gray and one blue. He was barely recognizable, every piece of civilized homo sapiens stripped away, a single consummate rage driving him forward, a keening emanating from a mouth whose lips were laced tightly back over the teeth.

The two colors crashed together, pinning him in their midst, where he slashed right and left with his saber, drawing blood with every swing, the men cringing in front of him, more afraid of the look in his eyes than the flashing blade in his hand. The onslaught proved too much for the Rebels, and they broke, fleeing in the face of this demon from Hell and his equally inspired minions. He could see himself barking orders to the officers still standing, and then spurring a bloody Charlemagne back to the center, the most direct path lying between the Union and Confederate lines. He was lying low over the neck of his horse, one hand clutching a handful of mane, the reins in his teeth, his saber pointing the way, racing back to his central command in the most direct route possible. The sound of cheering drifted up to his lofty perch, and he could see the Union soldiers waving their rifles, hollering for all they were worth, impassioned by the mad antics of their General, so recently on his death bed, scoffing at death. Then he realized there were others cheering, from the Confederate lines. They, too, were waving their rifles, yelling praise for one of the enemy, but a fellow countryman and human being whose bravery they could understand. The wind died, and he could feel himself begin to fall back to earth, taking one last look at his crazed self and the cheering Northerners and Southerners, united temporarily in their admiration of courage.

Charlemagne stumbled underneath Chamberlain just as they reached the sawdust pile back in the center of the lines. The horse then staggered, falling to his knees, Chamberlain leaping lightly to the ground with a bounce to his step that had been absent for quite some time, the adrenalin of battle surging hotly in him. "Somebody bring my horse to the rear and see that the wound to his neck is treated."

Emmett arrived soon after, realizing for the first time that Charlemagne had been shot. He had missed most of the fighting, merely trailing behind Chamberlain, who he was expecting to fall at any moment. He had no time to dwell on this, as Chamberlain had dashed forward into the midst of the battle to urge the soldiers on. The Confederates had now concentrated their pressure on the center of the Union forces, probing for a weakness to exploit.

"What in tarnation was that all about?" Daniel had spotted Emmett, and both of them were following Chamberlain into the breach.

"What?" Emmett was almost as dazed by the events as Chamberlain, unsure as to what part of all that was real, and what was not. He was hurrying to catch up to his mentor, but was still fifty yards behind him as the man was running as if possessed.

"The whole thing. I thought Chamberlain was dead, and then he goes charging off to the right. Next thing I know, he's racing between the two armies, and if my eyes and ears don't deceive me, both sides were cheering for him?" Daniel said gasping, breathing heavily from exertion.

"Did you hear them Rebels cheering, too?" Emmett asked. "I thought I was crazy. Hell, that was crazy."

"I guess the Confederates still have some American in them, enough to admire courage, whatever side it comes from." Daniel noticed that there was a red welt across Emmett's arm, the kind of welt left by a bullet as it grazed the skin.

"I don't reckon I know if it was courage or crazy, but it shore was something to see." Emmett grunted, raising his rifle and firing it for the first time that day, missing his target wide.

Everywhere there were wounded men, Union and Confederates alike, and often hard to tell who was who because of their dirty, grimy uniforms, and the smoke from the battle. Bodies hurtled forwards and backward around Emmett as he tried to find Chamberlain in the swirling mass of humanity. As he reached the front line, he suddenly caught sight of him leading a group of Rebel soldiers.

"Emmett, these men are my prisoners. See to it that they are brought to the rear under guard." And he was off again with his saber held high, encouraging men into the fight, on the one hand a ludicrous figure, and on the other, a macabre ghastly apparition not to be ignored.

"Who in hell is that?" One of the group of prisoners asked Emmett as he brought the men back through the lines.

"General Joshua Chamberlain." Emmett replied proudly.

"I thought that was a star I saw on his shoulder." Another interjected. "Couldn't rightly see it through all the smutch, guess that's how he fooled us into thinking he was one of us."

"Was he the dang fool idiot racing his horse up and down the line earlier?" Another of the men wondered aloud. "Was an act of God he wasn't shot out of his saddle, God knows we was tryin."

Emmett nodded. "That would be General Chamberlain."

"Is he loony?"

Emmett laughed, a harsh sound in the back of his throat. "I think he just got his dander up, is all. But maybe we're all a little bit loony." Emmett said, waving his arm at the death churning around them. And then, as if on cue, the fighting stopped, both sides pausing to take a breath. Emmett handed off the prisoners, returning to the sawdust pile in the center, where he found

Chamberlain standing in a small crowd of junior officers.

"It appears that Charlemagne slowed the bullet for me," Chamberlain was telling the group around him. "In fact, most of the blood on me is from him, poor horse. I do hope he will heal up."

"But you were briefly knocked out, sir. You must have been hit as well."

Chamberlain smiled wryly, pulling from his left breast pocket a leather bound book whose pages he used to send messages, and a brass pocket mirror. "It appears my wife saved my life by giving me this mirror as a gift. I thought she was commenting that I was vain about my appearance, but in reality it was a shield." He held up the mangled brass pocket mirror and the field book, the minié ball having ripped a furrow through the pages. The small crowd laughed in approval.

"It is also good, sir," one of the aides piped up, "that you have not had much of an opportunity to use your field book yet or it would have been much slimmer."

Emmett tried to stay quiet but couldn't help himself. "So the bullet went through Charlemagne's neck," he asked, "striking you below the heart but was deflected?"

"Emmett, glad to see you back." Chamberlain's eyes were still glazed over, his voice raw. "Yes, it appears the bullet deflected around my ribs. At least, there is a scorching groove along my side that makes me think this. After that it must have come out the back of my uniform where the Captain here claims there to be a hole. Somewhere in there it bruised my arm so that I can't even lift it. Good thing I don't have to shoot a rifle," he finished, laughing.

Ellis Spear appeared at Chamberlain's side, holding out a flask. "I have been saving this for a special occasion," he said with a smile, "and this seems to be it."

Chamberlain took a long swig from the flask, and Emmett watched the madness leave his eyes as the liquid trickled down his throat. Perhaps Ellis intended the offer to be a token sip, for his eyes grew narrow as Chamberlain tipped the flask to his mouth and drank deeply. "Major Spear," Chamberlain pronounced smacking his lips and returning the flask, "thank you for the spirits, they were just what the doctor ordered. I can always count on you and the 20th Maine when I need to."

The time for banter came quickly to an end, for a stirring across the way suggested a renewed attack from the Confederates. "Sir, I brought you a horse." Emmett said, handing the reins to Chamberlain. It was a mud-spattered white mare. He mounted and rode off to check on Major Sniper and the 185th New York. "Death on a pale horse," a watching soldier said, spitting into the dirt.

Emmett reflected on the truth of that statement as he spurred his own mount to keep up, racing this time to the rear of the left of the line where the 185th New York was.

"Colonel Sniper, how do we find you, sir?" Chamberlain asked, eyes sweeping the conflict that raged before him.

Colonel Sniper surveyed the men as they repulsed the Rebel wave, or rather barely stemmed the tide. With calm deliberation he turned to Chamberlain and replied. "One-third of my men are down, the rest have hardly any ammunition. We'll do what we can, sir."

Chamberlain nodded grimly. "The men are doing a wonderful job so far." He remarked while scribbling a note in the damaged field log. "Do you have a body who can deliver this? Perhaps General Gregory and the 2nd Brigade might give us a hand. Come Emmett, lets go see if we can boost morale some, get these boys to hang on."

The Union line bent back under the weight of the Confederate attack, until it was almost parallel to the Quaker Road. A messenger returned from General Gregory. The 2nd Brigade would not be able to reinforce them at this time. Retreat had never been an acceptable choice for Chamberlain, but sacrificing the lives of men unnecessarily was also not an option.

"Sir, here comes General Griffin." Emmett said pointing to the crest of a hill that Chamberlain had just been thinking might be a good fall back point.

"Let's go meet him." Chamberlain said, spurring his horse towards the division commander and his staff trailing along behind. "Maybe he has good news."

Griffin had seen the bent left flank from the hill, and the weight of Confederate soldiers pressing it forward still. "How bad is it Chamberlain?"

"We don't have much left, sir."

General Griffin respected the quiet officer from Maine; understanding that if he said there wasn't much left, than there wasn't much left. "I will get you artillery, and will put it there," he said, pointing to the hill he had just come over. "Just give me ten minutes. Hold for ten minutes. Can you do that?"

"Yes, sir."

"Just hold the lines, whatever it takes." And General Griffin went galloping away to call in the big guns.

"It will be more than ten minutes." Emmett said resignedly.

"I know." Chamberlain shrugged his shoulders, and then wheeled his horse to rejoin Colonel Sniper. The two men talked and then the order rang out. "Once more! Try the steel. Hell for ten minutes and then we are out of it."

Emmett dismounted and gave his horse to the care of a soldier who would stay behind. He drew his Enfield from its scabbard, making sure it was loaded, and carefully attached his bayonet. Every man was needed at this dire moment, and Emmett understood that it was time to lend his weight to the defense. As the word spread down the line, bayonets were fixed, and cheering, at first ragged and tinged with exhaustion, rose from the ranks, then building in intensity until the moment came to move forward, and as one mass the left flank of the 1st Brigade poured forth.

Emmett found that screaming as they charged forward gave courage to legs that were suddenly leaden. The noise helped to block the absolute insanity of rushing into Confederate fire with the intent of plunging their long steel blades into human flesh. It was good to have a man close by on either side, goading him forward against the wishes of his body. A bullet splatted into the shoulder of the New Yorker on his left, the sound a juicy smack, as if a watermelon being slapped by the flat side of a knife. Emmett's legs nearly buckled, but he managed to continue forward, driving towards the gray uniforms who were now pausing, surprised by the swarm of blue raging at them.

There was a boy no older than himself directly in front of Emmett, hastily loading his rifle as the distance closed between them. Emmett could see his blue eyes twitching as his hands raced to stuff the minié ball into place, slipping the percussion onto the nipple, hands shaking as he raised the rifle. The boy had lost his cap, letting his long blond hair spill out and around his shoulders, the hair as fine as a girl's. His shirt was torn and tattered, flapping loose from his left shoulder where a large rent spoke of a past injury.

The boy fired from the hip, not having time to raise the weapon to his shoulder, staring straight into Emmett's eyes as he did so from no more than twelve feet away. The bullet stung the side of Emmett's neck, pricking the skin like a wasp, and then he was on him, driving his bayonet into the soft belly, the steel ripping into his stomach, slashing his intestines, the blade twisting and turning as Emmett tried to pull it back out, the boy twitching like a fish with a stick through its gills, his eyes already going dull.

The Confederates broke in the face of the charge and ran back to their defensive positions just into the edge of the woods, the Union soldiers not pursuing them, content to have bought time. With little energy, ammunition, or desire to continue on, Emmett looked back to where the boy had fallen. He wanted to give him water, sit with him through the agonizing death that a gut wound ensured, find him morphine for the pain. Instead he walked past him, regained his mount, and sought out General Chamberlain. As he rode up to him, a horseman appeared on the hill, pausing, and then was joined by another. It was Lieutenant Mitchell and Battery B of the 4th Artillery.

Chamberlain spurred his horse with Emmett right on his heels, riding hard up to where Lieutenant Mitchell surveyed the scene. The thundering rumble of the twelve-pound Napoleon cannons being pulled up the hill echoed through the air. The six guns of the battery required 125 horses to pull the caissons and limbers, as well as the supply wagon, the forge wagon, and an ambulance wagon too.

Lieutenant Mitchell smiled slightly at the farcical figure that Chamberlain presented. "Tough day, sir?"

Chamberlain was in no mood for small talk. "Mitchell, do you think you can put solid shot into those woods close over the rebels' heads, without hurting my men?" The two lines were too close together to risk a shot directly at the Confederates, but Chamberlain wanted to spook them and keep them pinned down.

"Yes sir, if they will keep where they are."

"Well then, do it quickly. But be ready to stop on my signal so we can charge them."

When all was ready, Chamberlain gave the signal to Lieutenant Mitchell, and the fuses were lit, the crescendo of the huge guns sending death and destruction careening into the woods hiding the Confederates. A peach tree exploded, the spring bloom evaporating as if it had never been there, leaving a few jagged pieces of wood protruding no more than a foot or two out of the ground. Snipers, who had taken up positions in the treetops, plummeted onto the soldiers below, some merely shaken from their perch, others maimed and disfigured. The six twelve-pound smoothbores belching fire brought a cheer from the tired Union troops, but this cheer was short-lived as the Rebels, squeezed out of the woods, charged forward.

The Rebels focused their attention on the cannon battery on the hill, knowing that their very survival rested on removing that threat from the battlefield. A regiment of gray advanced up the hill, pausing at 200 yards to unleash a fusillade into the battery. The horses were the initial targets, the intent to stop the mobility of the smoothbores. If the battery could be captured, it could be turned upon the Northerners. And the South could win the day. The bullets took their toll, one such being Lieutenant Mitchell, who had his elbow smashed, leaving him ashen-faced, with his arm hanging by skin and tendon.

"You men come with me!" Chamberlain called, taking command of a group of New Yorkers who doggedly followed him to intercept the Confederates halfway up the hill. Emmett rode his horse through the gray uniforms, clubbing his rifle into skulls and shoulders until he was yanked from his saddle by a burly Reb who had lost his rifle, and who now pounced on Emmett trying to wrestle his from him. Emmett was pinned to the ground under the man's weight, gasping for breath, when suddenly warm ooze poured onto his face as if a bowl of stew had been dumped over him. Emmett realized that the man's eye was gone, and through the gaping hole brains were spilling out. He pushed the inert body off, struggling to his feet. He saw Chamberlain with the still smoking pistol in his hand nodding as if to say, we're even for Chancellorsville. The Rebels again retreated to regroup, the men from the North sinking to their knees in exhaustion.

General Griffin reappeared with his staff, and was aghast to see Chamberlain wavering on his feet. "General, you must not leave us. We cannot spare you now."

Distressed, Chamberlain replied in a strong voice. "I had not thought of it, General."

"I am bringing up three regiments from the 3rd Brigade under your command until General Bartlett arrives."

"That will be very helpful, sir."

Right on cue, a regiment of brightly colored uniforms appeared behind them. Emmett stared in astonishment at the sight of the 155th Pennsylvania Zouaves marching steadily forward. They wore French blue jackets with yellow trim, a false yellow pocket on the front for added splash. Red sashes with yellow trim were tied around the waists of the men, with pantaloons also of French blue puffing out from their legs. A red fez with canary trim and an indigo tassel toppled it all. The color guard flying the Maltese Cross of the 5th Corps broke apart from the ranks, following the Colonel of the regiment over.

"Colonel Alfred Pearson, reporting as ordered, sir." The man saluted neatly, brimming with energy and confidence. "What are your orders?"

General Griffin looked at Chamberlain. "You are in charge," he said.

Chamberlain nodded in return as he looked out over the surrounding farmland. "Colonel Pearson, please bring your men up the center towards that farmhouse there," he said pointing at the Lewis home. "You will find some fine boys from your home state hunkered down there. Pass by them, and then sweep to your left, and we will drive the enemy from the field. Do not stop until you have driven them from their breastworks on the edge of the woods. Understood?"

"Yes, sir." Pearson saluted smartly, wheeling his horse and galloping back to his regiment.

Emmett was content to remain with Chamberlain, Griffin, and their staff, atop the knoll, watching the gallant and colorful 155th Zouaves. On their left the 188th New York came into sight, pushing the Rebels back steadily. A roar caused Emmett to swivel his head back to the center, where the Zouaves were running full tilt to keep up with their battle flag, now being carried by Colonel

Pearson as he struck the Rebels a vicious blow. The 20th Maine appeared under Colonel Spear, and the three fresh regiments drove the Confederates from the field, pushing them back down the White Oak Road to the west, in the direction of Five Forks.

Later, General Warren found Chamberlain standing wearily at the back of the Union lines as they drove the last of the Confederates from the field. "General, these last hours you have done fine work, indeed. I am going to personally telegraph the President to tell him what you have done for your country here today."

"Thank you, sir," Chamberlain replied, ashen with fatigue and swaying slightly.

"You may pull your men back now and get some rest, General, for you look as if you might topple over at any moment."

Chamberlain smiled wryly. "People have been telling me that all day, sir, but here I am."

"I heard much about you today, General." Warren said, searching the other man's face. "Tales of some insane, blood-covered horseman from Maine daring the Confederates to put a bullet in him, but yet inspiring his men to greatness."

"There was a point there, sir, where I'm not quite sure what happened." Chamberlain murmured, barely able to stand now that the battle had wound down, exhaustion taking over his body.

"Sometimes sheer insanity is just what the doctor ordered." General Warren nodded his head approvingly. "Sleep, General, for hopefully we finally have old Bobby Lee in our net, and will be able to end this thing."

Chamberlain and Emmett returned to the Lewis farmhouse, having dispatched the rest of the staff with messages for the brigade. Emmett was looking forward to a night sleeping inside, hoping that a piece of the floor would be left for him under cover from Mother Nature. With these thoughts filtering through his exhausted mind, a fine mist that had been coating the air changed to a distinctive shower. They dropped their horses off in one of the barns, checking on Charlemagne at the same time. The horse had had a bullet pass through his neck, but somehow appeared to be in fine spirits, neighing loudly on seeing Chamberlain and Emmett.

"You get some sleep," Chamberlain said, grabbing a lantern.

"Where are you going?" Emmett asked, in his exhaustion even forgetting the "sir".

"The butcher's bill is not yet tallied, son." Chamberlain answered. "There are wounded who need water, and some beyond help who shall pass, but pass at peace with someone at their side."

With every cell in his body screaming, Emmett replied, "I'll go with you, sir, and see what comfort I might offer as well."

Chamberlain consented to the company, Emmett blindly following him as they tended as best they could to the wounded on the field, bringing solace and water as the fallen waited to be removed. Other lanterns pierced the night air as soldiers weary from a hard day searched for friends and kin scattered about the miles of farm fields. They passed a chaplain intoning a prayer over fallen soldiers, and then the rain began, soaking their clothes. With the wind, it set a chill to their bones; so that soon Emmett was no longer able to contain a fierce shivering that did little to warm him. Time passed, minute by agonizing minute, hours punctuated by horror after grisly horror. At one point they came upon the body of young Major Maceuen, who had been the darling delight of the entire regiment, courageous, gallant, pleasant, and good-humored. "Emmett, this man's father grabbed my shoulder in Philadelphia and begged me to take care of his only son."

"You cannot protect us all, sir. You follow orders. You fight. Some fall." He stopped, too exhausted to speak further.

"That doesn't make it any easier."

A voice came from the darkness. "General," it said kindly, "you have the soul of the lion and the heart of the woman."

"Who is there?"

"Colonel Sickel, sir." I am waiting for an ambulance to evacuate me. Now that most of the living have been transported to safety, it is my turn, I believe."

Emmett shone the lantern on the Colonel, briefly illuminating him in the flickers of light, his arm roughly bandaged in cloth strained red from the carnage of his arm. It seemed weeks ago that Emmett had seen the man go down, but in truth it had been mere hours. Sickel seemed at ease, the pain of the wound not yet coursing through his body. They gave him water and conversed briefly about the day's events before a stretcher arrived to carry him to the field hospital. Soon after, they went back to the

Lewis Farmhouse, where Emmett dropped to the floor in a corner.

Chapter Seventeen

My dear Susannah,

I hope that my addressing you thus does not offend you by its familiarity, but I am of the idea that we shared something special. From the moment I first saw you, I have been able to think of little else but you. When you invited me to visit with you, I thought at first you must be mocking me, but soon learned different. But yet, I have had but one letter from you in all these long months, and we could have been brother and sister for all that it said of the time spent at the Willard. Do you remember the picnic? The walks? Why is it that you have forsaken me? I believe that the war is drawing towards a close, and that I will soon after be mustered out of service. We are driving the Rebs before us like never before. Would I be welcome to call upon you in Washington when I am no longer tied to the army? Many such as us will be taking the end of this terrible war as a chance to start over. As will I. I imagine you have given some thought to a change of life as well. Might we start a new life together? I will find a job and support the both of us. I am willing to do whatever, just so long as we are together. Please write. Please let me know that you feel as I do. I will look daily for your words.

Yours,

Emmett

March 31, 1865

The sun peeked through the clouds late in the morning of March 31st, just two days after the battle at the Lewis Farm. Emmett hung his sodden blanket, along with his boots, socks, and coat over a stonewall that promised to catch some of its rays. He found Chamberlain on the straw pile that he had not left since falling into a deep sleep the morning before, waking to eat, but exhausted from his wounds, both old and new. His skin was as sallow as the hay upon which he lay, his body limp in repose, not yet ready to rise and begin preparations for the day. The 1st Division had been given a break, meaning that Ayres' and Crawford's Divisions held the front lines, all of them facing the White Oak Road behind which the Confederates lay waiting. The previous day had seen a soaking rain that had turned the area into a quagmire, the thick clay and water insinuating itself into every possible crevice of the body.

"Sir?" Emmett approached Chamberlain with a question on his lips, afraid to interrupt his recuperation. He hadn't spoken a word to him since the battle two days prior.

"Emmett, lad, I am glad to see you."

"I was wondering sir, if you wanted me to spread some of your things out to dry?"

Chamberlain looked up at the sun that was steadily driving a wedge between the dark clouds, bringing warmth with the light, and with it, life back into his exhausted body. "That would be very much appreciated." He rose, grimacing, and began to remove his jacket. "How are the men? Moaning like women as usual?"

"Improving, now that the sun is coming out and we appear to have a break from the fighting, for the time being at least. Everybody just hunkered down yesterday during the rain, but there is some stirring about now."

Chamberlain sat on the wall and shook the water out of his boots and pulled them on. "It seems that I best do the same, then."

"Sir? May I ask you a question? About the battle?"

"Go ahead," Chamberlain replied, struggling to his feet.

"Did you want to die?" Emmett blurted. The question had been haunting him for the past thirty-six hours.

Chamberlain chuckled, shaking his head, droplets of water flying from his mustache. "I most certainly did not want to die, but I don't suppose I gave much thought to it, either."

"It was as if you were no longer you, but some insane man charging around daring the Rebs to shoot you."

"I have to confess that I'm not sure what overcame me."

"The men all say they have seen few such courageous acts in this whole war."

Chamberlain stroked his mustache as he reflected upon his actions. "I guess there isn't much difference between fear and courage." He said finally. "I just got caught up in the moment and did what had to be done. I can't really explain it, but I could see the spectacle that I must have presented. Perhaps a man not quite possessed of all of his mental faculties." He cocked his head suddenly, his eyes searching the thick forest to the north and west.

"Did you hear that?"

Emmett followed his gaze and strained his ears to hear. "Is it thunder?"

"I don't think so." Chamberlain pulled his tunic on, buttoning it hurriedly. "I need my staff immediately. Have the bugler sound the call to arms."

The growing sound of rifle fire now became distinct, no more than a mile distant and approaching. The throaty screams of the Rebel yell slashed through the air from some engagement not far in front of them. Around the camp, men paused in what they were doing, some half-dressed, others sitting quietly drinking coffee. And then it became apparent that the entire mass of noise was moving towards them at a rather rapid rate.

Emmett found the bugler who sounded the call to arms and men sprang into action. The staff was now dashing madly around with orders for the two brigades under Chamberlain's command. Emmett rushed back to the stable to saddle two horses. He had originally planned to leave Charlemagne a few days to recover, but the frisky steed would have none of it, immediately rushing over and showing that his wound was of the past and that he was ready to go. The 1st Brigade was ordered forward to form up on the hill overlooking the stream of Gravelly Run below, or where the stream had once been. The swollen rainwater rushing between the banks of the stream was now a mass of blue humanity. What had been the forward brigades of the 5th Corps were now in total panic, retreating through the waist-deep water with a line of Confederates bearing down on them.

General Griffin was already on the crest of the hill with his staff. "Let them through," he shouted, "or they will break our lines!"

The 1st Division broke ranks to let the men through, there being no possibility to slow men pursued by terror, their momentum as uncheckable as a stampeding herd of cattle.

Chamberlain, with his staff in tow, rode hard to Griffin's position. "General Griffin, what has happened?"

"General Ayres," Griffin said hotly, "was probing the White Oak Road for strength when he was hit by an attack. Reports have it that it was Bushrod Johnson who hit him, surprised the hell out of him. I don't think he even had any skirmishers out.

They turned and ran, and in turn caused Crawford's men to flee as well. It is a complete embarrassment." Griffin had lost his hat and his bald head shone with perspiration in the sun, his thick beard quivering as his face contorted in anger at the rout.

Another group of horsemen galloped up to them with the commander of the entire 5th Corps, Major General Gouverneur Warren, in the lead. Warren was dashingly handsome, with sandy blond hair and a hawk-like nose over a strong jaw and a well-proportioned body to match. Usually of even-keeled demeanor, now his eyes flashed in anger at the embarrassment of having his corps broken and running in full retreat. Leadership was a tenuous business in the Union Army these days, and many a man had been broken in rank for far less. Warren was already on thin ice with General Sheridan, a powerful man who had the ear of Grant. "Griffin, can the 1st Division be counted upon to halt this charge, and then to take back the lost ground?"

"We will do our best, sir." Griffin's eyes peered intently down the hill. "But it looks as if Gravely Run has done the first part already." And sure enough, the momentum of the Rebel advance had halted on the far side of the stream.

"Grant will be furious when news of this reaches his ears." Warren spoke harshly.

"It is nothing that cannot be fixed, sir." Chamberlain said. Of the three, he was by far the calmest.

Griffin interrupted before Warren could reply, his face flat and without emotion. "General Chamberlain, the 5th Corps is eternally damned."

"Not till you're in heaven," Chamberlain replied, trying to bring a degree of levity to the situation.

"General Chamberlain," Warren said with the utmost gravity. "Will you restore the honor of the 5th Corps?"

Chamberlain bit back his immediate reply—that to suggest that the honor of the Corps had been lost in one small incident was ridiculous considering their actions of the previous days and months. He wanted to point out that his brigade had been decimated just two days earlier, losing 500 of its men in the fierce fighting at the Lewis Farm. But instead, he asked, "And what of the 3rd Brigade, as they are much fresher than my men?"

"We have come to you General Chamberlain; you know what that means."

"I'll try it then." Chamberlain nodded. "But don't let anybody stop me except the enemy, no half-measures here."

"You have my word." General Warren responded. "Give us an hour, and I will have a bridge built across the creek for your men to cross."

Chamberlain looked down on the rushing water that was now empty of men except the inert forms of the abandoned dead, twirling and tumbling along the banks. "A bridge might do for our return, sir," he said firmly, "but I do not think we will waste the time waiting for one now."

Wheeling his horse, he trotted off to find Major Glenn, commander of the 198th Pennsylvania Regiment, who had proven so effective two days earlier. He gave orders for Glenn to take his men across the stream while a protective fire would be set down by the 185th New York. "Have the men hang their cartridge boxes from their bayonet sockets and make sure to hold their rifles clear of the water, for you will need every shot that you carry before we are done today."

"Yes, sir." Glenn replied, rushing off to make the necessary preparations.

"General Gregory," Chamberlain said, turning to the commander of the 2nd Brigade, currently also under his authority. "You will follow behind in support as soon as New York crosses."

Emmett stood with Chamberlain watching as the men from Pennsylvania entered the water with their rifles held above their heads, at times elbowing floating bodies out of the way. Confederate snipers began shooting from concealed positions as the 185th New York tried to keep the enemy fire to a minimum with steady covering fire.

"Did General Warren choose the 1st Brigade to lead the attack because he trusts us the most?" Emmett asked.

Chamberlain smiled at Emmett, his eyes twinkling. "At a time like this, you put in your best."

Once the 198th had crossed the river and formed into skirmish lines on the far bank, the 185th followed them over with Chamberlain and Emmett in the first wave. Even on horseback, the water came above Emmett's boots at points, making him realize how cold it must be for those wading the stream. A man beside Emmett lost his footing, splashing underwater and losing hold of his rifle, but for the most part they made it through unscathed.

In the face of this counter-attack, the Confederates had fallen back to regroup, leaving just a thin line of soldiers to slow the Yankee's advance, which was hampered by the slick mud from the recent rains. The terrain was low bushes giving good cover to the snipers who would fire and then withdraw thirty or forty feet, reloading and doing it all over again, taking a toll with each shot.

Daniel Collins was in the front line of the advancing 198th Regiment, his eyes searching anxiously for signs of gray coats hidden behind trees, bushes, or in low hollows. A minié ball had ricocheted from the ground and struck his boot, its force already spent, but still a grim reminder that death lay just out of sight. A volley of rifle fire erupted from just ahead, the smoke rising from the ground, signaling that the Confederates were lying down under cover of a shallow ravine. He turned at a scream from his right, seeing a man he knew only as Saul staring in shock at his shattered elbow, blood dripping from the jagged bones.

"Forward! Drive them out!" Major Glenn shouted from close behind, urging the men not to waver.

Daniel realized he was standing still, while others pushed forward past him. He broke into a jog and then a run as they charged the soldiers in the ravine, crashing into the Rebel ranks before they had a chance to reload. He smashed his rifle into the side of a man. Realizing he had not yet fired, Daniel reversed the weapon, pressing the barrel against the man's chest, and pulled the trigger. The gray uniform caught fire from the spark, burning bright around the hole left in his chest.

"Forward!" The sergeant of his company called. Down the ravine, gasping for breath but fired with adrenaline, they chased the gray-coats. The advance skirmishers fell back to a supporting line of infantry, and another ragged volley tore into the Union advance. A bullet clanged against the barrel of Daniel's rifle, numbing the fingers of his left hand, but he barely noticed.

"Forward!" The officers ordered again, pushing the men in a mad dash to drive the Confederates before them. Their aim was not just to survive, but also to reclaim the honor of the 5th Corps in a brutal and overwhelming triumph.

They came to the breastworks erected by the Union soldiers of Ayres' Division just the day before, but which were now being used by the Confederates who had chosen to make their stand here, behind the hastily-built wall of earth and logs. A few hundred yards in front of the breastworks Daniel and the others finally paused to catch their breath, Daniel realizing that his ankle was tender, that there was blood, not of his own, splattered over his front, that his hand was numb, but that he didn't give a damn and was thankful just to be uninjured.

Chamberlain was viewing the Confederate defense with his field glasses when a staff officer rode up with a message that he took and read with annoyance. "Halt? We can't stop here." He spat. "I asked that we not be stopped by anybody but the enemy. Where is General Warren?"

"They are just about a half-mile to the rear, sir." The staff officer replied with deference. "I can take you to them if you want."

"Yes, I want." Chamberlain snarled, giving curt orders to several of his staff before calling for Emmett to come along with him and spurring Charlemagne in the direction the staff officer had pointed, forcing him to try to catch up to lead them.

General Warren and General Griffin were huddled together working a strategy that had yet to develop when Chamberlain rode up. He jumped from his horse, his anger overriding the discomfort of his wounds, and approached his two commanding officers. "The enemy is just on the other side of the White Oak Road, here," Chamberlain said, picking up a stick from the ground and jabbing the dirt, marking the ground with lines and symbols. "We will put General Gregory in the woods on the right of my brigade here," with another violent jab of the stick, "and General Ayres on the left, here. This will compromise their position and then I will charge and overrun them." Chamberlain looked up with flashing eyes, knowing that he was right.

"I am not sure if General Grant wants us to commit here." General Warren replied, hesitating as he studied the rough diagram in the dirt. He had recovered from the frustrations of earlier in the day, and was once again in command of his emotions.

"General Grant has said that we will attack wherever the

enemy is." Chamberlain stated simply. "And the enemy is here," he said, again jabbing the dirt. "I was told this morning that no orders would come to halt my advance. I cannot stay where I am, and if I fall back now I will lose as many men in doing so as I will in advancing. We must go forward."

General Warren seemed to ponder this for an eternity, then, finally nodded. "Very well then. We will follow your plan. General Griffin, see that Gregory and Ayres receive their orders. We will begin the attack in one hour."

Emmett rode hard to keep up with Charlemagne as they rushed back to begin preparations. Once again, they would be attacking fortified positions, charging into the very teeth of the enemy. Men would be maimed and killed on both sides as they fought over the strategic road, another step closer to victory, but no more than a step in a journey whose length they did not know.

On returning to the front, Chamberlain immediately began issuing orders. "Major, let the men spread into a loose formation for the charge. I don't much like charging a fortified enemy. But if we have to, that should help keep casualties down."

"Yes, sir." Major Glenn, with dark, angular features and black hair and eyebrows making for a rather grim countenance, looked the sort of man who seemed to enjoy charging into the thick of the enemy.

"General Gregory, you will start the attack with a demonstration on the right. Bring two batteries of artillery with you and make all the noise you can to draw their attention. Colonel Sniper, you will bring your regiment into the center, and it will be the spearhead of our attack. Major Glenn, you will come up on the right, between the 2nd Brigade and Sniper. When we hear the guns from Gregory, we will know it is our time."

Emmett found himself alone with Chamberlain as the others rushed off to prepare for the attack that all hoped would regain the honor of the 5th Corps. He pulled the Colt revolver from his waistband, adding a bullet to the cylinder so that it was fully loaded. Typically, he left the chamber under the hammer empty so that it wouldn't mistakenly fire when jarred. He held the pistol pointed up in his right hand while his left grasped the reins firmly.

Chamberlain looked at Emmett with a knowing glance. "You keep that pistol handy. I have a feeling you're going to need it real soon now."

With that, gunfire erupted to the right where General Gregory was to start the attack. Chamberlain raised his sword and the bugler sounded the forward. The New York Regiment started forward at a trot, the men breaking rank and spreading out as they crossed the open field toward the fortified guns of the Confederates. Chamberlain rode in their midst, urging them on, while Glenn and Sniper led from the front, the whole mass of men broken into skirmish lines and sweeping towards the Rebels, flags streaming, bugles playing, men whooping and hollering. A sudden volley ripped into the line of blue, sending some men crumpling to their knees with agonized looks on their faces. But the rest carried forward, letting their momentum drive them. Chamberlain pressed his spurs into Charlemagne's sides, and they bounded to the front, the horse as excited by the battle as the former professor of rhetoric from Bowdoin College. Waving his saber over his head to urge the men forward, Chamberlain dropped the reins and drew his Navy Colt, guiding the horse forward with only his legs, though Charlemagne appeared to know what to do without direction. A bullet whistled through the air past his head, a sound almost comforting to him as he searched for a worthy target. They leaped the breastworks of log and mud, Charlemagne rearing while Chamberlain fired into the soldiers closest to him. The men from New York came right behind, clambering over the walls and setting upon the Virginians with a bloodlust. A man drove his bayonet into the groin of another, and Chamberlain was unable to tell which color either man wore. A Union soldier had a Confederate soldier pinned to the ground with his hands grasping either side of his neck, choking the life from the already limp body. A Rebel slashed with a short knife, cutting, piercing—until a bayonet drove into his armpit and left him flapping on the ground, still clutching the blade. Everywhere he looked, Chamberlain saw men in blue attacking with a methodical savagery that brightened his hopes.

One such soldier was Private Augustus Zieber, a German from Pennsylvania who dreamed of a particular girl back in his hometown. In his dreams, he sometimes returned to her adulation after some act of glory, but other times, he died and enjoyed her mourning almost as much as if he'd lived. He saw his chance at glory as he leaped the breastworks and found himself face to face with the enemy's color guard. He fired his rifle point blank into the man, but the soldier clung to the flag, the heart and soul of his 56th Virginia Regiment. Zieber dropped his own rifle, wrestling the man with a bullet in his shoulder for the flag. The man molded his hands to the flagpole, refusing to relinquish it. With a quick movement, Zieber punched the man in the bullet wound with his right fist while holding on with his left. The man cried out but still held on. He pounded the man in the face and neck, but to no avail. And then a sudden hole appeared in the man's cheek, a bullet from nowhere ending his struggles.

As the Confederates broke and ran, Zieber found Brigadier General Chamberlain in a moment of calm. "Sir, I would like to present you with a regimental flag of Virginia."

"What is your name, soldier?"

"Private Zieber, sir."

"You earned the glory of that flag, son, so you hold onto it. I will be responsible for my own victories. Now, back to work."

In the swirling action, Emmett suddenly saw a gray coat rise up from where he'd been lying, a rifle nestled in his arms, standing not five feet behind Chamberlain with the barrel of the gun pointed directly at the back of the general's head. Emmett, remembering the forgotten pistol in his hand, brought the weapon in line, and without thinking, squeezed the trigger. The bullet tore the Rebel's jaw off, his face disappearing in a shower of red before he toppled over backwards. Chamberlain turned and looked at the man, and then at Emmett, giving him a slight nod of recognition, before continuing his pursuit. Emmett didn't have time to linger on the thought that he'd just killed another man. But that memory would return ensuring many a sleepless night in the future.

The Union eventually established a foothold on the White Oak Road as the Confederates were driven several hundred yards to the other side, and here Chamberlain checked the forward momentum of his men. They had effectively split General Lee and the Army of Northern Virginia from their cavalry, isolating each group from the other, and thus making both vulnerable.

General Warren rode up as Chamberlain was giving directions to his staff, his head cocked to listen to the sounds of distant gunfire. Warren was known for being an extremely sound commander, his leadership marked by caution and deliberation. He was not one to rush into battle until all of the options and possible outcomes had been examined. Once committed, however, he was extremely effective.

"Congratulations, General Chamberlain. You have done all I have asked and more. Hopefully this keeps that damn Sheridan off my back. He doesn't take well to setbacks." Warren smiled then, a bright and unexpected smile.

"Nor does Grant," Chamberlain replied, sagging slightly in his saddle. "But I might venture that I can't blame them for expecting success instead of failure. What with so much at stake." The fighting had only lasted about three hours, but he was not sure how much longer his exhausted body could continue.

Warren nodded his head to the southwest, asking, "General, do you think that gunfire is Sheridan?" The plan had called for General Sheridan to follow up this infantry movement with cavalry support, driving a wedge through the Confederate lines and further splintering the army of Robert E. Lee.

"It must be," Chamberlain agreed. As far as he knew, there was nobody else off to their left in the direction of Five Forks and Dinwiddie Courthouse.

"In your estimation, is the battle moving towards us or away from us on to Dinwiddie?"

"It sounds to me like it is moving away."

General Warren sighed. "That is what I thought. Where in tarnation could Sheridan be going?" He did not like unknowns, and did much to prevent surprises, but this significant mystery could only bode for the worse.

"I heard that George Picket and Rooney Lee are over there facing him. He might not be able to get to us."

"We might have to go and support him," Warren reflected, "wherever it is he is going."

"And give up the position we've carved out here?" Chamberlain tried to keep the disbelief from his voice.

"I can't leave the cavalry exposed, General. No matter what we thought the objective was, my orders are to report to

General Sheridan and support him."

"Is there no word from Grant?" Chamberlain wanted to advise this man whom he admired, but there seemed to be no right answer. As often was the case in battle, the objectives were ever changing and the communication sparse and muddled at best.

"I have had several messages, but they all seem to conflict with the last. First he sent word to halt the advance, then he said our flank might be exposed, and finally there was word to cross the White Oak Road if possible."

"What do you want to do, sir?"

"Give the men some rest, but be ready to fall back if we need to go find Sheridan."

Chamberlain set about establishing sentries to keep watch while the men bedded down. The Confederates were just through the trees and bushes, not far, probably within a few hundred yards, and he fully expected a counter-attack to drive them back from their advanced position. Emmett tried to grab some shut-eye, but slept fitfully, images of the man he'd killed flitting through his mind. An hour before dawn, he was shaken awake by Chamberlain.

"We are withdrawing to go aid General Sheridan who has run into trouble down by the Dinwiddie Courthouse. I have sent for Colonel Sniper but need you to go fetch Major Glenn for me."

The retreat was a delicate matter, as it would not do to have the Confederates realize they were leaving the field. Nonetheless, it was accomplished quietly and efficiently, and soon Emmett found himself shivering in the damp morning air as they marched south and west to find and support General Sheridan. In the distance, against the backdrop of the dappled morning, riders appeared in front of them. The men prepared to engage, but soon realized that the cavalry they faced was dressed in blue.

General Sheridan himself rode up to Chamberlain with his usual abrupt demands. "Where in God's name is Warren?"

"He is back in the rear, sir."

General Philip Sheridan was a short man, only about five inches over five feet tall, robust and dark skinned. Nicknamed Little Phil, he was a simmering ball of fire with a mustache stretched taut across his tightly-honed features. His arms dangled down on either side of him, to the point where Abraham Lincoln once remarked; "...if his ankles itched he could scratch them without bending over." He was an intense man who had won General Grant's approval for his no-nonsense, attack-at-all-times mentality. This powder keg now sat a horse in front of them as if he were trying to wrestle the beast to the ground instead of merely ride it. "In the rear is where I would expect Warren to be." He snarled. "Where the hell has the 5th Corps been?"

"We were engaged heavily in battle, sir." Chamberlain retorted heatedly. "We were ordered to create a breach between the Confederate lines, and that is what we did. Our expectation was that you would be supporting our left flank, and we did not receive new orders until just this morning."

"What is your name, General?" In a simmering rage he focused his full attention on Chamberlain.

"General Joshua Chamberlain, sir."

"I was told that you would be here by midnight, not mid-morning. Whatever the case, I am happy to see you leading the men instead of in the rear. There is a church about a mile that way," he said, pointing impatiently. "We will be meeting there as soon as the infantry is brought up into position." With that, the short, angry man rode off. Emmett wondered if he would ever get a chance to sleep again, more than a snooze in the saddle as they rode from battle to battle, anyway.

The meeting at the church was tense with General Sheridan stalking around like a caged beast just waiting to be unleashed to vent his fury on the Confederates across the way. To anybody that would listen, he blamed General Warren for being slow to bring the 5th Corps into position.

The new strategy was simple. General Picket's Confederate infantry was spread along the White Oak Road on either side of an intersection known as Five Forks. Sheridan's cavalry would engage the center and right flank in two places, Scott's Road and the Dinwiddie Courthouse Road. Meanwhile, the 5th Corps under Warren would strike the left flank of the Rebels and attempt to get around behind them, and then roll down the White Oak Road clearing the enemy before them. The upshot was that the 1st Brigade of the 5th Corps was again riding into battle, but this time supposedly in a supporting role.

Emmett had at least gotten to eat a few bites of food with

Chamberlain and General Frederick Winthrop of Ayres Division. The man had arrived on horseback, riding up in search of food, and the three of them had taken the opportunity to sit down and share a meal together. Chamberlain had sent Emmett to find what he could, and the young man had cadged some bread, jam, and even a bit of leftover chicken from the other officers' meager tables.

"This is delightful." General Winthrop replied, taking it in. "I am famished. Haven't eaten a morsel all day long."

"It looks like you'll be leading the Corps into the fray today, so it is the least I can do." Chamberlain was enamored of this articulate man, descendent of the famous John Winthrop of Massachusetts and whose family was the most influential name in banking and investment in New York.

"We are both commanders of 1st Brigades," Winthrop agreed. "I wanted to thank you for bailing us out yesterday. We went in blind, and, before we knew what was happening, the men had broken and run. Can't say that I blame them much."

Chamberlain nodded his head. "I am sure that after today, the reputation of the 1st Brigade of the 2nd Division will be without equal."

"I hope so," Winthrop agreed.

The two men shook hands, each having recognized in the other a kindred spirit in this short meal taken together. Much like Chamberlain, Winthrop had risen from a private to that of Brevet General for leading his men, and was revered for it. "I best be getting back. I imagine that General Warren has refined the plans for attack, and we will be going in soon."

"I know that he will have thought of everything." This overpreparation, Chamberlain knew, was a strength as well as a weakness of his commander. Preparing for battle was essential, but sometimes immediate action was what was called for, not hesitation.

"And then some." Winthrop said knowingly, smiling as he turned and mounted his horse.

The orders to move out came, Ayres' 2nd Division proceeding forward on the left and Crawford's 3rd Division on the right, with the 1st Division under General Griffin following behind. The plan called for them to turn to the west upon reaching the White Oak Road and roll down the enemy line dug in there. It was just after four in the afternoon with a warm spring sun on their left side.

Emmett rode his horse easily alongside Chamberlain. There was a tight pit in his stomach, but otherwise he was not affected by the impending battle. It was not quite that he had grown immune to the ordeal, but that his fear was no longer of that white-hot intensity of his first experiences. The screaming of the wounded and the ghastly sight of the dead no longer made him want to vomit, and the guns and steel blades of the Confederates, while scary, did not make every nerve in his body jangle nor his legs want to turn and flee.

"Sir, if you don't mind me asking, why was General Sheridan so upset with General Warren? We did everything asked of us. We took the White Oak Road. When orders came to withdraw and come to the support of Sheridan, we did. I don't understand."

"Take the stars off the shoulders, Emmett, and we are just men, same as everyone else." Chamberlain replied somewhat cryptically.

Emmett mulled that over a bit. "Are you suggesting that Sheridan just doesn't like Warren?"

"Not quite." Chamberlain said distractedly, his mind attending to the action all around him, one part having this conversation with Emmett, another part noting the movement of his own brigade, while yet other parts paid strict attention to the woods ahead, the surrounding divisions, the noises of the day. "What do you think that General Sheridan cares most about?"

Emmett almost made the mistake of replying without thinking that 'winning' the war was his main objective, but refrained to reflect first. "He seems quite concerned with what others think about him."

"Precisely. I believe that building his reputation drives General Sheridan. This is not a bad thing, as it coincides with the main objective of winning this war. But sometimes there are friendly casualties on the road to becoming a hero." They reached the White Oak Road with Ayres Division turning west just before reaching it and Crawford's Division sweeping left just past the road.

"If we had gotten here earlier," Emmett ventured, "we

would have surprised the Rebs and would have won a resounding victory, with General Sheridan reaping the accolades. Too bad we didn't even know we were supposed to be here until it was too late."

Chamberlain looked at Emmett with one raised eyebrow. "Accolade? Good word. At least your education is coming along." He nodded his head to the right. "Does it seem to you that we are losing touch with Crawford?"

Emmett looked around, so caught up in the conversation that he didn't even realize the battle loomed ever closer as they moved west into the Confederate lines. They heard sporadic rifle fire begin spitting in Crawford's position, and then a heavier fire to their left where Ayres was. "I don't know, sir."

"Let's go have a look." Chamberlain waved to a small hill to their right that was clear of trees. They galloped their horses to the top to find stretched out before them a rugged, but open field. Chamberlain swept his field glasses to the left and right, murmuring to himself. "Crawford is going too far right. He has split from Ayres, leaving him exposed to enfilade fire from the side." He turned his horse and they rode hard back to his command.

"We need to move left and fill the gap left by Crawford," he told two of his staff, sending them off to inform Glenn and Sniper. He grabbed another aide, directing him to tell General Gregory to follow them to the left in support. "Emmett, I believe Bartlett is following Crawford. Go find his command and let him know the battle is more to the south and west. Quickly."

Emmett galloped off to where he assumed Bartlett's 3rd Brigade would be when he suddenly saw a familiar figure. "Tom?"

Tom Chamberlain was moving forward, leading a group of men that must have been from the 20th Maine. Emmett recognized several of them, but it seemed that it had been eons since he had served with them. "Lieutenant Colonel Chamberlain," Tom said, beaming at Emmett. "Watch your manners."

Emmett stepped quickly down from his horse to grasp his friend's hand. "Good to see you."

"And you. How is my brother?"

"He is healthiest when we are going into battle. I have a

message for Bartlett that the 3rd Brigade needs to swing more west and south. Crawford has gone too far north and it is up to the 1st Division to fill the gap created."

"I will see to it personally." Tom turned his horse. "Give Lawrence my best."

Emmett watched him ride off, noting the ease with which Tom had become an officer. It must be something in the Chamberlain blood, he thought. He then turned and spurred his horse to rejoin his own brigade before the battle commenced.

"Is Bartlett all set?" Chamberlain paused long enough to ensure his message had been passed.

"I happened upon your brother leading the 20th Maine and passed the orders on to him. He sends his regards."

"God be with him." Chamberlain said softly. He then stood up high in his stirrups with his sword over his head and urged the men forward to catch the Confederates from the side. They moved down a gully through cat briars and blackberry thickets, hidden by the depressed ground from the action. Picket had refused his line north of the White Oak Road, bending it backward for 600 feet so that his front was now shaped like an arrow. It was into this refused line of men that Chamberlain drove his brigade, hoping to crush their left flank. The 2nd Division under Ayres was attacking directly at the angle created by the two lines, while Crawford had looped around behind.

Emerging into the field, the bugler sounded the charge and the men began a fast jog to cover the distance to the Confederate line stretching north from the White Oak Road. A crushing volley dropped scores of those in the front line but still they continued on. Emmett had his pistol out as he followed the men across the field. Before the Confederates, crouching behind the hastily-erected defense of rails and logs could reload, the 1st Brigade was into them, firing from point blank range as they reached the wall and then clambering over it in droves. Emmett's horse balked at the fence and he allowed himself to be turned by a tide of men moving southward while carrying on the battle with just a thin barrier between the two armies.

Emmett held the reins of his dancing horse tightly with his left hand and aimed his pistol carefully at Rebels on the other side, some hastily reloading, some preparing to fire, others wrestling with Yankees who had crossed the barrier.

A sudden blow from a rifle crashed into his shoulder and sent him tumbling to the ground, flashing lights exploding in his head as he struck the ground. The impact forced the air out of his lungs with a whoosh, leaving him helpless and stunned on the ground. A hulking gray-shirted man stood over him, reversing his rifle and raising it over his head to plunge the bayonet deep into him. Helplessly, Emmett watched, thinking detachedly that this is what death was, just a moment in time. The bayonet began its descent as the man over him thrust the weapon downward. Emmett was unable to look away, transfixed by the apparatus of his death descending into him, and thus saw the flash of a rifle that clubbed the man at the very last moment, sending him staggering to the side and causing the blade to miss Emmett by inches, piercing and tearing his uniform where it billowed out to the side, but not so much as nicking his skin. With no idea who it was that saved his life, Emmett rolled to his knees and crawled to where his pistol lay, plucking it from the ground and staggering to his feet. His shoulder was badly bruised, and his head was ringing, but he was alive. His horse, well trained for war, stood still where he'd fallen, and Emmett pulled himself back into the saddle.

Chamberlain rode up with concerned eyes, somehow seeing everything that took place on the battlefield at all times. "Are you injured?"

"I don't think so," Emmett replied, his body shaking slightly from the close call with death.

"If you need to go back for medical help, you may."

"I am fine, sir." Emmett suddenly gasped, pointing behind them. "We are being attacked from the rear."

Chamberlain jerked around to find himself pinched between two Confederate forces. He rallied a group of men to turn and face this new threat only to realize that they were actually surrendering, advancing merely to lay down their weapons. Emmett was dispatched to put together a band of escorts to take these new prisoners to the rear, hundreds of men who had seen no hope or reason to continue fighting.

The Confederates had fallen back from their breastworks to a stand of trees some 300 yards to the west, causing a lull as the Union reorganized their lines. The chaos of the battle had mixed the soldiers from various regiments, brigades and even divisions all together. Emmett hurried back to the front as soon as he'd deposited the prisoners with a detachment of troops held in support to the rear. He found Chamberlain at the same time as General Sheridan rode up with five or six staff members. The small violent man was in full frenzy as he approached, "General—what is your name?" He made no sign that he recognized Chamberlain from earlier in the morning, his eyes flashing murderously in his head.

"General Chamberlain, sir."

"I saw what you did, mighty fine work. Where is the rest of your division?"

Chamberlain replied, giving a rough account of where he thought Generals Warren, Griffin and Ayres were.

"It is time we smashed these Rebels." General Sheridan spit out. "Gather up all the infantry you can and sweep towards Five Forks where it meets the White Oak Road. I want you men to realize that we have a record to meet, before that sun goes down, that will make hell tremble! I want you there!"

Emmett was next to one of the staff officers who appeared to be not much older than himself. "What does he mean a record to meet?" He carefully whispered to him.

The young officer kept his face impassive, but his eyes belied his stiff demeanor. "Nobody knows what Little Phil is talking about most of the time, but everybody with an ounce of sense knows better than to ask."

"Is he as good as they say?"

"I'd rather be on his side than not." With that, Sheridan galloped off, presumably to find Warren, his staff flying along behind, hoping to keep up.

Emmett followed Chamberlain, gathering up infantry as they went, assembling all the men they could find, to push on towards Five Forks. With most of the 1st Brigade and various other regiments including the 20th Maine, they pressed on through the woods, chasing the enemy in a steady skirmish until the Rebels finally made a stand in a heavily-defended position. At this point, with their forward momentum checked, the men paused to catch their breath behind any cover they could find in the face of the massive volley that poured forth.

Emmett saw the 20th Maine flag and rode over to check in

with Tom. He found him hunkered down behind a log, chewing on some hardtack and sipping from his canteen. He motioned for Emmett to join him.

"I hear that Lawrence was up to his old antics at the Lewis Farm." Tom said, tipping the canteen to his mouth.

"He was pretty much out of his mind." Emmett replied, squatting down beside Tom.

"I only ever saw him mad as a hornet once. I was about four years old and Lawrence took me to visit some Penobscots who lived out behind our house. They would spend the summer there, and so we got to know them a bit. One day, some of the local ruffians were out there, provoking the Indians. Lawrence would have been about seventeen and there were three men in their twenties, but he ended up whipping all three of them. I was scared of my brother for a long time after that. He's not somebody to get on the wrong side of, that's for sure."

Emmett nodded. "I guess we got to be flushing them Rebs out of that grove of trees over there pretty soon. Sheridan isn't gonna let us sit around all day."

"Keep your head down." Tom cautioned as his friend rode off to find his master.

Chamberlain had spurred his horse over to the 198th Pennsylvania regiment, knowing that no amount of pausing would make hell tremble or General Sheridan happy. "Major Glenn, I will promote you on the spot if you take that enemy position." Chamberlain said, pointing to the grove of trees.

"Yes, sir." The man replied without hesitation. He wheeled his horse and shouted to his men, "To your feet. We have work to do." The Pennsylvanians rose to their feet as one. "We are going into them trees to persuade the Rebs they need to give up or move on. Loose skirmish line." Glenn rode his horse to the front of the regiment as the captains pushed and prodded the men into formation. As soon as they were in order, he had the bugler sound the charge. "Boys," he yelled, "follow me!" He spurred his horse and charged forward, sword over his head, heedless of whether or not any of his soldiers were following. The men, of stern mettle and well tested, followed with a cheer, charging along right behind him. Emmett watched them streaming over the open ground, the flag falling to the ground several times as the bearer was shot out from underneath it. Another would scoop it up, raising it to propel the men forward. The rest of the brigade swarmed after this marvelous charge, surging forward with unchecked momentum, a wave of humanity that no dam in the world could stop.

Glenn was the first into the trees, slashing with his sword left and right. A man grabbed his stirrup trying to upend him from his seat, but he drove the blade down through his shoulder. From the other side, hands grasped at him, ripping him to the ground, but he managed to keep his feet. He swung his sword in a wide swath, driving the circle of Rebs surrounding him backwards. A blow struck him in the back of the head and he twirled, swinging the blade. A bayonet was thrust into his leg, which buckled underneath him. Glenn sunk to one knee, remembering the forgotten pistol at his belt. He pulled the weapon free but a rifle barrel smashed into his forearm, forcing the revolver from his hands.

Just then the first of the 198th Pennsylvania caught up, sweeping into the trees and shattering the clustered Confederates. "Give em hell boys!" Glenn yelled from his knee, his left arm broken, blood flowing from his wounded leg, but still clutching his saber. He struggled to his feet as the Union soldiers drove the Confederates from their protected glade. A Rebel officer turned and fired his pistol, and Glenn felt a thud in his chest. Looking down, he was surprised to see blood bubbling from just below his heart, and then he fell.

Chamberlain found him where he had fallen moments later, carefully laid out with a tunic for a pillow, a few of his men around him. "That charge was a thing of beauty." He told the dying man.

"General, I did what I could."

"Colonel," Chamberlain replied thickly, emphasizing Glenn's new rank, "you can rest assured that you did all that was asked of you. I will remember my promise. I will remember you."

He looked up to see the lengthening shadows cast by the trees. The day was done. The Confederates had been routed and were in full retreat. The Union forces held the field, victorious as at no other time during the entire war. Chamberlain walked to the edge of the trees, watching the sun sink over the retreating Rebels. Glenn was just another name to add to the long list of men he'd sent to their death. He'd encouraged all he knew back in the summer of 1862 to join up, to come along to this Great War. Many of those men—students, neighbors, and friends—were now dead. He thought of that first night in Fredericksburg on the incline of Marye's Heights, sharing water, comfort, and companionship with dying soldiers. He thought of his near-fatal experience at Chancellorsville, saved by a boy he hadn't wanted to take along.

Another image flitted through his mind, Colonel Vincent telling him at Gettysburg to hold Little Round Top at every hazard. In war, failure was often worse than death, for failure meant defeat, and losing this war was unthinkable. He ran his hand down over his hip where the bullet at Rives Salient had mangled him for life, leaving him less of a man, but leaving him alive nonetheless. He had known then that he must still have a further purpose in this life. But was it to leave stragglers behind to have their throats cut by bushwhackers? Was it to rally the morale of the men and turn the tide of battle as at the Lewis Farm? Was it to send this brave soldier, Colonel Glenn, to his death on the White Oak Road at Five Forks? Was there something still ahead, some destiny yet to fulfill?

Chamberlain's musings turned to his baby daughter, Gertrude, and his other children Daisy and Wyllys. Was he being kept alive, to be a father and husband? But thousands and thousands had died, leaving young children behind. He wished that he were home with them. He would get a sailing ship and take them all into Maquoit Bay, much like his father had taken them down the Penobscot when he was but a child. He thought of his father and mother, living in Brewer together, worried about their sons, and stood for a long time after the sun had bowed down over the horizon leaving only darkness behind.

Chapter Eighteen

Dearest Lawrence,
Everybody says that this war is almost over. The newspaper tells of great victories on the White Oak Road and at a place called Five Forks. It relates the exploits of MY husband in glowing terms, 'What shall I say of Chamberlain, who beyond all question, is the first of our brigade commanders...the hero of both Quaker Road and Gravelly Run, and in this action of Five Forks making the air ring with the applauding huzzas of his soldiers, who love him?' It appears now that the South is finally broken, and the only question is when. I have begun to hope that you might indeed be returned to me, yet still alive. But at what cost? The goals you cherish have been achieved. Slavery will be abolished. Your precious Union will be preserved. But at what cost? You are no longer the man that you were, and I am no longer the woman that I was. I will not dwell upon the obvious, but more than the physical damage to your body, what of the damage to our life together? You will try to forget the battlefield and return to life in Brunswick. I will do my best to adjust to your return after so long of an absence and let go of my bitterness. Three years ago we possessed the idyll life, a life we can never go back to. As Ralph Waldo Emerson said, "What lies behind you and lies in front of you pales in comparison to what lies inside of you". So, I wonder, what now lies inside of you? What lies inside of me? And are those two essences still compatible? I am happy that the end of the war nears, but I am concerned about the next stage of our life. I am certain that your return will help allay many of my fears, so tarry not. Finish this WAR and come home to your wife and children.
Your loving wife,
Fanny

April 8, 1865

"Remember those first days with the 20th Maine?" Tom asked Emmett as they wearily chewed hardtack, the stale biscuit being the only thing they'd eaten for most of a week now. They were waiting for the 24th Corps of General Ord to continue moving, a delay they had been dealing with all day.

Emmett smiled in memory. "Our first day of marching we might of done ten miles and left half the regiment behind to catch up."

"It was the same thing with the 2nd when we first got to Virginia." Daniel Collins commented wryly. "Men that could cut lumber all day or lug bricks somehow couldn't walk ten miles." Emmett had been marching with the men today, having given up his normal mount to a foraging party trying to keep the army supplied.

"Do you suppose Old Man Lee is still just to the north of us?" Tom looked off to the right as he spoke, wondering if the entire army of Northern Virginia lay hidden just behind the trees.

Emmett thought back to breakfast before the sun was up, listening to the new Corps Commander, General Griffin, giving instructions to Chamberlain. "What I heard this morning," he said, "was that Sheridan has taken the cavalry ahead to try to cut off Lee's escape route west, while us and the 24th mirror his movements so he can't break to the south. The 2nd and 6th Corps are trailing along behind to make sure he don't double back."

"Lets just hope he don't go north then." Daniel was only half joking. The three of them had stopped in a grove of oaks dominated by one grand tree with limbs splayed every which way. It was almost comfortable leaning on the low limbs as they ate and drank. Sitting on the ground was forbidden because a halt had not been called, this being merely a pause to wait for the road ahead to clear.

"Rumor had it he was hoping to get supplied at Farmville but Sheridan intercepted the train. He must be headed for the railhead at Appomattox Station." Tom said, biting into the hardtack. "Didn't think I'd ever be happy with these rations the army gives us, but it sure must be a sight better than what them Rebs are getting right now."

Daniel nodded his head in agreement. "I heard a soldier from the 2nd Corps saying that most of them Rebs they captured when they split Elwell's Battalions from the main army were happy to lay down their arms as long as we gave them some food." Two days earlier at Sailor's Creek, Sheridan, along with the 2nd Corps, had captured three corps of Confederates, roughly one-fourth of the remaining Army of Northern Virginia, which was now numbered at roughly 25,000 men.

"It must have hurt Lee to have his son Custis captured." Tom threw a stick down the embankment, trying to reach the stream below. It was this stream that was holding them up as the 24th Corps struggled to get their supply wagons across it.

"I don't know about that." Emmett interjected. "It seems he might be happy knowing his boy was going to live. Soon the war will be over, and then he'll be let go. Until then he's safe enough, I guess."

"At least he don't have to march anymore." Daniel shifted his weight, leaning his rifle against the oak tree. "What do you reckon we've walked the past four days? A hundred miles?"

"Easy," Tom replied. "And we're not done yet."

"I'd still rather be moving than standing still doing nothing." Daniel took a few impatient steps, peering to the front, wondering when the march would continue, before suddenly swinging around and looking at Emmett. "Did you see Chamberlain get dumped in the river this morning?"

Emmett laughed involuntarily, glancing around to make sure they were alone. "I was right with him when it happened, as a matter of fact I'd just cleared the river and was looking back. Charlemagne went to take a drink, dipping his head down, and must have stepped in a hole. They went in ass over teakettle." He chuckled, trying to suppress his mirth, but unable to contain himself. "The muck was something terrible. It took three men to wrestle Charlemagne up the bank. General Chamberlain managed to get himself out, but looked like some sort of mud monster glaring at everybody, daring them to laugh."

Tom hooted loudly, the sudden loud noise scaring several crows from the tree. "I would've paid a good bit to have seen that. Ole' Lawrence dragging himself from the Buffalo River, probably trying to act all formal and dignified, with river muck dripping from every part of him."

The wagons must have finally cleared the stream, for the call rang out to continue onward, and the three dusty men left the shade of the tree and moved on. They walked several miles in silence, until Daniel broke the tranquility. "What you planning on doing when the war is over, Tom?"

"Don't rightly know." Tom said, chewing his lip. "I

thought I might look up John Marshall Brown back in Portland and see if he can help me get a job down there."

"Have you heard from Brown?" Emmett only knew that he had been wounded at Cold Harbor, about a week before Chamberlain's injury, then, sent home.

"I got a letter from him a few months back. He said he's doing better but still slow."

The three men continued on with their thoughts of how survival took many forms. The three of them were relatively healthy, Custis Lee's capture ensured that he would endure, John Marshall Brown had persisted despite his wound—they were the lucky ones.

"Halt and clear the way!" The call went up and down the line.

"What now?" Tom groaned.

Fife and drum music could be heard approaching. Down the road came a smartly marching regiment of soldiers in blue.

"They're all black," Daniel said, breathing the words that were on all their tongues.

"That must be Colonel Woodward's Brigade." Tom noted as the black men marched past, not looking left or right, but with eyes pinned straight forward.

A few observers made disparaging remarks, but they were half-hearted. These black soldiers were putting their lives on the line for the same cause as the rest of them. "I imagine that they can kill a man as good as any of us," Emmett remarked. He'd never seen so many black men in one place at one time, not even in Washington, D.C.

It was after midnight when they finally stopped, many of the men sinking to the ground where they were, falling immediately asleep. Tom had long since returned to his place with the 20th Maine, and Emmett had remounted to ride along with Chamberlain.

"We have marched approximately thirty miles a day for the past week and this on almost empty stomachs." Chamberlain said with wonder in his tone. "And while the men are frustrated being held up by bumblers, there hasn't been a peep about the length of the march or the lack of food." He twirled his mustache with wonder in his eyes and voice. "Human beings are certainly a remarkable species to adapt so to their environment."

"There was a pretty good brawl when the boys up front started moving those wagons themselves." Emmett grinned, remembering how the bands had been instructed to strike up a tune to drown out the disturbance.

"Can't say that I didn't agree with them." Chamberlain said. "Without this star on my shoulder I might have been up there myself." He smirked, needing to wind down from the day before finding sleep.

"They shore slowed us down some." Emmett agreed. "I think we're just in a hurry to get this darn war over with. The men can taste the end. They're starting to think about going home, seeing their families. Going back to their normal lives."

"It's hard to believe that three years ago I was teaching at Bowdoin College. Standing in front of boys no different in actual age than the soldiers who serve under me now," Chamberlain said, sweeping his arm around, "but far different in life-experience. What was I teaching that was so important? I can't even remember. It has all been overshadowed by our momentous task of the past years. No, I will not, I cannot return to that."

Emmett smiled in the darkness, but didn't immediately reply. Chamberlain often spoke as if teaching, waxing eloquently as if addressing a group of students hanging on his every word. "Do you think we'll catch ole' Bobby Lee tomorrow?" He asked finally.

"We may have caught up with him today if Ord hadn't slowed us down, but we can't worry about that. We will do our part, and eventually he'll be run to ground." Chamberlain stood with a groan that was barely audible, wounds and age making days in the saddle and nights sleeping on the ground all but unbearable. "I'm going to catch some sleep so that I'm ready for whatever the morning brings.

Emmett sat in the dark wondering what he would be doing once this war was over. Maybe he would stay and become regular army? If that was even an option, which it probably wasn't. Soon there would be no need for hundreds of thousands of soldiers. He couldn't see himself going to college, for much as Chamberlain had grown disinterested in the false world that a classroom represented, so had he. The past three years had been a classroom of real life that few boys had ever experienced, but what had it prepared him for? He had learned to read and write over the past few years as the college professor had insisted that he would have no illiterate for an aide. Winter camps had consisted of lessons and assignments and bivouacs had come to include a book and thoughtful discussions. The idea of being a writer interested him, perhaps for a newspaper or a magazine, writing about real things of interest. The sound of an approaching horse pricked his ears, and he looked up from where he now lay, aware that he must have fallen asleep.

"Where is General Chamberlain?" A sentry stood next to a courier, two shadowy figures in the dark. Emmett pointed and the three of them went to shake the general awake. "Orders, sir," the sentry said.

A match flared in the dark, briefly illuminating Chamberlain's mustached face as he read the note. "Emmett, raise the troops, get the buglers going, we are to be on the road again."

"What is it, sir?"

"General Sheridan has blocked the Confederates escape route and needs infantry assistance to pen them in. This could be it."

Within minutes the camp went from utter silence to controlled chaos with bugle calls splitting the air and the rustle and bustle of men rolling out of their blankets in the middle of the night. There were grumbles of sore feet and empty bellies, but all knew that the end was near, the excitement driving them on.

They marched through the wee hours of the night that strange time right before the sun rises when nothing seems real, but rather ghostly and surreal. Emmett rode next to Chamberlain in the vanguard of the brigade as they led the 1st Division forward. There was no talking. They could only see about ten feet ahead, Emmett hoping that Chamberlain knew where he was leading them. An owl hooted in the distance, the noise mournful accompaniment to the sound of thousands of marching feet. As the sky began to lighten with the promised arrival of the sun, Emmett wondered aloud where they were.

"Appomattox Courthouse." Chamberlain answered curtly.

At that moment, a staff officer came galloping up. "General, are you in command here?"

"I command two brigades."

"General Sheridan wants you to break off from your column and come to his support. The rebel infantry is pressing him hard. Our men are falling back. Don't wait for orders to come through the regular channels, but act on this at once." Emmett recognized the direct orders as the exact words of Sheridan, realizing that the man must have memorized them word-for-word.

"Let General Sheridan know that I will be there immediately." Chamberlain spun Charlemagne around to view his brigades in the morning light. "Emmett, tell General Griffin what we are doing and that Crawford should continue on."

Emmett was off like a shot, not wanting to miss the engagement while running an errand. Riding hard he found General Griffin in less than twenty minutes, conveying the message, and was back with the 1st Brigade in less than an hour. They were marching hurriedly through a thick forest, in search of General Sheridan and the combat beckoning them. Emmett had become familiar with the woods of Virginia over the past few years, its mixed stands of maples, alders, walnut, and hickory trees. What he missed was the green of the pines, the towering V-shaped hemlocks and fat balsams and white pine of the northern woods. He realized that the Confederate army must have passed through here, or at least a foraging party, because there were no hickory nuts or walnuts, not even windfalls from the previous autumn, the Rebel army so hungry they had scoured up anything edible.

As they approached a clearing, Emmett spotted a man alone, his back to them as he sat his horse, watching something that was out of their sight. They were almost upon him before Emmett realized that it was General Sheridan. The small man with the dark countenance sat his horse casually, watching the events unfold with silent satisfaction. When Chamberlain approached to receive orders, General Sheridan merely jerked his head with a small smile licking the corners of his lips, waving his hand in the direction that he wanted the infantry to go.

As they emerged from the forest and reached the ridge above the valley, Emmett, at first unaware that Chamberlain was hurrying off to arrange his brigades, halted his horse, stunned at the incredibly powerful scene in front of him. They were on the crest of an open expanse that was rounded like a bowl. At the bottom of the bowl was a seething mass of gray uniforms, like ants scurrying to find an escape route from some invisible threat. As Emmett watched the fleeing Confederates, he saw lines of blue appear behind them, pursuing down into the depression in the earth. Emmett realized that infantry ringed the valley, except for on one side, where only the thin ranks of a single regiment of cavalry stood between the Confederates and escape from the trap they found themselves in. It was this weak spot in the Union defense that the Army of Northern Virginia was now moving at a desperate trot. And it was to that same hole in the net that Chamberlain was to bring his two brigades of infantry with supporting artillery and in all due haste.

Major General Phil Sheridan sat astride his horse watching the final move of the war being played out, a forced checkmate against his nemesis, Robert E. Lee. Sheridan's impulsive and aggressive nature had often gotten him into trouble, such as the fight that had had him suspended from West Point for a year, or his refusal early in the war, as a quartermaster, to pay for stolen horses, a refusal that temporarily landed him in the brig. But it had also won him laurels, first in the western theater of Tennessee, and then as second-in-command only to Grant in the Army of the Potomac. He watched Chamberlain deploying his men to a supporting position behind the thin ranks of cavalry towards which the gray uniforms now scurried across the valley bottom. When his staff officer had returned to say that General Chamberlain was on his way with two brigades, he had finally relaxed. It had taken him some time, but now he knew that it was Chamberlain whose exploits he'd seen again and again over the previous weeks of fighting, a man who fought from the front, much like himself. Chamberlain's self-possession contrasted with his own Irish passion, but in the end, both led to the same positive results. As he watched, the two brigades of the 1st Division deployed themselves efficiently behind the cavalry, setting the teeth to the trap that was about to be sprung.

The Army of Virginia began the ascent towards the sparse ranks of mounted cavalry. They were men who had not eaten for days. They were men who had been constantly moving for weeks in a desperate attempt to escape the tightening noose. Many had

344

dropped out, unable to keep up with the pace, falling to the ground to be left behind, unable to rise even after a respite. Others had slipped away in the night to surrender, or to attempt to make their way home, or to find food, realizing there was no reason to return. Those who were left were the toughest of what had been an enormously powerful army. Men who had seen no break from fighting for four long years. These were men for whom the luxuries of life were no longer even a dim memory. Their hair was long and unkempt, and few had hats to cover their heads from the elements or boots for their feet. Uniforms had ripped and been mended, worn away and then darned, but eventually there had been no needles or thread, and for the most part, their clothes just hung in tatters, barely concealing the emaciated bodies beneath. Some of them didn't have any weapon other than a stick, and fewer still had any ammunition for the rifles they carried. There were no bedrolls or rations as they slept in their shredded uniforms under the stars, moon, and clouds. Onward came these men who no longer knew why they fought, other than for pride, for just plain old orneriness.

Chamberlain watched them jogging up the hill with their eyes downcast, refusing to look up at the cavalry above, and felt a burning admiration. They were proud men who didn't know how to give up. The cavalry suddenly peeled away as if opening a door, and Chamberlain gave the command to move up. Where there had been a few hundred men on horseback there were now 2,000 grim-faced veterans, each with a loaded rifle and all of them backed by several batteries of artillery.

"Drop some artillery onto them." Chamberlain commanded. The first shells missed their mark, going well over the Rebels heads but still had the desired effect. The weary men lifted their eyes to the infantry and artillery above them, and their steps faltered for just a moment. And then they continued forward with dogged steps of determination.

"I believe that was a peach tree in blossom and not a Confederate flag that your artillery was shooting at, General." General Griffin said, riding up with a smile.

Chamberlain stared in wonder at the unusual good cheer and then realized that Griffin was making an attempt at levity. He replied in kind. "I am sorry sir, but I am not used to fighting from such a long distance. I must get my eyes checked."

Emmett stared at the two generals as if they'd lost their minds. It seemed hardly the time for banter. A bugle call pierced his thoughts, and the Union Cavalry prepared to charge, the commander in stark contrast to General Sheridan, being tall with pure white skin and long blond hair that flowed back from his brow. The charismatic General Custer danced his horse up and down the line in front of the men. The sound of a cannon booming splintered the air, and then a momentary silence fell over the unfolding scene. The Confederates still moved relentlessly up the hill, and Emmett could see officers yelling orders, could see a canister shot rip through the ranks, but could hear none of it. There came the caw of a crow, as clear and pure as if Emmett were alone on this hill with the bird. In the distance he could see the Appomattox River serenely flowing, oblivious to the actions of man. Custer turned his horse and started careening down the hill directly at the approaching gray-coats, the rest of the cavalry following, horses scrambling for footing as they hurtled forward. As if someone had clapped his ears, sound returned as the first horses crashed into the Rebels, screams of agony, yells of anger and fear and cries of frustration filling the air.

Still the Confederates pressed forward, and Emmett felt sudden sympathy for them. The order was given to fire, and thousands of Union rifles puffed smoke and spat lead into the Rebels, dropping them in droves, but still they came on, reaching the top. Men swore, punched, kicked, yanked, and fought ferociously. It was the last gasp of an enraged animal. Emmett sat his horse next to Chamberlain and watched as the Union soldiers of the 24th Corps came to their aid and drove the Confederates back down the hill. They passed by a stand of silky dogwoods, their flat-topped blossoms shining white in the bleak valley of death, the men of the south pausing and massing just the other side of the trees. Emmett could see the prominent veins on the oval leaves of the dogwood, could somehow make out the most intricate of detail. On the right flank the cavalry under the leadership of General Custer began to re-form, preparing for the charge that would break the very soul of the South.

Suddenly, a rider broke from the Confederate ranks and rode straight towards them. The horse was thin, its ribs jutting, its

346

coat matted and dirty with grass, bramble stuck in its tail. The horseman held his mount to a slow walk, his back stiff and his face solemn. There was a dirty felt hat on his head with a brightly colored peacock feather jauntily perched in the headband and several emblems pinned to the brim. The Confederate officer carried a white cloth in his hand, so white and so strangely out of place in this grimy scene of two armies, exhausted and covered with dirt. "Where do you suppose a man would get a towel so clean?" Chamberlain murmured to Emmett as the man approached, dismounting and striding forward to where they stood along with several other staff officers. Not a man made a move to meet him, but merely waited, confused by this apparition in the midst of their battle.

"General Gordon wishes for a truce until he can hear further from General Lee about the proposed surrender." The man was tight-lipped and all business, either well aware of the shocking news he was delivering or so focused on the message that its words held no meaning for him.

Surrender? With enormous effort Emmett held himself still, fighting the impulse to throw his hat in the air and scream, to run around whooping and slapping people on the back while sharing the joyous news. He became aware of 50,000 eyes pinned on them, of the sun rising in the east, a dark morning cloud drifting lazily across the sky. The earlier silence had returned, and this time he believed it to be genuine.

Chamberlain remained dignified, stoic in all but the eyes, eyes that betrayed his jubilation. "General Sheridan commands the field. I will have you escorted to him." He waved for two aides to deliver the man to where Sheridan now stood with the 24th Corps and their flag. "Lieutenant Colonel Spear," he said, "would you make sure that nobody fires his weapon?"

Spear had recently become an officer in Chamberlain's brigade and was in command of the 198th Pennsylvania. How interesting, he thought idly, that his old student—whom he had enlisted with in the 20th Maine—should now be present with him while truce was being considered. It was amazing to think that the entire journey had been less than three years, for he felt the war almost Trojan in its span, a decade of strife and suffering. His journey home, he hoped, would be faster than that of Odysseus.

Up and down the lines, flags of truce could be seen waving. Chamberlain, for the time being, held the men in line, ready for whatever would come, awaiting the order to press on with the attack or to stand down. The minutes ticked by with the Southern and Northern soldiers standing just a few hundred yards apart, waiting for two men to decide their fate. A horse neighed, and in the distance a gunshot rang out. Union soldiers were talking excitedly and had to be restrained from crossing over to mingle with their Confederate counterparts. After what seemed an eternity, a staff officer rode up with a message from Sheridan to stand down for a truce, while Grant and Lee negotiated the terms of surrender.

"Have the men stack their arms and plant the colors." Chamberlain ordered his officers.

General Gregory, usually conservative and a bit of a sourpuss rode up and almost knocked Chamberlain from his horse in his exuberance. "Did you hear? It's over. Lee is surrendering."

Chamberlain grinned at the youthfulness that had overtaken his fellow brigade leader. "Well, let's try not to injure each other now, shall we?"

Gregory laughed loudly, spurring his horse off to share the joy with others. Ellis Spear returned, assuring Chamberlain that the men fully understood that a truce had been called. He sat his horse casually, as if this were just another day in the war, a small smile on his lips.

"I guess you'll be back to teaching schoolchildren in Wiscasset soon enough, Ellis." Chamberlain said warmly to his comrade.

"And you back to lecturing at Bowdoin." Ellis raised an eyebrow, suggesting that both of these things might not be true, that perhaps the war had changed them forever. "But let's not forget that even if Grant and Lee can work out this surrender, there are still several large Confederate armies in the field down South."

"If Lee indeed surrenders today, you mark my words, the rest will fall like dominoes." Chamberlain was watching various riders converge on Appomattox Courthouse, a village comprised of maybe fifteen or twenty structures at the most. "Ellis, you are in charge here. I am going to go see if I can find out more. Emmett, you may come with me."

They rode towards the formal courthouse that dominated the small town, a large brick building on the eastern side of the village, a scattering of shops and homes surrounding it. Various generals congregated around it, generals from both sides of the Mason Dixon line, all awaiting news from Generals Grant and Lee regarding the possible surrender. The two-story building had handsome panel doors flanked by tall sash windows. They started towards it but stopped short, Chamberlain veering off. He had spotted General Gordon entering the Clover Hill Tavern across the street from the courthouse. Inside a dozen or so men stood in clutches, some uniforms blue and some gray, conversing quietly. As career soldiers at West Point together they had been friends with one another, friends whose ties had been split these last four years by slavery, state rights, and secession.

"How about some whiskey?" A thin, uncomfortable-looking Confederate officer asked the barkeep. "Not the rotgut stuff, but a nice bottle of something to mark the occasion."

"I might have such a bottle but perhaps one of the boys in blue can pay for it?" Wilson Hix was the owner, bartender, and the entire staff of this tavern, a barren and cheerless place fallen on hard times with the war's tribulations.

"I've got money," the Confederate officer, Henry Heth replied. "I don't need any charity from the North."

General James Longstreet, Lee's right hand man turned his ponderous head like a bulldog might to view the scene. "I'm thinking he don't have much call for your Confederate paper, but would rather have some Yankee gold." Several men broke into guffaws.

Union Brigadier General George Sharpe stepped forward, laying a gold piece on the counter. "A glass for everybody." He said. The barkeep disappeared through a door beside the bar and they could hear the sounds of crates being shifted. Hix emerged a few moments later with a squat bottle of brown glass, its label nearly gone from dampness.

Once the brown liquor was poured, Union General Samuel Crawford raised his drink in toast. "To men of honor, blue and gray." Crawford had been at Fort Sumter as the first shots of the war had been fired four years earlier and was now here as the war wound down to its bitter end.

Sheridan suddenly burst through the door, muttering angrily to anyone who appeared to listen that the entire truce was a trick and that they should attack while they had the advantage. On his way into the village, it emerged; soldiers who either didn't know of the truce or didn't care to adhere to it had fired on him. Officers, both Confederate and Union, gave the turbulent man a wide berth, but he saw General Gordon sitting in the corner with one of his staff officers and immediately went over to join them.

"Is this the real thing, John, or just another ruse from that sly fox leader of yours?" Sheridan was the antithesis of the aristocratic plantation owner from Georgia across the table from him. Gordon was immaculate in his dress, the small goatee on his chin not quite hiding the scar from being shot in the face several years earlier.

"And hello to you, Phil. I see that your personality has not gained in subtly or tact over the last few years." Gordon smiled fondly at Sheridan. "But I do believe that as long as Grant is fair with his terms, that this may indeed be the end."

"Fair with his terms?" Sheridan spluttered. "I only hope that he lives up to his name and demands unconditional surrender. Anything less would be insulting."

"As would that," Gordon replied quietly, the smile disappearing from his eyes.

Sudden gunfire erupted from the direction of the Lynchburg Pike, and Gordon made a move to rise but was waved back down by Sheridan. "Oh, I know about that. Let em fight. Damn them." This was not reassuring in the slightest, but as there was no further noise of battle, all in the room returned to an uneasy truce. As the ceasefire's end rapidly approached with no word on an actual surrender, the gathering officers began to fidget. As the minutes ticked away, one by one they shook hands with their friends from across the divide and excused themselves to return to their men.

"Prepare the men to attack." Chamberlain told his officers once back in the field. The excited chatter died down as soldiers took up their arms with silent thoughts of their own mortality. None wanted to be like the young officer killed by artillery fire earlier, after the initial cease-fire had been called. To come this far, to have lived, survived, unscathed, and then to face death in an action that must certainly be the final of the war—it was an uneasy moment, even or especially to men so used to flirting with death. They checked to make sure their cartridge belts were full, not looking at each other. Orders rang out around the valley, feet shuffled, loads were rammed home.

Just as they were about to move out, a hush abruptly descended upon the valley. Emmett looked up to see what had brought this quiet to so many thousands. His eyes scanned the line of Confederates, realizing that they were all staring in the same direction. Riding out between the two lines of Americans, squared off against each other, was the regal figure of Robert E. Lee. It was as if a god had floated to earth and now approached. This man who had struck terror into the hearts of the Union Army throughout this Great War rode casually, serenely, as if out for a Sunday picnic. The Union lines parted to let the legendary soldier pass through. Somehow his uniform appeared brand new, bright gold striping and stars upon his shoulders. His sword had a jeweled hilt, and his shiny black boots were laced with a design in stitching of red. He rode his favorite horse, Traveller, sixteen hands high, iron gray, with dramatic black points.

Chamberlain tugged lightly on Emmett's arm and nodded his head across the way, and Emmett saw General Ulysses S. Grant approaching down another road. In stark contrast to Lee's impeccable dress uniform, Grant slouched easily in his saddle, wearing the uniform of a common soldier with three stars barely visible on the shoulder through the mud that splattered his entire visage. He wore simple boots with no spurs, his pant legs tucked into the tops. He could have been a private in the army except for the calm assurance and confidence that emanated from his being as his horse picked its way down the road. Emmett could not help but think that each embodied their region's culture, and very appropriately. Robert E. Lee, of almost royal bearing, was the quintessential gentleman of the South, while Ulysses S. Grant was the common factory worker or New England laborer who thought respect was earned through hard work and not birth.

The two men approached an ordinary house in the village center from opposite directions. They came from different backgrounds, opposing philosophies and upbringing, but both, still and finally, came as Americans. Lee arrived first, dismounting at the front gate, walking the last few steps to the front porch and entering with his chief-of-staff. Grant arrived afterward with about fifteen Union officers excited to be present at such a momentous occasion. The parlor on the first floor had been set up for the meeting with two tables, a small, plain brown table for Grant, and a grander, more ornate table for Lee.

"General," the almost forty-three-year old Grant remarked casually, "I met you once before, in Mexico when you paid a visit to Garland's Brigade." He was referring to the Mexican-American War in which both had served in the late 1840's.

"I have realized that we must have met, but have not been able to recall you in the slightest." Lee admitted. Grant had been a young quartermaster at the time, while Lee had been an older officer with much experience under his belt.

"You were a distinguished aide to General Scott, although your hair and beard were not quite so silver." They chatted for a few moments about that war.

Finally, Lee paused, then asked for Grant to write out the formal terms of surrender they had discussed over the past few days. Grant immediately picked up pen and paper, and began to write.

Appomattox Courthouse, Virginia April 9, 1865.

General: In accordance with the substance of my letter to you of the 8th instant, I propose to receive the surrender of the Army of Northern Virginia on the following terms, to wit: Rolls of all the officers and men to be made in duplicate, one copy to be given to an officer to be designated by me, the other to be retained by such officer or officers as you may designate. The officers to give their individual paroles not to take up arms against the government of the United States until properly exchanged; and each company or regimental commander to sign a like parole for the men of their commands. The arms, artillery, and public property to be parked and stacked, and turned over to the officers appointed by me to receive them. This will not embrace the side-arms of the officers nor their private horses or baggage. This done, each officer and man will be allowed to return to his home, not to be disturbed by United States authority so long as they observe

their paroles and the laws in force where they may reside.
U.S. Grant, Lieutenant-General.

General Lee read through the agreement, nodding occasionally. "Many of the men," he observed, "have brought with them their own private horses and mules. It would be important for them to keep them, especially for the farmers returning to plant their fields."

Grant nodded. "That would be agreeable."

Lee looked away, for the first time betraying his pride. "Most of the men have not eaten in days." He said simply.

"I will have rations for your numbers delivered to your camp immediately."

At about 4 p.m., General Lee exited the building between a multitude of Union officers who had gathered for the event. They silently doffed their caps in a show of respect and admiration, and he absently returned the salute. He mounted Traveller and slowly walked down the main street of the village. Several men whooped and threw their hats into the air, but General Grant, stepping out on the porch, stopped any such celebration immediately, suggesting pointedly that the work of reconciliation must start now.

The same reserve could not be said for the infantry soldiers who celebrated long into the night. Emmett ran around yelling, singing, hugging and crying along with thousands of other Americans unable to believe that this tragic conflict, while not yet officially over, had taken an irrevocable step in that direction. At some point, the celebration wound down as men, exhausted from battle, marching, and lack of food came back to earth.

It was into this lull that a message came for Chamberlain. A staff officer arrived with the request late that night, just as Emmett, Chamberlain, and the men of the 1st Brigade were preparing for their first night of relaxed sleep in four years. He was to call on General Griffin, post haste.

Chamberlain followed the officer back down into the town of Appomattox. He noted the ghostly signs, the smithies, the Plunkett-Meeks store, and the law offices of Mssrs. Jones & Woodson. General Griffin had taken up residence in the Clover Tavern to prepare for the surrender. Men were busy setting up printing presses for the 30,000 parole slips that would need to be printed from the lists of the Army of Northern Virginia.

"Good evening, General Chamberlain," General Charles Griffin greeted him.

"And to you, sir."

"As you know, I, along with Gibbon and Merritt, have been given the duty of preparing the details of the surrender. We have chosen you to command the ceremonial surrender." Griffin stared intently at this man from Maine who he'd come to respect so much over the recent years. He was by far his most trusted general, a man who, quite simply, had never failed to do what was asked of him. And he knew, too, that his men trusted him, and that the South admired him for his courage.

"I would be honored to do so, sir." Chamberlain replied calmly. Inside, his head reeled with the honor bestowed upon him, to preside at such a turning point in the history of his nation, not only the surrender, but also the reunification of the United States of America.

"General Grant has requested that the proceeding be calm and quiet and decorous, where it is clear that the Rebels have been beaten and surrendered, but in a manner that does not humiliate them."

"Of course, sir." Chamberlain replied. "After all, they are our fellow countrymen." It could not be like the humiliation faced by the British when they lost at Yorktown, but must be more amicable, requiring the Union Army to be humble to a humbled foe.

"That is why we have chosen you, General Chamberlain, because you understand the subtlety of things. It must be the professor in you."

"I don't know about that, sir, but I certainly understand that few men like to lose, and no man likes to have his face rubbed in it." A gesture needed to be made, something that did not lessen the fact that the Union had won, but an indication to the South that there was no shame in their defeat.

"Very well, then, you may begin the preparations for the surrender." Griffin turned his attention back to the pile of papers in front of him.

"Sir, if I may ask a favor?"

"Of course, General."

"For the surrender I would request command of the 3rd Brigade." The 3rd Brigade had incorporated the decimated 20th Maine's last men. It would be a touch of home to have those men from Maine at his back.

"That would be fine, General." General Griffin answered, smiling warmly at his friend.

Chapter Nineteen

Sae,

I am glad I was not tempted to leave the army this spring. I would not for a fortune have missed the experiences of the last two weeks. It seems like two years, so many, & such important events have taken place, within that time. Father said in his last letter to me that 'the glory of battles was over'. But if he had seen some of these we have had of late, in which we captured the enemy by the thousand & carried their positions by a dash, and at last at Appomattox Court House received the surrender of Genl Lee & his whole army, he would think differently....For my personal part I have had the advance every day there was any fighting—have been in five battles—two of them being entirely under my own direction and brilliantly successful—twice wounded myself—my horse shot—in the front line when the flag of truce came through from Lee—had the last shot & the last man killed, in this campaign...L[10]

April 12, 1865

Emmett woke at first light, but, instead of jumping up, as was his custom, he lay still and relished this moment, the day that the Army of Northern Virginia would lay down their weapons and surrender to the Union. According to the peace plan established over the last few days, the Confederates would surrender their weapons in a public ceremony. The southern delegation led by Robert E. Lee had requested a more discreet submission, but General Grant was of the notion that a public gesture was necessary to cement the bonds of peace. These weapons had been raised in violence against their country, and thus, must formally be laid back down in peace. It had been agreed that rebel soldiers could keep their horses, for these men would shortly return to their farms and to the work of the living.

The surrender was the beginning of the end of the war, but where did that leave Emmett Collins? His thoughts drifted back to his conversation with his friend Tom Chamberlain late the night before as they had sat by the dying embers of the campfire.

"You really think you might live in Portland?" Emmett asked Tom.

"I'll stay in the army if they let me." Tom said, shrugging his shoulders. "They might need to hang on to some of us volunteers to keep the peace in the South. I don't imagine everybody's gonna be just happy as pie with the new way of things. And there's rumbling about clearing out the Indians out west, too."

"I don't get the impression Southerners will much like having soldiers from the North keeping the peace, though."

Tom threw a small stick into the glowing red coals. "Abe Lincoln ain't gonna just let them work things out for themselves. Otherwise, what was this war about?"

"You think this war was about the slaves?"

"I been thinking on that since that regiment of colored soldiers marched by us a few days back. In uniforms, carrying guns, they sure didn't look much different than you or me. If the Southerners claim they were fighting for their rights, it seems to me that somebody had to fight for the coloreds' too, and freedom is a pretty simple one." Tom sighed, slouching on the stump he sat upon. "It seems to me that the South wouldn't have seceded unless they believed the North was working towards ending slavery. It all comes down to that."

"That's what I been thinking." Emmett replied. "I was talking to General Chamberlain earlier, and he was telling me about this new law President Lincoln is working on to create this thing called the Freedman Bureau. It's supposed to help integrate the coloreds into life outside of being slaves, or something like that. He told me that they been talking about putting General Howard in charge of it. Him being from Maine and all, General Chamberlain thought he could probably get me some sort of position helping out with that."

Tom nodded in the darkness, chewing over the words before answering. "You think that's what you're gonna do?"

"I'm not sure."

"You got that girl on your mind still, don't you?"

"Yeah," Emmett admitted. "I don't know why she hasn't been answering my letters."

Tom stirred the wood with a stick, and a flickering flame briefly illuminated his face. "What sort of future do you see with her?" He asked carefully.

"I thought we might get married." Emmett blurted out, his face burning red.

Tom considered his friend with no judgment at all. "That might be the problem right there." He finally said.

Emmett glared at him. "You don't think she wants to marry me?"

"I didn't say that." Tom responded. "I suppose if she did want to marry you, then you would get hitched right off?"

Emmett shrugged his shoulders. "I hadn't thought about it. I reckon we might take some time to get to know each other first."

Tom nodded. "And you wouldn't have any problem with her continuing to...work?"

If possible, Emmett flushed a deeper red. "She wouldn't be sleeping with men for money any more, if that's what you're talking about."

"How would she live? If she weren't married to you, and she couldn't work no more?"

Emmett started to reply, hesitated, and then fell silent. "I hadn't really thought of that. I guess we'd get married right off."

"It goes without saying that she would stop working, which means you'd have to get a job and support the both of you. What are you skilled at?"

Emmett thought on how he'd learned to read and write, but what good would that do him? He thought on how he'd become a fair to passable soldier, but that seemed to be coming to an end. "I know my way around a brick yard. I reckon we could go back to Brewer and live in my parents house, and I could work in the brick yard."

Tom stared straight at Emmett for his last question. "Is that what you want to do?"

Emmett squirmed uncomfortably. "I'd hoped to see a bit of the country first, maybe go to college, maybe find a job where I can write about things, maybe work for this Freedman Bureau for a bit, but I'd be willing to change all that for Susannah. I love her."

"And maybe she figured this all out a bit ago, and she don't want you to throw away your dreams for her. Could be she's just doing the right thing by you."

"Ain't that for me to decide?"

"You're seventeen years old, probably have a little bit of

money saved up, got yourself some education. Don't you think you should give life a chance before you tie yourself down to the brickyard in Brewer you vowed you'd never return to?" Tom stood up, throwing his stick into the fire. "But it ain't none of my business. I'm gonna get some shut-eye. I don't want to be too tired for tomorrow."

Emmett's sleep had been restless after that conversation, his heart longing for Susannah's love, his body aching for her touch, but his mind grappling with the truth of what Tom had said. He had been lying awake for the past two hours when Tom poked his head into the tent. "The war's not over yet, young Master Collins, so you'd best get yourself up and out here as we're about to go into town for the formal surrender."

The sun was not yet fully up as Emmett emerged from the tent, but in camp there was a visible current of excitement as men hurried here and there, ready for the surrender of this proud Army of Virginia. Emmett realized the sun would not be shining that day, as the sky was a thick gray, blanketing the countryside in a chilly embrace. It was as if Mother Nature had recognized the gravity of the event, providing the appropriate background for the somber day.

Chamberlain had called all of the regimental commanders of the 1st Division to his tent to review the details of the surrender. General Gregory was in charge of the 2nd Brigade, while General Alfred Pearson was filling in for Chamberlain in the 1st Brigade. Chamberlain would be commanding the 3rd Brigade, including the 20th Maine, as well as being overall commander.

"In one hour we will assemble on the Richmond-Lynchburg Road just east of the village." Chamberlain continued to issue orders, directing each brigade's deployment. "Any questions on the order of the brigades?" He finished.

"We will be arranged by regiment, east to west?" General Gregory wanted to clarify.

"Yes." Chamberlain responded. "I will be on the far right, the eastern most point of the 3rd Brigade, with my staff." He looked around at these officers with whom he'd shared so many hardships. His eyes paused on Ellis Spear, former student, now in command of the 198th Pennsylvania, and then moved on to Walter Morrill, former student, now in command of the 20th Maine.

"General Grant's orders are very specific: that we are to honor our southern brethren, and not humiliate them. There will be no celebrating today. There is plenty of time for that in the future. Is that understood?"

The officers nodded in agreement, though the expression on a few faces showed contrary feelings.

"The men will be in the order arms position. As the first Confederates reach my position, I will give the order for the bugler to sound the carry arms, we will perform the salute, return to order arms, and then parade rest. The Confederates will fix bayonets, stack arms, fold and relinquish flags, and then move on. These men have fought valiantly against us, and we will honor them for this. If there are no questions, see to forming the regiments in preparation for the march to town."

Chamberlain was all business, heavy with the burden of responsibility, realizing the importance of making this final act just right. His was not the manner of a victor, but rather, that of a man who knew the day's events needed to unroll precisely and flawlessly. History was watching. "Start the lines at the bluff of the stream there and stretch it this way into town." He ordered his officers as they crossed the shallow part of the Appomattox River. They lined up along the road, facing north towards the Rebels' camp.

Emmett could see the Confederates moving about their camp now; many of them hungry, the rations General Grant had ordered to be sent over to feed them having gone quickly. For many of these southern soldiers, it was the first meal they had eaten in a week. The few small tents were struck and put away, the men gathering their weapons in preparation for turning them over. As Emmett watched, they fell into columns of battalions, the flags marking the various divisions, and the entire gray mass of the enemy turned countrymen began the tedious march to surrender.

One such was Barney McNeil of Company G of the 15th Alabama, who had awakened before first light that morning. This was the day they were to turn over their weapons, surrender their flags, and then get a piece of paper saying they were paroled, and could return home. He had slept in his boots and clothes, what little was left of them. He had found a piece of leather a few weeks back that he had cut into strips to hold the soles of his boots on. He pulled tight the rope holding his trousers up, each day having had to pull it a little bit tighter. Looking closely, you could still see the red in his shirt that had at one point given his regiment the nickname, the "Oates Zouaves", but the color had long since faded. Today he would lay down his arms and get his first glimpse of the man who had fought the 15th Alabama so viciously at Gettysburg. Tomorrow he would begin the journey home to his wife and two daughters. Smoke curled up from several campfires, kindled for warmth rather than cooking as they'd gone through what food they'd received in a matter of hours. There was no coffee. Yesterday, the last of the hickory nuts had been boiled to create a bitter liquid that in no way resembled coffee, but was at least warm. As the sun peeked over the horizon, the warmth caused mists to drift lazily skyward from the cold ground. There was very little conversation, each lost in his own thoughts of surrender, defeat, and home. Captain Schaff gave the order for the men to retrieve their rifles. Barney McNeil, along with many in the regiment, carried the Springfield Model 1861. He grabbed a handful of sand and ran it up and down the barrel of the rifle, attempting to bring the shine back. He thought back to when he was first issued the rifle, and how he'd taken dirt to the barrel to achieve the opposite, not wanting the glint of the sun on the shiny barrel to give away his position. He ran his hand through his thick-black hair in an attempt to straighten it, and then his beard flecked with gray. He was thirty-four years old but felt like an old man.

The time was not long now as the call went out to assemble into companies. They formed their marching columns and then moved out for the last time as members of the Army of Northern Virginia, moving down the hill, crossing the Appomattox River, and approaching the gauntlet of blue that lay before.

At the head of the gauntlet, Chamberlain waited, giving the last orders. "When the first regiment approaches, have the bugles sound the order arms and carry, the marching salute. We will honor these men who have fought so valiantly as our enemies and are now once again our brothers." Chamberlain was reminding the men for the third time, speaking in a hushed tone, well aware that he might be criticized for this show of respect. What he knew, however, was that, while the fighting might be over, the long struggle to repair the shattered pieces of the country had only just begun.

As the first regiment of Confederates approached, Emmett strained to see these men who he'd fought against over the past few years. Truth to tell, they weren't much to look at. They walked wearily in defeat, hunger and exhaustion marking their steps. At the front rode General Gordon, leading the remnants of the famous Stonewall Brigade. The men stared straight ahead, doing their best to ignore the three brigades of Union soldiers they were about to pass through on the way to laying down their arms and battle flags. The only ones without beards were those too young to yet grow them, and of these, there were many scattered throughout the battalions.

General Chamberlain gave the order and the bugle sounded, the men of the Union Army snapping to attention to pay this one last honor to their vanquished foe. Like a wave traveling down the line, the Union soldiers went through the steps of the marching salute, the right hand grasping the stock with the left hand below the butt, and then the right hand dropping back to their side. The men then returned to parade rest with the butt of the gun back on the ground at their right side. Emmett stood with the men of the 20th Maine, rigid at attention as the men shifted and raised their rifles to mark the fighting spirit of their Southern brothers. The shuffling steps of the Confederates became lighter, and heads that hung in shame slowly rose.

General Gordon, the thirty-three-year-old Georgian, was the first officer to receive this salute, and thus, the first to realize the honor being bestowed upon the Confederate Army—that they were not being treated as vanquished foes and prisoners of war, but as men, as brothers, as fellow countrymen. There was not a man in the Confederacy who doubted the courage of their general. At Antietam, he'd been shot in the calf, and then again just above the first wound. Refusing to stop, he continued on, leading his men, a third minié ball piercing his arm, and then his shoulder, but still he continued on. It was only when he was struck in the face that he finally fell face down in his hat. The men who pulled him to safety realized that were it not for a hole in his hat, he might have drowned in his own blood.

But now, the enemy was celebrating his courage as well.

Not to be outdone, General Gordon wheeled his horse to face Chamberlain, touching his spurs lightly to the ribs of the magnificent beast, which reared up on its hind legs, before coming back down, bowing its head, Gordon's sword cutting a wide arc through the sky and gently coming to rest at his stirrup. He nodded, an almost imperceptible movement, and then gave the order for his men to return the marching salute, giving honor for honor.

On this thin, dusty road leading from the town of Appomattox east to Richmond some ninety miles distant, unfolded the surrender of the Army of Northern Virginia. Just fewer than 5,000 Union soldiers lined this road over which 25,000 Confederate soldiers were passing. Battle, time, dust, and weather had faded the blues and grays so that the uniforms of the two sides were almost indistinguishable. The flags of both sides, the stars and bars of the South with its diagonal cross and thirteen stars and the stars and stripes of the North all hung limp in the unmoving air. The Rebels had set their weariness aside, summoning up the last of their energy to march proudly through the lines of the Yankees.

As each Confederate regiment passed by, they returned the salute, honor for honor, turning and facing Chamberlain and addressing their lines. The regiment would then come up, the color guard laying down the company flag, and then each man coming to the fore to stack his rifle. As Emmett watched, he was particularly struck by the color guard of the 15th Alabama. The man, in his faded red shirt, a patch on the left breast that said 'Liberty, Equality, Fraternity', carried the Alabama state flag emblazoned with the words, 'Alabama, Independent Now and Forever'. He moved forward to the pile of flags already before him with slow feet, and Emmett could feel the heaviness in those legs at surrendering this symbol of his pride. With trembling fingers the man carefully folded the torn and tattered cotton cloth, tucking the corners, looking skyward for just a moment before gently laying his offering on the pile. His eyes were dry in contrast to many of the others, but perhaps he had no more tears to shed. The man bowed his head, and then returned to his regiment. Several others could not contain themselves as the flag was surrendered, and ran to the front, crumpling to their knees, grown soldiers crying like small children at being parted from the colors that they had carried so proudly for so many years. Yet, it was the original color guard of the 15th Alabama who would remain in Emmett's memory, an image so imprinted perhaps because the man looked exactly like his dead brother, William.

The formal surrender of flags and weapons had been going on for five hours already when Chamberlain heard a disturbance further down the line. He ambled his horse down to investigate. There appeared to be some dispute with the Confederate General Henry Wise and his own soldiers. In an attempt to avoid staining the day with an incident, Chamberlain approached the Southern general.

"General Wise," he said gently, "it bodes well for future relations between the South and North that both sides today have handled themselves so well, wouldn't you say?"

"Speak for yourself, sir, but I have been the butt of humor from several of your men already." Wise was indignant, the exchange having begun when his own men had mocked him for being a coward, one claiming this was the closest he'd ever gotten to a Yankee in this whole war. That had then progressed into jeers from the Union infantry as well.

"I am sorry to hear that, sir. What exactly has been said to you?"

"There were calls of 'who killed John Brown?', and 'where did you steal your coat?'" Wise spoke in a shrill voice, his white hair in disarray on his head, tobacco spit spotting his chin.

Chamberlain remembered that Wise had been the governor of Virginia who had officiated at the conviction and hanging of John Brown some six years earlier. He also noted that Wise wore a dark blue coat with shiny gold buttons, more in line with a Union uniform than that of a Confederate officer. "I am sorry to hear that, and will have it looked into." Chamberlain had no intention to, but rather was struggling to keep a grin from escaping in the face of this ludicrous figure with the thin skin.

"You see to it, then."

"I hope to get a chance to visit with you after the war is over, General."

Wise spat a stream of tobacco juice to the side in disdain. "Let us be clear, sir, that I hate you, as I hate every living person in the North, and your visit would not be welcome and I'd rather go to Hell than cross over the Mason Dixon line."

Chamberlain choked back a biting response, and made to turn his horse away, reflecting to himself that, while the fighting might be over, peace was still a long way off.

General Wise rode on, and Chamberlain returned to the head of the line as the surrender of weapons, munitions, flags, and men continued on. It was sunset before the last of the Confederates came through, a special headquarters guard. The color bearer gravely handed the flag over. "This ain't the first time you Yankees have seen this flag. I have carried it into many a battle, always at the front, many times leading to Southern victory."

Chamberlain looked behind the man, realizing this was the last, and that the day was finally over. The road behind him to the east lay empty, as quiet as it had been the week before, and probably would be a week in the future. "I am sure you speak the truth, and it is in this bravery and spirit that we welcome you back. If it were within my power to grant you this flag as an honorable keepsake, I would do so. But alas, I cannot, and so I grant you my respect." The man seemed satisfied with that response, turning and continuing down the road.

With that, the last of the Army of Virginia had surrendered. Chamberlain gave the orders for the weapons to be gathered in preparation for shipment north, oversaw the careful boxing up of the battle flags to send to the capital, and finally the destruction of the unusable portion of the munitions. As the sun began to descend over the horizon, he found himself alone on the Richmond-Lynchburg Road. His eyes lifted up to a small knoll, just a slight raising of the ground where a single solitary figure stood alone. A small girl, no more than four years of age, he thought, stood there in a white dress, blond curls swirling about her features, lips pressed together tightly and no hint of smile on her face, merely a look of fascination tickling her eyes. She held a small wreath of flowers in her two tiny hands before her, freshly picked flowers from a nearby field. It was impossible to tell where her sympathies lay—whether it was with the North and union—or whether it was with the South and secession. To her, the victors and the vanquished were all the same.

Author Notes

I have wanted to be a writer for as long as I can remember, but it was not until college that the concept of writing historical fiction began to germinate within me. I was a history major at Trinity College, fascinated with the subject, but well aware that most history books were, well, quite frankly, boring. It was the passion of a history professor at Trinity, coupled with the sweeping sagas of James Michener that made me grasp the novel concept that history could be entertaining as well as insightful. In choosing historical fiction, I hoped to fool the world into learning about the great people and events of the past.

In 1989, fresh out of college, I researched and wrote a historical novel about the Cuban Revolution of 1953-1959. Much like *At Every Hazard*, I used a fictional character who followed Fidel Castro as he led a small group of revolutionaries to power. Upon beginning my first edit of this manuscript, I realized that never having been to Cuba, the novel lacked sincerity, and I deposited the pages on a dusty shelf until I could visit that country.

In the meantime, I became a middle school history teacher and published two mystery novels, *Mainely Power* and *Mainely Fear*. I chose to write mysteries to further hone my writing, all the while searching for the 'just right' topic for more historical fiction. As is often the case, the subject matter lay right before me. Joshua Lawrence Chamberlain was from Brunswick, Maine, the town in which I live and teach. He was a Civil War officer, an American hero. His house is now a museum in Brunswick. Here was my main character, the events of the Civil War providing the bones of the book.

The problem with historical fiction is untangling the real from the embroidery. How much of *At Every Hazard* is historically accurate? The simple answer is, all of it. The life of Joshua Chamberlain and the events of the Civil War are entirely factual, and can be used to glean a better understanding of the man and of this crucial period in American history. That being said, history is also an interpretation, an attempt to untangle various accounts of what has happened in the past, to sift through what was known and merely hypothesized, to distinguish the truth from opinion and hearsay. A significant amount of what we know about

Joshua Chamberlain was from his own pen, as he wrote prolifically about himself and the war until the day he died in 1914. His was the flowery prose of a poet, and he more than likely exaggerated his own heroics. It was important to balance his recollections on the war with other material to try to get to the central truth of what actually happened.

All the same, historical fiction does permit certain liberties that nonfiction does not. The Collins family is fictional, but is also representative of a typical family from Maine struggling to get by during this difficult war. The prostitute, Susannah, is also fictional, used to portray the difficulties often faced by women, particularly widows. A few of the common soldiers in the pages were fictionalized to portray the average Union soldier. While the battle scenes are entirely accurate in the big picture, the individual details of soldiers fighting I created so that the book would be readable. Some of the letters and newspaper articles I likewise created to discuss and explain actual events of the war without the reader having to wade through the long, often tediously detailed newspaper articles of the day. All of the dialogue is my own, created to push the story forward, but strictly in keeping with what these characters would have said or thought. At the battle of Chancellorsville, Joshua Chamberlain did indeed have a horse shot from underneath him, but not exactly in the manner I describe.

Things of particular note are that Abraham Lincoln did consider creating colonies of black people in South America. That the term "hooker" did actually precede General Hooker, but the large following of prostitutes around his camp brought a resurgence to the term. Mary Anne Hall was a famous Madame of one of 450 brothels in Washington D.C., her establishment catering largely to politicians. Eliza Thomas was the Madame at 62 Ohio Avenue where Nellie Star was the favorite prostitute of John Wilkes Booth. The aurora borealis truly did streak the night sky in Fredericksburg as the 20th Maine was burying their dead. Walt Whitman was a nurse and paymaster in Washington, but as far as I know, never fixed up any soldiers with 'soiled doves'.

Why Emmett Collins? This is a book for adults, but I also want it to be accessible to younger adults, believing that the coming of age of a young boy would engage high school juniors while learning about the American Civil War. But I also needed a character who could cut through the flowery prose of Joshua Chamberlain and get to the real dirt of his life and the Civil War. That it was not pretty but ugly, that it was not good versus evil, but some murky concept in between. Emmett Collins allowed me to show Chamberlain as a real man instead of the fictional character he created for himself through his writings after the war. He was a man who struggled at sending boys to their death in astounding numbers, and attempted to reconcile his romantic Sir Walter Scott version of war with his actual experiences on the battlefield. He was a man who was wounded six times during the war and fell gravely ill twice. The wound at Petersburg would cause him incontinence, infection, and agonizing pain for the rest of his life, and would eventually kill him forty-nine years after the end of the war.

And what of Joshua Chamberlain and the almost fifty years of his life following the Civil War? He used his hero status in politics, being elected Governor for four one-year terms from 1867 to 1870. In 1871 he was named President of Bowdoin College, serving in that capacity for twelve years, modernizing the curriculum by adding practical sciences and engineering. He also instituting mandatory military drilling, a concept initially embraced by the student body, but eventually so controversial as to be discontinued. True to his promise to Emmett, he bought a twenty-six-foot sailing sloop named Wildflower, and then later on a ten-ton ship he called the Pinafore. He built a summer home, Domhegan, on Simpson Point in Brunswick. It was here that his favorite mount from the war, Charlemagne, was buried, having survived numerous wounds and dying peacefully of old age. He also moved his house down Potter Street to the corner of Main Street, raising it up to add a new first floor underneath. Fanny made it her mission to decorate the enlarged home with artwork and antiques.

In 1878 Chamberlain was appointed to go to France to represent the United States in education at the Paris Universal Exposition. He took Fanny, Daisy, and Wyllys with him, spending several months traveling the continent after the exposition. In 1880, as the commander of the Maine militia, he was called upon to restore order when political scandal in Augusta threatened violence and civil strife. With a small staff headed up by his old

20th Maine adjutant, John Marshall Brown, Chamberlain settled the dispute peacefully. As the decade progressed, Chamberlain became involved in real estate deals in Florida and various businesses, spent a great deal of time in New York City, continued to lecture at various organizations, and was on the board of many educational and artistic programs. In 1898, Chamberlain volunteered his services for the Spanish/American war but was turned down. He was sixty-nine years old and still struggling from his Civil War wounds. Fanny suffered from failing eyesight, eventually going blind. Their marriage continued to be a tumultuous affair, with good times and bad—at one point divorce was even contemplated—though they ended up staying together. She died in 1905 after complications arising from a broken hip. Chamberlain's time was marked by the wound received at Rives Salient, causing him torturous pain for the remainder of his life, forcing many operations to alleviate the suffering, and finally leading to his death from infection in 1914. At his bedside was Abner Shaw, the 20th Maine surgeon who had initially operated on him after he fell outside of Petersburg, prolonging his life by almost fifty years.

Tom Chamberlain had a more difficult time adjusting as a civilian, never really becoming comfortable in a life outside the army. It is possible that he suffered from Post Traumatic Stress Disorder, long before it was called that. There are rumors that he struggled with alcoholism as well as difficulty with his lungs. He went to work for his brother, John, in New York City as a clerk in his business. When John died in 1867, Tom took over his business, eventually marrying his widow three years later. There are some signs that he struggled in business as well as matrimony until his death in 1896.

As for Emmett, well, he adjusted to life after the war, becoming a journalist and then a novelist. He married the woman of his dreams and had eight children.

Joshua Chamberlain During the Civil War

* *Reports to Camp Mason in Portland in August of 1862 as a Lieutenant Colonel of the 20th Maine, a regiment formed from all over the state*
* *Reports along with the 20th Maine to Washington D.C. for orders in September, 1862*
* *Plays a supporting role in Battle of Antietam in September, 1862*
* *Fights in the losing effort at the Battle of Fredericksburg in December, 1862*
* *Minor involvement in battle of Chancellorsville in May, 1863*
* *Promoted to full Colonel in 1863 when Adelbert Ames himself was promoted*
* *Receives Congressional Medal of Honor for heroics at Battle of Gettysburg in July, 1863*
* *Court Martial Duty in Washington D.C. recovering from illness in January, 1864*
* *Gets shot in the hip during the Siege of Petersburg at Rives Salient in June, 1864*
* *Is promoted on the battlefield to Brigadier General when most thought he was dying*
* *Goes home to Brunswick to recover from injuries in September, 1864*
* *Is shot through the side during the battle of Quaker Road in March, 1865*
* *Is promoted to Major General on March 29, 1865*
* *Wins valuable ground at Battle of White House Road and Five Forks in April, 1865*
* *Is chosen to accept the Southern surrender at Appomattox Courthouse in April, 1865*

Joshua Chamberlain After the Civil War

* *Serves four consecutive one-year terms as Governor from 1867-1871*

* *Serves as President of Bowdoin College from 1871-1883*

* *Delivers the state oration at the nation's centennial in Philadelphia in 1876*

* *Serves as U.S. Commissioner to Paris Exposition in 1878 and composes long report to government on education system in France*

* *Prevents civil unrest when called upon to settle angry dispute over state election in 1880*

* *Receives the Congressional Medal of Honor in 1893 for his heroism at Gettysburg*

* *Organizes a land development company in Florida called the Homosassa Company in 1885*

* *Is President of Institute for Artists and Artisans in New York City from 1892-1893*

* *Volunteers for service in the Spanish/American War of 1898 but is turned down due to age (69) and poor health*

* *Is appointed surveyor of Port of Portland in 1900*

* *Dies at the age of eighty-five in 1914 from an infection of the wound he received in the Petersburg Campaign, making him the last person to die from Civil War injuries*

374

Work Cited

Chamberlain, Joshua. *Bayonet! Forward; My Civil War Reminiscences*. 2nd ed. Gettysburg: Stan Clark Military Books, 1994. Print.

Chamberlain, Joshua. *Blessed Boyhood! The Early Memoir of Joshua Lawrence Chamberlain*. 1st edition. Brunswick, ME: Bowdoin College, 2013. Print.

Chamberlain, Joshua. *"Joshua L. Chamberlain; A Life in Letters."* Trans. Array *Joshua L. Chamberlain; A Life in Letters*. Oxford: Osprey Publishing, 2012. Print.

Coggins, Jack. *Arms and Equipment of the Civil War*. 2nd edition. Mineola: Dover Publications, Inc., 1962. Print.

Conforti, Joseph. *Greater Portland; History and place in northern New England*. 1st edition. Durham: University of New Hampshire Press, 2005. Print.

Desjardin, Thomas. *Stand Firm Ye Boys From Maine; The 20th Maine and the Gettysburg Campaign*. 2nd edition. Oxford: Oxford University Press, 2009. Print.

Furgurson, Ernest. *Freedom Rising; Washington in the Civil War*. New York: Random House, Inc., 2005. Print.

Leech, Margaret. *Reveille In Washington 1860-1865*. Alexandria: Time-Life Books, Inc., 1980. Print.

Longacre, Edward. *Joshua Chamberlain; The Soldier and the Man*. Cambridge: Da Capo Press, 2003. Print.

Lord, Francis. *Uniforms of the Civil War*. 2nd edition. Mineola: Dover Publications, Inc., 1970. Print.

Loski, Diana. *The Chamberlains of Brewer Maine*. 1st edition. Gettysburg: Thomas Publications, 1998. Print.

Lossing, Benson. *Matthew Brad'ys Illustrated History of The Civil War*. 2nd edition. New York: Random House, Print.

McCutcheon, Mark. *The Writers Guide to Everyday Life in the 1800's*. 1st edition. Cincinnati: Writers Digest Books, 1993. Print.

Nesbitt, Mark. *Through Blood & Fire; Selected Civil War Papers of Major General Joshua Chamberlain*. 1st edition. Mechanicsburg: Stackpole Books, 1996. Print.

Pullen, John. *Joshua Chamberlain; A Hero's Life & Legacy*. Mechanicsburg: Stackpole Books, 1999. Print.

Smith, Diane. *Fanny & Joshua*. Gettysburg: Thomas Publications, 1999. Print.

Stein, Gloria. *Civil War Camp Life; Sutlers, Sex, and Scoundrels*. 1st edition. Xlibris Corporation, 2008. Print.

Trulock, Alice Rains. *In the Hands of Providence; Joshua Chamberlain & the American Civil War*. Chapel Hill: The University of North Carolina Press, 1992. Print.

Tunis, Edwin. *Frontier Living*. 1st edition. Cleveland: World Publishing Company, 1961. Print.

Varhola, Michael. *Everyday Life During the Civil War*. 1st edition. Cincinnati: Writers Digest Books, 1999. Print.

Varhola, Michael. *Life in Civil War America*. 1st edition. Cincinnati: Family Tree Books, 1999. Print.

Wallace, Willard. *Soul of the Lion; A Biography of General Joshua L. Chamberlain.* Gettysburg: Stan Clark Military Books, 1995. Print.

Ward, Geoffrey. *The Civil War.* 1st edition. New York: Vintage Books, 1990. Print.

Notes

1   P. 17   Trulock, Alice Rains. *In the Hands of Providence; Joshua Chamberlain & the American Civil War*. Chapel Hill: The University of North Carolina Press, 1992. Print.

2   P. 31   Smith, Diane. *Fanny & Joshua*. Gettysburg: Thomas Publications, 1999. Print.

3   P. 55   Smith, Diane. *Fanny & Joshua*. Gettysburg: Thomas Publications, 1999. Print.

4   P. 79   Trulock, Alice Rains. *In the Hands of Providence; Joshua Chamberlain & the American Civil War*. Chapel Hill: The University of North Carolina Press, 1992. Print.

5   P. 117   Chamberlain, Joshua. *Bayonet! Forward; My Civil War Reminiscences*. 2nd ed. Gettysburg: Stan Clark Military Books, 1994. Print.

6   P. 219   Desjardin, Thomas. *Stand Firm Ye Boys From Maine*; The 20th Maine and the Gettysburg Campaign. 2nd edition. Oxford: Oxford University Press, 2009. Print.

7   P. 233   Desjardin, Thomas. *Stand Firm Ye Boys From Maine*; The 20th Maine and the Gettysburg Campaign. 2nd edition. Oxford: Oxford University Press, 2009. Print.

8   P. 267   Trulock, Alice Rains. *In the Hands of Providence; Joshua Chamberlain & the American Civil War*. Chapel Hill: The University of North Carolina Press, 1992. Print.

9   P. 272   Smith, Diane. *Fanny & Joshua*. Gettysburg: Thomas Publications, 1999. Print.

10   P. 357   Smith, Diane. *Fanny & Joshua*. Gettysburg: Thomas Publications, 1999. Print.

About the author

Matthew Langdon Cost lives in Brunswick, Maine with his wife, Debbie Harper, and has four wonderful children—Brittany, Pearson, Miranda, and Ryan. Prior to focusing on writing, he taught middle school social studies with an emphasis on American history. Cost has two previously published mystery novels, *Mainely Power* and *Mainely Fear*.